The King's Corpse

The King's Corpse
by
MJ Jones

www.penmorepress.com

ISBN-13: 978-1-950586-91-2(Paperback)
ISBN: 13: 978-1-950586-92-9 (E-book)

BISAC Subject Headings:
FIC002000 FICTION / Action & Adventure
FIC009080FICTION / Fantasy / Humorous
FIC014020**FICTION** / Historical / Medieval

The Book Cover Whisperer:
ProfessionalBookCoverDesign.com

Address all correspondence to:

Penmore Press LLC
920 N Javelina Pl
Tucson AZ 85748

Dedication

To the memory of my parents
Thanks for all the love and all the books

Acknowledgements

My thanks

— to the Conrad family, who let me fish for the Muse at their cottage on Lake Wisconsin;

— to Carol Mueller, who provided her house in the woods where I could hunt plot and trap words;

— to Laurel Yorke and all her workshop writers, who joined me in the chase and gave me good counsel along the way;

— to "Ladies Must Write"—Jan Levine Thal, Gail Sterkel, Linda Woito—guides and companions, who keep me from stepping in my own snares and pull me out when I do;

— to Elizabeth, whose aim is always true.

"For the Snark's a peculiar creature, that wo'n't
Be caught in a commonplace way."

— Lewis Carroll, <u>The Hunting of the Snark</u>

Notice to All People

A.D. 978. This year was King Edward slain, at eventide, at Corfe-gate,

On the fifteenth day before the calends of April.

And he was buried at Wareham without any royal honour.

No worse deed than this was ever done by the English nation since. they first sought the land of Britain.

Men murdered him but God has magnified him. He was in life an earthly king—he is now after death a heavenly saint. Him would not his earthly relatives avenge—but his heavenly father has avenged him amply.

The earthly homicides would wipe out his memory from the

earth—but the avenger above has spread his memory abroad in

heaven and in earth. Those, who would not before bow to his

living body, now bow on their knees to his dead bones.

—*The Anglo-Saxon Chronicle*, Version C, Abingdon Chronicle II mid-11th century

PART I

Kingdom of All England
Anno Domini 979

CHAPTER ONE

The guards in front of Wilton's earthen walls stopped me at the gate. "Tryff Tewdwr, you are. Come to steal our saints," said one, a runt of a fellow made big and important by his coat of chain mail. And his spear, which he used to twiddle my beard.

I slapped it away, choked back some choice words, and handed over my travel warrant. I could have told him I wasn't after Wilton's saints because I wasn't a relic thief anymore. But he looked like a man lacking even a mote of Christian charity. He'd likely figure "once a thief, always a thief." And no such vermin would come creeping into holy Wilton. Not on his watch, anyhow.

He took his time with the warrant, staring hard at the parchment and moving his lips so I'd think he could read. Then he ran a stubby finger over the seal. Since any stupid Saxon—Englishman, that is—can recognize the royal seal, that should have been that. But off he stalked to the guard hut, leaving his mates to see I didn't make a dash for Wilton Cathedral's reliquary.

Presently, another man came out of the hut, warrant in hand. "Off your horse, Welshman."

He was as blond as the guard, but taller and better dressed. His wool tunic was thick with gold embroidery, his helmet so polished you could see yourself in it. He wore a long sword in a silver-chased scabbard and an aristocratic manner to go with it.

I got off Tom Tub, my big chestnut horse, then turned him loose so he could help himself to some green shoots sprouting from the wall.

"I'm Leofric of Salisbury, the watch commander. Says here ..."—he rattled the parchment—"says you're ... um ... um ... By all the saints, what kind of name is this?"

Why can Saxons never get my name right? "I'm Tryffin ap Tewdwr. That's Tryffin as in 'roughen,' Tewdwr as in 'ruder.'"

He eyed me for a moment, then looked back at the parchment. "You're Tryffin ap Tewdwr, relic merchant."

"Warranted by my noble lord, and the king's own reeve."

Lord Leofric stroked his whiskers like he was thinking the situation over. Then he ran his eyes up and down me. What he saw was a big, black-haired Welshman with a bristly beard and a nose like an ale bucket. I'm no beauty, that's for sure. On the other hand, I was wearing my best tunic, the one with indigo-blue embroidery at its hem, and a cloak lined in soft, warm weasel hide. See you, the relic trade turned a nice profit.

After he finished inspecting me, Lord Leofric said, "My yeoman claims you've a bad reputation. For holy thievery. Along with stinking drunkenness and wanton wenching." The lord's fair mustache twitched. "You do all that?"

"I don't steal saints no more. As for the rest—"

"Come to Wilton on business?"

Truth be told, I didn't exactly know why I'd come to

Wilton. Only that the prioress of St. Finella's nunnery sent a message saying to meet her there.

"The yeoman thinks you're a menace to the morals of our fine city and shouldn't be admitted, no matter you carry a royal warrant." Leofric rolled up the parchment. "However, I've never heard of you. And the warrant's valid."

He handed it over, threw me a wave, and strolled back to the guard hut. When I was aboard Tom Tub, about to ride through the gate, the yeoman sent me a wave, too. The one-fingered kind.

I gave him another good cursing, then gave myself a better one because it looked like I'd ridden three days on a fool's errand. Half way across England in a cold, wet winter just to meet a nun. "On a matter of the gravest importance," her message claimed.

Bandits had set on me not once but twice. I'd fought them off both times. No trick that. I'm a travelling man, have been most of my life. I know how to take care of ragged peasants armed with nothing but billhooks. But the second lot nabbed my bag of hardtack and I went hungry 'til I found a hare dumb enough to hop in my net.

When I'd come in sight of Wilton's walls, I'd sent up a happy prayer to St. Christopher. Wilton's an important town, sitting as it does where two rivers and three highways come together. It was the royal seat of Wessex before King Alfred moved to Winchester, and they even named the whole shire after it.

I hadn't been to Wilton for over two years, not since the great hunger. That was when a spell of bad weather, failed crops, and starved livestock had England living on nothing but bugs and weeds. Wilton's markets had been empty then, its smithies still. The only sight seemed to be funeral processions, tolling bells the only sound.

Sin was what caused all the trouble, clerics had claimed. England, they said, was full of grievous sin. Of miserable sinners, too, starting with young King Edward himself. But, praise God, that was past. Now, with a new king soon to be consecrated, the land waxed fat again. Wilton, too, and why not? It had a royal hall, a cathedral, and a nunnery, even a mint. And every one stuffed with silver.

On either side of Wilton's market square stood the big cathedral and an even bigger royal hall, timber-sided and straw-roofed. The cathedral bells rang out above the clang of the square's smithies, the squeals and bleats and bellows of its slaughter pens. The mint sat in the square, too, busily pounding out coins bearing the new king's silver portrait.

Past the square, in a maze of crisscrossed rivers and streams, stood the town's houses, churches, and nunnery. Beyond all that lay three suburbs with mills and slaughter pens of their own. A big, prosperous place was Wilton.

Now Tom Tub and I joined the crowd surging along East Street. It was the usual town mixture of country churls in torn tunics and muck-matted leg bands, their cattle dogs frisking alongside. Clerics, too, in cowls and black robes, and townsfolk in fine wool cloaks closed tight against the hard February wind.

I pulled my own cloak up to my chin while I watched a brown dog chase its tail and once again asked myself what the prioress could want with me this time.

In Minster Street we came to the royal hall where I was supposed to meet St. Finella's prioress. You'd think a visiting nun would stay in a nunnery. But Wilton Minster and St. Finella's had some trouble 'twixt them. I don't know whether it was church politics or just woman fuss. But, whichever, they wanted nothing to do with each other. Hadn't for years.

Behind the royal compound's picket barrier stood its big, slate-roofed timbered hall and collection of wattle sheds and stables and bower houses. White smoke, hard whipped by the wind, rose from a round cookhouse. Royals rarely used the place, but it still had household guards and servants living there. It also provided lodging for visitors to Wilton's cathedral.

I found the prioress and her companion nun in the royal hall's second-best guest bower. The best bower, the one with the white-wash and the cushioned furniture, went to thegns and bishops when they came visiting. Simple nuns and retired relic thieves got damp walls, bare stools, and a scarred oak table. Oh, and a jug of that tasteless slop the English call ale.

"St Finella be praised!" the companion cried out when she saw me. Then, nun or no, she threw her arms around me.

And near cracked my ribs because this was Sister Hrothbeort, and Sister Hrothbeort was the biggest woman I ever knew. But I was damn glad to see her. Even if my sides would ache for a week.

When she finally let go, Sister turned to the other nun. "Looky, Prioress, our Welsh rascal's come after all."

The dim light cast by smoky tallow candles showed the prioress at the table, busy pouring ale into clay cups. Like Sister Hrothbeort, she wore a long grey tunic, her hair hidden by a headdress of the same grim grey. But the prioress held hers in place with silver pins. Silver embroidery crusted the sleeves of her tunic and still more silver—gold, too—circled her fingers.

"Hello, Prioress," I said. Her name was Æthelthryth, but that's one of those English names I have trouble saying, so I didn't try. I just called her Prioress. "You've come a long way down here from St. Finella's. But it's a wasted trip. For both of us."

Prioress didn't say anything back, only pursed her lips. It was a habit I wished she'd break, giving folk that sour pout, because behind it there was a fine-looking woman. She was about my own age, thirty-odd, a bit slim for my taste but with wide dark eyes and a complexion that put me in mind of a pink Tuscan peach. Too bad she was nowhere near so sweet.

"A wasted trip," I said again.

Which she already knew because when I first got her message, I sent back my reply in good, clear English: "I don't steal saints no more." Maybe I should've said it in Latin, too. Or Welsh. "*Hir ladrad, i grog,*" I could've told her. Long thieving leads to the gallows.

Wouldn't have done much good, though. Not in any language. Not with Prioress. "Greetings in Christ's love," her return message had said. "Meet me at the royal hall in Wilton on Candlemas, the second day of February. I have an important business matter to discuss with you."

My travels have often taken me to Francia and Navarre and Italy, so I can say that in most places you wouldn't find a nun meeting somebody in a worldly spot like this one. Or any place outside their nunneries. In Europe, they keep the *religeuses* wrapped tight in what clerics call strict enclosure. But here, nuns go wandering around the countryside like they own it. Which they do, come to that. Their families do, anyhow. There isn't a nun in England that's not rich or noble, and usually both. Prioress herself came of a family laying claim to half the land in Kent. No wonder she was St. Finella's prioress, its second in command, outranked only by Mother Eada, the abbess.

Anyhow, that second message, the one mentioning business, did it. I gave in and saddled up for the ride from Southwark, where I was staying, out west to Wilton. So I could meet a nun in some second-best guest lodge—where I now watched her pour ale into little cups.

"I quit stealing saints. Not their bones nor their garments nor the tiniest speck of dust off their tombs."

The prioress took a swig of ale. "But you're still in the relic trade."

"And doing fine, I don't mind telling you. Just last month I delivered St. John's shinbone to the abbot of Ramsey. He was so grateful he told me he'd say a prayer for me every day."

He'd also handed me a plump bag of silver. "But I didn't

steal St. John. I'm not Holy Church's *fidelis predo*, not her faithful thief any more. I quit sneaking around churches at night, snatching saints out of their reliquaries. No matter how many clerics ask me to."

Or how much they offer to pay.

"The abbot of Ramsey, eh?" Prioress squinted through the bower's greasy candle smoke. "Perhaps that's why you're looking so prosperous."

Giving her my biggest, dumbest grin, I asked, "What you want with me, Prioress?"

She shoved a cup of ale across the table and bade me sit and drink with her and Sister Hrothbeort. The ale was as thin as I'd expected.

When we finished it, Prioress refilled the cups. I said, "Ain't you supposed to be fasting this time of year?" It would be Lent soon.

"We are travelling and therefore dispensed."

"Those rules of yours bend easy as a Surrey snake."

A little smile cracked the edge of her lips. "For a spoiled monk, Tryff, you've certainly retained a most active interest in the monastic life."

She said that just to tease me. I was never a monk, though I lived and studied at my uncle the abbot's monastery from the time I was ten 'til just after I turned fourteen. Got sent there as an oblate, a gift to God. That's what my *tad*—my father—claimed, anyhow. Fact is, the brute didn't know what else to do with me after he sold my mam into slavery.

The nuns and I lapped up the ale for a bit, until Sister Hrothbeort began telling me all about recent events back at the nunnery. "You remember Father Langdun, our chaplain, don't you? Well, his wife had a new baby and—"

Prioress cut her off. "It's time we got down to business. Your noble lord has sent us to speak with you."

That's the trouble with being in a lord's service. They can summon you anytime they want, order you to do your duty, whatever, whenever, wherever. Put you in harm's way, too, if they like. Still, a man's got to have a lord here in England and anyplace else, lest folk think you're some kind of outlaw they can chase down for the price on your head.

"Where is my lord, by the way?"

Prioress took another gulp of ale. "Unfortunately, she couldn't come with us."

Like I said, you've got to have a lord. Mother Eada, abbess of St. Finella, was mine. Maybe some folk would mind having a woman for their lord. Not me. Mother Eada's nunnery may have been little, but it was wealthy. It owned half a dozen nice estates and had a saint that pilgrims from all over the country came to pray to. And leave money with. Best of all, Mother Eada was kin to the king. So I didn't care if my lord was a lady. In a business like mine, a man needs all the protection he can get.

In return, I owed her what's called gesith service. Carry her messages and see to the bridges on her estates, guard her on her travels. That's what English law said I had to do for her. The law also said I owed military service in her name. I said I'd rather lay my tongue on a blacksmith's anvil than spend so much as an hour in a Saxon army.

"Mother Eada's duties keep her at St. Finella's, but she is well and sends you greetings in Christ," the prioress said. "She wants you to find something for her."

St. Nicholas save me. Last time these nuns wanted me to find something, I got beat up, locked up, and all but drowned. "Like I keep telling you, Prioress, I don't steal—"

"It isn't holy relics we've come to you about."

I was afraid of that. Because whenever the nuns at St. Finella's sent for me, they didn't necessarily want me to bring them a saint, or fix their bridges, or carry their messages, or guard them on their gadding about. Sometimes they wanted to put me to work tracking down bad folk.

Ordinarily in England, if somebody gets wronged or harmed or even murdered, their family has to go after the evil doer and bring him to justice. But the victim's brothers and cousins can't always move as fast or as far as a guilty man. A lone hunter who knows his way around people and places does a lot better. And who would know better than a relic thief? At least that must've been what the nuns thought, because whenever they found out about trouble in their neighborhood—and not just in their neighborhood—they sent for me. Most times I didn't mind. As long as I got paid. Trouble was, sometimes I didn't.

Now Prioress glanced at the door. "Before I proceed, we need to make sure we won't be overheard by some snooping servant."

She gestured to Sister Hrothbeort, who went and shut the heavy oak door, then planted herself in front of it. No one would come bothering us now. Sister's bulk could keep out Satan himself.

Prioress poured another cup of ale. "As I said, Mother Eada, your noble lord, wants you to find something."

"I'm her radman, not her hunting dog."

"Mother Eada wants you to find her cousin."

"Which one? She's likely got them a dozen to the acre all over England."

"Actually, she wants you to find her cousin's body."

I set my cup on the table. "You don't mean a dead body, do you?"

She nodded.

"I'm no grave robber."

"Mother Eada wants you to find the body," Prioress said, "the dead body of the king of England."

"I didn't know King Ethelred died," I said.

"Not Ethelred. His brother."

"You mean King Edward, the lad who got killed last year?"

"Who got murdered," Sister Hrothbeort said.

"That's just gossip," snapped Prioress.

Official word was that King Edward, sixteen years old, had died in a hunting accident. Thrown from his horse while visiting his half-brother, Ethelred, down in Dorset. There were rumors, though, that the king hadn't met with any accident.

"It's not murder we're here to discuss, Hrothbeort. So do not interrupt."

The big nun obeyed her superior and clamped her mouth shut. The only sound out of her was the grinding of her teeth.

"You know, of course, about the recent succession crisis?" Prioress's tone implied that of course I wouldn't.

But I did. About four years back, King Eadgar the Peacemaker had died at the age of thirty-two. He'd left behind his widow, Queen Ælfthryth, and two past wives, one of them a nun. There was also a child by each wife. First came Edward, then a girl, Edith. The third was Queen Ælfthryth's son Ethelred.

The choice for a new king had been 'twixt Edward and

Ethelred, both of them still young boys. I don't know what all went on, but Edward got to be king. Not because he was the older, but because he was considered more throne-worthy. This though he'd just turned thirteen and, so I heard, was one of the nastiest boys God ever made.

Worse yet, the church had all but said his parents' marriage wasn't valid. And that meant a lot of folk didn't consider Edward legitimate enough to be king. Even so, he was backed by some very powerful thegns and bishops. After a good bit of political hubbub and horse-trading, the Witan—the council of bishops and thegns and abbots that elects English kings—decided on Edward. Besides, Ethelred was only nine.

I rubbed my eyes. The greasy smoke was making them sore. "The way I got it, last March King Edward's half-brother, Ethelred, and his stepmother, Queen Ælfthryth, were at the royal hunting lodge in Dorset. What's it called again?"

"Corfe Gate," the prioress said. "It's pleasant there and the hunting's good."

"King Edward went to visit them. And, right near Corfe, got himself killed."

"Got murdered," muttered Sister Hrothbeort, blunt as a smith's hammer.

There's always gossip when a royal dies in violence. So it wasn't surprising that stories went around about Edward being murdered. There were even some good reasons why he might've been. For one thing it seemed he followed his father in the way he felt about clerics. He liked giving them land and taking their advice. That's why some said he was killed by disgruntled thegns looking to punish a king who favored church over man when he parceled out the royal property.

"Queen Ælfthryth did it," Sister Hrothbeort said, in no uncertain terms, "so's her son Ethelred could be king."

Prioress turned a hard look on Sister Hrothbeort. "You know perfectly well some men are afraid of the queen's power. That's why they tell so many ugly stories about her."

Power, indeed. The queen came from a family that owned half of Cornwall. She was also a force to be reckoned with in her own right, a woman who knew how to deal with thegns and clerics. Kings, too, if Eadgar was any example. He'd turned over the whole of Dorset for her to rule.

But even if I agreed with Prioress about the gossip, baiting her was still good sport. "Heard Eadgar killed Ælfthryth's first husband so they could be together."

"That evil woman's the killer here," Sister Hrothbeort let us know. "She murdered King Edward."

Sister's hardheadedness so exasperated Prioress that she ordered her to go fetch more drink. "Good ale this time. Not this meek ale."

"I ain't leaving," Sister Hrothbeort said.

Here's the thing about English nuns. They take a vow of obedience, but, aristocrats to the core, they sometimes act like obedience is for churls and children.

"Remember your vows, Hrothbeort," Prioress said, "or you'll find yourself excluded from the oratory."

The big nun still didn't move.

"And from the refectory," Prioress added.

Sister Hrothbeort went to get the ale.

I didn't know what to think about this idea of murder. But I did think it peculiar that Edward had had no funeral. Not a big, impressive one anyway. The English like to bury their mighty in high old style. King Eadgar's funeral procession had stretched damn near three miles, and the drinking damn near three months.

"They interred Edward near Corfe Gate," Prioress said. "Where he fell."

"Just stuck him in the ground?" I was honest-to-God shocked. Even Saxons have better morals than to treat their kings like dead dogs.

"Of course not. I told you he lay in Dorset. In Wareham church. Until he was stolen."

Stolen? This was something new. "Who'd dare do such a thing? And why?"

Prioress shook her head. "Those are questions I can't answer. And they don't matter, really. Mother Eada just wants you to find King Edward's body so he can have a proper funeral."

"He died almost a year ago. When did his body go missing?"

Prioress hesitated, then said, "I don't know. But we heard about it a few weeks ago."

"How come you're just now getting around to looking for him?"

"You know that Ethelred is to be crowned in early May, two weeks after Easter?"

"Going to be a big celebration," I said. "In London. They're already filling up the ale kegs."

"It would be a much happier occasion if the late king were properly interred, don't you agree?"

I shrugged.

"And a much holier one, too," she went on, "since the coronation is after all a religious ceremony. That's why

Mother Eada wants you to launch a search for Edward's body."

"Dead kings aren't in my vocation," I said. And meant it. Because by now I could tell we were talking dangerous business.

"King Ethelred must've set people looking for his brother's body right away," I said. "Seems like the whole of Dorset should be ploughed up by now."

Prioress folded her hands around her cup. "The king's agents have had no luck."

Now I knew this was truly dangerous business. For one of two reasons, either of them lethal. *Primus*—If all the king's men couldn't beat or bribe their way to Edward's body, then somebody very powerful was behind its theft. And would do what he—or she—had to to keep the corpse right where it was now. Which would for sure include—what's the fancy word? —eliminating anybody caught looking for it.

Or, *secundus*—What if all this talk of a religious ceremony was just so much holy smoke? What if the real reason Mother Eada wanted me to find her cousin's body was so everybody could see he didn't just fall off his horse? What if her family had vengeance in mind?

I sure didn't want to get in the middle of any royal feud. So I said, "I'm not going anywhere near Corfe Gate."

Sister Hrothbeort returned then, with two good-sized ale horns. She handed them to us and again took her place by the door, where she stood with arms firmly crossed over her broad bosom, mumbling and sighing and rolling her eyes.

"Ah," said the prioress when she sampled the brew, "this is better."

I took a sip, then a mouthful, and nodded my agreement.

"You're a stubborn man, Tryff Tewdwr." Prioress took another gulp of ale. "And I can see that no appeal to honor will convince you to do your duty. Therefore, we may have little choice but to call in the archbishop's reeve."

The archbishop's reeve? What had I done to be hauled into court? Or, worse, off to jail, which is what reeves do with you.

Prioress refilled her ale cup. "There's that little matter of Our Lord's shroud."

The archbishop of Canterbury used to hire me to find relics for him. Until what happened in Constantinople. But I could explain that. "About me losing Christ's shroud. See you, the dice were loaded and—"

"I'm afraid Archbishop Dunstan still finds the incident rather disturbing."

To say nothing of sinful, sacrilegious, and downright criminal. Still, let Prioress turn me over to Dunstan's reeve. It would be better than getting mixed up in the death of King Edward. I was willing to count on an archbishop's mercy over a king-killer anytime.

"I should probably get hold of the shire reeve, too," she said. "Since you've refused your lord's command."

I gave another shrug.

She stared at me over the rim of her ale horn, waited a couple of heartbeats, then said in a voice laden with threat and omen, "Remember, you do not have the rights of an Englishman."

"Do what you got to. I said I'm not looking for Edward's body." My words sounded a lot braver than I felt.

In one stiff-wristed swoop, Prioress knocked back her ale. *That woman can sure put it away*, thought I. And, as if to prove it, she told Sister to bring the keg. Sister gave us each a glance, then followed orders without argument.

When the door closed, Prioress turned back to me. She said nothing for a moment, then reached into the pouch that hung from her belt and pulled out a little roll of parchment. "This," she said, "is a letter from the queen of England."

I'd done good work for King Eadgar on not one but several occasions in the past. So getting a message from his widow didn't surprise me much. I took the parchment, peeled off the thick red seal, and rolled it open. It was in Latin but not in the queen's own hand, though she knew how to write Latin. This was the script of the royal chancery in Winchester, handsome and easy on the eyes.

Queen Ælfthryth first offered me Greetings in Christ. Then she ordered me to find "the precious body of my dear son, Edward, may his soul rest in peace."

Since when was Edward her son?

I looked up at Prioress. "Like you Saxons say, 'No.' I'm not getting involved in anything that dangerous. Not even for the queen of England."

"Read the rest."

Queen Ælfthryth went on to say that this service "will exempt you from military duty."

I laughed and shook my head in wonder. A sneakier plan I never heard. Sometimes I just don't know about women, be they royal or religious. But I did know I wasn't having any of it. Not even after I read on to where the queen said, "I understand you well enough, Tryff ap Tewdwr, to assume that by now you have refused this summons to service at least twice, if not three times. Do not be afraid. The good Lord will protect you."

The queen's letter went on to say that not only was she ordering me to find King Edward's body, she wanted it done before Shrove Tuesday. That was when the Witan would meet to elect Ethelred king. "So you must deliver Edward's remains before Lent."

I dropped the page on the table and took a long slug of ale. Then I said, "For the last time, Prioress, I won't risk my life for any dead Saxon king. No matter who orders me to, what they threaten me with, or how much help they say I'll get."

The door clattered open and back came Sister Hrothbeort, balancing a middling-sized wooden keg on her shoulder. She swung it to the floor next to the prioress.

Prioress rose from her stool. "I will make one final appeal to you."

She motioned to Sister Hrothbeort, who hoisted the ale keg and set it end-up on the table in front of me.

The thing was about the size of a butter churn. Big enough for me to get plenty drunk on its contents. Before I went to the gallows.

Prioress lifted off one of its end pieces. "Look inside," she said.

The keg was filled with silver pennies. More silver pennies than I'd ever seen in one place. Enough to buy horses and houses and ale sufficient to keep the whole of Southwark drunk 'til the millennium.

Enough, praise God, to buy my mother out of slavery.

I set the keg end gently back in place. "Where do I start?"

St Finella's nuns had packed me off to all kinds of strange lands—Jerusalem, Tripoli, Denmark. And I found relics for them in all those places. So now it might be Ultima Thule or Kievian Rus or, for all I knew, King Arthur's Avalon.

As it turned out, this time the nuns weren't sending me to the far ends of the world. "You start right here in Wilton," the prioress said.

Thank St. Christopher—I wouldn't have to brave any more of England in this cold winter. Maybe good luck was catching up with me.

"You may come to wish you were at Corfe Gate after all," Prioress said as she and Sister went out the door. "Or anywhere else."

"What's that supposed to mean?" I called after her.

"Sister Hild will tell you after Sext."

Sister Hild? What was that old thing doing here? Why wasn't she in Rome or Salerno or wherever it was she went to show off her cures and nostrums? The old physician, healer, hedge doctor—whatever she called herself—was even more aggravating than Prioress. The two of us had been like a pair of cats in a barrel since back when Mother Eada hired me to save St. Finella from the wicked monks that stole her.

For some reason Sister Hild didn't like me. Maybe she didn't approve of my line of work, even though the rest of the Church did, pope right down to pastor. I was what the Church calls *Fedelis Predo*, a Holy Thief—someone who makes sure saints are in the place they want to be. And, believe me, saints know what they want.

It doesn't take any decree from a pope or bishop to make a saint. Saints are just specially close to God. It's that simple and it's what makes them able to work their wonders—healing and prophesying and such, even talking to the animals. Their miracles are a sign they can intercede with God on behalf of us poor supplicants. They don't have to be dead to do it, either, but it doesn't matter if they are. A saint's spirit is alive both in heaven and in the tomb. It's like what's on St. Martin of Tours's gravestone: "Here lies Martin whose soul is in the hand of God. But he is fully here, present and made plain in miracles of every kind."

The business of a *fedelis predo* is to move saints wherever they think they can pass the best miracles. In St. Finella's case, it was with the nuns. How could Sister Hild find fault with the man who'd rescued St. Finella from her kidnappers?

By now the guest bower's lamps' greasy green smoke had begun to turn my stomach. I needed some fresh air. So I headed to the stable and made sure the ostler was treating Tom with all due respect and lots of oats. Then I went to find an alehouse where I could wait 'til after Sext—in England that's what they call the mid-day church service. I hoped there'd be some men in the alehouse. I was tired of women, 'specially bossy ones.

As I paused for a cup of water at the trough on West street, a commotion busted out just the other side of the city wall. It sounded like somebody was trying to break down the gate using curses for a battering ram. When the gate-keeper swung open the doors, a horseman rode through.

"Where's he at?" he yelled at the gatekeeper. When he didn't answer quick enough, the horseman slashed open his cheek with an iron-tipped whip. "Where is he? Where's Wynstan? Where's that miserable liar?"

His eye fell on a grey-clad woman heading for the gate, basket over her arm, walking stick in her hand. "You, old woman, take me to the Lady right now or I'll have your sagging tits for a coin purse."

What kind of a pig was this? "Oy, there! Watch your tongue," I called out.

But the man paid me no attention, just glared at the woman. As for her, she gazed at him a moment, then turned her back.

He raised his whip to her.

I started across the gravel street on the run. But the woman must've had eyes in the rear of her headdress. When the whip slashed down, she stepped away.

That gave me time to jump the bastard. I wrenched him off his horse and slammed him face down into the gravel. Then I gave him the pounding he sure deserved and I sure enjoyed. His nose spouted blood the color of haws in autumn. His whip arm damn near left its socket.

He was a fighter, though. Bucked like a stallion under me. An old stallion, I noticed when his cap fell off to show a shock of white hair. He didn't quit struggling 'til I tugged his big scramseaxe out of its sheath and put it to his throat.

He held still then, except for his heaving chest and his cursing mouth. I would've given him shit for shat except next thing it was me with a blade to my neck. I looked up to find myself surrounded by a whole swarm of armed Saxons. The gate guards, Lord Leofric in command, had finally decided to earn their mead.

"Drop the knife and let him go." Leofric's sword point twitched against the back of my neck.

I did like I was told. After I breathed a fine Welsh curse into the horseman's ear. And after he yelled a few English ones back at me.

When we finally stopped to draw breath, Leofric said, "Know who this is?"

"A thing that's manners come out his bunghole," I said. In Welsh.

"This is Lord Ælfhere Alvarsæt, ealdorman of Wessex and Mercia."

I looked at the white-haired little man now leaning against a wall while he swiped blood and snot off his beard. He sure didn't look like much in travel-stained cloak and tunic, leg-bands sagging into his shoe tops. More like a churl —a peasant—than a nobleman. And sure not like any ealdorman. Leave it to me to knock down an ealdorman, the king's own man and the chief officer of an English shire— governor, geld collector, top general, and probably the biggest land owner.

Leofric gave me a boyish grin. "An ealdorman's a judge. Know that?"

I did. I also knew he only presided over the shire courts, where the big landowners came to settle their disputes. But that didn't mean he couldn't send me to where regular law and order got dealt with, further down the legal ladder in the Hundred courts. That's where Saxons take care of their local miscreants—cattle rustlers, man killers, those sorts. In the Hundred courts, justice runs down like water the way Scripture says it should. Except when you're an outlander, like me. Then you can get stoned to death. On the spot.

Now the ealdorman waved Leofic away, told him to go and stand with the gate guards. Leofric touched his breast, then hustled to his men.

So he was an important man, this Ælfhere Alvarsæt. One of his shires, Mercia, was the biggest in England. So big it used to be a kingdom all of its own. He was a dangerous man, too. Liked to sack monasteries, beat up the monks. Then he'd take away their gold-leafed books and their embroidered vestments and every acre of their land—the deeds, anyhow—and leave the monks behind, bleeding in the snow. Killed one or two with his own hands. Or so gossip had it.

There were other stories about him, too. Not just gossip, either. Seems that in the big royal mess of twenty years before—there's always some new royal mess in England—in that fight, Alvar kidnapped the reigning king's own mother-in-law. Brought her to the marketplace in Gloucester, where the townsfolk promptly strung up the greedy slut. No trial, no mercy. I knew a man from there who said Alvar himself tied the rope round her neck.

Lucky for me he was alone now, without his spear band. And where were they? How come he'd ridden into Wilton with no companions at all? It just wasn't like an ealdorman. Usually, they couldn't get off their manor without enough soldiers, horses, carts, priests, and treasure to make you think the Second Coming was at hand.

I was also lucky Alvar seemed less interested in hanging

me than making a plea to the old woman. He dropped down on one knee and asked for her blessing. When he got that, he went for her forgiveness. "Christ, Sister, I'm—if I'd knowed it was you … "

It was Sister Hild. But whatever bad blood might've flowed 'twixt her and me, Alvar was damn lucky I hadn't spilled any more of his own blood. I should've hacked him head to heel.

For her part, Sister Hild gave Alvar a brief nod that wasn't quite absolution and leaned down to examine his nose. "It's not broken. Nor is your arm. So get up now."

Alvar stood up and shifted his shoulder around. Satisfied his arm was indeed unbroken, he set to grubbing at his nose with a tunic sleeve. "Is Wynstan in there? In the royal hall, where I can yank the lying tongue right out of him?"

Before anyone else could provide an answer, Sister Hild spoke up. "All in good time, sir. How is your son getting along?"

A huge grin cut through Alvar's blood-stained white whiskers. "Them potions you sent made him fit as any lad in Wessex."

"Let us give thanks to the Lord, then." Sister Hild cast a look at Leofric and me that made us bow our heads, though neither of us had any idea what demon she and the Lord had cast out of the ealdorman's son.

When the prayer was done and Alvar's head came up, it swung my direction. "What we got here?"

His voice made me afraid that the penitent had all too soon been replaced by the judge. And it was me in his dock.

To my surprise, Sister Hild jumped to my defense. Sort of. "He's St. Finella's radman."

Sister must've known I'd need a sturdier defense. "His name is Tryffin ap Tewdwr and he's the nephew of a Welsh king."

Alvar's eyes slewed in her direction. When they returned to me, there was a different cast to them. "Christ, man...I mean, hell, I'd've done the same thing—worse, likely, if somebody jumped Sister."

Did Alvar believe this apology would save his people from being fallen on by hordes of savage Welshman bent on avenging the honor of one of their princes? I damn near laughed out loud at the notion. King Brynmor hadn't seen me since I was ten years old. I doubted he'd thought about me since then, either. Nor had that brother of his, my bastard of a father. There'd be no Welsh hordes raging through Alvar's shires. Not even if he nailed me to my uncle's gate.

Alvar eyed me up and down. "Say your name again, only slow-like. So it don't sound like a cat hawking up something she found in the yard."

This time I shouted it very loud and very slow, which is what you have to do with Englishmen. "Tryffin ap Tewdwr."

He started to try it out, then stopped. His eyes narrowed. "Ain't you some kind of relic man?"

I took my time deciding if I should admit to it. The ealdorman had a lot of churches in his keeping, monasteries, too. And who knew how many of them I'd moved saints out of?

While I was trying to think of a way to cover my backside, he said, "We done business together, though you may not know it. Last year, one of your... uh... agents helped St. Potamiaena escape from the Pope. Brought her to Hadley

Minster that I'm patron of. Now the saint's happier and holier than ever."

The ealdorman turned to Sister Hild. "Christ, Sister ... I mean, hell, Sister, I should've carried a piece of the saint down here with me. She's a mighty good healer. She could've helped you fix the Lady."

While I was wondering what he meant by "fix the Lady," Sister honored him with the same thin smile she gave the convent dogs when they rolled over on command. "I'm sure St. Potamiaena would be most beneficial. But even though she's not here, let us pray for every suffering creature."

She raised her hands to heaven and presently everybody was praying up a storm. Me, too. Though I was asking that saint to throw a fit of forgetfulness over Ealdorman Alvar. He was too much of a Saxon to long overlook a Welshman that beat him up, no matter how many saints I'd brought his monasteries. Nor how many prayers Sister Hild might throw betwixt us.

When the prayer got done, Alvar plucked at his mustache a while. Deciding, I figured, if he should thank me for bringing the saint to him or sentence me for beating the hell out of him. But when he spoke, it was to Leofric. "Get your troop back where they belong. My men'll be in Wilton presently. See they're treated proper."

Behind Leofric, his half a dozen guardsmen still stood leaning on their spears, still all a-grin, happy to see the Welsh pig at bay. They were as surprised as I was when from around the alehouse charged a band of men armed to the eyebrows and in full battle cry.

"Northmen!" someone yelled.

At a shout from Leofric, the guardsmen snapped into a

solid line, shields up, spears bristling at the ready. It was the Saxon battle-hedge that had skewered invading Vikings for centuries. I hoped it would again today.

But before the battle could get started and before I could decide which way to run, Alvar let out a sharp whistle. The Northmen stopped like so many sheepdogs.

Turned out they weren't Norskers after all, only Alvar's spear band. They'd spied their chief on his knees in front of a cloaked stranger and come to his rescue. Fortunately, Leofric followed Alvar's lead and called off his own troop before a tide of blood washed over the streets of Wilton.

During all this, Sister Hild, the cause of the commotion, had never stirred, had barely blinked. Now she cast a withering eye on the guard captain and on the ealdorman, but said nothing. She didn't have to.

Leofric shouted an order to his men, who snapped into rank, spears ported smart against their coats of mail. While they marched back to the town gate, Alvar's spear band trooped past them, to take their place by their lord and give him a protective escort all the way to the royal hall.

But Alvar pointed to his horse. "Take him to wherever you left yours," he told his men. "And stay there 'til I say different. Only me's going in the royal hall."

He picked up his whip from where it lay by the water trough and slapped it across his thigh. "That bastard Wynstan's in there. And I'm going to tear out his lying tongue and feed it to the pigs for breakfast."

Without a glance at me or Sister Hild, the ealdorman started toward the hall gate. But if he thought the old nun would follow meekly behind, he sure didn't know Sister Hild. She gave him a hard poke with her cane that brought him up short. "It's time, Alvar, that we had a little chat."

Then she turned to me and, under her breath, hissed, "You have been exceedingly stupid today. I hope you will be a trifle more clever, never mind discreet, in finding King Edward. Of this, I will have more to say later."

With that and in a swirl of grey cloak, she swept through the hall gate followed by Alvar shaking his head and rubbing his backside.

"When you want me, Sister, you know where to find me!" I called after her. It got no response, but if she wanted me she could look for the sign of the green bush. I was going to the alehouse. First, though, I stopped at the town gate and offered to stand Leofric a drink. He'd saved my bum not once but twice that day.

Leofric took me up on my offer, ten times over and with strong Wiltshire ale. I matched him gulp for gulp there in the dark little alehouse that smelled like a whole tribe of mice had died under its floorboards. It wasn't long before we were the best of friends and had all but raked up kinfolk. He told me that his grandfather's land sat hard by Clawdd Offa in Shropshire and the old man, his mother's father, spoke Welsh. He'd even taught Leofric a bit, which Leofric demonstrated by saying my name right and reciting a couple of Welsh riddles.

You could tell he was the kind of man who liked to show off. He wore his blond hair and beard cut short. Like a soldier should, he might've claimed. I figured he did it to display his fair face. When I'd first seen Leofric at the gate, I'd taken him to be just another conceited Saxon, likely as soft in the head as in the spirit and only playing soldier 'til he could get back to his real duty, screwing slave girls on his father's manor.

But when we got to that point in a drinking bout where you start talking about life and love, it turned out he had notions as dark as any churchman's. Only they didn't involve sin but Fortuna. He quoted from Boethius. "Fortuna's most friendly and alluring to the ones she seeks to deceive. Until she overwhelms them with grief beyond bearing, by deserting them when least expected."

I've read my Boethius. But the Master's too deep for tavern talk and it's hardly news that Fortuna is a lying slut. I first found that out as a boy when I begged her to help me find the Great Harp of King Arthur. Folk say he hid it in the mountains of my uncle's kingdom and claim it'll make the one who finds it into a new Arthur. Maybe it will. I looked for his harp often—and so did my countrymen. Nobody found it, I reckon. Or at least no new Arthurs stepped forward.

As for Leofric's disappointment with Fortuna, I figured he was just bored. As who wouldn't be stuck in a guardhouse for months at a time, with nobody to talk to but blockheads like his little yeoman and a town full of clerics. So I let him run on, and amused myself with making eyes at the serving girl. Then I found out she was the ale keep's daughter. There'd be no luck here, either.

"Have you ever known love, Welshman?"

"Uh ... "

"I have. I do. A love full of the 'darkness of ever treacherous passions,' as the Master says. But I tell myself it's as he says, 'Who would give a law to lovers? Love is unto itself a higher law.'"

Boethius also said, "He suffers from lethargy, an illness

common to distracted minds." I signaled the ale keep to bring the barrel.

By the time we left the alehouse, West Street had somehow turned into a rolling ocean and I a yawing coracle. Leofric was just as bad off, and seasick on top of it. But after he puked up a couple gallons of the Wiltshire ale, he felt better and we helped each other navigate the heaving street.

We weren't too clear about where we were headed or what we'd do when we got there. Drunk as I was, I could hardly appear before Sister Hild. And since Leofric was supposed to be on duty, we couldn't use the guard hut to sober up in. So we roamed around Wilton, sang a few tavern songs, flirted with some girls washing clothes by a bridge, and finally ate two big mutton pasties apiece.

When we kept both down, we decided we'd successfully ridden out the storm. But neither of us was sober enough, or willing enough, to get back to our duties. We headed away from the town and the hall, toward one of the suburbs. Leofric knew a house out that way where lived a woman who understood how lonely a soldier's life could be. And she had a friend.

As we were passing alongside the high holly hedge that surrounded Wilton Minster, we heard a shout. And the unmistakable sound of marching men, the thud of their boots, the ca-chink of their chainmail. Sure enough, around a corner came Alvar's spear band, his one-eyed captain in the lead, the flag of Mercia flying. They filled the street.

When they saw us, the captain snapped out a command and the whole lot of them hitched up their spears and their shields. They came charging straight at us. "Insult! Dishonor! Vengeance! Welshman!"

I stood there with my mouth hanging open, still too drunk for even mortal danger to register on me. Good thing the soldier in Leofric came to about then. He grabbed me by the tunic sleeve and yanked me along with him through a gap in the hedge.

We crawled out of the hedge into a patch of gravel and the stink of a latrine yard. Leofric pointed at the little wicker-sided privy. "In there."

When I didn't move fast enough, he gave me a hard shove. I stumbled through the door, and caught my foot on the lip of the latrine hole. I would've fallen—and likely knocked down the whole building, it was that small, that frail—but Leofric grabbed at my belt to keep me upright. I stayed on my feet all right, but what he'd caught was the leather tube I kept my travel warrant in. Its laces tore loose and the tube vanished down the hole.

"Shit," I said.

Damned if Leofric didn't giggle. And us wedged in a latrine stormed by English warriors, never mind my travel warrant stuck and stinking down below. I was just about to bust him in the mouth when we heard a soldier slash his way through the hedge, pause, then call to his comrades. "Nobody here. And I ain't waiting around to look at the nether parts of no nun."

"Nun?"

Leofric shushed me and we stayed quiet until the soldier and his spear band marched off.

"Sorry about that," Leofric said as I dropped to my knees,

held my nose, and peered into the hole. "But I can hang onto you if you want to try and reach for it."

I prayed for the forbearance not to drop him on top of the warrant. On the other hand, here was a chance to gain some honor. "Accidents happen," I said with a grin as I got up. "Nothing for it but to give the bitch Fortuna a good cursing. Besides, you saved me from the wrath of that ealdorman."

I added that I'd find some way to manage without my warrant. And I would, at least until next I came on pen, ink, and a bit of red wax. Then I'd fool 'em like I always do. I'd make a new warrant, complete with a lovely new royal seal. Meantime, I wanted to know where in hell we were.

Leofric ran a smoothing finger over his mustache. "In Wilton Minster."

It was all I could do not to trample him. We'd landed inside the nunnery. And not just any old nunnery. We'd come up in Wilton Minster, the most royal convent in England. Which was saying something. They were all full of thegns' daughters, and their widows, too. But Wilton held the daughter of a king—Eadgar's second child, Lady Edith. And one of his wives—Wulfthryth, now no less than the abbess of Wilton.

Here we were, huddled in their privy.

I asked Leofric how he knew about that gap in the hedge. He gave me a sly grin. "We can hide in here 'til dark. By then Lord Alvar will either have forgotten about you or he'll be too drunk to care."

That part sounded good because we couldn't just crawl back through the hedge. Alvar's men might still be nearby. But I wasn't sure I wanted to spend the day in a toilet. 'Specially one that belonged to nuns. "Who knows how they might act if they find a man in their jakes?"

Leofric peeked through a chink in the privy's wattle wall. "Looks like everybody's in church, servants included."

As they were for all eight canonical services. In England the prayer day starts a couple of hours past midnight with the service called Nocturns, then rolls through the other services—Matins, Lauds, Prime, Tierce, Sext, None, Vespers —to Compline in the late evening. Bedtime's a little later. In between services there's work, meals, even a nap right before None, which comes mid-afternoon.

Problem was that after None, the service going on now, they'd have their eyes wide open. If they saw us, we'd be hauled off to court and charged with invading a convent. The English are serious about protecting their female religious and really know how to punish a man. If you got caught in a convent, you'd have to pay 120 shillings. That much silver could buy a dozen good horses. I sent a prayer to St. Mark, who's always helped me out when I have trouble with the law.

Leofric eased open the privy door and peeked out at the nunnery grounds. "We should be able to get to the gatehouse before None ends and from there we can sneak back into the street. If anybody sees us, we'll claim we're waiting to visit the chaplain. You sell relics to priests sometimes, right?"

"I generally like to tell 'em I'm coming, though. Otherwise, they tend to think I'm looking to ransack their relic racks."

Leofric assured me no such thing would happen at Wilton Minster. "I'm well known here."

Unfortunately, so was I. But the ale still sloshing around in my belly convinced me the abbess had forgotten by now.

Forgiven, even. As for explaining to her how we could've gotten past the troll wife at the gatehouse wicket—all nunneries have a troll wife at their wicket—well, Leofric could handle Abbess Wulfthryth if, God forbid, it came to that.

Staying close to the hedge, we slipped past the whitewashed stone church. Inside it, the nuns were starting a psalm. "How shall we sing the songs of the Lord in a strange land?" That's usually a thorny question for music-deaf Saxons, but these women sounded pretty good. I almost stopped to hum along. I didn't, though, and we made the gate with no trouble.

But it turned out to be locked—the wicket, too. The best that could be said was the troll wife had gone to church with the rest of the nuns. I gave the wicket an aggravated rap and felt like giving Leofric another. "You damn well better know another way out of here."

He said not to worry, he knew the guards that patrolled outside the minster. They were likely catching a nap in their hut in Minster Street while None was going on. They'd be back presently and he'd signal them to let us out. "Meantime, we can hide in the gate's shadow."

A thing easier claimed than accomplished. The shadow was short and None could go long—it takes a while to sing your way through a dozen psalms. So I decided to look over Wilton Minster. Its layout wasn't much different from St. Finella's. Besides the church-house, there were half a dozen stone and timbered buildings strewn around inside the hedge—kitchen, chapter-house, dormitory, refectory, a few sheds, and what looked like it could be a brewery.

One thing was different here at Wilton, though. St.

Finella's smelled like a farm, which it was. But Wilton smelled of incense, sweet and spicy and very expensive. I took its rich fragrance for a sign that the narrow notions of the monastic reformers in Canterbury and Winchester hadn't yet arrived, that maybe all that nonsense about poverty, obedience, and chastity hadn't taken root. Matter of fact, the new rules hadn't made it as far as St. Finella's, either. I always figured its barnyard reek kept poverty and obedience a proper distance away. Though don't misunderstand, there was plenty of chastity. More than enough, if you ask me.

And probably was here, too, even if not all the women were nuns. Thegns' daughters came to be educated at Wilton and, sometimes, to avoid unwanted marriages. With no compulsion to take any vows, they'd tuck themselves away until all marital danger passed. Later, when something better came on offer, they could get back in the market, no worse for wear. Meantime, their fathers would be sure they stayed safely cached 'til needed.

When the bell rang to mark the end of None, the guards still hadn't gotten themselves back to the gate. Worse yet, a procession of women came snaking out of the church-house. Now folk would be going back to work all over the minster, spinning and weaving, making ale and bread. I pushed further back into the shadows and called Leofric a few names for getting me into this mess. But truly there was nothing for it except to figure out which women were the nuns and which the ones here just to learn a little Latin. That way I could at least enjoy some pretty girls, and without guilt.

Only, everyone was cloaked to the eyebrows against the February wind. That didn't matter to Leofric, though. He all but panted as he watched the women parade past. When he finally pulled himself together, he said, "We'd better get closer to the gate before someone sees us. Sees me, I mean. I'm rather persona non grata here in the nunnery."

He'd said he was well known in Wilton Minster. But he never bothered to say it was for something that caused him to use the kind of Latin you hear in a law court. And now one of the older nuns had peeled off the line, coming right at us.

From the grand staff she carried, and her even grander manner, I knew her to be Abbess Wulfthryth, the second of Eadgar's three wives. She fairly burst across the cloister, the low afternoon sun behind her, every bit the royal she'd once been. Following her came a younger woman, no doubt her daughter, Lady Edith.

Wulfthryth, in spite of her proud bearing, wore a dull brown wool cloak over a tunic of even duller brown. Her daughter, on the other hand, looked as if she'd been dipped in a rainbow. She wore a violet headdress, shot with silver thread, and was pulled away from her face to let twinkle the emerald pins in her fair, curly hair. When she and Wulfthryth stopped to say a few words to each other, her scarlet cloak fell open, showing its ermine lining and the sapphire crucifix that lay on her gold-embroidered breast.

Leofric couldn't take his eyes off her. He looked like a cross 'twixt a whipped hound and a hungry wolf. For the poor lad's sake, I wished Lady Edith were just at Wilton for the Latin. But I knew that after King Eadgar had set Wulfthryth aside, he offered to make Lady Edith, only a few months old, the abbess of Wilton and two other minsters. She declined them or, rather, her mother did. Except for Wilton, where Wulfthryth became abbess and where the two had been ever since. But, if her dazzling clothes were any hint, maybe now, at eighteen, Lady Edith had grown weary of her heavenly bridegroom and longed for one a trifle more earthy. Maybe that's what Leofric hoped, anyway.

Forlornly, it looked like. Lady Edith stood silent and with downcast eyes as her mother reminded Leofric he was not welcome within the nunnery precinct. Her nose wrinkled as if the putrid smell that had arisen came from him and not the wind blowing off the jakes. She pointed to the two big guards who had just then come through the gate. "And if you do not leave forthwith, I shall be forced to have you arrested for rape."

Rape? My God, what rape?

Or maybe she meant that with the big scramseaxes strapped to our hips we looked like brigands. Or maybe she just meant we were men.

The abbess took a menacing step forward. "I know all about your disgusting ways, what kind of things you've done."

Did she mean at the ale house or with his lady friend? Leofric must've known because he straightaway took to his heels. I turned to take off right behind him—in England, raping a nun was almost more serious than committing murder—but the abbess touched my arm with her staff. To my surprise, she said, "Do not be alarmed. This has nothing to do with you."

She bared her teeth in what might have been a smile, so I gave her the half nod I always give Saxon royalty. If any of them have ever figured out my bow is a mite less than sincere, they've never said.

The abbess's tone wasn't exactly warm, but it was nowhere near the icy bath she'd dumped over Leofric. "We do not abuse the laws of hospitality here in Wilton Minster. However, I must tell you that we cannot offer you accommodation, if that is what the captain told you. I suggest you try the town's alehouse. They take in strangers and—"

"But we're not strangers, are we, Tryffin ap Tewdwr?" Lady Edith said with a welcoming smile.

I didn't think she'd remember. She'd been barely more than a child when we'd met. "Long ago and under unhappy circumstances, I'm afraid," I said as I dropped to one knee before her.

Lady Edith, who as a child had often been at her father's court, knew that he'd called on me to find the truth about his own father's murder. I'd succeeded, though justice had come at a price almost too steep even for a king.

"You did the right thing." She spoke in the same decisive but gracious tone her father always used. "Now I have to stir the soup for supper. Come join me. I love talking to strangers. And the soup is very good."

With her father's restless energy, she strode off, leaving her mother to wave forward the two guards. "My men will accompany you," the abbess said. "I have other duties."

The two guards were a pair so lumpishly English that one was scratching his ass while the other picked his nose. I almost broke into a run to catch up with Lady Edith.

In the yard we passed women and girls hard at work before nightfall, packing up the many looms that leaned against the buildings. Others hurried to unload wooden casks from carts drawn in front of the stone brewery. Since there was still some sun, two nuns remained at a trestle table copying from books propped up by other books. They had on heavy tunics and thick wool shawls, but I noticed that the hands holding the quills were all but blue with cold.

In the kitchen yard a huge iron vat sat over a fire that had burned down to embers. Lady Edith dipped a finger in the vat, tasted of the soup—it smelled like pig-tail. She licked her finger, pointed it at the two guards, then at the stack of wood by the stone kitchen house. They hopped to immediately, moving the wood, feeding the fire, fanning the flames.

When the fire was right, she picked up the big stick that lay across the vat, thrust it into the soup, and gave a stir or two. She again pointed at the guards. The ass-scratcher took the stick and started stirring. Lady Edith motioned me to the stools that sat in the lee of the kitchen house.

She had a hundred questions about my travels in faraway lands. Was it true that in Ireland women studied law? Had I ever been in Cordoba? Did I know the poet Ezter there? "Her husband's a poet, too, but it's Ezter's poetry we have here at Wilton. In Hebrew. Can you read it?"

While I tried to keep up with her questions—no, I couldn't read Hebrew, yes, the sea can freeze over, no, I'd never seen a dragon—she combed her fingers through the curly blond forelock that crept from beneath her headdress. She'd pulled off her cloak by then, and under it she wore a blue wool tunic that fell to her ankles. With its golden yoke and jeweled crucifix, the tunic looked far too expensive to be a nun's. So did her fur-lined boots.

Nor was I the only one to think she didn't dress the way a nun should. But I had the sense to hold my tongue. Unlike the bishop of Winchester, who'd once berated her severely and at length for her extravagant dress. To which Lady Edith responded, "God regards the heart more than the garment."

That shut him up.

But however she was with the bishop, she was nothing but kind to me. As evening came and the soup began to bubble, our talk grew more serious. We spoke of God and Fortune, then she read from her copy of Boethius. We talked of his conversation with Lady Philosophy and how she taught him that the contemplation of God is the highest good and reconciles a person to misfortune.

"You must know that, Tryff. You've had your own misfortunes. Your father ... "

My father... It's a tale I dislike telling, but I all at once found myself telling it to Lady Edith. I don't know why, except she had a way about her. And that way was why, during her father's lifetime and even still, she received ambassadors from France and Germany, from tough Norsker kings and faraway Byzantium. They came for Lady Edith's wisdom, of course, and her kindness. Later in her life, I heard, they came to hear her talk of the art of rule, its moral dangers along with its worldly rewards.

Me, I told her my story because Edith was a pretty girl and I like pretty girls.

After I finished, she said, "Let me see if I've got this straight. Your father—a prince, is he?"

That'd be one word for him. And even it is way too grand. His brother's realm is just some high hills squeezed 'twixt a pair of rivers. But I agreed that, yes, my *tad* was a prince.

Now Lady Edith looked me over tip to toe. She didn't say it, but I could tell she didn't think I looked like any prince's son, even a Welsh one. "So your father came home one day and found your mother in bed with his court clown."

"His name was Fynach the Funny. The clown, I mean. My

father's name is Tewdwr ap Callwen—Tewdwr, son of Callwen." Like I'm Tryffin, son of Tewdwr. A thing I've never denied. Blood is blood, more's the pity.

"And for punishment," Lady Edith said, "your father had the clown burned in a wicker cage. Then sold your mother into slavery."

A lot of women would've touched me then, to show their sorrow over such a thing and offer a little sympathy. But Lady Edith just looked into the fire and pulled at her hair. When she spoke, her voice was brisk as the winter wind. "How could he do that?"

Something I'd been asking myself most of my life. "There's an awful lot of evil here below, I reckon—"

She waved that aside. "I mean how could he do it under the law? You do have laws in Wales, don't you? She was his wife, for heaven's sake. She had rights, didn't she?"

Now wasn't that just like a Saxon, royal or not? Always worrying about the law. Of course, there were laws in Wales, even for women. Better than most, too, you compare them to France or Italy or Spain.

"She wasn't exactly his wife," I said.

If Lady Edith was shocked, she didn't show it. Just blinked her indigo eyes a couple of times when I quick-like added, "I'm his lawful son, though."

And I am. Tewdwr never denied it and he used his own goods to raise me. Among the Welsh that made me his, just like the sons of his wife.

"So your mother was his concubine—"

"A very fancy Latin word," I shot back, in case she was trying to make fun of me. She wasn't, though. She said, "Therefore, your mother had no rights, no protection."

"If my mam had stayed in his bed for seven years, she would've been all right. As safe as his wife. Not that Tewdwr ever treated Gwyneth any too well, either."

"Didn't your mother's kin try to protect her? They should've marched—"

"My father bought them off. They were barely more than slaves themselves. Thought a stretch of property to call their own was ample payment for somebody they said was nothing but a woman of bush and brake anyhow."

And maybe she was, though she stayed under Tewdwr's roof for better than six years. I can't figure why. Likely he kept promising her he'd put aside his wife. Though that would've been pretty hard, since he'd already been married to her for seven years. After that, divorce gets difficult in Wales. And expensive.

Or maybe my mam just wanted the comforts of Caer Tewdwr. Being with a man of stock, even a cruel one like my father, was sure better than life in a peasant hovel.

But I didn't think it was worth getting into all this with Lady Edith. And what would the king of England's daughter care anyhow? So I was a little surprised when she all of a sudden leaped up. "How could he do that? She was a Christian. Even in Wales it must be illegal for one Christian to enslave another."

"Not when you're dealing with Irish slavers."

"Where did the Irishmen take her?"

I shrugged.

"You knew the king my father. You performed great service for him. Why didn't you ask him to send his men to find her?"

I shrugged.

"Or now you could ask my brother," she said. "Why does Ethelred or that mother of his not find her? That is what I would do were I sovereign in this realm."

And she probably would've. Too bad the thegns and bishops hadn't had the wisdom and courage to elect Lady Edith queen. It wasn't unheard of in England. King Alfred's daughter ruled Mercia. And there'd been one named Seaxburh, I think, right there in Wessex.

Lady Edith sat down again and in a sad voice said, "Wherever your mother is now, I know the Lord soothes her poor, wounded soul."

We both fell silent and I got up to toss another log on the fire. By the time she spoke again, her voice was cool and under full control. "If you'd like to tell me more, I'd be glad to listen."

I poked the fire 'til sparks shot up into the growing dark. "He swapped her, if you want to know. For two copper pots and a tall grey dog."

"And you? What of his son?"

"Sent me to his brother the abbot."

Lady Edith waved the guards away from the fire and came and stood beside me, her arm through mine. "Do you know where your mother is now?"

"In Navarre, I've heard. Or Italy. Across the whale road, anyway. Or maybe only up in York. I've heard that, too."

I paused for a breath or two, then got down to business. "You've been so kind as to let me tell you the miserable story of my life. Now may I ask you something? Your brother King Edward's remains seem to have—"

But before I could say "disappeared," Abbess Wulfthryth burst into the yard.

"What are you doing with my daughter, luring her into this solitary place? She asked you to stay because she remembered you as the man who once rid England of a king killer. Now here you are, acting the brute."

"Mother—"

Edith tried to get a word in, but Wulfthryth was in full cry. "You are a scoundrel and a thief as well! Oh yes, I remember your visit to our reliquary two years ago. And now I see my first thought about you today was right."

She turned and barked at the guards who dawdled behind her. "Kene! Wilfrid! Take this thing away."

A frog-march to the front gate, a hard shove, and I was face down in the cold mud of Minster Street.

I limped back to the royal hall—cold, wet, and with my uncle the abbot's voice in my ear, half whine, half whip like it always was when I failed at some task or duty. "Your sins will find you out, boy." And he was right. Because of robbing Wilton Minster's relic box two years ago, now I'd never find out what Wulfthryth and her daughter might know about King Edward's body. Besides that, I hadn't even made a decent profit off their saint.

But if none of the saints were smiling—Fortuna, neither—somebody else turned out to be ready to point me in the direction of the royal cadaver. The guard at the royal hall's gate said Sister Hild was waiting in the guest bower. I found her there without a companion nun, only a carved cane across her knees. When I sat down at the battered oak table, she offered me neither respite nor solace. Nor information.

"Throw some water on your face," she said. "And put on a clean tunic, if you have such a thing. We will see Lady Flæda now. She wants to help you find King Edward. He was her son, after all."

"Lady Flæda? By St. Helena, what've I done to deserve another dead royal? Will I have to look for her or have you got her someplace cooling nicely?"

Sister pursed her lips. "Must you always play the fool?"

I sure felt like one when Sister informed me that Lady Flæda, King Eadgar's first wife, most certainly wasn't dead. "In spite of what the king claimed, she did not die shortly after Edward's birth. The king sent Lady Flæda to Wilton."

And that would've been just about the time he took up with Wulfthryth. "No wonder she lives here in the hall and not at the Minster," I said. "Eadgar always did take good care of his women."

Sister Hild banged her cane on the floor hard and suddenly enough to make me jump. Sister was damn near the oldest woman I knew. Well past fifty, I think, and lumbered with that stick. Which I'm not sure she needed. Sometimes she leaned on it like it was the only thing 'twixt her and the Hereafter. Other times she hustled around like a girl of twenty. And she was forever on the road, travelling in search of charms and herbs and whatever else she needed to cure folk of what ails them.

"Now," she said, "besides being in Wilton to meet with you, I'm also seeing to Lady Flæda's leprosy. "

I damn near choked. "Leprosy? By St. Lazarus, no wonder Eadgar sent her away. She was lucky he didn't lop off her head."

It's well known that leprosy is caused by lust. Which, come to think of it, was probably why Eadgar married Flæda in the first place. He liked the ladies, liked them lots and often, the lustier the better. But what of Flæda herself? What if the royal member couldn't satisfy her? What if she went looking for her bliss under other tunics? Me, I'd never known the lady—in any way—so I couldn't say for certain she was a whore. Nor had I heard it of her, either. But now here she was with leprosy.

I started to ask Sister Hild if Flæda had come down with it before or after King Eadgar met Wulfthryth. But all of a sudden, I remembered what they said about leprosy in Constantinople, where it was a common thing. They said no matter what its cause, it was a plague even the Arab doctors, best in the world, couldn't tame once it broke loose.

That made me jump right off my stool. "You want me— ME!—in the same room with her? The same hall? The same town?"

Sister Hild jabbed her cane my direction. "You've already come down with lust, Tryff. And if the disease's cause lies elsewhere, you'll still not be stricken. I've not been and I've dressed her poor leg for years."

But I was already breaking for the door. I had it flung open when Sister Hild reminded me that Prioress had taken the keg full of silver away with her. "To be kept by Wilton's bishop until you've delivered King Edward's body."

I glanced at Sister, thought of my mother, then heaved a sigh and returned to the stool. "So let me get this straight. Lady Flæda didn't die, like King Eadgar put about. But she couldn't be the king's wife anymore because she's a leper." And, it went without saying, a whore.

"He had little choice but to repudiate her and send her away from the royal court."

How much had his household's silence cost him? How much more the Pope's? And maybe the situation had cost Eadgar more than money. During my time of service with him, I'd only heard him speak of Lady Flæda once. I forget his exact words, though I remember his tone being both sad and tender.

Nor had he disowned their son, unlike another father I

could name. "But he didn't have any other sons at the time, did he?"

Sister Hild shook her head.

"How did he know Edward was even his? Under the circumstances, I mean."

Sister poured a cup of wine and pushed it my way. "You served King Eadgar. So you know very well he kept his wives all but prisoners, with only women around them until they were safely with child."

I knew no such thing. "Queen Ælfthryth went where she wanted, when she wanted, with whoever she wanted. And whether or not she was with child. Still does, I imagine."

A grin cracked through Sister Hild's wrinkles. "I'd forgotten you only met the king after he discarded his first two wives. But you're right, Ælfthryth constitutes a separate case."

And Sister should've known. For one thing, she'd midwifed both their sons, first Edmund, then Ethelred.

"If only Queen Ælfthryth had sent for me in time, I could have saved poor little Edmund. Or, barring that, she could have taken the lad to the nuns in Wareham. He only had a touch of winter cough. But, no, she let some dreadful local woman talk of worm and elves and treat him with cow patty. And there Ælftthryth stayed, out in Dorset until ... "

Before Sister Hild went on one of her tears, I brought her back to King Eadgar and Lady Flæda. "Why'd he choose the Wilton royal hall to stash her in? Why not someplace truly remote like York? Anybody can find out she's here."

"She would have come to St. Finella's if I'd had my way. But our prioress said we couldn't risk it."

Well, someone had to show a little common sense. And I

noticed it wasn't Prioress who was now parked in this little room in Wilton, waiting for the leper queen.

And waiting. Lady Flæda didn't send for us until well after the cathedral bells chimed Vespers. We'd missed our suppers, though I don't think I could've eaten anything anyway. The guest lodge's green smoke was bothering me again, never mind the leftover Wiltshire ale still sloshing around inside my head.

Lady Flæda met us in her bower, a small timber building separate even from the rest of the hall bower. It was good-sized, though not a room meant for confab, more a space for cold-weather work at the loom taking up almost the whole of one wall. A fire pit sat in the middle of the room, its embers barely aglow. Next to it was a small oak table, without, I noticed, any cups on it or an ale horn. The only seating were a few stools and a high-back chair carved from tree trunk. A thick wool curtain separated the chamber from a sheepskin-covered bed.

Any light came from the beeswax candles that only a queen could afford. Otherwise, the room would've been far too plain for a royal bower without the ornate dragons on the plaster walls. They wound and hissed and spat fire, even slithered onto the plank floor.

The Lady sat in the tree trunk chair. Though I wouldn't have had to, and hadn't for Wulfthryth, I dropped to one knee before her. I was finally learning you can never overdo it with women or royalty. Now if I could only learn to govern my tongue.

Her full name was Æthelflæda Eneda and she was sometimes called the White Duck. If you thought about it,

Lady Flæda really could put you in mind of a white duck. She was that fair and that plump. She also quacked. Or maybe her ugly northern accent and the flat pitch of her voice made it sound so. She was a fetching woman, though, with eyes the color of a summer sky and a lovely big bosom straining against her green tweed tunic. Her only jewelry was an elaborately wrought gold brooch sweetly perched on the mound of her breasts. I didn't see any signs of leprosy, but her hands remained hidden inside the long sleeves of the tunic.

After she bade me stand up, and while I was trying not to seem too interested in her bosom, she turned to Sister Hild. "Have you become a wandering entertainer, dear Sister, that you come before us leading this black bear?"

"He's Welsh," Sister said, as if that explained all.

Lady Flæda laughed, and it was more ripple than quack. "A most musical folk, the Welsh. What is it you call your scops? Bards? Eadgar was always so fond of your bards and their strange stories."

She bit her lip. "But that was long ago. Now I have some things to tell you which need to be said in private. Go see to it that the guards or my women or some servant hasn't found cause to be about."

I went to the door, opened it, peered up and down the hallway. Except for the smoke from its lamps, it was empty.

"But we must keep close watch." She nodded at Sister Hild, who slipped into the hallway and took her place in a leather chair just outside the bower door. "Because if I know Ealdorman Alvar, he'll come sneaking around. Or send one of his henchmen. He's like a child. Always thinks somebody might be telling secrets."

Her blue gaze brushed over me. "But what I'm going to tell you is no secret."

Then why put on such a show about it? Maybe Lady Flæda missed life in a king's court, where secrets were served with ceremony and gossip dripped from every courtesy.

She folded pale, smooth hands over her bosom. "It's no secret—although Alvar, for instance, would never admit it— that my son, the king of England, was a complete ass."

So much for courtliness, never mind mother love.

"Edward was foul-mouthed, hot-tempered, pig-headed, and completely self-engaged. A disappointment as a son and as a sovereign."

She held up a hand as if to stop me from disagreeing. "You wonder that a mother would say such things about her boy. Or a subject about her king. It's true, however. And I know why."

I expected her to pause for effect. But she flew on, her voice rising first to quack then to hoot. "He was a royal prince eligible for the kingship. But his father never recognized him as heir. As his throne-worthy successor."

Sires are that way sometimes, as I had cause to know. 'Specially if there's something wrong with the dam.

"It wasn't enough for Eadgar to ignore my son when that woman cast her spell over him. No, he sent Edward away, too. To Cliffden, for the monks to rear. Oh, he sent servants with him. And horses and silver. All the things a prince could ever need. Except respect. Regard. Recognition as the heir."

By now I was confused. "What woman cast what spell?"

"Ælfthryth, of course. Queen Ælfthryth, she likes to call herself. As if she was ever anything but what I myself was. The king's wife. No more. Nor less."

"And a spell-caster, you say?"

"A speaking-woman."

That's what the English call someone who does business with Satan.

"Ælfthryth's a speaking-woman." Lady Flæda pressed her hands together and took a deep breath, like an entertainer does getting ready to sing in a crowded mead hall. "You may think I'm only a woman scorned. But this is why I wanted to speak with you alone. To warn you to be careful of that woman. She really does traffic with Satan. Have you never heard what she did to the abbot of Ely?"

"I been out of the country a while. Haven't kept up on all the royal gossip."

"This isn't gossip. I swear on the Gospel-book, this is truth. Ælfthryth cast a spell over the abbot of Ely and it killed him."

She glanced at the door and her voice fell to a whisper. "Ælfthryth killed him right there in the royal hall in Winchester."

I raised my eyebrows in silent question—why?

"Because one day he caught her changing herself into a horse."

Well, well. A woman of some parts, is our Ælfthryth. Shape-shifter and spell-caster, too. "A horse, you say?"

"A black mare, to be precise."

"She do that often? Or just for passing abbots?"

"Then before he could inform King Eadgar about her vile practices, Ælfthryth cast a spell over him."

"Over Eadgar or the abbot?"

"Both. But you know very well that just now I'm talking about the abbot. Ælfthryth cast a spell over him that made him come to her bower, where she killed him. Had him killed, I should say. Her serving woman took red-hot shears to him. First she burnt open his stomach, then she cut off his privates."

If she expected me to quake and quail in fear for my manhood, she was sorely mistaken. Ælfthryth was no witch. That I knew, though I wasn't so sure about her serving women. They could cast spells over a man all right.

Anyway, I'd known that abbot of Ely. Did business with him when I was a young fellow just starting out in the relic trade. It wouldn't have taken any magic spell to send the abbot into a woman's bower. Besides, I heard he dropped dead at his own altar.

Lady Flæda leaned forward in her chair. "No one knows this story but the monks at Ely and myself."

"So why are you telling me?"

"Because you need these." She plunged a hand down her tunic front.

I watched the movement of her hand as it worked between her breasts. What was she offering me?

When the hand reappeared, it held nothing but a leather pouch. "You need the protection of my charms," she said as she dumped the pouch's contents onto the table in front of me. Out fell a yellow tooth and a leathery grey disk.

"They belonged to St. Apollonia and St. Agatha. Take your choice. They're all good against witchcraft. Ælfthryth's witchcraft, anyway."

I reckoned they must be good protection. If they weren't, Lady Flæda would be dead instead of divorced. I chose St. Apollonia's tooth, mostly because it was small. Besides, St. Apollonia looks after teeth, which I have a full set of, and St.

Agatha is in charge of women's ailments, which I have none of.

"Splendid," she said with a satisfied nod. "Now I can direct you safely to Edward's body."

The tooth almost flipped out of my hands. Did she already know where Edward's body was? If she did, what was all this prattle about? Why not just send Ealdorman Alvar or one of his men to find it?

A little smile came to her lips, but she promptly smothered it. "What I should say is that I myself don't know where Edward is, but I know the man who does."

"Then send *him* after it."

"I have done just that. But Wynstan is a man who cannot always be trusted. I mean, he sometimes does foolish things. It is needful that you help him."

That didn't sound right. "You saying you don't trust your own man?"

She didn't really answer, just said not to let him know I was watching him for her. "Wynstan is a man of great pride. I would not want to injure it. But you must find him. And my son."

When I could not find a reply, she said, "I know Ælfthryth has already bade you search for Edward. I have added money to pay Wynstan for his knowledge."

What choice did I have? Because just then Sister Hrothbeort came in, rolling the keg of pennies. Astraddle it rode my saddle bags. They were full of Flæda 's silver.

Next dawn, Tom Tub and I passed through Wilton's gate, off to find Wynstan. Leofric wasn't on duty nor was his yeoman. I did, though, catch a glimpse of Ealdorman Alvar slipping into the cathedral for Prime. A busy man, our Alvar.

Wynstan, Lady Flæda told me, was in Winchester, less than a day's ride away. So by nightfall I should have been safely tucked in a Winchester bed. But Fortuna's wheel turned again. On the section of road that sprouts off just south of the London Way, I dismounted at a little valley stream and both Tom and I put our mouths in the icy water. All at once something heavy, a cloak maybe, fell over me. Then my head got pushed hard into the water and held there.

The problem with struggling while somebody's trying to drown you is that it'll drown you. And I was struggling hard enough to make exactly that happen when the attack stopped, just like that. I heard the slosh of feet through mud and the wet clatter of horses scrambling out of there.

By the time I'd thrown off the heavy cloak, all I saw was a pair of churls the size of oak trees standing by a mound of slush. They were too dry to be the ones who'd held me down in the stream. And if I knew country men, there'd be no point asking whether they saw who did. They wouldn't give away their neighbors. Besides, there was something more important just then. "Oy! You two thieving Saxon assholes! Where's my horse?"

I didn't think they'd stolen Tom, but he was nowhere to be seen and I had to take my fury out on somebody. One of the churls shrugged while the other picked a flea out of his beard and crushed it with his thumbnail.

I hurled the cloak to the ground—it stank like a hundred dead polecats. Then I hurled every curse I knew at the Saxons and a few I made up on the spot. They just stared back at me, both of them with that empty English look and the one still clawing at his whiskers. Just as I pulled out my scramseaxe and started for them, Tom came loping back.

He was fine, only a little spooked, and let me climb aboard without too much fuss. As I passed the churls, the mighty flea slayer wrinkled up his nose. "Man," he said, "you sure do smell ugly."

I grabbed Tom and swung into the saddle. Time to be off for Winchester. Lest I start carving up some Saxon flesh.

CHAPTER SIX

I hadn't been in Winchester for years. But Fortune had found me there before, and looking around now I could see the place was still *Felix urbs Winthonia*. Lucky Winchester-town, with its royal hall, its cathedral, three rich monasteries, and its bustling economy—and the ruckus, even on so cold an afternoon! Men and animals hollering, clerics braying out their prayers, church bells going off the whole livelong time.

Tom and I pushed through the crowd surging along Cheap Street, where kilns and smithies pumped smoke into the winter air while fishermen hawked their pickled eel and butchers their frozen mutton. Next to a baker's stall that smelled like Eden must've, a juggler and his little troupe worked the crowd. They were too bundled up to put on much of a show. He dropped as many balls as not and his girl dancer did little more than shuffle across the icy dirt.

I felt sorry for them, 'specially for the small boy who thrust out their begging bowl. It's hard to live by your wits. But I had no time for charity. At least not 'til I found the man who would lead me to King Edward's body.

Lady Flæda had said to meet Wynstan in the alehouse where he sang. But she didn't say which alehouse, and Winchester was full of them. In the first two I tried they'd never heard of him and at the third the ale-keep burst out laughing and said he wouldn't let "that broken-down old stinker" under his roof. It was almost dark before I finally came on him in an alehouse that seemed nothing more than the ale-keep's hovel.

It was a windowless room lit by oil lamps stuck in its log walls and only big enough to hold a dozen or so customers, some wooden barrels, and a manger for the cow and her spotted calf. So this was what he'd come to. Wynstan Wing-tongue, who'd struck the harp before prince and prelate, now sang for his supper in a low Winchester tavern.

Tonight it was packed with English throwing dice and swilling ale. They were churls, and not very prosperous ones by the look of them. The room was hot and they'd pulled back their cloaks, so I could see their torn tunics and trousers and their filthy leg bands and mud-crusted clogs. Poor they might've been, but they were merry with drink and their own good company. The smoky room rang with laughter and rich English oaths. In one corner, two red-faced women ladled ale—the ale-keep's wife and daughter, likely—laughing and dripping sweat into every cup of brew they handed off.

They say there's no bargaining with God. But when I saw Wynstan the poet sprawled on the floor with blood oozing out of his dirty white hair, I sure gave it a try. "Dear Lord, don't let this old man be dead and I promise I'll split every saint I ever sell with you, right down the middle."

The old man lay by the far wall. Though his big belly and poet's triple-pointed beard told me this was Wynstan, I called out his name good and loud just to make sure. A half dozen Saxon heads swiveled in my direction. Their owners looked none too friendly, but one of them pulled a finger out of his nose and pointed in Wynstan's direction. As I shoved through the crowd, a curly-headed blond fellow stuck out a leg to try and trip me. "Dirty Welsh shithead," he said.

Every Welshman knows it's true. *Mynd at Sais i ddysgu moesau.* You don't go to a Saxon to learn manners. Still, what made the mannerless oaf know I was Welsh? Maybe because I'm so dark, all black hair and beard. Eyes, too. My mam used to say they were black as an Englishman's heart.

Not that I was bothering this Englishman, or his heart. But some chaps need an ale barrel to draw their manhood out of. I kicked him in his and, while he lay groaning at my feet, I threatened his mates with the same or worse if they tried to make a feud of it.

They mustn't have liked the look of a lad the size of me. Or maybe it was the size of the scramseaxe I pulled out. Anyway, they went right back to their drinking and dicing, to hell with curly-head slumped in the dirt.

Knife still in my hand, I knelt beside Wynstan. "Dear God," I prayed again, "don't let this old boy be dead. And if he's not, Lord, please let him know where Edward's body is."

When I turned Wynstan over, his mouth dropped open and his eyes rolled back in his head. A cut on his forehead oozed blood and a line of yellow spittle drained down his chin. He wasn't breathing, either. But I've known men without breath whose hearts still beat hard as a ram in rut. I put my ear to his chest. He stank like a tannery.

"Is he dead?" said somebody at my shoulder.

My knife and I spun around to find a girl kneeling beside me. She had wide green eyes and her headdress had fallen off tangled red hair that hung to her waist. She could've been any age from twelve to twenty.

"He's dead drunk," I said. "Who're you?"

The girl glanced at Wynstan as he took a loud snort of air. "Do you know him?"

"I do. If it's any of your concern." I stuck my knife back in my belt, then pulled a wad of yellow mess out of Wynstan's mouth. I flicked it in the direction of the curly-haired Saxon.

"When'll he come to?" she asked.

"I don't know. Maybe tonight. Maybe not 'til tomorrow."

She looked around the tavern. At the gamblers crouched over their noisy game of knuckle-bones, the pair of women at the barrels, the curly-haired churl now sitting up and sucking ale from a leather bucket.

Turning back to me, she said, "You should get him home."

"What do you care? You the ale-keep's daughter or something?"

"His."

"His? Wynstan's, you mean?"

The girl widened her eyes and gave me a smile that would've brought a hallelujah even in the halls of hell. She was definitely older than twelve.

"Wynstan's," she said and peered around the tavern again.

When I did the same, the curly-haired Englishman cast me a wicked look. Maybe he'd had his eye on the girl and figured I might give him some competition. But presently he shrugged and went back to his ale.

"That man is not Wynstan's friend," the girl said. "They had words earlier, while Wynstan was singing his story."

She touched the wound on the old poet's head. "That's

how he got hurt. We really must take him home."

Likely he and the girl had a room somewhere in Winchester.

"All right, let's go." I took hold of Wynstan's feet. She shoved her cloak under his head so it wouldn't get scraped while I dragged him along the rough dirt floor.

As we passed, Curly-hair glared at us, then stuck his nose back in the ale bucket. No one else tossed us so much as a look. Wynstan must've given the customers a good performance, though. The ale-keep didn't try to collect even an extra penny for all the ale the old man had drunk.

Outside, I asked the girl, "Is it far?"

"Oh," she said, "far."

In the yard Wynstan came around enough to mumble a curse, then pull himself more or less to his feet. Before he could fold up again, the girl and I draped his arms across our shoulders and lugged him to the ale-keep's shed, where Tom Tub was munching oats and stamping his hooves on the cold ground.

"Look, girl," I said, "I'm going to tie Wynstan in the saddle, then get on behind to hold him aboard. I won't be able to use the reins, so you'll have to take Tom by the halter and lead us. You'll have to carry the lantern, too."

"My name, sir, is not 'girl,' it's Kyre." Her tone made her sound like the first-born daughter of one of the king's own thegns.

When I had the lantern lit and Wynstan and me where I wanted us, Kyre caught hold of Tom's halter and we set off through the dark streets of Winchester. When she led us toward the town's north gate, I asked her if she and Wynstan were staying out in the country instead of in Winchester.

"In a barn," she said. "Don't worry, it's quite warm there."

"But is it far?"

From under her hood, Kyre threw me that delicious smile again. I lapped it up like a kitten at the cream bowl. "How old are you?" I asked.

"Nineteen," she said. "Maybe twenty. If it's any of your concern."

I relaxed. At least it wasn't somebody still in swaddling clothes I was just then lusting after.

I put away that notion quick as I could. This was no night for thoughts of the flesh. Unless they had to do with keeping it from freezing solid.

Neither of us spoke as we went through the town gate, nor out in the cold, empty countryside. Behind us Winchester's bells tolled Compline.

A few miles later, we went past a silent hamlet and its barns. "How come you stay such a long way from town?" I asked.

"He wants it so."

That didn't sound much like the Wynstan I remembered. He was like other travelling poets—scops, the English call them. He wanted people around him, people who cheered when he took his place in a crowded mead hall. People who fell silent when he struck his harp-strings and yelled out to them, *"Hwaet!"*—"Listen!"

And the people would hold their breaths as he began the story their lord had hired him to sing. They'd set down their ale cups and mead horns—the ones still sober enough to listen, anyway—so they could better take in his tale of men and monsters, of kings and killing, of golden gifts to loyal hallmen. Of all the stuff of Saxon dreams and Saxon honor. Then, when he finished, the people would shake the rafters with their clapping and shouting. Afterwards, he'd receive his own gifts. Not always golden, but worth enough to have made Wynstan Wing-tongue the richest scop in Britain.

That was a long time past. Now he was an old drunk reduced to selling secrets. And I hoped he'd come around soon, so he could sell one to me.

On the other side of the hamlet lay its landlord's hall, a sprawling pile of dark buildings set high up a slope. Dogs barked as we passed the wooden walls. Just beyond them was a fine, big barn filled, I figured, with lots of warm straw. But Kyre didn't turn Tom into its lane, just kept marching along the road.

A mile or so later, Wynstan favored us with a loud "*Hwaet!*" followed by the word "Murder" and then, "Poison!"

"You've been poisoned, all right," I retorted. "By English ale and your own gluttony." From the look of the puke that lay frozen on his cloak-front, Wynstan had downed the best part of a mutton leg and a chicken or two before he'd laced into who knew how much ale.

"Murder!" he yelled again.

"Look there!" Kyre cried. Up ahead, a few yards off the road, was the dark shape of a building.

"St. Christopher be praised," I said. I meant it, too, because the sky had grown cloudy and a hard wind carried the smell of snow. But when we got to the round, picket building, it turned out to be a wayfarer's hut roofed over by thin thatch.

"This isn't any barn."

"The barn is much further and the weather's turned."

Kyre was right about that. The wind had not only blown out the lamp, it now carried ice. Still, the prospect of sitting out a storm in this place didn't please me much. It seemed barely big enough for three humans, never mind Tom Tub.

But the hut turned out to be better than it looked. Its swept dirt floor bore a rock-rimmed fire pit, a goodly stack of dry wood, and enough hay to keep Tom from starving to death. Lucky, too, that the door was high enough to let him through, though we had to drag Wynstan in.

While Kyre got her father stretched 'twixt a couple of thick layers of straw, I took out the bits of firestone I carried in my pouch. The good folk who kept up the place had remembered to leave tinder, so before long we had a nice fire.

They'd also left a wooden bucket full of water, now mostly turned to ice. I handed Kyre a sliver and sucked on one myself. After the rest melted, Kyre wanted to give it to the old man, but I let Tom have it. When Wynstan woke up, he could slake his hangover with half the snow in Wessex.

Kyre and I huddled by the fire, warming our hands and feet and watching smoke curl through the hole in the ceiling. I'd unsaddled Tom and covered him with his blanket. Now he chomped at the hay, while Wynstan mumbled in his sleep. Outside, the wind howled around the hut like a hungry wolf.

Finally, Kyre said, "You're a good friend to Wynstan, Taff. And God bless you for it."

"Tryff," I said. "Name's Tryff Tewdwr."

"Well, whatever it is, you're a good friend to take so much trouble for Wynstan."

"We're not exactly what you'd call friends, but we've done some work together." We hadn't, of course. But she didn't need to know that. "Maybe he's mentioned me."

"He tells me very little," Kyre said with a sad shake of her head.

She was a pretty girl. I like talking to pretty girls.

There came a hard pounding at the door.

"Murder!" Wynstan sat straight up in the straw. "Murder! They're trying to murder me!"

I peeked through a chink in the wicker wall. But I couldn't see a thing for snow blown against the hut. No matter. Whoever was out there couldn't get in. I'd barred the door by setting Tom's saddle in front of it.

The pounding was getting harder now and a man was yelling. Cursing, too, claiming to be about to die of the cold. I stood up and drew my scramseaxe. Kyre, too, now held a knife. You never know who you might meet up with in a traveller's hut like this one. Once, in northern Italy, I opened the door to a pack of bandits who robbed me of St. Barbara's backbone and all of St. Moldadus. I've heard of folk who had to spend the night with elves and pookies, even a troll or two.

On the other hand, you can't leave somebody out in a storm. I shoved the saddle back and slid the door open a crack, careful to keep my shoulder to it so I could slam it shut if there was a snow-demon on the other side. A gust of wind blew it open anyway.

A body fell in.

CHAPTER SEVEN

The thing that landed on the hut floor wasn't a corpse but a young boy, alive and bawling. He wore a rough wool tunic and his cap had slid back to show fair hair and red ears.

The door banged open again. A cloud of steam and snow burst into the hut, followed by a man in a billowing black cloak. "By Satan's boots, it sure as hell took you long enough to let us in."

"St. David preserve me," I said out loud. He was the Saxon I'd tried to unman back at the alehouse.

"Thank God we come on this place." He swept back his hood to show hair matted with ice. "It's a rough night out there."

While my mouth hung open in surprise, he knelt by the boy. "You all right, Cuthred?"

The child stared at the Englishman with eyes blue and clear as a day in June. "Wannh," he howled. "Wannhstan."

"He's here," the Saxon said to the lad. Then, to me, "Ain't he?"

"There." I nodded at the mound of straw next to Kyre.

Her mouth was a thin crease and her knife remained in her hand. So did mine. I've done some knife-fighting in my time and if this Saxon had come for vengeance, he'd soon be chasing his guts across the floor.

"Is Wynstan all right?" the man said.

"Who wants to know?"

Eyes on my knife, he said, "Put that thing away and help me with the lad. Then I'll be happy to tell you whatever you want to hear."

Help him do what with the lad? By now we were packing the hut like pigeons in a pie.

Fortunately, Kyre had the sense to put away her knife and pull the bleating boy to her. She touched his face. "Brave lad," she said. Then she gave him that hallelujah smile, which even small boys couldn't resist. He grinned back, snuggled up against her, and fell asleep.

"About what happened back at the alehouse," the man said with a lopsided grin, "my mates put me up to it. They don't like strangers and I was drunk."

If that was an apology, it was a mighty thin one. But I let it pass. Just kept my knife where he could see it and asked him who he was and why he was out in the storm with the lad. Whoever the lad was.

"My name's Beorn. Boy's called Cuthred. Leastways that's what he said when he come flying out from the ale-keep's cowshed, hollering for Wynstan."

I looked over at Kyre, to see what she might think about all this. But she was fast asleep.

"Reckon I was a little light in the head, to do such a thing," Beorn said. "Grab the boy and carry him out of the tavern." Drunk, he meant. It sure wasn't his head I'd kicked him in. "But I felt sorry for the lad. You can tell he ain't full-witted."

Far as I could tell, Cuthred was like any other Saxon sprig —snot-nosed and whiney.

Beorn said that when the two of them got away from the tavern, he told the boy he'd seen Wynstan go off with a woman and a Welshman. Cuthred went back to bellowing, up and down Goldsmith street so loud it brought householders to their doors and drunk Saxons streaming from the tavern. "Surprised you lot didn't hear. I seen you lingering at the north gate. Figured I could catch up. But Cuthred don't move so quick and I didn't know the weather'd come on so bad."

The story smelled funny. "Live in Winchester, do you?" I asked him.

"Staying there. But I come from the Wye Valley."

That explained how he knew I was Welsh. Along the Wye, Cymry and Saxon have been living plunk up against each other time out of mind. Not always too happily, either.

"I come down here," Beorn said, "to see if I could get on with the monks at the cathedral. Heard they liked to have men with my talents around." His hands darted beneath his cloak. Before they could come out holding something wicked, I brought my hawk-hilted scramseaxe alongside his jaw.

His Adam's apple hopped up, then down, and his hands moved real slow as they pulled forth two combs and a small bone ball. "I'm a bone and antler man. Carve combs, buckles, handles. Even gewgaws like this." He ran the ornately carved ball back and forth along his knuckles.

I pulled my knife away. "Who's this Cuthred?"

"The old man's son. Who's the woman?"

"His daughter."

"You don't say." Beorn's pale eyebrows shot up and he glanced at the sleeping Kyre. "Glad I ain't got a daughter like her. That'd bop me over the head with an ale cup, make the blood go flying."

Now what was this? Kyre said Beorn had hit Wynstan. Now here was Beorn claiming she did it. I would've pursued the matter right then, only I was worn out. I had to get some sleep. But what to do about this Beorn? The best I could think of was to tie his hands and feet, then for Kyre and me to take turns watching him. I woke her and she agreed, even said she'd take first watch. I was too tired to argue, though I went to sleep wondering how an honest merchant like myself got mixed in with a washed-up poet, a champion sniveler, and at least one lying Saxon.

When I woke next morning, Kyre was sitting in the straw with Cuthred on her lap. "It's all right, love," she said as she pulled boy's cap down over his ears. "He'll be gone just a while."

Seeing I was awake, she said, "I let that other man loose and he's been decent enough to go see where we've landed. Maybe he'll find us something to eat."

"Landed? What do you mean, landed? I thought we were near where you lot live."

"Well ... "

"You saying we're lost?"

She didn't say.

"Aren't we on the main road?"

She still didn't say.

"By St. Christopher, how could you go and get us lost?"

She opened her mouth to say. But I told her not to bother. *"Ni ddiffyg esqus ar wraiq,"* I said. A woman never lacks an excuse.

Through the smoke-hole, I could see dawn coming up. And no snow falling down. The wind had dropped, too, though it still blew hard enough to make Beorn a brave man for going out in it. "Wynstan still asleep?"

"He's been twisting around a while, muttering about murder again."

She settled Cuthred back in his place next to Wynstan, told him to stay put, then swept up the water bucket and made for the door. As she stepped into the wind, Wynstan popped out of the straw and yelled, "Cuthred! Has God preserved you through the evil of the night?"

That brought the boy up, too. "Wannhstan," he cried and threw himself atop the old man's big belly. They hugged and kissed, then went to picking the straw out of each other's hair with a sweet care that surprised me. I didn't know the English could be so affectionate.

Presently, Wynstan jabbed a finger in my direction. In a voice commanding enough for King Eadgar himself, he said, "For all the love you bear the dear Lord above, help me and my boy outside."

Up, Wynstan looked ready to topple straight into the pit of hell and be glad of it. But the arrogant old bastard wasn't so hung over he couldn't eye me like I was the most disgusting churl ever to crawl out of an English dung heap. "By St. Nicholas, if it isn't my very favorite failed *fedelis predo*. Still running from the archbishop, are you?"

I hadn't seen Wynstan since Eadgar's coronation in Bath, six years before. But he seemed to have kept up with all the gossip. I said, "Where's the king's body?"

Wynstan's bloodshot eyes swiveled my direction. "More to the point, where are *we*?" He pushed open the hut door.

An ugly day was coming on. The clouds were low and grey and they slunk out of a raw, pink horizon. There'd be another storm before long. Pray God we weren't too far from someplace safer than a traveller's hut. The wood supply was running thin. Besides that, we didn't have any food, and eating snow will neither fill you up nor quench your thirst.

Figuring Edward's body could wait 'til I took care of mine, I swung my eyes across the countryside in all directions. Except for Kyre scraping snow into her bucket, I saw only high hills and dark woods and blowing snow. Couldn't even locate the road, it was drifted in so deep. Beorn was nowhere to be seen, either, though what was left of his footprints led west and disappeared in a clump of scruffy yew.

I sent St. Christopher a little plea for help. Would've sent one to St. Jude, too, except Jude's the lad I save for when the water in the well's to my chin and they're hauling up the ladder. Things weren't that bad yet. If Beorn didn't return presently, I'd go look for help myself. Though I sure didn't want to leave Wynstan, now I'd finally found him.

As he and Cuthred started through the door, Wynstan said, "That attractive young woman out there. Who is she?"

It was time for St. Jude. "Please don't let Wynstan be out of his mind," I prayed. "Please don't let him be so old he can't remember his own daughter. And please do let him remember King Edward's body."

"Woman," Wynstan demanded when we were all inside again, "just who are you?"

Kyre blinked twice, then the truth poured out. Through sobs and hiccups and a storm of tears, she said she was a runaway nun. "Please, good sirs, don't make me go back. They'll beat me and starve me and make me pray 'til the Second Coming."

St. Jude save us, now we were in for it. Even if she'd gone over the convent wall on her own, I know how clerics think. They'd accuse us—me—of kidnapping her. And what was the penalty for kidnapping a nun, anyway? Just a fat fine, I hoped, and not a trip to the gallows.

But while specters of debt and death danced through my head, Wynstan whooped with delighted laughter. "Now here's a daughter a man could be proud of." He planted a sloppy kiss on her cheek.

Kyre drew back—the old man stank—and gazed hopefully at him. "You'll let me stay with you, then? Until I can go home?"

Wherever that was. And if they'd take her back.

"Of course, you can," Wynstan said. "A monastery's no place for the living."

That was something I could agree with. And, besides, Wynstan had made up his mind. So I said nothing. I'd ask him about Edward's body again as soon as we were alone. If, that is, I could ever get him alone. We'd damn near swollen to the size of a threshing party.

Kyre smiled—oh, that smile of hers—and dried her tears and told Wynstan she was sorry she used him as excuse to get away from the tavern. She might've said more, maybe even thrown me a "Sorry, sir, and thankee," but Beorn burst into the hut in another mighty cloud of steam.

"There's a manor just over the hill behind us," he said with a self-pleased smile. "Last night, I thought I seen a lane turn that way. Sure enough, there 'twas. Leads to a big, timbered place. Lots of nice warm smoke coming out the roofs."

I just wanted to make some money, not parade around

the countryside with a runaway nun in tow, nor waste time in some countrified Englishman's hall that'd likely have as many cracks in its walls as this hut. Bugs, too. I thought about telling Beorn and Kyre to go by themselves, Wynstan and I were staying put 'til the weather changed. But I figured he wouldn't let Cuthred go cold and hungry. Nor send the boy off with that peculiar pair.

Still, bribery's always worth a try. While the others packed straw into their boots, I pulled Wynstan next to me by Tom's flank, where they couldn't hear, and whispered, "What about King Edward?"

The old man blinked his rheumy eyes at me. He never answered, even when I said I had a whole keg of silver and he could have half. A smile cracked through his whiskers, though. He leaned close to my ear. "We'll speak of this later. Meanwhile, I must get my son—flesh of my flesh, blood of my blood—to safety."

I could see that no amount of silver would change his mind. Praying for patience, I picked up my saddle and swung it onto Tom's broad back.

We got cracking right away, me leading Tom, Wynstan loaded on top of him, and Kyre hand-in-hand with Cuthred. Beorn insisted on walking alongside Wynstan, to keep the old man firm in the saddle, he claimed.

Wynstan looked down at him, belched a time or two, then asked, "And who is this little fellow? Another of my daughters?"

I believe if he'd said that to me, I'd have dumped him on his fat butt and kicked him 'til his belly bud sprang loose. But Beorn answered by launching into his whole genealogy, plus a description of every scop he'd ever listened to.

"Not a poet amongst them," Wynstan said with a sniff. "Mere gleemen. Reciters of rotted rhyme and scurrilous verse. My God, what English song has come to since good King Edmund went to his eternal reward."

Edmund—King Eadgar's father—had been dead for years and never had much of a reputation as a patron of poetry anyhow. But that dismal truth didn't stop Wynstan from conjuring up the shade of a splendid past. He waved a paw at the white countryside. "Where?" he asked in his best bass. "Where are the snows of yesteryear? Where the treasure-giver? Where his horse? Where his men? Where the feasting, where the joys of hall?"

He went on that way for quite a while—no wonder some folk called him Wynstan the Windy—'til I halted Tom so Kyre and Cuthred could catch up. As we waited, Beorn said, "By St. Cecilia, the man's a wonder, ain't he? Never a poet the like of him. I could listen all day."

Well, at least he wasn't on about murder.

Wynstan, mercifully over his poetic fit, turned to Beorn. "The hall we're headed for, it's a well-made one? Generous in proportion?"

Which meant, did its owner look to be rich and open-handed. Beorn said it could belong to a king's thegn, an ealdorman, even, so handsome it was. Wynstan belched in satisfaction.

When Kyre and the boy came alongside us, Wynstan asked him how he fared. Cuthred grinned wide and patted Kyre's arm. She assured the old man that all was well and we started up again—into swoop on swoop of wind that slashed us with hard, blinding snow as Wynstan sang of English honor.

The King's Corpse

The storm had let up by the time we got to the manor. It was a big place—a thegn's hall, for sure—but without a wall protecting it, just a broad ditch and a thick row of bushes and hawthorns. I guessed the only enemies that ever threatened this place were a few stray cattle and the odd wolf. No savage Vikings, anyhow. Or if they had, they'd just strolled in through the wicker gate, then carried off the gold and the girls with a "Thankee, sir, we can find our own way to Winchester."

Covered in snow and cold to our bones, we hove to in front of the wicker gate and said a prayer of thanks. After which Wynstan raised his big voice above the wind, begging hospitality. While we waited for the gate to open, he said, "I've no idea who these people might be, but I intend to bestow on them the gift of song and story."

So they'd bestow a few gifts on him. Which, to judge from the size of the buildings peeking through the trees, they could well afford.

"I confess," Wynstan went on, "of late I have been somewhat slim of purse. And, if I may say so, the rest of you look none too well off yourselves."

When no one seemed willing to argue, he said, "Thus, I propose we perform ensemble for these people. I will spin my best tale, a lovely long one about the Norsker wars. Cuthred will tell his riddle. Likely, Beorn owns a few jokes, and you, Welshman, can no doubt sing. Something suitably fierce and foreign, of course."

He turned to Kyre. "What about you, my dear? Can you carry a tune? If so, do it. If not, simply favor our audience with a smile."

Before anybody could say him nay, Wynstan threw back his head and shouted into the cloudy heavens, "It's Wynstan and Company, oh Lord. Be with us, All-father, when we put on such a show as will itself become the stuff of song and story." He flung out his arms and gave his hands that little flip like entertainers do when they figure they've said something grand enough to bring down the hall.

Tom had had enough. He did some flipping of his own. Pitched Wynstan head first in a snow bank. Cuthred went out and out crazy. Tore loose from Kyre and took off across the snow toward Wynstan.

Of course, the gate swung open then.

Out leapt a huge, snarling dog.

It lunged straight at Wynstan, ready to shred him for sausage.

I stumbled backward. Beorn let out a curse. Tom screamed and ran in the opposite direction.

A hard snap to its chain stopped the dog just short of the kill.

"Down!" commanded a voice beyond the gates.

The dog—a hairy, big-headed black thing—dropped in the snow as ordered. It continued, though, to eye Wynstan like he was a specially large and very toothsome haunch of ham.

Kyre, the only one with her wits still about her, strode past the beast, planted herself in front of the gate, and loudly demanded to know just what kind of hospitality was being offered. "Is this a Christian house? Will you do your duty to strangers?" she called out. "Or are you but heathen Northmen?"

A man stepped through the gate. In one hand he held the dog's chain, in the other a sword. So much for Christian hospitality.

He had to be as old as Wynstan. But with his burly build and mass of grey hair and beard, he looked solid as an oak tree covered in mistletoe. I knew at once that he was master here. "Well, well," he said. "We got us a pack of bandits or just the leavings from some churl's wake?"

That made Kyre start to call him names and demand he let us in straightaway. A brave lass, but when she commenced telling him where he could put his sword and his dog, I clapped a hand over her mouth. "Go get Cuthred."

To my surprise, she did as I said. And so did Beorn when I told him to find Tom. Wynstan, meantime, had hauled himself out of the snow bank. Now he was on all fours next to it, throwing up.

The black dog, more interested than ever, inched forward.

A woman appeared from behind the gate. She was tall and wore a dark red cloak with a fox-fur hood. "I told you it wasn't the king or we'd have heard horns all the way from Winchester," she said to the swordsman. "And it isn't snow elves, either."

This had to be the lady of the manor. Now we'd see Christian duty. And some good manners, too.

Wynstan, finally done puking, got to his feet and, never mind the dog, lumbered toward the woman. Falling on his knees in front of her, he flung up his arms and cried, "Praise the Lord from the earth, ye dragons, as the psalmist says. God has indeed brought us through snow and vapors and stormy wind, fulfilling his holy word."

The woman said, "What do you want, Wynstan?

CHAPTER EIGHT

The woman hadn't bothered to keep the sneer out of her voice. The swordsman shouted with joy. "Wife," he told her, "ready the hall—Wynstan's here! Now we're going to have us a time." He hauled Wynstan to his feet and they embraced. Or as much as two men the size of farm carts can embrace.

"Hunwald!" Wynstan cried. "Hunwald, my comrade, my countryman, my friend!"

Beorn and Kyre crept back then, Tom and Cuthred with them. The boy's eyes got wide when he saw the big dog. But, with Kyre's hand on his shoulder, he bravely walked past the now calm beast as Hunwald waved us through the gate.

"A feast's already laid," Hunwald said. "For young King Ethelred himself. We've not just killed the fatted calf for him, neither. Whole herds got slaughtered. Half the geese in Wessex. But looks like the storm's delayed him. We might as well enjoy the food ourselves. There'll still be plenty for the king here at Thornholt."

His wife—her name was Bathilda—looked none too happy about this new plan, but she remembered her manners enough to bid us follow her and the dog across the hall-yard to the mead hall.

Through the falling snow, I could see the timbered,

shake-roofed mead hall, the bower house where Hunwald's family slept, and a good-sized stable. Next to the hall stood the half-finished stone watchtower English kings bade their thanes raise. And next to the tower was a stone building with a tile roof and glass windows. Little wooden dragons—or maybe they were angels—flew along its eaves. Further away, outside the enclosing bushes, stood barns, sheds, and a kitchen marked by the smoke rising through its thatch. I thanked St. Christopher for bringing us to someplace where we'd be warm and safe and fed. And where I could finally talk to Wynstan in private.

When Bathilda—with Wynstan clinging to her arm, talking ten leagues to the mile—and the others started toward the mead hall, Hunwald apologized for having no one to take care of my horse. I told him I always put Tom away myself. He said he didn't blame me, Tom was a fine piece of horse flesh.

"That he is," I said. "Calm and willing as he is handsome. Best horse I ever rode."

Hunwald decided to join me in the stable. Not to help, of course. Just to talk horses. And talk and talk and talk. Country men get lonesome, I reckon, with nobody around but their kinfolk. So I let Hunwald run on about every nag he'd ever fed a handful of oats, until he finally finished and said, "Been with Wynstan long, have you?"

I didn't know how to answer that, so I said what a fine hall he had here.

"Oh, this place? It's Bathilda that likes Thornholt. Got me five big estates up north, every one better than this one. But she'd rather live down here where it's warm."

He told me his family had held Thornholt since King

Alfred had given it to them as reward for fighting back the Northmen. "Oh, eighty, ninety years ago. I battled a few Norskers in my time, too," he said. "Wynstan and me both. Just boys we were."

I suspected they'd been a bit more than boys. They were both well past fifty winters and the Norsker kings of York had still threatened England only a couple of decades back.

Hunwald gave Tom Tub a scratch behind his ear. "Didn't recognize Wynstan at first. Used to be a skinny fellow. Well, so did I used to be slighter than I am now. A pair of willow wands, we were, when we carried the spear for King Edred. Fought in his last battle forty-some years back, up at Stainmore. You maybe heard Wynstan sing about how we killed us five Norsker kings, Erik Bloodaxe amongst 'em, the murdering bastard."

He told a few more war stories—some even Wynstan must not have known—'til I'd finished with Tom and we stepped back into the stable yard.

The snow had quit, so I got a better look at Thornholt and was surprised not to see a churls' village nearby. "It's yonder." Hunwald waved a paw into the storm. "Over the stream."

As we plowed across the snowy hall-yard Hunwald again asked if I'd been with Wynstan long. I figured I'd better give some kind of answer this time, so I explained I wasn't an entertainer, just a merchant who had business with Wynstan.

"A merchant, eh?" Hunwald slapped me on the back. "Fine life, that, travelling around, meeting every manner of folk. You could say I was a merchant myself, back in my youth. Dealt in horses mostly, a few cattle. And, during the

Norsker wars, in slaves, of course. Heathens make good—"

I didn't pay much attention to the rest. I'd already learned more than enough about Lord Hunwald of Thornholt.

Whose mead hall was not what I'd expected—not a rich, elaborate affair, lit by a dozen flaming torches and lined with silken wall hangings. Though it did have windows—glass ones, no less. They and the few oil lamps stuck in the timbers showed only a long, oak-floored room, bare except for the hearth in its middle and a trestle table surrounded by a few benches. The heads of dead animals lined the rafters. An open staircase led to a sleeping-loft above and some weapons leaned against the far wall—spears, mostly, and a battle-axe or two.

I'd expected to find a mob of folk laughing and drinking. But Hunwald said his eldest son and the rest of his hallmen had gone out hunting and, he figured, gotten caught in the storm. They were laid up someplace safe, no doubt, like his churls in their village. Soon as the weather changed, they'd come swarming back.

People in this part of the world weren't used to snow. Not like Norskers, anyhow, who'd suck down a bracing draft of cold air then strap a couple of slats on their feet and be off across the fields, smooth and proud as swans gliding over pond water. All these folks could do with snow was stand bewildered in their doorways, blinking like strangers set down in a world they'd never seen before and hoped never to see again, here or hereafter. That was why, besides Wynstan and Company, who still hovered by the door with Lady Bathilda, the hall held only a serving woman and a young monk.

The grey-eyed serving woman—Irish, maybe, but fine to look at—turned when we entered, then quickly returned to tending the hearth. On its spit turned a whole raft of roasting, sizzling geese. The black dog soon took up watch over them, tongue lolling out in sloppy expectation. I knew how he felt.

The monk sat in a carved chair. He held a gilt-chased drinking horn in manicured fingers and was reading noisily from a large, leather-bound book perched on his knees. He was a well-tended fellow—for a cleric, anyhow—with his tonsure making a neat circle in clean, dark hair and with jaws that looked like they'd once known a razor. His long black tunic fell over pointed black shoes.

The book was Aldhelm's *On Virginity*, which he read ever more loudly, never looking up. Not even when Wynstan left off his chat with Lady Bathilda and explained formally to her and her husband just how thankful we were to be there.

Made quite a fine speech of it, Wynstan did—a long one, anyhow—explaining that the rest of us were his troupe, God-inspired performers all. I had to give him credit for thinking on his feet, a skill stropped in a hundred mead halls. But I also had to wonder what we were in for when he bowed to Hunwald and said, "I well remember your deeds against the Northmen. Included some of them in my poem 'The Great Battle at Stainmore.' Which I sang before King Ethelred and his lady mother Queen Ælfthryth not long ago, by the way."

I doubted that. Ælfthryth had too fine an ear, and too little time, for the likes of Wynstan the Windy. But I reckoned the old man was as much trying to compliment his host as brag on himself. When you live off your wits, like Wynstan and me, flattery's likely not your worst sin. And it must've worked, for Hunwald bade all five of us sit at table with the quality.

Wynstan grabbed me by the arm and pulled me behind the staircase. "I always heard you had a good amount of Welsh luck on you, Tryff, my lad. And now I see it's so. Do you know what's here at Thornholt?" Wynstan sidled closer. "It's here. King Edward's body is here."

I was surprised—and not just at the possibility of the body being at Thornholt. I hadn't had a chance to talk to Wynstan about King Edward, didn't know if he suspected I was after the king's bones, too. Or if he was aware that Lady Flæda had asked me to keep an eye on him. Maybe he really had been entertaining Queen Ælfthryth and picked up a rumor in her court.

But why would the king's remains be here, anyhow?

Before I could find out more, Lady Bathilda swept around the staircase. "We're waiting, you know."

Wynstan courteously begged her pardon, then followed her to the table. On the way, he whispered, "Plenty of time for our work later. Meanwhile, let's have some fun, eh?"

I could hardly go traipsing off to hunt a corpse just then. And I certainly couldn't demand to know where it lay. If it was here at all. I'd have to wait 'til everybody was down for the night. Then I could root around, especially in that little stone building next to the hall. I figured it for a church-house, just the place to stash a king. Meantime, I'd have to settle for Wynstan's fun.

Lord Hunwald had settled himself onto a bench at the middle of the table, the black dog by his feet. He waved Wynstan to his right and Lady Bathilda his left, Kyre across from him. So he could look at her, I figured, not that I blamed him any. Next to her, facing Wynstan, went Beorn. Cuthred was on Kyre's other side and I sat by Bathilda.

When finally the monk—who turned out to be Hunwald's younger son, Petroc—joined us, he did a thing I'd never seen before. He brought his book along. And there he sat, at the end of the table with the book propped up against a carved ivory drinking horn. Except for the loud mumble of his reading, he never said a word. Nor ate either, far as I could see, through the whole of supper.

And that was a mighty long time. The handsome serving-woman brought on the food a little past noon and kept on bringing it 'til what seemed like midnight. Only it wasn't any fatted calf or herd of cattle, just boiled parsnip and roast goose. But the goose dripped fat and there was lots of it. The serving-woman passed around lots of ale, too, and it was a cut above most English drink. Which I proved by pouring down plenty, though not as much as Beorn. Not nearly.

"If he keeps on the way he's started," I said to Lady Bathilda, "he'll be snoring under the table with the dog long before he gets to tell his jokes." A good thing, too. We wouldn't have to bear any of that dry dust Saxons call humor.

For his part, Wynstan worked his way through a flock of roast geese and a brew house of ale fast as the serving woman could hand it to him. That is, when he and Hunwald weren't talking. The way they carried on, you'd have thought they'd been in every battle since the rebellion of Satan. And on the winning side.

Ignoring their palaver, Lady Bathilda tucked into her food with the gusto of a woman who knows how to compliment her servants with more than words. She was perhaps fifty and almost as tall as her husband, though darker of face and far more elegantly dressed. She'd cast off the fox-ruffed cloak to show her blue wool dress and yellow headdress, both thickly embroidered in scarlet silk. Likewise, her fingers glittered with gems of red and blue.

For a long while, she ate and drank without saying much, though I noticed she was giving me and the rest of Wynstan's troupe a good eyeballing. When finally she'd eaten up her trencher and licked the goose grease off her hands, she turned her eyes on me. "And are you some vagrant like the rest of this miserable lot—lordless, kinless, landless, kithless?"

Kyre started to say something, but I got her stopped before she let Bathilda know she'd been a bride of Christ, even if they were divorced now. Instead, I rushed to tell Bathilda what a splendid hall this was, like the rest of Thornholt.

"Who is your lord?" Bathilda snapped.

I couldn't have her thinking I was an outlaw. She looked just the kind to call in the shire reeve. "Eada, Abbess of St. Finella's."

Bathilda nearly fell out laughing. "Crazy Eada?" she said when she got her breath back. "The one who keeps more wild animals than nuns in her convent?"

Maybe Eada did keep a zoo. But at least she didn't abuse her guests.

"Hunwald!" Bathilda shouted over the table din. "This fellow here is your cousin Eada's man."

His cousin? And Abbess Eada was cousin to the king. That made Hunwald a royal. So maybe Wynstan was right about Edward's body. English royals, even half-royals like Hunwald, do love relics.

The company was still having a high old time. While Hunwald slopped more ale into Wynstan's cup, Kyre and Cuthred laughed and giggled and flung bread pellets at each other. One landed in Wynstan's ale cup, splashing him good. He gave the boy a dark look. Then, seeing Cuthred so happy, he started tossing pellets, too. Finally, even Hunwald joined the fun.

Brother Petroc was still hidden behind his big book. Except for his manicured hands, which rested elegantly on the table top. Next to him, drunken Beorn waved his cup at Hunwald and demanded a refill. But then his eyelids fluttered shut. His cup dropped onto the table, followed by his head.

Eventually, the game at an end, the dog snuffled up bread pellets under the table and the gorgeous serving woman poured drinks all around. Lord Hunwald stood up, eyes flashing with good cheer, and flung his ale horn high above his head like he was offering a toast before the king himself. "Wynstan Wing-tongue will now recite for us. Let's hear 'The Warrior and the Troll Wife,' eh?"

A line creased 'twixt the poet's eyebrows. "I was thinking you'd like something more up-to-date."

That brought Brother Petroc out from behind his book, which he now closed and lay on the table. "My father wants 'The Warrior and the Troll Wife'."

Wynstan gave him a stare as icy as the weather. But then he must've remembered he was a guest. He shrugged. "It's rather slipped out of my repertory. People have gotten so they only want stories with happy endings."

Hunwald shook his head and handed Wynstan another cup of ale. "Has public taste sunk so low? Well, in this family we maintain the high standards of old. Words won't fail you. Nor good ale."

Wynstan laughed as he slugged down the ale. "Very well. 'The Warrior and the Troll-wife,' it is. Shall we get right to it, then? With no prelude from our Welsh friend. Or that one."

He pointed to Beorn, still face-down in his trencher, then turned to Kyre. "Nor from...uh...the lady."

Her shoulders slumped in relief, but Cuthred jumped up and demanded to recite his riddle. Kyre pulled him onto her lap and assured the lad he would be allowed to tell all the riddles he wanted after Wynstan got through with "your favorite story."

The boy seemed ready to object, but Wynstan let out a "*Hwaet!*" loud enough to set the whole hall ringing. "Listen! We have heard of the glory of the kings of the Spear-Danes! How their princes did glorious deeds in days gone by."

Then he started the royal Dansker genealogy. I prayed it wouldn't go on too long. I had no desire to hear about everybody from Scyld to Beow to Hrothgar. Along with their wives and, if I knew English poetry, their swords and halls and horses, too.

As it turned out, there wasn't much to hear. Before he even got to the murdering troll-wife, Wynstan stuttered to a stop. Without another word, without another sound, the old poet dropped down dead.

CHAPTER NINE

It was like a spell had been cast over that mead hall. Nobody moved, nobody spoke. Even the dog stopped worrying his fleas. All we could do was stare at Wynstan crumpled on the floor.

Then everybody came to at once. And, oh, the noise of it. The dog went to barking, Cuthred to howling, Hunwald to shouting. And me, I was praying at the top of my lungs. "Don't let him be dead. Don't let him ... don't ... "

Ale cups clanged as we threw them down, benches crashed as we leaped from the table. Hunwald and I got to Wynstan at the same time and for a moment stood peering down at him. A thin line of yellow spittle oozed out of his open mouth and into his whiskers.

"Dead, eh?" Hunwald said.

It sure looked like it. And when I knelt down beside him to put my ear to his chest, I heard nothing, just as in the Winchester alehouse. But this time Wynstan's eyes had gone dim, lifeless. I crossed myself and stood up. "He's gone."

Hunwald took my word for it, crossing himself, too. "Sad thing. Him so young and all."

He shook his head and a tear leaked out of one eye. Then he straightened his shoulders, sucked in his gut, cast a commanding look around the mead hall, as if daring anyone to ask why a man of his own years would just up and drop dead. Besides, there was business to take care of.

By now, the women had Cuthred more or less quieted down, but the black dog stood in the middle of the hall, barking his head off.

As for Beorn and Brother Petroc, they were where they'd been all along—at the table, Beorn still out cold, the monk's manicured fingers still around his ale cup. His crooked little smirk made him look both amused and disgusted.

And disgusting. Why wasn't he at his clerkish duties, sending Wynstan to the other world with some proper prayer?

Hunwald must've wondered, too. "What you doing still on your arse, Petroc? You may be no priest yet, but you can at least see a Christian soul goes to his Maker riding on the right words."

Brother Petroc shrugged, set down the cup, and lazily rose from the table. The smirk never left his face. The dog went on barking, setting Cuthred off again. Kyre swept the sobbing boy into her arms.

"Shut up!" Hunwald roared at the dog.

He turned to the serving woman. "Get him out of here, Thrima, before I rip his sodding head off."

Thrima, the serving woman, set the big ale horn on the table and led the dog out of the hall.

Bathilda marched over to take a look at Wynstan. "He's dead for sure?"

"Far as I can tell," I said.

Bathilda stooped down and ran her jeweled hands over Wynstan. Then she opened the pouch at her waist, poked in it, peered into it, shook her head. "Thought I had a looking glass in here. To put under his nose, you know. Make certain he's not breathing."

"Man's dead," Hunwald told her in the same irked tone he used to tell his son to get praying.

"I believe he is," Bathilda said with a deep sigh. She closed her eyes and made the sign of the cross, then stayed on her knees by Wynstan while Brother Petroc finally said the *Commendatio animae.*

Meanwhile, I thought about the possibility that Wynstan's death might not have been natural. If it wasn't, I had even more cause to search Thornholt for King Edwards' bones. I touched my hawk-hilted scramseaxe in its sheath at my side and the two smaller knives wrapped tightly beneath my legbands.

After he finished up his prayers, Petroc said we should move the body into the church-house. "At least 'til the weather breaks. Then I suppose we'll have to bury him here on the estate."

He glanced at his father, who nodded glumly. Nor was Hunwald's next thought very happy, either. "What about the boy?"

All four of our heads swung toward Cuthred. He was perched on the staircase with Kyre, quieted by the bannocks she was feeding him.

Hunwald pulled at his beard. "Likely he'll start up bawling again soon's we lay hold of Wynstan. You better put him in a shed, Bathilda. Give him one of your potions, get him settled."

Bathilda's eyes narrowed down like a cat that's ready to start hissing. But before she did anything Cuthred leapt up from the stairs and tore out of the mead hall, Kyre right behind.

For a little, the four of us stared after them, then at each other, then down at Wynstan. Finally, Bathilda started in laughing.

"Wife," Hunwald said in a shocked tone, "have some respect for the dead."

That only made her laugh louder. And she was still laughing when Hunwald sent her out to find Cuthred.

Beorn had come around by then and now stood next to the table, picking goose flesh out of his beard. Hunwald wheeled in his direction, jabbed a fat forefinger at him. "Get out of here, you! Your woman and whelp, too! Now!"

Beorn didn't argue. He straightaway grabbed the troupe's pack and ran for the door.

I hoped I wouldn't be asked to leave, too, now Wynstan's soul had departed. What if he'd been right and King Edward was at Thornholt? I needn't have worried, because Hunwald clapped me on the back, damn near knocking me halfway across the hall. "Better stay 'til tomorrow, good friend. It's dark out and the way back to Winchester ain't fit for travel."

A nice offer, though it wasn't quite the bargain it seemed. In return Hunwald expected me to help cart Wynstan's big, floppy carcass to the church-house. We rolled him up in his cloak and dragged him there. We, meaning Hunwald and myself. Beorn had gone who knows where and Brother Petroc had actually produced a breviary. It turned him into cleric enough to be the leader of our little cortege as we scraped Wynstan across the hall's rough floor and out the back door.

No snow fell now, but the night had grown so black the

buildings had all but disappeared. We passed a wicker fence that, from the stink, I knew must surround a latrine. The church-house, Hunwald said, stood just a few steps beyond.

It was more than a few steps and we'd pitched Wynstan in the snow a few times before Thrima appeared with a pair of torches. She said the dog and Cuthred were safely penned up in a woodshed.

Grabbing one of the torches, Hunwald gave his son a shove toward the church-house. "Best you and me go in first, have it all lit and fit for good Wynstan."

When the two of them had disappeared through the church-house door, Thrima turned to me. "*Eitr.*"

"Afraid my Norsker's gone rusty on me." It hadn't, but I wanted to find out more about this woman. With those light eyes in her dark face, she looked like a she-wolf. And made me feel like a wolf myself. A hungry one.

"Poison," she said, still in Norse. "Thy bard was poisoned."

Her elegant court speech surprised me. Thrima was dressed like any other woman-churl, dirty wool dress covered by an even dirtier wool cloak. Her hands were raw and red, nose likewise. But she carried herself like a woman who'd known more than small ale and cold beans.

"She poisoned him," Thrima said in English. "She, Bathilda."

Uh-oh. Crazy woman here. Must be, to accuse the lady of the manor of such a thing. Well, I'd likely go crazy, too, if I was stuck being a scullery churl. But she was like no other churl I'd ever met, 'specially when she jammed her fists on her hips and said, "Bathilda is having good cause to kill him, *ja*. And easy means, too. Shed is full of hemleac."

Now it was Thrima's words that had my full attention. Bathilda not only had the means, she also had opportunity to poison the old man. A long day of passing around the ale horn had provided that. "Even so," I asked, "why would she?"

Thrima never answered because just then Hunwald came bounding through the church doorway. "What you still doing here, woman? Get in the hall, fix us up something to eat. We'll be hungry after."

As Hunwald and I picked up the tails of Wynstan's cloak, Thrima said it again. "*Eitr.*"

The church-house sat apart from the half-finished stone tower and was barely more than a wooden box. No wonder I'd first thought it just another shed. But Hunwald had a priest for his church. Or he would once Brother Petroc had turned thirty and gotten himself ordained. So it was a pretty expensive set the lord of Thornholt had—church-house, tower, mass-priest—though he likely wouldn't have to pay Petroc, him being hand-raised for the job. Still, if Hunwald had started life as a slave trader, he sure had come up in the world.

"Going to build me a stone church, once the tower's done. Bell for the tower's already ordered. Be next year afore it comes, though. Fancy brass wonder, all the way from Paris. Hate to say it, but them Frankies are the only ones that—"

His son gave him a priest's chiding glare and Hunwald hushed. The look on the old thegn's face dangled someplace between anger and embarrassment. It must be kind of hard for a man to go from absolute lord to just another servant only because he's passed under an arched lintel. That's why Mass was likely something Hunwald most times avoided.

Not that I blamed him. Who'd want his son over him, even on Sunday? 'Specially this son.

The church nave was as bare as any I ever saw. Not that I saw much—no glass covered the half dozen skinny windows, just dingy flaxen cloth and it none too clean. The plank walls were adorned by patches of damp and an oil lamp or two. In one corner stood the baptismal font. It looked more like a hogshead of ale than a holy vessel.

Nor was the chancel any prettier. In it stood a stone altar bearing a wooden cross and a single candle. And that was all. No gold or silver vessels adorned it, no fine linen, and no— here's the sad part—no reliquary. But maybe King Edward had been hidden under the altar.

After we rested the body just inside the church-house door, Brother Petroc turned Wynstan's cloak into a shroud. He folded the hood over the old man's face, then pulled the whole thing square and made sure it covered all of him. A bit of a trick it was, too, Wynstan being so fat. But Petroc finally got him fixed up so he didn't look too much like a pig sacked for the smokehouse.

Then Petroc said a few words in that garbled mess English clerics call Latin. I crossed myself and muttered the responses while Hunwald blew on his fingers—it was colder in the church than it was outside. A good thing, though. Otherwise, Wynstan might go off, be spoiled meat by the time they could get him buried.

When it was all done, I said I'd like to stay with Wynstan a while. "Pray for his soul." And look for King Edward. I didn't mention that. Nor did I mention my growing suspicion that Wynstan's death might've been murder after all.

The two men thought praying proper enough, and so,

having no desire for a long night's vigil in a cold church, they left me on my knees by Wynstan.

I stayed put 'til they were likely back in the hall, all the while thinking how I'd find Edward's body. No matter what relic you're after, you'd better bring the right kind of tools. You can't always sneak into a church or abbey after Nocturns at midnight, toss a couple of bones down your tunic-front, and be out of there before Matins, three hours later. And what if the saint's in the churchyard? You have to dig. That takes a spade and a while, though you won't have too much trouble with a wooden coffin even if it's fallen apart. But if the coffin's made of marble, you'll need a grappling hook and an ox to haul it up. Better to just stand in the hole and prise the lid off. Bit of a trick, I can tell you, on a wet, moonless night.

Same when the saint's enshrined inside a church in a stone box or under the altar. You'd better have a big sack, even if it's just a bunch of bones rattling around in there. You wouldn't believe how many bones a person's made of. You get mighty uncomfortable, too, bent over picking up toes for an hour with the rats scurrying across your feet.

There weren't any reliquaries in this church, stone or otherwise. Nor had the folk at Thornholt blazoned their relics with a shrine out on the green. If Edward was around, he'd be under the altar. That's why, before we'd carried Wynstan to the church-house and on the excuse that Tom Tub needed seeing to, I'd taken the small pry bar from my saddlebag and tied it against my chest. The only problem I figured on would come if Edward hadn't gone to bone—I planned to use my cloak for a sack and I didn't look forward to sticking something nasty in it.

Except for the bit of light thrown by the oil lamps next to the door, the inside of the church seemed as dark as any other grave. I didn't want to use a light because even the smallest taper would set up a glow that could be seen through the windows. And you never know who might see it. Sure, peasants are usually long asleep by that hour. But a man can still be up and about for a lot of reasons. He might be sneaking out a widow's door. Or exchanging his sick sheep for a neighbor's sound one. Or the lord could be checking on the gold he buried next to the well. And if this night-prowler saw a light moving through the church, he might get curious. That's why I never use a lamp, just creep along in the dark with only the saints to preserve me.

I crossed the nave's dirt floor onto the flagstone of the chancel, passed an open doorway and moved toward the altar. The chancel felt unused. Abandoned—if not by God, then by man, and for a long time. There was a faint, sweet smell. Of incense and mildew, maybe. Or rotten flesh.

Taking out my fire-stones, I scratched up some sparks. The saints were with me and the altar candle caught right off. I set it on the floor and got to work.

I gave the stone altar a hard shove. It didn't move. I'd have to lever it off the floor. Nor could my little pry bar lift it up. So I braced my back against the wall, set my feet to the altar, and shoved again. I said my regular prayer, the one I always make when I'm helping out a saint. It's to St. Nicholas, who's the helper of thieves and merchants both. I ask him for his protection and then promise to visit his tomb down there in Byzantium. I will, one day, and bring him a bag full of presents.

Betwixt my praying and the loud screech of the altar as it

moved off its mooring, betwixt the clang of the pry bar when I accidentally dropped it on the flagstone floor, betwixt my huffing and puffing and panting and cursing—the noise in that church could've woken the Seven Sleepers and King Arthur, too. But eventually I opened a gap big enough to stick my fingers in. Praise heaven, the altar had a space beneath it. A mite more toil and travail and my hand was on King Edward. Or rather on the embroidered bag that held him, which I pulled out and opened. Inside, were the dry, sweet-smelling herbs that bodies are often buried with.

And that's all. The bag was empty.

After I ran through every curse I knew or could invent, I blew out the candle and, leaving the pry bar by the altar, crawled back to Wynstan by the church door.

He wasn't there.

That's the last thing I remember for a while. For how long a while I don't know, but when I came around I felt like somebody had pitched me into the sea off Land's End. My head was full of roaring surf and shifting sand.

When finally that tide went out, I knew I was still in Hunwald's cold, dark church-house. But I also knew I wouldn't be for long. I'd be away from Thornholt quick as I got to the stable and jumped aboard Tom Tub—the hell with this whole business. The queen of England could hire some other fool to look for her stepson's body. I'd find some other way to buy my mother free.

When I stood my head still felt fuzzy and I was stiff as an old boot. At least whoever'd stolen Wynstan's body hadn't killed me, though they'd taken my cloak, my pouch, and all three of my knives.

I didn't think it had been Wynstan's troupe. They were likely locked up in the shed with Cuthred and the black dog, a stout churl leaning against the door. I had no doubt Hunwald and that son of his were responsible. They'd likely stolen Wynstan's body so they wouldn't have to bury him at Thornholt. Later they'd sink him in a bog or float him down the River Itchen all the way to Southampton.

The evil ones had left me my neck sack. I pulled it open

and touched the sliver of St. Veronica I kept there. The Gospel-books said she'd been a kind woman and I knew she'd take good care of me now I had no weapons, no cloak, and, soon enough, no money. And if not Veronica, then Fortuna would. I hoped.

I decided I'd better wait 'til dawn to escape from Thornholt, when I could see if anybody was lurking around outside. If nobody was, I'd hide in the shadows of the buildings, then tear across the green and into the stable. I'd toss Tom's blanket around me for warmth and we'd slip through the manor's hedge, off to ... it didn't matter. So long as it was somewhere besides Thornholt.

First, though, I had to make it to morning without freezing to death. A simple enough task. I went to the sacristy and wrapped myself in long albs and heavy chasubles, some of them embroidered in gold. Then I curled up in a big wooden chest, pulled close the lid, and thought about Wynstan and King Edward's body.

Had Wynstan been murdered to keep him from telling where it was? If he had, why wasn't I killed, too? After all, he might already have let me in on the secret. Or maybe Wynstan's death had nothing to do with King Edward. The folk at Thornholt had known Wynstan for a long time. Maybe they'd avenged one of his past misdeeds. Or maybe Thrima was right about Lady Bathilda—she just liked to poison people.

What if King Edward's body really was somewhere at Thornholt? Maybe I could just take a short look and .... That witless notion made me pull the chasuble around my ears and launch into my prayers. I thanked God that my headpan was still whole. And pleaded with Him, as I always did, not to let me die on Saxon soil.

When I woke to the sound of trumpets, I knew God had punished my sins. Gabriel's horn was blaring forth with me stretched out on English dirt. But how did I get past St. Peter dressed in priest's clothes?

I crawled out of the chest to find light showing under the sacristy's outside door. From beyond came the noise of trumpets and the hubbub of men and dogs and horses. Easing the door open a bit, I peeked out to see three trumpeters, followed by a brace of armed men, then a herd of monks and a tall, skinny bishop. All of them were mounted, as was the next group—four mailed warriors tucked up close to a fair-haired boy in a wolf-pelt cloak. The dogs, a good dozen or so, came last, tended to by green-clad men on foot.

I'd never seen this king of England except in profile on the coins of his realm, and then all too seldom. But I knew right off the lad in the wolf cloak was King Ethelred. What other curly-headed stripling goes hunting with three trumpets and a bishop? And, anyway, I recognized the woman riding next to him, Queen Ælfthryth, his mother.

Lord Hunwald came tumbling out of his mead hall, all a-grin and more than a little drunk. Behind him, Lady Bathilda dropped a dramatic curtsey and Brother Petroc bent his head. I heard Hunwald claim King Ethelred could expect the best hunting in Hampshire. "I only wish both my sons were here to join us. My eldest is many miles away ... "

While Hunwald prattled and the king's party dismounted, I eased the sacristy door shut and wondered what to do. I could hardly barrel into the mead hall and accuse its lord of murder. Not while it held the king of England and the bishop of Winchester both. But when I thought harder, I knew now would be the perfect time to look around the rest of Thornholt. If I found Edward's body, I could hand it over to Queen Ælfthryth in front of king and bishop and thegn. Then the trumpets' fanfare would be for me. And I could collect my silver and be off to find my mother.

The snow had begun to melt but still made for good tracking. Ethelred and Hunwald would be hunting soon—along with everybody else, including Bathilda, Bishop Æthelwold, and the queen. That would leave only Thornholt's churls. They were back from their snow-bound village now and would be busy with their chores. If I was careful, I could search the hall, the bower house, the sheds, even the latrine. If one of the churls asked who I was, I'd claim to be the king's man left behind to make sure no enemy came creeping up on him.

The royal reception rituals would take a while. Instead of waiting them out in the cold church-house, I decided to head for the stable. Even if I couldn't escape right now, I could at least look in on Tom Tub. He'd likely been fed and watered along with Hunwald's horses, but his saddle and my saddlebags were too valuable to trust around churls—including the kings'. The price they'd bring in the back streets of Winchester would feed a family of ten for the rest of the winter.

When I opened the sacristy door, I saw the snow outside had been churned up, and by more than one person. A trail of footprints came from the direction of the mead hall while other tracks veered off toward the bower house.

I wasn't surprised. I'd already figured out whoever had knocked me over the head must've been hiding in the sacristy while I looked for King Edward under the altar. Then they hit me and grabbed Wynstan. But what next? Wynstan wouldn't be an easy load to stash.

I'd taken on a boatload of ale at Hunwald's table. So on the way to save my saddle, I stopped by the latrine. Before I left it, I looked down the hole. Of course, Wynstan was too big to be in there and I sure didn't expect to see Edward's anointed body. But in a lifetime spent searching for things folk deem precious, I'd found stuff in stranger places.

As I lurked behind the latrine's lattice gate, I heard the king release his bodyguards from their duty of standing at his back while he feasted. His mother whispered to him and he added, "We are with Lord Hunwald now, safe as if Christ himself were by our side."

A bit extravagant, even for an English royal. But in his heart, what Saxon doesn't think he sits at the right hand of God?

For their part, the bodyguards seemed delighted that they could spend some time drinking and even dicing if they wanted. The rest of the royal party wasn't so pleased. They milled around the hall-yard, looking cold and resentful. Soon they'd be bored enough to start making sport of the yokels, me included.

Worse yet, there in the stable doorway, yawning and scratching his behind, stood the little yeoman I'd met up with at the gates of Wilton. A man who doesn't want you in his town sure won't want you near his king. And there was no telling how he might go about preventing it. I could see that the choices were my saddle or my hide. I chose hide.

The nearest door led into the larder at the rear of the mead hall. Where I ran straight into Thrima. Lucky for me she was alone, stacking loaves of bread onto the big trestle table that ran down the middle of the room. When she saw me, she jammed her fists onto her hips. "Why are you in larder? Why are you not with your friends?"

Before I could find an answer, half a dozen men pushing ale kegs came in from outside. "It is about time," she told them in her mangled but haughty English. "They almost are dry in there."

She hoisted a tray of bread onto her shoulder and joined the other churls as they rolled the kegs through the larder door. I watched her for a while, thinking of … But I could dally no longer. I had to find Edward's remains now. If I presented them to the queen in a moment of magnificent surprise, my reward would be just as magnificent.

Not to be seen beforehand presented a bit of a problem. To get to the hall's far door, the one without the yeoman lurking outside it, I would have to go past the several trestle tables Hunwald had brought in for the royal party. But I was accustomed to slipping through difficult terrain. Fact was, my little trip along this hall would be a stroll down a country lane.

To plan my passage, I sidled up to the larder door and, through the big gaps between its boards, peeked into the hall. At the center table with Hunwald and his family sat the king, his mother, and Bishop Æthelwold. Someone must've decided that Hunwald was not St. Joseph after all, for against the back wall stood four armed men. Except for the black dog and the servants, no one else was in the hall.

Just as on the day before, the table was heaped high with boiled parsnips and roast goose. Now that fare was joined by wheels of cheese and loaves of bread. When the churls tapped their kegs, cascades of ale flowed into cup and horn. As I watched all this disappear, I wondered how they could take on such a load, then spend the rest of the day in the field. But the English are a greedy race. And a drunken one. Including the clerics. Brother Petroc and the bishop drained their ale cups fast as the churls could fill them.

It seemed that everybody had been well fed and watered. So just then Hunwald jumped up to announce there'd be entertainment. At that, the larder door flew open and the churls streamed out of the hall, grumbling because they'd been sent off to feed the king's men and would miss the show. I thought about leaving with them, hidden like a herring in its school. But then I heard the jangle of a tambourine. What was this, now?

Still at the door, I saw that down the loft stairs skipped little Cuthred, grinning broadly and banging his tambourine for all he was worth. Behind him came Kyre wearing a shimmery gown and a grin as broad as the boy's. At the top of the stairs, Beorn bounced on the balls of his feet a time or two then launched himself into a pair of spinning mid-air somersaults. He lighted just in time to reach for Kyre's hand and lead her onto the hall floor.

There, while Cuthred slapped his tambourine and Beorn did back flips from one end of the hall to the other, Kyre sang about love and loyalty. A pretty tune, and no wonder. It was Welsh.

The king clapped his hands in happy surprise. He'd probably never expected to find the like of such minstrels out here in the backwoods. Neither had I. 'Specially since they'd claimed to be a bone-carver and a nun.

Kyre was sure no nun. I could see that now, and hear it.

Nuns didn't sing about what she did right there in front of the king of England. It near burnt up my ears. Nor was Beorn any bone-and-antler man. Or, if he was, he'd juggled as many knife handles as he'd made. For that's what he was doing now—tossing knives in the air, then catching them and never dropping a one nor cutting himself, neither.

After the little boy did a few cartwheels and Kyre sang another song, Beorn took to conjuring. It was pretty ordinary stuff. He didn't make the dog disappear or cut the child in two. He only did tricks you can see in any town on any market day—knots that vanished from the string, a cup that disappeared into his cap only to reappear in Cuthred's pouch, five wooden balls that came and went between his fingers then out his ears.

There was nothing here to get the clerics worried, though I've seen country priests fall to their knees just because an acorn vanished out of a mummer's fist. Petroc and Bishop Æthelwold were too worldly to think Satan had taken the stage at Thornholt. They laughed loud as anybody when Beorn snatched a Frankish centime from King Ethelred's ear, then in a trice changed it to an English penny.

"We should find you work in one of our mints," Queen Ælfthryth said, laughing, too.

"You might not want that, Lady," Kyre said and began to sing "For he's a wandering lad and light of finger as of heart."

Beorn shot her a look and gave a quick shake of his head. In return, she gave him a satisfied smirk. Then the two of them turned toothy grins back to their audience and got on with the show—more songs by Kyre, with the boy pounding his tambourine while Beorn juggled cups, then cups and platters, at last adding the big drinking horn and King

Ethelred's own silk cap.

Like the Romans say, it was a *grande spettacolo*, and the audience loved it. They clapped and cheered and hollered for more. The dog barked and the king even put his fingers to his mouth and gave out a noisy whistle.

As the smiling entertainers took their bows, the mead hall door banged open. In poured a cloud of steam that smelled like a latrine in July. Out of it, arms spread wide, stepped Wynstan.

CHAPTER ELEVEN

What do you do, what do you say when somebody up and rises from the dead? The Thornholt folk—man, woman, and monk—leapt to their feet, let out a trio of strangled squeals, then fell back onto their benches, Hunwald and Bathilda with a great moan, Brother Petroc with an even greater curse.

The queen and bishop jumped up, too— she commanding the bodyguard not to kill Wynstan, he demanding to know just what was going on here. The players stood with faces still as the animal skulls that lined the walls.

Me, I'd gone stumbling through the larder door and onto my knees. Thrima snatched me back before God or Queen Ælfthryth could see me, then got us stationed where we could once more safely peek out through the gaps in the door.

When King Ethelred set to laughing and his three bodyguards looked less murderous, Wynstan trotted to the front of the little crowd. "*Hwaet!*"

The fire pit and a space the length of a good-sized yew lay 'twixt us and the quality folk. But the pit's flames lit the hall well enough to know this Wynstan was the real Wynstan.

I was someplace between awestruck and furious. "In the name of all the saints, how did this happen?"

Thrima gave a sage nod and said she knew the reason Wynstan had come strolling back to us from *purgatorium*. "Not miracle. Man has likely been into Bathilda's henbane. It will put you down for a right long nap, *ja*. Kill you, you don't watch out."

"What about the cloud of stink? He set the latrine alight, too?"

Thrima didn't answer because King Ethelred was speaking. With his elders finally calmed down and settled back at their table, the boy asked Wynstan if there'd be more magic. "Merry tricks and such?"

Wynstan threw up his hands. "Tricks? No, lord king, I'm no wizard, no sorcerer, no heathen conjurer. The business at the door was only a bit of foolery no different from Beorn's sleight of hand. It was only to capture your attention, only to amuse, only to startle then delight. And have I not done so?"

King Ethelred sent up a roaring "YES!," followed by "MORE! MORE!"

"Of course, my king. Anything—anything you like," Wynstan said with a deep bow. "But first I have something new I'd like to try for you. Something quite amazing that I learned in a faraway land."

"I think we've seen quite enough," Bishop Æthelwold intoned. Æthelwold was always a champion intoner.

Not used to having his wishes squashed, the young king cast him a bewildered look. Then he turned to his mother. Her will, as the boy well knew, would cancel out any old bishop's.

The queen didn't so much as glance at Æthelwold. "You may proceed, Wynstan."

With a satisfied smirk, Wynstan motioned for Beorn,

Kyre, and Cuthred to get ready. As Kyre disappeared under the staircase, Wynstan whispered to Cuthred and pointed in my direction.

I damn near sucked down my tongue. Was Wynstan sending the boy to fetch me? Did he have some foul trick for me to perform? I let out a mighty gust of relief when Cuthred raced right past me on his way into the larder.

By now—and none too soon, either—I'd figured out that Wynstan had lied to me and, most serious of all, to Lady Flæda. He no more knew where King Edward's body lay than I did. Furthermore, his current scheme—and he had one, of that I could be sure—was well afoot. I'd no idea what it might be, but by now I didn't care. I had to get the hell out of Thornholt. If the king's remains were indeed here I could come back for them, my deal with Queen Ælfthryth still on and my hide still intact.

I slithered out of the larder and into the deep shadows along the wall. They were a better hiding place than the larder, and if I was careful I could get to and out the little door under the loft stairs. From there, I'd have a fair chance of making it to the stable without the yeoman from Wilton noticing me.

Meanwhile, Beorn hauled one of the smaller trestle tables in front of the crowd. He hoisted a leather stool onto it, then draped the stool in a purple cloth, a Tyrian purple cloth. What had these backwoods buskers done? Robbed the royal clothes hamper?

Presently, Kyre, also draped in purple, swept from behind the staircase, leapt onto the table, and seated herself on the stool. In her hand she held some kind of stick, or maybe it was supposed to be a wand. Anyway, the thing was wrapped in what looked like dirty leg-bands.

I kept creeping along the wall, paying close heed when I reached the big hall door because it let in light. Good thing I did, too. It saved me from tripping over the iron pot that lay next to it. The pot reeked, and so did the puddle it sat in. That was how Wynstan had brewed up his stinking white steam—some snow, some pee, a cold draft. I could only hope I'd be well out of Thornholt before Bishop Æthelwold caught on, never mind the queen.

Cuthred came out of the larder carrying a broom and ran to Beorn and Wynstan who were by the table. It would have been an impressive tableau with gangly Beorn and vast Wynstan beside the tiny lad, splendid Kyre behind. It would have been, except that dried green puke still clung to Wynstan, from his three-pointed beard all the way down to his knees.

He gave the royals another deep bow. "As I said, my king, I have something novel for you. As I said, it came from a land far away, but not so far that you have nothing to do with it. Nor was it devised by a wizard or a witch." He shot the bishop a disdainful smile. "In fact, I learned this new way of performing from a nun."

Now it was Bishop Æthelwold's turn to try on a disdainful smile. For her part, Queen Ælfthryth was busy trying not to look bored. She'd probably heard more than one scop boast of novelty, only to have to fight off sleep while yet another hero slaughtered his way to glory.

"Yes, a nun. A German nun called Hroswitha. I spent last winter as a guest in her minster there in Saxony, in Gandersheim."

Oh Lord, not prattling Hroswitha. I met her once, when I

sold Gandersheim a drop of saintly blood, I forget just whose. Clever enough woman, I'll warrant, but she never kept still. And what new way of performing could Wynstan be talking about, anyhow? I never saw any performances at Gandersheim, unless you count the one at Easter Matins, and that's the same little show they do in half the minsters in Christendom. Fact is, Bishop Æthelwold even made up the one at Winchester: "Whom do you seek?" a priest dressed as an angel asks at Christ's sepulcher, and the Three Mary priests answer. Then ... well, it goes on and on. You ask me, the whole thing's just a bit of mummery barely different from what you see at any market fair betwixt London and Constantinople.

In case his audience hadn't heard him, Wynstan repeated himself. "A nun there in the dark Germanic forests, in the heavy Teutonic mists. A nun has conjured something novel, something fresh, something new under the sun."

At this second rapture over nunly doings, the bishop's face switched from mere disdain to real disgust. But Wynstan gained the queen's full and approving attention when he explained that this Hroswitha belonged to the religious community headed by the king's own cousin.

While Ethelred was likely wondering why he should care, Wynstan bellowed "*Hwaet!* Let the performance begin!"

He paused for effect while Cuthred darted into the shadows along the far wall and Beorn flexed his fingers. "In that year King Eadgar died, protector of Mercia, ruler of Wessex, sovereign over all of England. Lord of triumphs, hallowed king. His earthly dreams were at an end and he sought another light. The rewarder of heroes resigned his life, his throne."

Ethelred jumped up and waved his cap. "Huzzah! Huzzah! My royal father!" He likely would've joined Kyre on the table if the queen hadn't put one jeweled forefinger on his shoulder and the other on her lips.

Wynstan waited 'til the king settled down. "Then young Edward, his son, of royal race and prince of men, came to England's throne."

From someplace, Beorn produced a horn that looked suspiciously like the ones that had announced the royal hunting party. He put the horn to his lips and blew a hunting call. Onto the floor trotted Cuthred, wearing a parchment crown and straddling the broom like it was a horse.

So this was how it would go—Wynstan telling the story and his troupe acting it out. What was new about that? I settled further back in the shadows to find out.

Beorn pretended to lead the pretend horse and pretend king to a place in front of Kyre, who now also wore a parchment crown. She stood and bowed to the boy. He gave her a brief bow in return and, at Wynstan's nod, began to dismount from his stick-horse. "King Edward reigned, then died—"

Beorn caught hold of the boy's arm and began to wrench it. Or so it seemed when the boy cried out, then dropped the broom and fell on the floor. "Murdered! Murdered!" Wynstan sang. "At Corfe Gate on the fifteenth day before the calends of April, at even-tide."

What was Wynstan up to? Still sticking to the shadows, I moved closer to the action.

Kyre, still in her purple drape, jumped from the table and, as Beorn held the boy down, shook the wrapping off her wand. It was a scramseaxe. She plunged it into the boy. "No worse deed," Wynstan cried, "was ever done since men first sought our British land."

I was at first too startled to move. Then too surprised. The big knife had safely lodged between Cuthred's chest and arm. But with its hawk-shaped hilt, I knew it was mine.

The Thornholt family seemed shocked silent, as did Bishop Æthelwold. The young king looked like he was waiting for more action. Queen Ælfthryth simply appeared confused.

The players held their places while Wynstan stared accusingly at his audience. "The king's bones have disappeared," he sang out. "The morth-slayers would wipe his memory from the earth. But—"

Before I could follow this new idea, the queen spoke up. Her voice was soft and mild. "Perhaps, dear Wynstan, this kind of show is a little too novel for a simple Englishwoman like me. Whatever your Germans might relish, I would rather not have children murdered before my very ..."

The queen sprang up so fast that her headdress dropped back to show hair the color of pitch and a face suddenly warped with fury. She pointed a finger at Wynstan. "You!" She made a sweeping gesture that included Wynstan's troupe. The Thornholts, too. "You have contrived to accuse me of murder. And not just any murder. Of regicide."

Now came fierce shouts and a tumult of toppling benches and falling ale-horns as thegn and bishop, wife and monk sprang to their feet. Only young Ethelred stayed where he was, bewildered, I reckon, by the sudden chaos.

Meantime, hearing the noise in the hall, the king's bodyguard rushed inside, swords drawn, ready to defend the royals. But even as they formed a shield-wall around

Ethelred, their eyes darted from the Thornholts to Wynstan to Bishop Æthelwold to young Cuthred—all of them so still now that they might've been nailed to the floor. It was obvious the guards hadn't any idea who they were defending against.

That's when I understood it all. This whole show, the whole journey from Winchester, was a sham, a deception. Not only had Wynstan never known where King Edward's body was, he'd concocted the whole scheme so he could get to Thornholt and accuse Lord Hunwald of murder. Cuthred was meant to represent King Edward, Beorn was Hunwald, who, Wynstan's show was saying, killed the king.

But as soon as the thought formed in my mind, I realized it couldn't be that way. First off, why would Wynstan accuse Hunwald of murder? More importantly, it was Kyre who held the knife, Kyre who stabbed the boy. Kyre. Draped in royal purple.

"And take him," Ælfthryth shouted as she turned and pointed in my direction. "Him! The one hiding in the shadows."

I wanted to roll myself up like a scared hedgehog. What in hell was going on here? And how did *I* get involved?

Well, I wasn't going to let another Saxon lay his hands on me. And I could see only one way to keep that from happening.

I tore up to the queen and dropped on my knees. "You know me, Lady. Have for years. You know the service I gave King Eadgar and—"

"Arrest them," the queen ordered. "All of them. And that includes the child and this..."—she ran her icy Saxon eyes up and down me—"this filthy creature."

Before I could do, say, think of anything to save myself, it seemed like half the English army jumped on me. They trussed me up good and tight, then threw me into a corner of the hall with the purple drape over my head and those dirty leg-bands stuck in my mouth.

There I stayed while the screaming and cursing came to a halt and the hall grew still and cold. I shivered and gasped for the rest of the night, until the king's men put me in an ox cart with Wynstan and Beorn, bound for Winchester. Alongside us, a squad of English soldiers slogged through the melting snow. Their spears glistened in the morning sun.

CHAPTER TWELVE

February's cold and dark enough without spending a week of it in a Winchester crypt. Better to be in that crowded outdoor thieves' gaol in Fleshmonger Street than underground with only dead saints and live rats. When the king's soldiers first went to shove me in Old Minster's crypt, I raved and roared and tried to take a few of them with me down that black hallway to hell. But they stove in a rib or two and stole my shoes.

That shook the grit right out of me and I started brooding on the scripture my uncle the abbot used to read out loud in the refectory. He liked the thundering prophets, Jeremiah and 'specially Amos, telling us, "He that is courageous among the mighty shall flee naked."

Fleeing naked in February held little temptation for me, not with ribs that hurt like sin. So I lay down on the straw pallet the monks had tossed in a corner, to chew on my own favorite scrap of scripture: "Better a live dog than a dead lion."

Only, you don't have to be a lion to find yourself at the end of a rope. When I was on my way to meet the nuns in Wilton—just one week before—in bleak boundary land 'twixt two shires, I'd come on a crowd clustered round a gibbet.

Funny how folk act at a hanging. Some laugh, some pray, some cheer, some weep. Others just stare, maybe thinking what it'd be like with their own necks in the noose.

I didn't know if the churl on that gallows had dared plot against his lord or was just a common morth-slayer, but his end drew a good audience—merchants and churls and churchmen. Soldiers stood there, too, maybe even a thegn or two. A woman passed through the throng selling pasties, and in a nearby field a troop of minstrels were setting up for a show.

On the scaffold a pair of clerics moved to either side of the churl and began to pray. Three women at the edge of the platform wept and keened and howled. Finally, the hangman dropped the noose over the head of the white-faced churl, who looked more angry than scared or sorry.

The crowd pressed forward as the last prayer was said, but my nerve failed me and I turned away. Instead of taking the churl's death as a sign and heading someplace far away like I should've, I bought a pasty and headed toward trouble.

After I'd spent a day or two in the crypt under Old Minster's church, monks took over from the soldiers guarding me. Nobody'd yet come to haul me off to the gallows, so I mustered nerve enough to ask for a candle. The monks brought one and even something to read when they found out I knew how—a book of penances that promised a year's fast for fornication and three for murder. But reading it was better than counting fleas and dreaming about the scaffold.

The monks' food wasn't so bad, either, if you didn't mind nothing but eggs, boiled parsnips, and Saxon ale. I bolted it all down fast as it came, which wasn't often enough, and even though they were likely just fattening me up for ... what? Killing was the least of what the English would do to a Welshman they thought plotted against their royals.

What plot was I supposed to be part of, anyhow? Wynstan had put on his act to accuse the queen of murdering her stepson. Since most of England had already convicted her, it couldn't have come as any shock to Ælfthryth. Still, maybe arrogant old Wynstan thought that after his grand show she'd be so overcome with guilt that she'd just up and confess. But I really didn't fancy Wynstan as a redeemer of souls.

And why put his plot in motion at Thornholt? Didn't he know he could get his old friends—and, more importantly, me—in trouble if the thing failed? Maybe he thought if he faked his death, we'd look genuinely shocked when he came through the door in a billow of hell-spawned steam. Or maybe he was just an entertainer that liked to make a big impression.

All this I mulled over for days and days as I ate the mushy parsnips and swallowed the miserable ale. From the length of time it was taking to bring me up before my betters, I began to have the feeling that the betters had no more notion of what was going on than I did. The time had come to hatch a plot of my own.

The crypt wasn't much of a burial chamber for the minster's saints, with only thick oak tree trunks to hold up its vault, half-plastered walls, and a pounded dirt floor. It also had a narrow staircase that ended at a locked oaken door. Worse yet, it was empty. No altar, no reliquaries, just me and my straw. A pretty grim spot compared to St. Swithin's fancy mausoleum outside on the green. But maybe the monks had emptied the place just to store me there.

Anyhow, it offered no weapon. I'd have to rely on fists alone. The first day that my ribs felt better, I waited for the monk who carried me my supper of watery parsnips heaped on a bread trencher. He was a tall, pale-haired young fellow sporting a stained habit and a badly barbered tonsure. He also reeked of onions and his own unwashed body. But his shoes were stout, dry, and, best of all, big.

"How 'bout a nice mutton haunch for tomorrow?" I said. "Like your abbot gets."

The lad bristled as if I'd accused his abbot of denying Our Lord's divinity. "We follow St. Benedict's Rule here. And eat no flesh."

"Neither did Judas Iscariot."

The young monk's eyes got wide and his Adam's apple went all a-quiver. Why is it folk think they're holy, sanctified, and can't sin just because they don't eat meat? I almost spoiled my plot by busting out laughing. But then I told him to set the parsnips down and be gone. "By the bye, I'm done with the Penitential. Next time, could you bring me something a little lighter? The Office for the Dead, maybe?"

I held out the book with one hand, ready to grab him with the other. His scrawny neck would snap easy as a pullet's. But he waved the book away. "You're to be in the abbot's lodge after None."

In another eye blink, I'd have had the lad on his back and howling for the whole Company of Heaven to come deliver him. But now I reconsidered. Escape was dicey, 'specially with a monastery full of monks and me without a weapon.

On the other hand, maybe the abbot's lodge wasn't on the

highway to the gibbet after all. A new way out might be presenting itself. I said, "Did St. Nicholas have a chat with your abbot, tell him I'm only a relic monger? Or maybe St. David came and explained I'm a tame Welshman."

The lad gave me a good glare. "Somebody's come for you, all right."

"And who would that be?"

"I can only pray it's the king's jailer to take you away from here."

"Now, now, Brother,"—I shook a finger at him—"maybe you ought to check and see if your Rule has a little something to say about Christian charity."

He shoved the parsnips at me and without so much as a *Benedicte* stalked out.

Had the king sent his man? Or, rather, had his mother? If so, what for? To say all is forgiven, or to ready me for the noose? And if not the king's man, then who? The possibilities were endless—and endlessly awful. But I've a tongue in my head and, if I'm honest, it's usually a better weapon than my fists. I'd take my chances on whoever I'd meet in the abbot's lodge.

After the minster bells tolled None, a soldier clad in chainmail and wolf skin put me in fetters—and new shoes— then marched me across the cloister to the abbot's lodge. Even scared half witless, I could tell it was big and comfortable as a nobleman's mead hall. My stomach started to unknot when I saw the fire blazing in the hearth, the cushioned chairs, the many-colored tapestries. A big table fairly groaned under flagons full of drink—ale and mead and cider and spiced wine—along with half a dozen platters heaped high with sweetmeats.

Next to the fire stood a stocky little man with narrow eyes and a nose that had been broken more than once. He wore monkish black, though he had no tonsure. Instead, his head was completely bald, whether by razor or nature, I couldn't say. But, all in all, he put me in mind of a particularly vicious blackthorn cudgel. "Unbind him," he said to the soldier. "Then go."

The man wasn't the abbot—that would've been Bishop Æthelwold—and I didn't think I knew him. He seemed to know me, though. He called me by name anyhow, and gestured to the chair next to the fire. "Sit down, Tryff. Help yourself to food and drink."

The ale was Welsh and strong enough to make me guzzle two cups straight down in hopes of drowning my terror. It didn't help much, so I said, "Pretty fine treatment for a prison rat. Or is this my last meal?"

"You don't seem to remember me from your time with King Eadgar. And I shouldn't wonder. I was only a lowly bower-thegn back then. Now I'm *consillarius* to King Ethelred."

He smiled broadly and slapped me on the back. "I'm Siward of Gloucester. And of course this isn't your last meal. If it were, do you really think you'd be enjoying it in an abbot's lodge?"

Instead, it appeared I was to enjoy an interrogation. I asked when he'd be breaking out the thumb-screws.

Lord Siward's smile never slackened. "Do you remember the celebration King Eadgar put on after you brought him his father's killer? I, for one, stayed drunk a full week. And you? You couldn't even mount that fine chestnut horse the king gave you. How many times did you miss the stirrup?" Now he laughed. "I was one of the folk who finally heaved you into the saddle."

So I could canter through the royal pavilion facing that horse's fine chestnut butt. It'd been no way to thank so generous a king. Good thing Eadgar had been as drunk as everybody else.

For a while, Siward and I told tales of Eadgar, *god cyning, god mann.* But Saxons rarely wax so jolly without some dark purpose. I played along until Siward at last turned to the business at hand. "As you may have surmised, Queen Ælfthryth has sent me. She knows Wynstan tricked you into joining in that foul trick he tried to pull off at Thornholt."

Had Fortuna's wheel spun my way at last? "Then let me go now," I said.

Siward swiped a hand across his glossy head. "Wynstan naturally claimed it was a mere entertainment. Some old Dansker story he picked up in York. Nothing to do with Queen Ælfthryth. He'll be hanged before Lent."

It was no surprise, but I choked and gagged and spewed anyhow, 'til I could finally ask, "What of Kyre? Beorn? The child?"

Siward's brow knitted up and he shook his head in a show of perplexity.

"Then where's my horse? My fine chestnut horse?"

More brow knitting, head shaking, even a display of shrugged shoulders and up-turned palms.

I was still puzzling over this harebrained attempt at deception when the lodge door opened and through it ducked first a head, then stooped shoulders, then the whole of Lord Ordwulf, the ealdorman of Devon and Cornwall. He was Queen Ælfthryth's brother, wicked as the gallows and just as deadly. He tossed his cloak onto a chair. Its ornate silver clasp was worth a pasture full of chestnut horses.

Me, I never believed Ordwulf was the tallest man in England, like folk claimed. He was just a long rake of a man topped by dark hair and a mouth full of buck teeth, out of which now roared a forest fire of curses. Siward barely glanced at him, just set to picking through the sweetmeats.

When the smoke from Ordwulf's blasphemy cleared, he came and stood over me. "My sister the queen has never seen you for what you are, a thieving vermin that battens off holy treasure. But even she would like to know how you could have fallen in with the likes of Wynstan the wanking Windy."

Meanwhile, Siward sucked mutton fat off his fingers and I helped myself to another cup of ale. I was proud that my hands hardly shook. But I couldn't summon any voice at all.

"My sister knows, by the way, that you did not see fit to visit her when you were here in Winchester last week. Instead, you sought out a low tavern and even lower company."

So someone had informed on me. I wasn't surprised. England was full of folk too poor to resist the king's silver. Me, for one. But how did this spy know what brought me to the tavern in Goldsmith Street? And did he know Lady Flæda had sent me?

Siward set the sweetmeats aside, satisfied, I reckon, that he'd found all the best bits of kidney. "I've told the Welshman that the queen doesn't believe he had any part in Wynstan's plot."

Ordwulf shook that off with a flick of his hand. "Paul's balls, man, Wynstan wasn't the prime mover in this treasonous folly. That we know. Wynstan, however, hasn't told us all he knows. I could not attempt to extract more, lest the old man die short of the hanging he damn well deserves."

He took my ale cup and turned it upside down on the table. He said, "This bastard here, as we shall see, can be pushed as far as flesh will bear. He will plead for death, then plead some more only to find the dark angel has resigned him to me."

I reached over to right the cup. Now my hands shook for sure.

"So, you Welsh weasel-dick, would you like to tell us what you were up to in Wilton? I mean besides cheating nuns as usual."

I dropped the ale cup. It rolled into a corner as I admitted to visiting Lady Flæda.

"Ah yes," Ordwulf said. "Flæda. Our plump White Duck, too diseased to fly away, too well to keep still. She suggested you find Wynstan?"

I spent a moment pondering live dogs and dead lions, then nodded.

"Flæda sent you to Wynstan because he allegedly had knowledge of the whereabouts of King Edward's body." Ordwulf had stopped asking questions. "Nor was that all you did in Wilton."

He surely knew I'd beaten up Ealdorman Alvar, so I admitted that, too, and added I'd talked to Abbess Wulfthryth.

Ordwulf slewed his eyes toward Siward. "The wretch has already told us more than bloody Wynstan did after a full day under the scourge."

Siward pointed a greasy finger at Ordwulf. "No whip for

this man, hear? He's a Welsh prince. More important, he was a friend of King Eadgar's bosom. Your sister the queen would never countenance it."

I could tell I wasn't the bone of contention here. This was a feud 'twixt royal thegns that was about to turn deadly. Ordwulf made a sound low in his throat. Siward jumped up from the chair, his lip curled back. The two glared at each other, tall wolfhound and squat terrier ready to row. But no matter how high they stood in the world, neither one had been allowed to carry sword or knife into the minster. If they were going to fight, it would have to be hand to hand, tooth to tooth.

Me, I sidled to the door for a peek into the hallway. Dog fights generally end in blood and I didn't want any of it to be mine. But the hallway was chock full of soldiers. I'd be better off where I was. If the thegns killed each other, I could slip away in the confusion.

When I turned from the door, they'd backed off a fight. Neither of them looked any less angry, but presently Siward returned to his place at the table and Ordwulf poured down a hornful of wine. "Get back in that chair," he told me.

I went almost eye-to-eye with him and he wanted his usual edge, looking down on his quarry. That tempted me to stay standing, but Siward wisely shoved a chair my way. After I took it, he said, "Did Lady Flæda give any reason, other than a mother's love, for wanting her son's body?"

I asked what other reason there could be and Siward said not to treat them like fools. He said we all knew that if Flæda got hold of King Edward's body, she might put it somewhere so secret no one would ever find it again. "And," he added, "Ethelred's consecration as king would not be valid."

"My lords, I don't know where the king's body is. And I don't think Wynstan does, either." It was the bare truth, likely too bare for polished courtiers like Ordwulf and Siward. I could tell neither believed me. And Ordwulf would still put his faith in a good beating.

I tried to pour more ale, but once again the beaker shot away from me. This time, it flew into Siward's lap. He leaped up, now ready to turn his anger on me. But he laughed instead. "Let us go to Queen Ælfthryth. She will be better able to deal with our Welshman. As you say, Ordwulf, he's a prince. His royal blood will out. He will not lie to a queen."

Ordwulf looked like he wanted to let loose a fatal round of curses. Instead, he settled for "Your own royal blood has never stopped you lying to her."

I didn't know what that signified, but once again the two thegns started to snarl at each other. Only they didn't just say hard words this time around. Now they growled, making gnarly sounds down low in their throats like a couple of riled-up hounds. Finally, Siward tried to sink his fist in Ordwulf's middle and Ordwulf reared back, ready to knock the little *consillarius* to kingdom come. Blood would flow in a trice.

That's when I had the chance to escape—out of the abbot's lodge, across the cloister, and over the wall before those two brawling curs could stop to draw breath. Then I thought about what would benefit me most—and stepped betwixt them.

I don't know which one blinded me with a thumb to my eye. But I can tell you the water from that wounded eye rolled down like justice. I lowered my head and rammed it into the nearest belly.

Siward went down like a busted sack of grain and Ordwulf went to laughing. He would, he claimed, still be laughing when he led me before the queen of England.

But that would come later, Ordwulf said. Now he sent me back in fetters to the crypt. I complained bitterly, of course, much good it did then or later while I shivered in the dark, barefoot now—and furious.

From the church-house above me, I could hear the monks at their psalms, chanting the hours—Sext, then None, and finally Vespers. I say again, Saxons' singing is as dreadful as their cooking. But not near so dreadful as the words Ordwulf said to me before he left me there in the crypt. "In spite of what Siward told you, we ... my sister has decided that the royal house is no longer in need of your services. However, as I told you, we do need to know the begetter of your treasonous plot."

The smile he cast my way was so grim it almost covered his buck teeth. "Say your prayers tonight, Welshman, because tomorrow you'll have breath only for confession."

Whatever Queen Ælfthryth had ordered or not ordered, it was clear Siward had abandoned me. And Ordwulf's eyes held a mad, murdering malice that told me he'd beat me to death with his own fists.

I splattered a curse over him as he left the crypt. Then I started my prayers, just as he'd bade me. But they were in a different cause. After the yellow-haired young monk came in with the parsnips, I'd escape from Winchester. And not just from Winchester, but from the pursuit of King Edward's remains. Let the English track down their own royal carcasses.

It was a terrible decision and that keg of silver pennies rolled in and out of my mind while I made it. But a dead man can't buy his mother out of slavery, not with all the silver pennies in the world. It was that simple. And another simple thing—it was time, past time, that I set out to find her. I even knew where to start. The slavers my father had sold her to had likely taken her to Bristol, just across the water from Wales, and there auctioned her off.

I've been in Bristol when a boatload of slaves comes in. The slavers—Danskers mostly, these days—march the merchandise off the boat and make them crawl onto slippery planks perched high above the wharf where everybody can see them. Then the slavers start singing out their praises. "Step right up, folks. We got girls today. Girls. Big ones, blond ones, strong ones. Girls today. What's that you say? Are they Christians? Now, sir, would I try and sell you a Christian? These ones are guaranteed heathen from heathen lands. Girls. We got girls today."

The Irish slavers would've done the same with my mother. No matter that she was a Christian. But I know the kind of people who live off slavers—the men who sell them drink, the women who sell them pleasure, the priests who sell them absolution. Those people had the kind of memories that a cut penny could jig even before it left your hand.

Like the psalmist says, weeping endures only for a night. My new resolve came as joy comes in the morning. Still, I prayed for the strength and courage to do whatever had to be done to escape from Winchester and get to Bristol. Then I added a few more prayers because I'd have to go back to Thornholt first. I sure wasn't leaving Tom Tub to the Saxons.

The question was how to pay for all this. I had a little of Lady Flæda's silver left. It wouldn't go far, though, what with bread and bribes. I could always pick up some relics, of course. But that's a chancy craft at best. Saints don't always want to move, not from magnificent cathedrals or comfortable country churches, either. And I needed a great deal of silver soon. Gold, too, if I could get it.

A solution, though, was at hand. The Great Harp of Arthur still lay somewhere in the lands of my uncle, King Brynmor. I could find it before autumn, God—and Fortuna—willing.

First, I had to get out of the crypt, then out of Winchester itself. The young monk who guarded me would present no problem. In the world beyond him, though, I'd need a weapon, a good sharp one, and finding such a thing in a monastery would be a bit of a trick. Monks weren't allowed to carry real weapons, neither sword nor seaxe. But even the meekest would have a knife to use at the refectory table. Problem was, the things broke apart on anything that wasn't bread or over-cooked chicken. I wanted something sturdier and whole a lot sharper. So I sent up a prayer to St. Peter, who knew how to use a blade, and he answered.

I figured from the young monk's ink-stained hands that he wasn't a jailer by vocation. He likely spent his days tucked in his cell copying holy manuscripts so all those new churches going up around England would have proper gospel-books for their mass-priests to read from. His desk would be littered with pots of ink, a stylus or two, pages of parchment and an awl to mark them with. He'd also have a stout penknife. And if he was like the scribes I grew up with, he'd keep it on him to trim his iron-hard toenails or stab a rat under the refectory table.

I hadn't planned to cut the lad's throat, but it was a temptation because when he came in he refused to speak in words. He just made signs. I knew that finger talk from my own time with monks and I didn't appreciate being called names in any language. I made a gesture even a cleric could understand, then a fist that spelled out my meaning on his jaw. Like I'd predicted, he was no problem.

Sure enough, he had a penknife in his relic bag, along with the usual bits of saintly bone and a few twists of holy hair. What surprised me was that he also carried some cut pennies in there. This fellow was in obvious need of help with his vow of poverty, so I helped myself to his silver, his penknife, his black cloak. Oh, and his shoes.

Outside in the minster's cloister, I found that the recent days of sunless warmth and melting snow had turned Winchester into a foggy quagmire. But, miserable as the murk and mire were for everyone else, they were a good thing for a fugitive like me. No one could see how ill my monk's clothes fit, nor how my new shoes had turned into slabs of sludge. And even if a man stood next to me, and was tall enough to see, he wouldn't be able to tell if that naked patch atop my head was tonsure or bald spot.

As it turned out, I didn't have to use the penknife on the monk at the minster gatehouse. He'd been brought his supper and was too busy with it to notice me. But once past him I still had a problem—two, in fact. The first was getting out of the city. The guards at its gates might wonder why a monk needed to take a walk in the countryside after Vespers.

Another problem was that even if I got through the gate, I couldn't go around Wessex with only a penknife for protection. Naturally, I'd find a stout stick lying about in the countryside, or at least a rock. But a stick and a stone wouldn't take care of bandits. Or village toughs that think you've no business strolling down their leafy lane. I needed another knife, better yet several of them.

Stealing a knife out in the world would be no easy task. Sure, everyone—man, woman, and cleric—carried an edge of one sort or another. But knives are expensive and well-tended. If I sidled up to somebody on the street and tried to ease their blade out of its sheath, it'd be 'twixt my ribs in a twinkling. Better to filch one from a smith or a crowded butcher's stall. I remembered both in Cheap Street.

On the other hand, I didn't want to brave a smith the size of an ox or a butcher armed with a tool that could fell an ox. And I couldn't just stroll up to the knife-maker and buy a knife. The man might remember a monk who carried silver. Maybe I'd better stick with the penknife, do the best I could until I got to Thornholt. I'd find plenty of weapons there.

I pulled my cowl over my head and headed for the arched gate in the north wall. There, I lingered at a little shrine to St. Helen, praying and such while I waited for the guards to turn their attention to what guards most like to do—showing off how important they are. Sure enough, it wasn't long before they pounced on a trio of churls they claimed they'd never seen before. They likely knew exactly who the poor devils were, where they came from, why they were at the gate. The guards tormented them anyway, out of boredom and the conceit of officials the world over. But that was the churls' bad luck, not mine. In the commotion, Fortuna came to my aid and I slipped right past.

The road looked even less welcoming than it had at dusk the night Kyre led me into all this trouble. Heaven help her now, her and her man and her boy. Wynstan, too. They were probably in far worse distress than I was. They'd danced on the edge of treason and Queen Ælfthryth wasn't the sort to permit an encore. But maybe Wynstan would call in a few markers—believe me, a travelling man has them out there— and everyone would be off to distant Orkney to entertain the Norskers.

By now it was all but dark and I decided to find a place to stay in the little suburb just beyond the gate. It was a marketplace where the vendors lived as well as worked, in huts with their stalls out front. Everything was closed now, the people asleep, though the sweet smell of new-baked bread lingered. I headed for the baker's stall with the big warm oven I could spend the night beside. The baker'd be up at first light, maybe even before. But I'd be gone by then, and his biggest knife along with me. I found a good spot behind the oven and slept almost as soon as I'd drawn the monk's cloak around me.

I woke up with a blade at my throat. Likely I would've woken up dead if the fellow'd just gone ahead and stuck the knife in. But instead he squatted down behind me and leaned over me to cut my throat and take my neck pouch in one swipe. The stink of him was what brought me to. The man smelled like a dead rat. If he hadn't been trying to kill me, I would've puked all over him. Instead, I grabbed his knife arm with one hand and his beard with the other, then took to wrenching both. Next thing, we were rolling around in the dirt, howling and yowling loud enough to wake the whole of Wessex. And sure loud enough to wake the baker and his wife.

I admit they saved me. Drove the man off with pitchfork and broomstick. I went after him, of course, but he was down the dark road before I even made it to my knees. And he knew the place, likely, and I didn't. Maybe he was just a common thief, interested in taking my pouch and not my life. At least I hoped that's all he was because the stink he left behind smelled as putrid as the one that'd bloomed up when I was attacked outside Wilton.

In thanks for the baker's help, I pressed a cut penny into his hand. He gave it back, calling me Brother and mumbling about the rules of hospitality. He even asked for my blessing. So I said I'd exchange the silver for one of his knives, the big one he used to chop the beef and turnips for his pasties. He handed it over with a grin, relieved it was his knife and not his hospitality that had a price on it. His wife didn't care about rules or hospitality or anything but that coin. It was worth enough to buy a whole crate of knives, thrice over, and a couple of cows to use them on. She grabbed the coin, tested it with her teeth, then stowed it 'twixt a set of tits so sweet I dared not look. I lowered my eyes—the baker still held his pitchfork—and gave them a cleric's blessing.

The road north was a half-thawed bog. Its thick, cold mud would suck, cling, soak, and finally kill. I decided to take my chances cross country, where I'd be more or less able to choose what I stepped in. What I didn't choose too well was the way to Thornholt. I had only a dim notion of where it lay. I'd gone there staring into a snowstorm and left staring at the floor of an oxcart. I knew it couldn't be far but still I spent the whole day climbing from one hill to the next, fog-girded and soaked through. The only good thing was that if the stinking lout from the baker's stall—or anyone else—was following me, he'd be as wet, tired, and ready to quit as I was.

I decided to find a swineherd's hut to spend the night in. The pigs had finished foraging in the oak forests at the New Year, so no one would try and kill me for a pig-rustler. Now the swineherds were back at the estates they worked for, enjoying the fruits of their labor—pig-tail soup, pickled trotters, fried chitterlings. My stomach growled with envy. Since yesterday's parsnips I'd only eaten a few acorns and they half-rotten. Then from where I stood on an oak ridge, I caught sight of a half-built bell tower and its unwalled manor in the valley below. I'd be at Thornholt before nightfall, feasting on Thrima's good food and good looks.

I'd no idea what had happened to Lord Hunwald and Lady Bathilda. Were they due for the gibbet like Wynstan? Or had the queen forgiven them for the fools they were, so easily taken in by Wynstan's winged tongue. And if she hadn't pardoned them, who was in charge at Thornholt? Their sons, slimy Brother Petroc and his no doubt even slimier elder brother? Or were the royal reeve's tough troopers on guard?

But Thornholt seemed as unprotected as ever. I slipped through its thick hawthorn and spindle hedge—where I left my monk's cloak hidden in the brambles—and onto the muddy green. Across the green lay the mead hall and its bower house, the tower, the stable, the church-house. The whole place was silent. But that meant nothing. For all I knew, half a hundred troopers squinted at me through the Wessex dusk. And notched the arrows in their bows.

I started for the stable anyhow. My skin crawled at the thought of Saxons riding Tom, though I never had any doubt he was well fed and cared for. Whatever the English are, they know better than to mistreat good horseflesh. Even so, I was ready to charge to Tom's rescue with Red Dragon banners blazoned. But as my mam used to remind me, "*Haws dywedyd 'mydydd' na mynd drosto.*" It's easier to say 'mountain' than to climb one. I decided it would be best to go to the churls' village and find out the lay of the land before I let English arrows make me look like a Welsh St. Sebastian.

I slopped past the dark blur of the mead hall and around its dung heap. At the track that led to the village, I looked back to see if anyone was following. The only thing behind me was the bower windows' dim glow splashing onto the muddy hall-yard.

Where to stay 'til morning? Nobody'd mentioned any night-spirits lurking around Thornholt, but you never can tell. So I didn't want to spend the night in its woods, even if I could find a spot where I wouldn't die of the cold. A barn would do fine. I'd just have to take my chances some churl wouldn't find me asleep in his straw and plant a pitchfork in my backside.

I moved past some ramshackle sheds and the threshing barn—too big and too bare—'til I came to a three-sided wattle ox house. The pair of beasts inside twisted around and gave me a look that made me very respectful when I slid in with them. I didn't want to find myself sharing the small space with half a ton of horned and unhappy animals. But when I dropped into their straw, they only mooed a mite. The sound was comforting and so was their smell. I fell asleep straightaway, warm enough to dream of summer and my *mam* at our cow camp in the mountains.

Next thing, sunlight licked through the chinks in the wattle wall. And somebody else was in the ox-house. Then two somebodies. They pelted past me, first a speckled hen, then Thrima, the Norsker woman. I don't know which of them squawked loudest, and the only reason I understood Thrima better than the hen was that I've heard the cursing at Norsker ale-benches. Those folk never stop 'til they've called down the abjuration, imprecation, commination, and execration not only of every saint in heaven but the whole of Satan's army, too. And that's what Thrima did to that speckled hen.

When it headed to my corner of the shed, I ducked back under the straw. Too late. "You," Thrima cried. "You there, catch hold of thing."

I tried, I promise I did. But when I came out of the hay, I found myself beak-to-beak with the hen. She threw a hard peck, then slipped past me while I clutched my nose. Meantime, the two oxen broke loose and took off after Thrima.

Now every creature in the yard was on the move, oxen bellowing and running after Thrima, who cursed and chased the hen, which was screeching and flying out the door. I leapt from the manger, caught a toe on its front board, lost the baker's knife, and sprawled in the ox muck. Just in time to see Thrima and the hen disappear around the corner of a shed, oxen lumbering behind.

But now a new combatant was about to enter the fray. A hulking troll of a man slopped through the muddy yard, an ox goad in his meaty hands. While I wondered what ale-soaked Norsker epic he'd dropped out of, he threw down his goad and grabbed the dun ox by the horns. The beast gave a startled moo. Before it could think what to do about this monster twisting its horns, it fell onto its front knees, then all the way down into the mud.

By now, the other ox had forgotten what it was mad about and stopped to stare at its mate struggling up from the ground. About that time Thrima came around the corner of the shed, hen held high. The churl picked up his ox goad and hoisted it like a spear. Then he and Thrima roared out a northern victory cry so fierce it might've raised King Alfred from the grave. When the two turned their savage eyes towards me, all I could think of was the prayer said in half the churches in Christendom: "Spare us, oh Lord, from the fury of the Vikings."

Thrima looked at the squawking hen clenched in her fist. Then she looked at me, then at the big churl. "Jump on it," she said, waving the hen my direction.

The big man and I answered at the same time. "Me?"

"You, Hauk. Jump on him."

The man cocked his head like a puzzled hound.

"Hauk, jump on thing from ox-house. Then throw him over wall."

She didn't mean the chicken, but Hauk was flummoxed enough for me to get a word in. More than a word, truth be told. I shouted over the shrieking hen in my best Norsker. "You remember me, Thrima. From last week when you told me Lady Bathilda poisoned Wynstan Wing Tongue."

Thrima looked me up and down while it dawned on me I shouldn't have mentioned her mistake. "I mean, when you warned me there was trouble here at Thornholt."

Her dark eyes narrowed. Her lip curled. "I know you, *ja*. You are trouble here. Hauk, tackle him."

I was saved by the speckled hen, who wrenched herself from Thrima's clutches. As the hen bolted toward the open fields, Thrima shouted some terrible northern curse and tore after her. "Hauk, kill!" she yelled over her shoulder.

Neither Hauk nor I moved, only gazed at the woman and the hen in the field, both mud-sodden and struggling. If I tried to run that's how I'd end up, and with no guarantee I wouldn't die face down in an English barnyard. Words would have to save me now. "Looks like I'm less important to that bossy old hag than her chicken."

They weren't very true words. Bossy Thrima might've been, but she was likely no older than me. And she sure wasn't any hag. Still, true or not, more words rushed out. I piled them higher and deeper. "Seems like she's crazy. Possessed, even. Ever hear her chatting with Satan?"

Hauk brought the ox goad level with his broad chest. He held it like a two-fisted battle axe.

Maybe I'd gone a bit far. I'd try reason instead, put to use the Augustine and Jerome and Ambrose that my uncle the abbot had pounded into me. "What you say we talk this over, man to man?"

Hauk took a step closer. "That's my mother."

He might've been lying, of course. Thrima didn't look old enough to be the filthy lump's dam. But I know two things about this fallen world. One is that when a large man with a weapon in his hand and blood in his eye advances on you, words probably won't stop him. The other thing is that cold cash tops filial feelings every time. I yanked my neck sack from under my tunic and dug out a cut penny.

Hauk continued his advance. Maybe he was as crazy as his mam. But he slowed down and eyed the coin. When his eyes set to gleaming bright as the silver itself, I knew Hauk for a sane man. I tossed it to him. He snatched it like a dog does a scrap of meat. And his weapon splashed into the mud.

After a while, Thrima returned from her hunt, the hen in her hands. She found Hauk and me in the threshing barn, mugs of mead in ours.

CHAPTER FOURTEEN

After Thrima had stomped away, loudly complaining to both Freya and the Virgin, I asked Hauk when he thought I could sneak into the stable. "So the Thornholts or their spear band won't see me take my horse and get the hell out of here."

"Young lord and his men all gone hunting over to Sudholt. Brother Petroc, too. Be gone three, four day. Nobody up to the hall now."

He didn't look too sorry about it, either. But, my God, what if they'd taken Tom Tub with them?

I grew even more worried when the only creature in the paddock was a dun-colored old she-mule. But Tom was inside the otherwise empty stable, as glad to see me as I was him. His ears twitched forward and he gave out a good loud nicker. The dried apple in my hand was well met, too. He curled his big, soft lips around it and all but purred.

While he worked on the half-dozen other apples I'd brought from the village, I looked around to make sure he'd been properly cared for. The stalls were clean and sturdy, with buckets of clean water and plenty of dry hay.

Tom's hooves looked fit. He'd been groomed regularly, and had no sores. He'd recently dug quite a neat little hole in the stall's clay floor, but that was just Tom and not to be held against the brothers Thornholt. They seemed to have taken decent care of him, which wasn't necessarily any great credit to their generosity. With their father accused of treason, they'd need to hang on to everything they owned and anything they happened to find.

Tom took the saddle easily and acted quite the gentleman on the way out of the stable. Once in the yard, he might've wanted to take off right away, but I walked him around before I tightened the girth. Then I swung aboard for a gentle trot to the village so I could thank Hauk and Thrima for their hospitality. After that, praise St. Christopher and all the saints, I'd be on my way to Bristol.

Tom hadn't taken more than two steps when he came up lame. A storm went off inside me. Thunder cracked in my ears, white streaks flashed before my eyes, a scalding torrent burned through my head. And over it all came the roar of my voice cursing Saxons all the way back to Adam and forward unto generations yet unborn. What had they done to my Tom?

When at last the tempest let up and I merely quivered in anger, I dismounted to look at the hind leg giving Tom his trouble. I searched for a crack in the hoof, heat in ankle and hock. But truth be told I was still too vexed to play horse leech. I'd find Lord Hunwald's smith. Likely, he'd know what ailed Tom.

I gave the big chestnut a pat of apology for leaving him with these evil worms, then charged into the village and found Hauk. I demanded he produce the smith. When he said the man'd gone out with the hunting party, I damn near foamed at the mouth.

Hauk's brow knotted up. "Worried about your horse, are you?"

By then my fury had taken me beyond words, but Hauk somehow found the sense to add, "Heard Odo smith tell Brother Petroc the new horse had a stone bruise. He be fine in a few days, but best leave him home for now."

I tore back to the stable, hoisted Tom's hoof, poked and prodded for myself. When he didn't kick me across the paddock, I figured the smith was right. Tom would be fine in a day or so and we could go to Bristol. Meantime, I was stuck at Thornholt with a village of peasant simpletons and a woman who seemed to want me dead.

After I unsaddled Tom, brushed him down, said I'd be sleeping with him tonight—his peat moss looked a lot more inviting than the oxen's foul straw—I headed back to the village to find out when the royal reeve would be coming round to lay hold of Hunwald's property. I'd have to be gone beforehand.

The village was a mean little place, only a ragged row of houses, barns, and sheds strung along a muddy track. But it had a shake-roofed church, though barely better than a shed itself. I wondered how such a tiny building could hold the horde of churls that now poured out its door. There were at least two score men, women, children wearing more-or-less clean tunics and really clean headgear—brightly colored caps on the men, embroidered headdress on the women, freshly washed hair on the young 'uns.

It looked like a funeral, with the wake to follow. But I soon realized this was the annual blessing of the village fields, one of the happiest, most hopeful days in a farmer's life. It's a moveable feast, depending on when the ice has fled and the ground is soft enough to plough. This year the fields were blessed in February, "Mud Month," as the English say. And a good time everybody was making of it, laughing and singing and cavorting along the muddy track, led by a red-haired lad of about twelve who carried a long pole with a wooden cross at its end.

The priest came just after him. He was a burly redhead—that was probably his son with the cross—and no manicured monastic. Hauk told me he was one of those clerics who loved his people as he loved his God. He rejoiced with them when Fortuna smiled, wept with them as they mourned, listened to them when they grew old. He'd drink at their weddings, play with their children, and pray hard for every single one of their souls. Today, he danced right along with them, even while the white ends of his alb went dragging in the muddy road.

Everybody was in such good humor that they let me join them. It surprised me because peasants can be chary of strangers, especially ones as big and dark as me. But I knew Hauk, and they didn't object when he went to pull me into the procession. *I* objected, though. "I'd rather stay in the barn. The fewer folk that see me—well, too many eyes, too many mouths."

Hauk brushed away that notion. "You worried about Lord Hunwald's sons—they called Petroc and Immin. They be to Sudholt for days. Weeks, if they be bagging enough heads for the meadhall walls. Plenty boar about this year. Yesterday the two of the beasts dropped down the trap we made in yon wood."

Hauk tugged at my sleeve. "There'll come ale and boar

meat later on. Dancing, too, you of a mind." When I still hesitated, he said, "We won't tell nobody you here. We don't tell on folk."

By now, the parade was headed toward a dozen or so brown and white oxen and as many lads. The oxen, heavy ploughs already hitched behind them, stood calmly chewing their cuds. The plough boys, on the other hand, were shouting, laughing, leaping over ploughs and beasts. It's the same everywhere, come spring. Before plough boys crack their whips, they crack jokes like it's a game they're off to instead of the hardest work on the farm.

When we reached the ploughs, the priest spread salt and fennel and incense on them. Then he stuffed a loaf of bread into a newly cut furrow and asked the All-ruler to make the fields flourish. Finally, he made the sign of the cross over field, furrow, oxen, people. "Grow in the name of the Father. Be blessed and may the eternal Lord grant that neither cunning-man nor speaking-woman nor the evil elves overturn these words."

He went on quite a while—something about the earth mother and bright crops—until he finished up with *In Nomine Patris* and everyone shouted "Amen" and "Amen" and "Amen."

Then the churls got right to work. The men, priest included, went to their ploughing, the women to spinning, milking, and minding the two boars turning on their spits. Only the very old men could make a real holiday of it. They tapped into an ale keg, then settled on the village green to talk and drink and celebrate the tilled fields of yesterday.

Hauk said since I was a guest I'd not be expected to take a turn behind the plough. Just as well, too. Learning to plough was the only thing my father ever spared me. So I meandered back to the village, where I stayed away from the old men, who'd surely have had hard words for a fellow big as me not out doing a man's work. The women weren't too friendly, either, maybe for the same reason, or maybe because a travelling man's good enough at a celebration but considered a menace when he's on his own.

They could flatter themselves all they wanted, but I wasn't interested in a passel of Saxon women. I was, though, interested in Thrima. Not the Thrima who used barnyard curses to order her son to kill me, but the Thrima who'd warned me about Lady Bathilda in the language of a woman raised in the house of a *jarl*. I'd taken a fancy to her frosty Norsker looks and, I hoped, frisky Norsker ways.

I trailed her to the hall kitchen. It was timbered like the hall itself, only with a reed roof. When I'd ducked under its lintel and blinked away its smoke, I saw it was dirt-floored and filled with the usual sacks, cupboards, cooking utensils. In the middle, beneath the smoke-hole in the ceiling, a fire blazed and likely had all day, making the place cursed hot. Maybe that was why Thrima, bent over the fire-pit, had stripped off her tunic and worked in her sooty and sweat-soaked shift. I prayed to St. Valentine that the flaxen shift would be wet right down to her breasts.

I greeted her with a lively "*Heil!*" But when she turned and saw me, she snarled a warning that she'd have no truck with outlaws. I lingered at the door, to gawp at her breasts and consider my tactics. I already had it worked out that Thrima wasn't the sort for a quick spot of slap and tickle. I'd have to woo her.

And that might take some doing, since the next thing out

of her mouth was, "I am not feeding outlaws." She spoke in English now.

I gave her my most fetching grin. "Sure hope you won't outlaw me looking at you."

No response, neither frosty nor frisky. Just flinty silence. On the other hand, she didn't toss me out of her kitchen. Or threaten to kill me.

I took a small step closer. "Like I told you in the larder the other day, I'd be good for you. And you've already been damn good for me."

The only sound was the hiss of the hearth's flames.

"I owe you my life. Twice over," I said. "And a good thing, too, lest I wouldn't be here gazing on the most beautiful—"

"You are not getting around me with words of honey. I am not peasant chit starving for fondness." She stood facing me, one hand on her hip, the other perilously close to a large metal poker.

"See you, it's the Irish that shovel on the tripe. I'm Welsh."

"Welsh, eh? Just different word for polecat."

Arms spread wide, I moved even closer. "Here now, I smell good as sweetbrier in June."

She jumped back like she'd grabbed a fist full of thorns. And found the poker. "Keep distance."

"Ah, now, love..."

"Love me no loves, Welsh polecat outlaw. I am not having time for you."

She hadn't picked up the poker or ordered me out of the kitchen. Still, the look on her face told me I'd best be gone, if I knew what was good for me. I was almost out the door when she said, "Sit over there, *ja*. And keep still."

She pointed at the oak stump that served as the kitchen's only chair. Then, without waiting to see if I obeyed, she returned to the soup. I sat down and kept still. I also kept my grin.

When she was done settling the soup on the hob, and I'd served my time on the stump, she pointed at the wood pile. "Feed fire."

While I tossed a couple of logs into the flames, she opened a cupboard. Inside sat all manner of pots, horns, baskets, even a small vessel made of glass. They couldn't all hold dill and chervil and parsley. They had to be medicines for man and beast.

I went and picked up a little pot, took a whiff. It all but snapped off my nose, so sharp was the smell. "Thought you said it was Bathilda that served up the poison here at Thornholt. Smells like you got some nasty potions of your own."

Thrima made no reply, only scooped a handful of herbs from one of the baskets, dumped them into the soup, and gave it a hard stir.

I set the smelly little pot back on the cupboard shelf. "Hope you don't decide to serve this Welsh polecat outlaw some of your Norsker poison."

Thrima straightened up, put her hands on her hips and stretched. She turned around, breasts straining at the wet shift. "I am surprised your wife is not already putting poison in your porridge."

"Don't have a wife."

Before she could chew that over, I said, "Maybe I was the one that put the poison in the porridge."

"Then she is smart to eat it."

I burst out laughing and presently a smile broke open Thrima's face and then she was laughing, too. Next thing, I had a spoon in my hand, a bowl of fragrant bean soup on my lap, while Thrima talked to God. "Why, Lord?" she said. But she laughed when she said it.

Presently, music started up outside, fast and fine, from drum and pipe and flute. Everybody was singing along, of course, and Thrima said we should, too. So we went and joined the churls on the green, men and boys back from the plough, girls and women unfettered from their chores, old men drunk and noisy.

I'm not much of a singer. But I can play the jaws harp, so I borrowed one and busted into a lively tune with Hauk blowing his bagpipe and the priest's wife pounding a tambourine. Before long the dancing started, first with a stately circle, everybody putting their best foot forward. Next came line dances with promenades, then a few hands across, pivot and bow.

Thrima said she wanted to join in, and hauled me along with her. And I mean tugged, pulled, dragged. I'm an even worse dancer than singer and I didn't fancy setting these Saxon oafs all a-snicker. But Thrima steered me through a prim promenade or two, some circle dances, and a thing she called the willow branch, though busted stick better described my part in it. As the ale kegs dwindled, strings of people, arms across each other's shoulders, went dancing through the village, becoming just two people, like Thrima and me, arms around each other, surprising the village and maybe ourselves.

There were other surprises that night and more well into the morrow, surprises and sheer bliss. When we could finally leave the warm straw of her bed, I persuaded her to cast aside her chickens and her chores to go walking with me. She didn't object and we moved through that fine morning like sovereigns on a tour of our realm.

After a while, as we passed the church, I said, "I'm headed to Bristol. Come with me."

To my surprise, she wrenched her hand from mine and looked as if she'd cry. I figured she'd next be telling me I couldn't go, couldn't leave her. So I started to tell her what I tell all weeping women. That their tears can no more move me than they could a mountain in Wales. But somehow this woman and these tears would. I wrapped my arms around her and, though she did not cry, held her close.

After a while she said, "There is thing I am not telling you. That nobody is telling you."

Here it came at last. Just as I feared, she was about to tell me about the husband off selling sheep in Winchester. Or her crazy daughter hidden in a hut down by the river. I rushed to say it didn't matter. "Just get you a divorce. I know a couple clerics that'd be glad to help." After I deposited something grand in their reliquary, say the middle toe of the Magdalen.

Thrima gave her head a hard shake.

"Or if there's somebody you don't want me to see, well then, I just won't look."

"Be quiet and listen. I cannot go with you because"—she broke off to take a huge gulp of air which she let out in a long gasp—"if I am leaving here, Lord Thornholt will take away our oxen and our acres. My sons and wives and children will be slaves."

It could happen. I'd heard of poor peasants turned into slaves. In England, in other lands. I said, "But you won't be a slave. You'll be with me."

"Hunwald will hunt me down like red deer in winter. You could not stop him. He will be bringing royal reeve. They will make me slave. Or kill me."

She paused. "Or kill all my family, even."

A lot of women have told me a lot of things when they didn't want to tell me the truth. And most times I've pretended to believe them. But this. By St. Patrick, this was an insult. Somehow she'd found out about my mother and thought she could use it to twist me around, make me have sympathy for her even while she told her lie. "Bullshit." I shoved her away.

She put her hands together, twisted her fingers 'til the knuckles showed white. "Hunwald was slaver. You know, *ja*?"

When I nodded she went on. "Ware was radman to him. Hunwald came to Thorpe and took me from the bishop's manor. He did not make me slave because Ware wanted me for wife. Hunwald gave me to him but made Ware swear oath if I hurt myself or ran from Thornholt, then his children—my children—would bear punishment of death."

I was astounded. "That sounds like something they do down in Constantinople. And why did Ware want to marry you, anyway? I mean he could have just—"

Thrima first looked insulted, but then she laughed. "Ware was strange man. He wanted only me, *ja*. I do not know reason."

"Did he keep you locked up? Some men are so jealous that ... "

"Nay. And he was as other men in bed. He did not beat me or children. Oh, once, maybe, when ... "

"Did Hunwald ever bother you?"

"Nay."

"How about that wife of his? Or the sons?"

"Nay."

"But I still don't understand why Hunwald made Ware swear this oath."

Thrima shrugged. "I would not be slave. But Hunwald must have *gield*."

She said *gield*—payment—in a way that made me understand she was done with my questions, that she'd told me all I needed to know. Anyhow, it's all she ever said about her dead husband. Elsewhere I learnt he'd been a man who came to love dice and drink more than his wife and sons. He'd died the winter before, in a fall from the top of Thornholt's all but finished stone tower, which, on a drunken dare, he'd tried to scale. Not only had the fall killed Ware, it toppled the upper part of the tower. Lord Hunwald was waiting for the bad luck to ebb before he raised it again.

Suddenly a ruckus of screaming came from the woods— hoots and honks and howls. "Pig!" Hauk yelled and, waving his axe at his brother, took off for the trees. "Pig in the pitfall!"

He and his brother and everyone within hearing distance stopped what they were doing and, like an army summoned to battle, headed for the boar trap. And, like an army, all had their duties—men brought axes, women came with pots and knives, the children dragged lengths of rope. They all cheered, too, and called for the kill.

By the time I got there, Hauk and another man were pulling away the brush and branches that had fallen into the sunken wooden trap with the quarry. I could tell from the way the trap swayed and quaked that something big was in there. Something big and noisy.

Something called Wynstan Wing-tongue.

CHAPTER FIFTEEN

I figured the churls would stone Wynstan out of their village for raising false hopes of a month full of pork. But they knew him. He was their lord's friend and came to Thornholt often. The village headman, a wiry fellow with intelligent eyes, called out a glad greeting and the rest of the villagers, plough ceremony mood still on them, cheered as Hauk hauled Wynstan up. They yelled even louder when he stood, arms spread wide, on the edge of the pit bellowing *"Hwaet!"*

I could tell I'd have to stone the old buzzard out of the village by myself. Because what was he doing here? How'd he get out of Winchester? And who was right behind him, ready to lead us both back in chains?

But the answers would have to wait. The stoning, too. The crowd were all but carrying him back to the village, though he told them he didn't have his lyre along. They let out an "Ahh" of disappointment.

"No, no, do not fear. I've many a tale to tell. They'll strike awe into your very souls. But first finish your work, I will meet you on the green just before sundown."

His power to control a crowd, at least a sober one, amazed me. Or maybe the churls figured Lord Cat's away, here's our chance to play. Once in the village, huge grins on their faces, they went back to weaving and ploughing, sharpening tools and fetching cows, and all the mucking out and chopping up that go on in farmyards on a cold day in late February.

I followed him to the green, where he rummaged around in his pack. "Herein is all the music and the magic of the spheres," he said.

His grin was so smug I grabbed him by the beard to wipe it away. "How much of the English army do you have behind you?"

Wynstan took my hand, eased it out of his whiskers. "Do you think I would be so dense as to leave Winchester under threat of imminent recapture? Please, my boy, give a man who's lived through wars and plagues and three marriages more respect than that. Lord Ordwulf won't realize I'm gone for days. He'll be too busy overseeing the restoration of the beams that hold up his house, a story you will hear later. For now, however, you can fetch me some ale."

"What do you mean—'beams,' 'restoration'? By St. Joseph, man, what have you done?"

Leave it to Wynstan to concoct an escape far more elaborate than just socking a monk. But whether this grand scheme had really gotten him out of Winchester was another question. What was clear was that Wynstan wouldn't be leaving Thornholt for a while. Not with the whole village gone thoroughly lovesick over the old loudmouth.

I felt considerably different. "What are you doing here, Wynstan? With or without an English army on your tail."

"All in good time, my boy. All in good time." He hauled a dry, withered apple out of his pack, then chomped down on it with strong yellow teeth.

I knew I'd get no further with him 'til after his performance. So I asked Thrima if there was some way to post a watch, in case the royal guards were headed this way after all. She said there wasn't. "No one is wanting to miss Wynstan's singing. But leave if you are afraid."

Instead, I went for the ale.

The headman put a couple of torches alongside the table, though there was still plenty of daylight left by the time the villagers crowded onto the green. They stood six and seven deep, shivering with cold and excitement. The old men and the children sat on blankets in front, so they had the best view as Wynstan cried "*Hwaet!*" and then told a story about a boy and a beanstalk. He'd claimed it would involve the amazing, the astonishing, the impossible. It didn't, but at least it was short.

Later, after the crowd finally let go their darling, I said, "You didn't come to Thornholt just to tell a story even churls have known since before they cut their teeth."

"You've found me out, clever lad. I've brought news. And a wonderful new story, too." Wynstan peered into his now empty bucket of ale.

"So what's your news?"

He waved toward Thornholt's mead hall. "Let us eat first. Lady Bathilda's table was always the most sumptuous in Hampshire."

While I fumed and cursed, Thrima caught my elbow and spoke under her breath in Norsker. "I know these old poets. I heard them in the bishop's household and even more in Thornholt. They will tell nothing until thou endures their wretched poems and claps thy hands so hard it raises blisters. Only then will they tell the news they bear."

So, in the end, it was Tryff Tewdwr who did the amazing, the astonishing, the impossible. I sat down to eat with Wynstan and Thrima in the mead hall at Thornholt. At the high table, no less, spread with a cloth of fine linen, well fit for a woman raised in the house of a Norsker bishop and a man with an opinion of himself high as the ceiling.

I don't know how Thrima had gained it, but she wielded a good deal of authority in Thornholt village. The headman leaped to obey her, and even the women liked her. So there was no problem with the churls when she decided we would take our supper in the mead hall. She didn't ask, just informed the headman. He gave her a renegade's grin and said the hall was mighty cold, he'd send some lads to light the hearth and lug in a keg or two of ale, would Thrima like a girl to serve the guests? When Thrima said "yes" to the lads and "no" to the girl, the headman went off to tell the hall servants that as hall cook Thrima would see to supper on her own.

I didn't like this one bit. Lord Siward's men—the English army, too, for all I knew—were likely on the move, searching the whole of Hampshire for Wynstan. And me. I'd rather have had our confab tucked away in the threshing barn, even the ox-house. But Thrima told me to be bold, and Wynstan all but laughed my cowardice to scorn. So I surrendered— and bade the headman keep close watch.

In the hall Thrima brought on the big, ivory-lipped ale horn, then poured drink for Wynstan and me. He'd shucked off the adulation of the mob and now looked old and tired. But not so old and tired as to forget his oily courtesy. "I've eaten with some curious folk in my time, though perhaps with none more curious than a woman-churl who speaks

Norse like a queen anointed." He flung out his arms. "Join us, lady. It is our honor and our joy."

Somehow satisfied by this nonsense, Thrima signaled the larder. Two young churls carried in platters of stewed rook and half a haunch of boar left over from the plough ceremony's festivities. Wynstan smacked his lips like a hungry dog.

He and Thrima ate and drank deeply and noisily. Not me. I was too busy praying the English army had dropped in a bog and that the brothers Thornholt wouldn't all of a sudden return with swords drawn, spear band charging. Before long, though, I'd calmed down enough to eat and found the vittles as good as if the lord and lady of Thornholt sat here with us instead of in a Winchester jail.

When we'd eaten our fill and laughed our loudest at the story of Wynstan's escape from Ordwulf and Siward—just as he'd claimed, it involved low cunning, high courage, and a very good saw—he let out a prolonged burp, then hauled his bulk off the bench. "Let me pay for this exquisite food with a poem that will awe you. It's the one I've composed for King Ethelred."

My laugh was long and loud. Nor could Thrima quite smother hers.

Wynstan looked hurt. "You think I'm just an old has-been, don't you? A windless pipe, a stringless harp. You think my poetry long ago dissolved at the bottom of an ale barrel."

Maybe we didn't think it in exactly those words, but that was the general idea.

One hand on his ale cup and the other flapping the air, Wynstan winged on. "You don't believe an old man can remake himself. But he can, you know. Just as the poet revises a poem that no longer suits either himself or the occasion."

My first reaction to this performance was to give Wynstan the slow, sarcastic clapping of hands that my father's poets used to insult a colleague's paltry efforts. "Remade or just warmed over," I said, "you're as full of shit as ever."

But by now Wynstan was in full flight. "A man can take the parts of his old life, like a poet lifting a good line from this poem, an apt image from that. Then he works them into a new shape, finds a different meter, invents a better trope. It takes sweat, of course, and imagination. Maybe even the breath of God."

He brought his ale cup down on the table so hard that the ivory-lipped serving horn went sailing and ale rained over the linen cloth. The horn clattered across the table and into Thrima's lap. She knocked it away with the kind of curse they don't teach you in a bishop's palace.

Wynstan greeted the commotion with a triumphant smile. "I tell you, I'm a new man. With a new poem I'll recite for King Ethelred after we have come to him with news of where his brother lies."

That "we" had an evil sound. Wynstan had already led me into more trouble than I'd known since I left my uncle's monastery, maybe my mother's womb. There was no telling what grief "we" might come to next. Better I should just look for my mam, Satan take these royals and their lost corpse. It was the living I needed to seek.

"My poem, Tryff, will bring joy to the king, as I said. But first it will bring you treasure from his mother. And not only that. It will enthrall you, inspire you, bring you honor, bring fame, bring all that a man—"

I jumped up, pulling Thrima up with me. The old fraud could damn well make somebody else his fool for a change. I wasn't going with him to find King Edward's body, no matter how fine his story or how splendid the reward he promised.

But a man who lives by wits learns to change direction fast as any weathercock. In a trice Wynstan saw how the wind blew. He began to speak as plainly as I'd ever heard him. "Sit down, my lad. And you, too, lady. I have hard truths to tell you now."

Thrima righted the ale horn, wiped its ivory rim, turned to Wynstan. "I am wanting to hear poem fine enough for England's royal ears." She smiled at him. "And ears of whole world, *ja*."

That was all the old bag of bluster had been waiting for. Wynstan marched to a seat by the hearth. Majestically, he lowered himself into the carved chair. It gave a wicked creak, and for a moment I thought it might collapse under the vastness of the man. No such luck. This wasn't going to be a night for comedy.

As Thrima touched my elbow and guided me back to the table, Wynstan went on. "Tryff," he said. "You can't stay at Thornholt. Word of your whereabouts will soar to Siward and Ordwulf like a leaf in a storm."

Nor, he said, could I rush off to worlds unknown. I was no longer a free man. Fortune had taken me hostage. "I see how it is between you and the woman," he said without looking at Thrima. "But she's bound to Thornholt. Or rather to her sons and her grandchildren. To her acres and her chickens and ... "

I glanced at Thrima, mopping up the spilled ale. All along, I'd had it in my mind that we'd just up and leave

Thornholt when the time came. But Wynstan was right. Thrima was bound to Thornholt.

Wynstan twiddled the three points of his beard. "It's well known that the king—rather, the king's mother—is ready to revoke Lord Hunwald's hold on this land. You could perhaps someday own Thornholt."

Thrima's eyes met mine and we both laughed.

Then Wynstan said, "May I remind you that I know where the king's corpse lies."

I sat down. "All right. You win. But none of your poetic embroidery, just your story simple as you can weave it."

After Wynstan made sure the ivory horn had ale sufficient to accompany him through his tale, he began by saying he'd been with King Edward for several days before his death. "A fine time we had of it, too, there at Kingston, his lodge in Dorset. I was singing for the king, his bodyguard, and his royal thegns during the March boar hunt. Lord Leofric, for one, and Ealdorman Alvar. You'll remember them from Wilton."

I remembered Alvar all right. And I was sure he remembered me.

Wynstan continued, "Later in the week, we were supposed to go hunting with Ethelred and his mother at Corfe Gate. Kingston's only a few miles away. As it turned out, though, I couldn't go on the Corfe hunt. I stayed at Kingston, felled by, of all God-cursed things, a bellyache. We got into some bad eel at supper the night before, half of us, and spent two whole days heaving up our innards."

He shook his head as if he still could not believe what occurred next. "It seemed simple enough. Everyone said so. On the morning of the calends of March, King Edward and

Ethelred went hunting. Ealdorman Alvar went, too, and Ordwulf, along with their men. But apparently the woods were thick and the day foggy. The hunters got separated. Nothing to worry about, they figured, happens all the time. Besides, they had their horns along. With everyone giving a horn-blast from time to time, a man couldn't get too far afield."

He paused as we refilled our ale cups. When we'd drunk, and drunk again, he said, "On top of the bad weather, the hunting turned out to be terrible. So, by late afternoon, Alvar and his men had come straggling back to Corfe Gate with only one boar amongst them. Then Ordwulf and a very wet Ethelred rode in together. Not only were they empty-handed, Ethelred had taken a fall into a pond. King Edward didn't return at all."

I asked if the folk at Corfe hadn't been a mite concerned about the king.

Wynstan shrugged. "At seventeen Edward was a man grown. Besides, it wasn't the first time he'd spent a night alone in the woods. The king was the sort that just couldn't come home empty-handed. He'd claim another man's downed animal as his own and if he couldn't do that, he'd rob an unguarded cache. Even if it took all night."

Wynstan stopped to drink again, but found the ale horn drained. Holding it up, he looked at Thrima. She ignored him and it was me who tapped a new keg.

We filled our cups, once, twice, three times before Wynstan took up his story. "Early the next morning, Queen Ælfthryth had the horns blown from atop Corfe hill. Surely, she said, King Edward would hear them and they'd guide him safely home. Then, about noon, his horse came limping in. Before long there were half a dozen search parties roaming the Purbeck hills."

Wynstan paused, waited, spoke. "But it wasn't the queen's men who found him."

What was this now? I thought nobody found Edward. That's what all this whole thing had been about—Edward was missing, who knew how or where. "All right, Wynstan, I'll play along. Who found him?"

"I did."

And I'd thought he could tell the truth. That he wouldn't lie just for the fun of it. Only the whole company of heaven prevented me from hammering the old swindler into the floor.

"I mean," Wynstan said, "that I found Ordwulf and Ethelred. 'Twere they who found the king's body. But then they lost it."

One more silly word out of him and nothing in this world or any other would have saved the man. But Wynstan didn't seem to notice my rising exasperation.

"Seems it'd been a day for finding things," he said. "Ordwulf and Ethelred had just found each other, poor young Ethelred soaking wet and shivering from a tumble into a pond. They were heading home past a marsh when they came on Edward. Found him on his back in a patch of trampled grass, peaceful as if he were taking a nap. Except he was napping in a puddle of blood. At least that's what Ordwulf told me when I met up with him a little while later."

Ordwulf said he'd jumped off his horse and gone to Edward. But it was the work of only a moment to know the lad was dead, killed by a sword. Or maybe a scramseaxe. Something sharp, Ordwulf said, that had caught him under the ribcage and gone in deep and mean.

"Was the king in a fight?" I asked, again caught up in the situation.

"Not with swords, apparently. Or at least his sword hadn't been in a fight. It was still sheathed. His scramseaxe, too. That I saw for myself."

Ordwulf told Wynstan he'd left the body where they'd found it because by then Ethelred was shaking so hard he could barely sit his horse. Nothing could be done for King Edward, so Ordwulf decided it was more important to get his nephew—king now—someplace warm and dry. Nor did he want to sling the royal body across a horse's butt.

Me, I would've done the same as Ordwulf. A wet man can die of cold in the middle of a summer's day, and returning with two dead boys—royal boys—was not how Ordwulf wanted to end this day. But why hadn't he sounded his horn, brought the other searchers to him? They could've carried the king's body back to Corfe Gate.

As for Wynstan, he said he'd met up with Ordwulf and Ethelred shortly afterward, heard the story, and decided he would be the one to bring King Edward to Corfe. But when he found the bloody, trampled spot by the marsh, the king's body was gone.

"Is that when you finally figured out Ordwulf had been lying to you?" I asked.

"As it happens, he did not lie. Bear with me a little longer and you can judge his honesty for yourself."

I put a hand on Thrima's. "Had enough of these circles inside circles?"

Thrima patted my hand, removed it from hers, told Wynstan to go on.

"I looked all around," he said. "Spent half the afternoon wandering those woods. I even waded into the marsh right up to my knees. Found nothing except hoof marks likely put there by Edward's horse, and Ethelred's and Ordwulf's."

Wynstan beckoned us closer and dropped his voice. "I found nothing. But I saw something."

He paused. Only when he knew his audience could bear the silence no longer did he continue. "I should say I saw someone."

"And who was that?"

"A woman."

Did any of this really happen? Or was Wynstan just telling the kind of story he brought out for children when the dogs and the grownups were fast asleep.

"A woman who dwells in those woods. An evil woman, some say. But one who can foretell the future."

"So can I," Thrima said. "But is it coming true?"

That broke the spell. I laughed and so did Thrima.

But Wynstan wasn't amused. "You may laugh now. But you will not when you meet her."

"Meet her? Is she here?" I pointed at his sack. "Is that why you've been so worried about that thing? Dump her out, why don't you. Let's have a look."

"This woman—her name is Crawe—this woman has King Edward."

That brought me around. I quit laughing. "What do you mean 'has him'? Has his body, has his bones? Is he still alive and she's holding him for ransom? Or his remains?"

"The king is dead. Nor does Crawe want to ransom his remains. It's worse than that."

Wynstan's fingers flicked across the strings of an

imaginary lyre. "It is King Edward's body that allows Crawe to foretell the future."

Thrima sucked in her breath. And I didn't blame her. Wynstan was saying the woman was a waker-of-the-dead.

The fancier word for them is necromancers, folk who steal a fresh corpse, conjure up the soul of the dead person and make it go back in the person's body. After the person rises again, the waker starts asking questions about the future, or maybe where some treasure's buried. I've heard tell they can even make the person attack their enemies.

"So you're telling us this Crawe took King Edward's body. Where?"

"To her lair." Wynstan hauled out his neck pouch and kissed it. "I know because I followed her. I saw Edward in the grass outside her hut. I would've fought her, I swear I would've taken the king up and fled but for the spell she cast over me."

That did it. I had no time for another of Wynstan's outrageous stories. I was already out of my chair when Wynstan stuck his fist in my face. Before I could react, he opened the fist. On his palm lay a thick gold ring set with a blue-purple stone.

I'd last seen that ring on the hand of the king of England.

CHAPTER SIXTEEN

When we left Thornholt next morning, Wynstan said some things were beneath his dignity and riding the dun-colored old she-mule was one of them. Couldn't say I blamed him. Her name was Lady Philosophy, though she didn't seem to take a very philosophical view of life. I've ridden many a mule and I don't care how stubborn they are, or how pouty, as long as they're a little affectionate along with it. This old mollie spit my offering of a dried apple right back at me and then tried to bite my hand off. She didn't like Wynstan, either, and I came near to pounding her with a barrel slat just so she'd let him in the saddle.

Presently, though, it became clear they were suited to each other, their arrogance in perfect tandem. He found the wisdom to call her the rose of Sharon and the lily of the valleys, fair as the moon, clear as the sun. "Make haste, my beloved," he whispered into her long ears. And she did, prancing along like it was her own father who'd carried Our Lord through Jerusalem on that Sunday before Easter.

I'd left Thrima at Thornholt's gate, fists jabbed on her hips. "Do not expect tears," she'd said. "And do not promise to return."

So I made no promises and she shed no tears. Something

Wynstan couldn't help but comment about. "That's one hard woman," he said. "I'd have thought you'd choose something at least as tender as—"

"Shut up, Wynstan, or I'll tear out your tender tongue and feed it to you with supper."

The old man threw me a look that was half amused, half amazed, but protected his tongue by shutting his mouth and keeping it that way 'til we stopped to decide how best to proceed. The queen had ordered me to produce King Edward's body by the Witan's Shrove Tuesday meeting, less than a fortnight away now. Getting to Dorset by road was a three-day trip, even in the best of weather, even by the highways and bridges so well maintained as part of a thegn's duty to his sovereign. To add to the problem, neither of us had a travel pass. Some thegn or his radman or his priest or his churls might think they'd found a better paying duty and claim they'd nabbed a pair of outlaws. We'd have to use cow paths and deer runs—and time, a week in any case, a month if Lady Philosophy had her way.

We needed to find a safer, faster way to get to Dorset. So we decided to go south of Winchester, then down the River Itchen to the Solent and across Poole Bay. We'd first have to spend a while on deer and cow paths, but we both knew men who could run a boat down the Itchen in a few hours and others who could have us out of Southampton on the first tide, to hell with the weather as long as the money was right. Such are the boons of travelling men.

Right after we got started, so did a heavy rain that I called lucky because it hid us from our enemies. According to Wynstan, though, "This weather could conceal the Heavenly Host. But it covers the king's men, too. They might break through with a strength that could toss the Itchen from its bed, serve us up like gill-netted fish, flopping and gasping and dying."

We didn't talk much after that, huddled deep in our wet cloaks as we were. But I did ask Wynstan about the big news he'd claimed he carried when he came to Thornholt. "What was it?"

A rumble of laughter shook his cloak. "Just that I already knew Tryff Tewdwr would sooner or later be on his way to Dorset."

The deceitful serpent had duped me into joining him. For what wicked purpose I could not fathom, but I knew we'd come too far to turn back. It was a good thing my hands were so cold I couldn't reach for the Thornholts' scramseaxe sheathed against my back.

When we came to the river, we began to search for a boatman waiting out the rain under a bridge. The one we found was a Frankie, greedy like all his race, and demanding damn near our last penny. What we could offer wouldn't have been enough but for Wynstan's winged tongue. The old villain's voice dropped to a honeyed murmur as he swore he was the brother of Wareham's mint master. "And I know where he keeps the key."

The little Frankie might've been greedy, but he wasn't dense. "Like hell you do."

Wynstan dug under his sopping cloak and into the pouch at his waist. To the surprise of both the Frankie and me, his hand held a golden coin. "Look closely. Does it not say Wareham right there beneath King Ethelred's picture? How else would a penurious fellow like me come by such wealth?" To demonstrate his poverty, Wynstan stuck a finger through a hole in his cloak.

Greed and pride fought it out in the Frankie's face. He could no more read what was written on that coin than I could've pulled down the peaks of Yr Wyddfa. But he knew English gold when he saw it. Or thought he did. The coin was merely polished bronze. I don't know whose face was on it. He snatched at it anyhow, just as it disappeared from Wynstan's hand. With a murderous howl, he went for the old man.

"Now, now,"—I hoisted the little fellow by the chin 'til his shoe tips scraped the boat's planks—"just get us to Dorset. We'll settle up then. Meantime, you have my silver and Wynstan's good word."

The Frankie began to choke and his eyes swiped wildly across the deck. His three crewmen weren't in sight. Wynstan told me to set him down, a strangled sailor would do us no good. "Besides, I take these drama-laced gurgles and burbles to mean we have a deal."

Two days later we landed on the Dorset coast, only a few miles from Corfe Gate. It'd been smooth sailing all the way, skies clear and the wind fair. The boat was a good long one, seaworthy and wide enough in the beam to hold men and mounts as easily as it might a load of millstones. Once we got Tom and Lady Philosophy aboard—she put up fewer objections than we'd feared—Wynstan and I ducked into the tent on the aft decking. We slept a lot on the trip, the Itchen and the Solent and Poole Bay rocking us as sweetly as ever our mothers had our cradles. I dreamt of Thrima, of course, even saw her weeping for me. And, of course, saw myself returning to Thornholt in triumph, the keg of pennies tied oh-so-tightly to Tom's wide butt.

On the morning of our second day at sea we broke fast, sitting in the tent with the bread and chopped chicken Thrima had sent along and a pint or two of the Frankie's sour red wine. All that food and drink must've thickened my wits because I went stupid enough to ask, "You got a home, Wynstan? I mean, someplace you stay when you're not on the road?"

"Home? And what is that these days?"

Good question. I wasn't sure I knew myself. But I tried anyhow. "A hearth to call your own, I reckon. Woman to go with it maybe."

Wynstan's eyes narrowed. "Say you're a Welshman, do you? Have you no songs of loss in Wales? No elegies for a time, a place long gone?"

I felt a poem coming. He'd be off and reciting if I didn't stop him right then. I drew breath. Too late. Wynstan's big voice was on. "Has no weary Welsh poet stirred his hands in icy seas far from home? Has none journeyed down the black paths of exile?"

My cup needed re-filling. Only, when I tried to go out to the wine barrel on the deck, Wynstan grabbed my sleeve. "Has never a far-wandering Welshman dreamt of his own lord's mead hall? Where once again he feasts with his friends, his comrades, his kin. Hears their laughter, knows their love. Greets them with songs."

"Why don't you spend all that breath telling me where Edward's body is?" I knew he wouldn't, maybe even couldn't. So I bolted out of the tent into the Solent's hard wind, drew down another flagon of wine, and would've gotten happily drunk but for Wynstan joining me at the gunwale.

"You're a travelling man. You know what the road is like. At the mercy of mud and man and the moonless night. England can be paradise on a warm day in June—the road winding out in front of you, the scent of gorse in the air, the hum of bees in the heather, the cool of an oak copse to rest in, the laughter of villagers in their fields. Such a day can make you forget that in winter the road turns to mud. That is, when there is indeed a road beneath you and you're not wandering lost in some black marsh."

"Where is King Edward?"

The sea wind howled loud around us. But Wynstan was louder. "As for the people along the way, some are grand, generous of heart and purse. Then there are the others. Churls so ignorant they barely know they're Englishmen. Bandits willing to slice you asshole to eyeball just to own your shoes. Monks that'll make you confess to every sin since Cain before they offer a bite of bread. Thegns who expect your woman along with your poem."

"Where is he?"

Wynstan turned out of the wind. "You may ask why I'd take a woman with me on my travels. Easy enough question to answer. First, she was part of the act. A singer. She was also my only love." The old man waved a hand into the wind. "She came from a fair land far away. Lovely girl, slim and blond and nimble. Joy was her name."

"Shut up, Wynstan. I'm interested in King Edward, not your lost loves."

He began to recite anyway, bawling about Joy, then a dark thicket and Christ in stone. "Ancient is her earth hall ... in a black bog beyond Wareham town." On and on and on. I went back to the wine barrel.

The Frankie delivered us to Dorset's western shore, and sailed north as soon as Wynstan had handed over his golden coin and whispered the secret whereabouts of the keys to Wareham mint. We headed into Purbeck, the steep and sinister land between us and Corfe.

Wynstan, who claimed he knew this country, said we should aim for the high ridge straight ahead. Problem was, this route lay along a boulder strewn lane. Then the rain came again, first a fine mist, then a downpour that made the road more river than the Itchen had ever been. Tom slogged along manfully, and even Lady Philosophy stepped lively through the sucking mire. Only Wynstan complained, yowling like a wet cat until I wanted to tie him in a sack and drop him off the next bridge.

Next thing, Lady Philosophy decided to turn the cold slog into a summer stroll. She ambled along at her leisure to browse the little Snowdrops peaking out from the rocks. No amount of cajoling or scolding or out and out threatening could hurry her. When Tom took a notion to join the fun, I told Wynstan I'd meet up with him at Corfe, then told Tom to leave off the greenery and walk on.

Alone in a foggy valley, I turned coward, huddled into my cloak, pulled my hood to cover all but my nose, and let Tom find the way. He did a good job of it until a noose dropped around my neck.

I'd been half asleep, cradled by the saddle. So I was plenty surprised to wake flying, bouncing, skidding, choking on mud and curses, and finally on fear. I came to a halt bang up against a chunk of Purbeck marble. Heavy mud saved me from anything more serious than cracking my funny bone.

There's nothing funny, though, about a noose around your neck, 'specially when somebody's pulling it tight.

I grabbed it and pulled back. I held on with one hand, went for my seaxe with the other, figuring to cut the rope before my captor, a man on a dark horse some five yards away, could fasten it to his saddle. Then I'd go for the man himself.

And maybe I would've. But the curtain of mist broke open and out charged Lady Philosophy, long ears laid back, teeth bared, legs churning the mud. Wynstan was braced in the stirrups, brandishing his walking staff like a spear and screaming like a Norse berserker.

Man and mule swept clean past their quarry and disappeared back into the fog. They did, though, startle the horseman. He dropped the noose and his horse bolted. By the time I hauled myself out of the muddy track, Wynstan was back. Walking staff again lashed to his saddle, he was clapping his hands and howling out a hymn of praise to himself and telling Lady Philosophy, "The scent of thy garments is like the scent of Lebanon."

The smell in the air wasn't mule hide, at least not living mule hide. It was the reek of something dead, long dead. Wynstan wrinkled up his nose and made a face. "Great God, man, have we landed in the midst of an execution cemetery? Someplace where they only half bury their corpses?"

I started to tell him that I'd smelled this stink off and on ever since I'd left Wilton. It had been in the air every time I'd been attacked. But I decided to say only "Let's move along."

And we surely would have, except now a pair of armed horsemen rode out of the hills. Before I could go for my seaxe, before I could do anything except blink rain out of my eyes, their spears were at my jaw. It wasn't going to be any kind of contest. So I clasped my hands on top of my head and yelled "I give up" in English, Irish, Dansker, and, just to be safe, Latin, too.

Wynstan didn't wait for a reply. He put his heels to the mule's ribs and took off. The horsemen didn't even turn their heads to watch the mist swallow him up. Instead, and to my surprise, they pulled back their spears. Blinking the rain away, I took a good long peek. They looked like soldiers right enough, in their mail coats and pointed helmets. They carried swords, too, and shields hung by their saddles. But I couldn't tell if they were English or something even worse because the shields were plain round ones with no metal boss to proclaim their realm.

"Who are you?" one of the soldiers asked me. In English, I was glad to hear. At least these two weren't northern savages or Irish slavers. But they might not be soldiers at all, just very well dressed bandits. Whatever they were, I was at their mercy. They demonstrated it by circling Tom and me like we were a herd of desperate captives instead of just a man and his mount, both soaked and shivering.

One of the men reached over and gave me a pop that sent me flying onto my backside in the muddy road. It was a good tumble, though. I landed in mud soft enough to break my fall and firm enough to give me something to fling along with my curses. I planted a glob of mud on each of their fancy Saxon helmets. For answer, they pulled their swords and got ready to run me through.

"Don't!" came a man's shout. "Or you'll answer to King Ethelred."

A third man rode up. The other two snapped their swords

to their nose guards in salute, then swung their mounts away from me. They didn't, though, put the swords away.

"And you, Tryff Relicman," the man said, as he dismounted and came toward me, "where in hell have you been?"

The fright drained out of me. It was Leofric of Wilton, who'd saved me from killing Ealdorman Alvar back in Wilton. Now it looked like he'd gone and rescued me again. Before I could answer, he ordered the two surprised—and still angry—soldiers to put away their swords. Sweeping off his helmet, he ran a hand through his damp hair, then gave me a grin before he pulled on his hood. "When our coast guard saw you come ashore, he sent a message to the queen. Of course, he didn't know who you were. But when Queen Ælfthryth heard about the pair described as a tree and a barrel, she sent us out to locate Tryff and Wynstan."

Leofric looked around. "Where's the windy one got to, by the way?"

"Am I under arrest?"

"Holy Mary, what gave you that idea? You're going to meet with the queen."

Here, in the royal service, Leofric seemed much more the soldier than when we'd gotten drunk together in Wilton. Gone was the high, gold-adorned saddle he'd had then. This one was plain brown leather and only the reins had any decoration. If decoration is what you'd call lines festooned with human ears.

"Bandits," Leofric said when he saw me staring. "Killed a dozen, all told—took an ear apiece. They're getting rather old, though."

Which I could tell, now that I looked. The ears had

started to mold. Stink, too, now that I sniffed.

"Cleared out their nest just after I came down from Wilton," Leofric said. "No more've been around since then, glad to say."

He tapped the ears with his whip, totting up the kill. "Took this one first. And this one's their leader. This is a woman they had with them. This one—"—he paused over it—"can't recall, but this next chap's a pirate."

The ear looked like a terrier had had his way with it. "Bastard came out of a longboat that chased us on our way here. Arrow to the eye. Must've been their chief. The rest fled, anyway, after *he* got it."

Leofric said all this with a sweet smile and boyish pride in those soft blue eyes. I quick-like sent up a prayer—"Spare me, O Lord, from the fury of the English." But it was the fury of English weather that truly concerned me. The fog turned to sleet and we folded our hoods over our faces. Then the wind began whipping sleet into our horses' eyes so hard that we had to lead them all the way to Corfe. I thanked St. Christopher for bringing Leofric my way because without him I would've been thoroughly lost. Maybe even dead.

Did I say that the first pair of soldiers, the ones Leofric saved me from, were not alone? They'd formed the vanguard of a travellers' escort. Now, from out of the fog, there appeared two more soldiers and an ox cart full of nuns. My nuns.

St. Finella's prioress, along with Sisters Hild and Hrothbeort, looked almost as unhappy to see me as I was them.

CHAPTER SEVENTEEN

We trudged on for miles, the nuns and soldiers and I, our eyes covered against the hard wind, which only dropped as we came to the high, rugged mound that plugs a gap in the Purbeck Hills. It's called Corfe Gate. Atop it perched the royal hunting lodge—and Queen Ælfthryth.

As if sitting high above Dorset wasn't enough for English royals, they'd built their lodge's stockade of solid timber buttressed by rock, and studded its sharp pickets with wolf skulls. Some of the beasts had their muzzles thrust upward as if in mute howl. From other jaws, open and still fierce, icicles dripped like frozen blood.

Once upon a time, wolves had served King Eadgar as a grim emblem of his sway. He had their images stamped on his saddlery and woven into his wool. Their heads bedecked royal barricades from Cornwall to Northumbria. Sometimes he even collected wolf carcasses instead of taxes. But now, not even three years after his death, the wolves at his ramparts were crumbling to ruin.

One, though, had not. When the lodge gate swung open, there stood Lord Ordwulf, slavering with laughter. He ordered his men to pull me off Tom and take me to the queen. No one, neither thegn nor nun, tried to stop him. The nuns disappeared as completely as had Wynstan.

Queen Ælfthryth's enemies describe her as low, dark, and common. None of it was true. Not if low means short and common means ordinary. She was tall like her brother and this day wore a long green tunic crusted with gold embroidery. The wool of her headdress was shot through with gold thread and framed a face the color of thick, fresh cream. I'd have called her beautiful, except her for eyes. They were pale as the belly of an eel.

She received me in her bower, where she stood at an embroidery frame, needle in hand. "Received" was what she said, though I'd been all but flung there. Laughed at, too, by Ordwulf and his whole spear band as they did the flinging. But like King Eadgar, her late husband, Queen Ælfthryth was as generous in words as purse. On one knee, I saluted her in Welsh, Latin, and English. When I was done, she bade me rise, even gave me a thin smile.

Did that mean I wasn't going to the gallows after all? Or was it just a last kindness for the condemned man? She didn't tell me to sit down, and Tyne, that serving woman of hers, lurked in a corner—talk about somebody short and common. The best to be said about the situation was that the queen ordered Ordwulf to leave. While he put up honorable if futile resistance, I looked around. If I had to leave in a hurry, a second door would come in handy.

You'd think a queen's parlor would be something grand, but this little room was so plain as to be downright grim. It had no other door, nor even a window to let in God's light. The candles and wall lamps—they smelled of beeswax— showed only table, chair, and a wooden prie-dieu. The flagon and cups on the table were made of silver, but the chair's cushion looked prickly as a hair shirt and the prie-dieu hard enough to flay the flesh from your knees. The walls had only two adornments. One was a spray of garlic and wormwood threaded with a vine called venom-loather, both good remedies for maladies caused by demon elves. Opposite hung a big crucifix the like of which I'd never seen. Its dying Christ wore the vestments of a priest and his head was circled not by thorns but a royal crown.

When Ordwulf had finally gone, Queen Ælfthryth joined me before the crucifix. "Very English, don't you agree?"

Before I could answer, she dropped a deep genuflection, whether to Christ or to England, I couldn't decide. I bent my knee anyhow. Then we both made the sign of the cross and said a Pater Noster. I added a quick plea for protection against evil beings. After all, Queen Ælfthryth had that reputation for being what the English call a speaking-woman, someone who does business with Satan himself.

When we were done praying, she sat down in the chair by the table. I started to explain about my part in Wynstan's trick at Thornholt manor. After a silencing wave, she began to pour from the silver flagon, something that amazed and frightened me. Tyne was in the room and half a dozen servants stood on the other side of the door. They could've done the pouring. Should've done. Who did the dowager queen of England think she was, dumping out drink like a churl's woman? Or was it like Satan's woman.

"Something to keep the cold off." She pushed a cup my way. "A potion of my own making. Pray God that it's as efficacious as it is delicious."

Pray God it's not poisonous. I dipped my tongue into the cup. The stuff tasted like maggots and mold, but surely she wouldn't murder me right there under her crucifix. Tyne smirked over in her dark corner. I emptied the cup in one gulp.

Queen Ælfthryth gave a sharp nod, then said, "I assume the nuns explained why we found it necessary to hire a man like you."

What was that supposed to mean? The queen knew me from when I used to find saints for King Eadgar. And from when I found the evil serpent that killed his father and had likely meant to kill him, too.

Once again her pale eyes flicked to the elf herbs. "You're a man who can deal with forces visible and invisible."

I'd heard that before. Clerics can be mighty generous of tongue when the relic you found for them passes a miracle and the pilgrims start flocking in. But want to know the truth? Most forces are way too visible. Still, it never hurts business to let people think you've got all manner of skill, in this world and any other.

"Or so Sister Hild claims. You may thank her for your life, by the way," Queen Ælfthryth said. "At least for the moment."

She couldn't scare me because now I knew what we say in Wales is true. *Gwell cr yn llys nag aur ar fys.* A friend at court is better than a gold ring. And if that friend's a nun of St. Finella's Minster, so much the better.

The queen rose and moved back to her embroidery stand. "I suppose you truly do believe I murdered poor Edward."

Everybody from Land's End to Holy Lindisfarne believed it. Oh, they allowed as how she likely didn't stick the knife in herself. But they figured she sure told somebody else to. Otherwise, however would her son have gotten to be king?

She glanced up at the elf remedy. "I've my own notions about what happened to Dward, which I will tell you later."

It was about time she told me something. Though in truth just telling me I wasn't headed for the gallows should've been more than enough.

The queen extended her hand toward Tyne, who gave her a threaded needle. "First let me tell you what I've put together from speaking with those who hunted with Dward that day last March."

I was a little surprised she hadn't gone along. Queen Ælfthryth had always been an ardent hunter of boar.

"Not many people went at all. For one thing, it was a rough day. Cold, wet, windy. I've quite lost my taste for haring around Dorset in the rain. Lord Siward and I stayed here. And another thing—when Dward arrived the evening before the hunt, he was alone."

Alone? King Edward likely hadn't been alone since he left his mother's belly.

"I mean except for Felding, his huntsman. And, of course, his dogs."

I started to ask about Leofric and Wynstan, but let it go. No point bothering the queen just then. Instead, I asked if King Edward hadn't been staying at Corfe Gate.

She was bent over her embroidery now, plucking at it, smoothing it, completely absorbed. After a while, she nodded sharply, stood straight, plunged the needle into the fabric. "Dward had been several weeks at Kingston, his estate a few miles south. So besides Dward and Felding, only my son and my brother went hunting that day. Oh, and Alvar." She mentioned the ealdorman in the same tone she had the dogs.

"The hunters left at first light. Not that there was much of that. Such a cold, foggy morning. And it stayed that way. A thoroughly dismal day. That's probably why they got separated. Oh, they each had a horn, of course. And I had horns blown from Corfe hill so they could find their way home. There really wasn't much danger they'd get lost. But, as I said, they did get separated."

She said nobody seemed sure what happened after the hunting party had ridden down Corfe hill, along the little river that winds around the bottom of the hill, and into the woods. But they lost each other. "Their horns told me something was wrong. All afternoon I could hear them sounding and sounding and sounding *Ta-ta-tahh, Ta-ta-tahh*. That was the special call of the king's hunting party. Every royal hunting group agrees to one, in case they get separated in the field. And each member has a special answer so the rest will know he's all right. Dward's was *Ta-ta*, sounded three times."

But though the *Ta-ta-tahh, Ta-ta-tahh* came over and over and over, King Edward never blew his answer.

"Perhaps he couldn't. When his horse finally came in, a day later, we found his horn still laced to the saddle." Ælfryth's eyebrows drew together. "Funny, that. The horn was almost the only thing left on his saddle. It had been stripped of all ornament, the reins, too. And his saddle bag was gone."

A simple robbery, then? Maybe somebody didn't know who they'd killed. It wouldn't have been hard to pull off. You wouldn't even have to be a regular bandit. You—a churl, say, even a slave—you hear the horns, figure the grand folk are out hunting. You know all the forest paths. You go to one and climb a tree with a nice overhanging branch. It's foggy, so you're well hidden. A lone hunter comes riding by. You drop down on him, wrench him off his horse. He resists. You run him through with your knife, then grab what you can and take off. Of course, you could've been hurt, broken a leg, gotten run through yourself. But you're a robber and that's the cost of doing business. Even so, you might've panicked, dropped the lad's body down a hole.

When the queen said there'd been no blood on the king's saddle, I asked if anyone else ran into trouble on the hunt.

She pulled her needle out of the embroidery, thrust it in again. "Ethelred and Diggy—that's his hound—came back by themselves that evening. They were both wet through. Ethy had fallen into a pond. My brother was with them."

So far her story pretty much matched up with Wynstan's. Now all I had to do was act like I'd never heard it before. "How'd they go in the pond?"

"Ethy'd left Ordwulf at the boar run to get in place for the kill. Apparently, Ethy went further than he intended."

"Your brother let him do that? Run around the countryside on his own? Get near drownt?"

Queen Ælfthryth gave me a puzzled look. "Why not? He was almost twelve, nearly a man." She paused. "And a king's son."

"That's just it. How come him and King Edward were out there in the woods on their own? Bandits don't know kings' sons from plough boys; they catch the gleam of silver."

She shrugged and returned to her embroidery. Maybe she didn't believe there were any bandits in her Dorset. Maybe she thought she'd turned it into a real live peaceable kingdom. But what about all those rogues whose ears lined Leofric's reins? And all those longboats full of Danskers making regular runs along the coast? Everybody knew it wouldn't be long before they came ashore, started in looting and raping. If they weren't already.

None of that was what concerned her now, if ever. "As I said, when Dward's horse came in the next day, almost everything had been stripped off the saddle except his sword. It was still in its saddle-sheath. Clean and with its silver hilt intact. At least whoever killed him showed some respect for the sword of majesty." The queen closed her eyes and, needle still in her hand, crossed herself. "But his scramseaxe and hunting knife were missing."

"His horse came in by itself? How come you didn't have half Dorset looking for the lad by then? And the horse?"

"Of course I sent out a search party. Several, in fact. No one found Edward."

"And his horse never found the searchers."

The queen cast her cold eyes my way. How could a woman so beautiful make my skin crawl? "They find anything at all? Or they still out riding around in the fog?"

She glanced at the crucifix, then at the herbs. "All kinds of evil might have come to Dward. In any case, it was clear someone besides my brother needed to search for him. Ordwulf was utterly useless. He did tell you that he led the original search?"

I studied my shoes, the ones I took off the monk in Winchester. I've never had a pair fit so well before or since.

The queen went back to her embroidery, now stabbing her needle hard into the flaxen cloth. "And I suppose he also told you that only a few people know the king's body is missing?"

"Lord Ordwulf said it's still like what was in your message

to me. That just you and him know. And Lord Siward and maybe a couple others. Everybody else thinks the king's body's in the church at Wareham, waiting for his brother's coronation."

I tapped a finger to my lips before I said, "But it isn't in Wareham and never has been."

The queen nodded, said, "Nor has Ethy—King Ethelred been told that. He loved Dward dearly and I didn't want him upset any further."

As well he would be, once he found out his coronation might not come off as planned.

The queen needed a new piece of yarn. She handed the needle to Tyne, who threaded it. "You do understand that no one, no one must be told otherwise?" Somebody'd sure been told otherwise. Or somehow found out. Wynstan, for instance. And if Wynstan knew, the crowd in every alehouse in Winchester might.

"Naturally," the queen said, "I told Dward's mother. I had to explain why she couldn't see her son's body, and I did not wish to lie."

I already knew that. What I didn't know was just how she thought I could find out anything more about the body. "You sure you still want me looking for him?"

"Of course. Ethy's—King Ethelred's consecration depends on it."

She had more confidence than I did. Especially if Wynstan's story about the waker-of-the-dead was true.

"I'll need to poke around, talk to folk. They may figure out there's nothing in Wareham church but an empty box. That going to suit you?"

Her strange eyes went paler, colder. "You have a

fortnight. Until Shrove Tuesday. Until Lent, that is. As I told you in my message, I will not permit you to disturb our time of prayer and penitence."

The threat went unspoken, of course, and I didn't linger over it. I still wondered, though, why so little time. Ethelred wouldn't be consecrated until two weeks after Easter. That was over two months away. But maybe the queen just didn't want me disturbing forty days of good, soul-saving starvation. Or maybe she just wanted to scare me. Ælfthryth was good at scaring folk.

I dipped my head obediently, then told her I'd need to talk to her son about the hunt. "Him and the rest of the hunting party, so I can figure out where they might've wound up that day. 'Course, I won't say anything about King Edward's body."

The queen began to sew again. "You may ask whatever questions you need to, of whomsoever you need ask, King Ethelred excepted. He's quite distressed enough."

I decided not to argue. I'd go to the men—Ordwulf and Siward—let them convince her I should talk to the young king. But Queen Ælfthryth must've seen into my mind. She looked up from the embroidery, first at Tyne there in the shadow, then at me. "In regard to King Ethelred, do not seek help from my brother or the *consillarius*. They both agree he is not to be further tormented in this matter."

The queen's gaze near turned my bones to frost. She said, "There is something else you should understand. No member of my household murdered King Edward. Nor did I."

She glanced upward. Whether at crucifix or elf herbs, I couldn't tell. "I would not commit murder. Not even for my son."

"I never—"

"You never said such a thing. But others do."

CHAPTER EIGHTEEN

I needed to head somewhere and have a good think. The hill above the hunting lodge, with vast Purbeck spread out below, would be just the place. Along the way I went past Ordwulf and Siward conspiring over an ale horn in the mead hall. They gave me curled lips and wicked looks, but let me pass unharmed.

On the hill's top, I sucked down the cold air like it was strong drink. Then I found a spot out of the wind, where I commenced to seriously ponder how to find the king's body. It wasn't just the old question *Cui bono?*—Who benefits? Everybody who'd come for the hunt, along with an untold number of other folk, had reason to kill King Edward. And they sure had the weaponry. If I were obliged to figure out if the lad had been murdered and who might have done it, I'd be scurrying around England into the millennium. Nor did I want to worry about who'd benefit from hiding the king's body. There was a simpler way.

When my father's cattle got rustled, he used to ask just one question—where were the neighbors that night? He never stopped to wonder which of them might do such a thing. He knew they all would. And he knew they had the men to round the beasts up and a good place to hide them.

So when he had the answer to his question, more often than not he had his rustler. And a dead neighbor.

That's what I decided to do. I figured it was the neighbors who took Edward's body. In this case, that'd be the noble folk in Dorset who'd come for the hunt—Alvar, Leofric, Siward, Ordwulf, the queen. Now all I had to do was ask where they were and what were they up to when King Edward disappeared. I'd ask each one where they were, and about the whereabouts of the others. I'd get more from Wynstan, too. If I could find him.

They'd lie, sometimes just for the sake of lying. But they weren't the only ones chasing boar that day—the bush-beaters and the dog-handlers and the horse-holders had been there, too. Churls see more than the nobility ever knows, and remember it longer. Sure, they'll lie, too. And why not? They know which side of their bread's got the dripping on it. I'd start with the higher ups, though. The highest, in fact. King Ethelred. Only how would I convince his mother to let me at him?

The answer came struggling along the lodge's rough walkway. I jumped up. "Can I help you, Sister Hild?"

Sister waved away my offer of help. Staff tucked under her arm, she strode to the hilltop. There she stood in that hard wind with her grey headdress flying falcon-like behind her.

I wasted no time before I asked her to intervene for me with Queen Ælfthryth. But she said the queen's word was law. I wouldn't be seeing Ethelred. Besides, Ethelred wasn't a well lad. In fact, that's why she was at Corfe, to try and heal him. "Which I shan't be able to do if the likes of Tryff Tewdwr is pestering him."

So I offered to free St. Agnes from the Vatican and bring her to St. Finella's. "Where she's always wanted to be."

Sister tapped her cane against my chest. "I thought you were retired."

"Relic men can no more retire than nuns. I'll have her to you by next Agnes Day."

Saint Agnes was an inspired choice, if I do say so. Her feast was just a few days past, so I had a full year to make good on my promise. And I also wouldn't have to break my back lugging her across the Alps. The Vatican only had St. Agnes's head.

Did Sister Hild hesitate? If you think so, you don't know ecclesiastics. Across the water in Flanders, nuns and monks have been stealing St. Gislenus back and forth betwixt them for nigh on two centuries. Sister snapped up my offer like a badger does a beetle.

I don't know what she said to the queen, but likely she stirred ethos, pathos, and logos into an elixir no mortal could refuse. Anyhow, the queen must've swallowed the argument and within the hour I stood with a fuming Lord Ordwulf in the torch-lit hallway outside the royal apartment.

"King Ethelred fell into a stream on that evil hunting trip," Ordwulf said. "He's not been well since. And he certainly won't feel like talking about his brother's death. Especially now, with its anniversary coming up in a few days. And what with you being a stranger, an outlander, a ... a ... whatever bloody kind of thing you are."

So I didn't expect much from the boy. But I put on my most winning smile as Ordwulf pushed open the door and said my name.

Inside the room bearing little furniture and decorated

with only one or two animal heads, King Ethelred sprawled on a cushioned chair by the hearth. Next to him a tall, bearded dog crouched on its haunches, jaw resting on the lad's shoulder. It was some kind of hound, a lean, grey creature with the most sorrowful eyes I'd ever seen on man or beast.

As for the boy-king, he looked more boy than king. He was a gangly lad, and no part of his body seemed to fit with any other part. He had ears like plump little mushrooms and long slats for feet. Out of his tunic stuck spike-sharp knees and hands big as plough-shares. When he opened his mouth, there showed forth enough teeth for two people. But King Ethelred wasn't so much ugly as just thirteen—tall with fair, curly hair and deep-set blue eyes like his father's. Full-grown, he'd be a presentable enough likeness for England.

If he lived so long. Right now, you didn't have to be a leech to see something ailed him. He was almost as grey as his dog. I couldn't tell if he had some bodily affliction or if he was just lonesome. Like they say, heavy is the head that wears the crown. 'Specially if you're only a boy and maybe still grieving for your dead brother.

He gave Ordwulf and me a courteous royal welcome in a firm, deep voice that deserted him half-way through. He finished up in a high-pitched crackle and a toothy smile.

The dog showed teeth, too. And growled. A low, serious growl clearly aimed at Ordwulf. "Easy, boy," the king said, patting the beast's grizzled head.

"Get that thing out of here," Ordwulf said in a growl as serious as the dog's, though he lingered in the safety of the door frame.

Ethelred made no move to do anything of the kind.

Instead, he and his uncle took to glaring at each other like men and boys do the world over. Me, I went up and bowed to the king. I was relieved when the big dog didn't show teeth or fold his ears back or turn away.

"Careful there, Welshman," Ordwulf said as the beast took a wary sniff of me. "The thing's vicious. I don't know how many times I told King Edward to have him put down."

"He got a name?" I asked King Ethelred.

"Deorward Deer-slayer. But I call him Diggy."

I stuck my hand under Diggy's nose and when it remained attached to my arm, I gave his chest a good scratching and finished up with a tender pat to his head. With a deep sigh, the dog once more rested his head on the king's shoulder. His eyes returned to Ordwulf.

"Good hunter, is Diggy?" I asked.

A grin broke out on Ethelred's face. But before he could tell me all about his hound's prowess in the field, Ordwulf broke in. "My king, this is the man your lady mother told you to expect."

The boy's grin disappeared. "I don't want to talk about that."

He lapsed back into what I could now see might not be sickness so much as a good case of the sulks. The only thing he showed any interest in was the scramseaxe at my belt, one I'd taken from Thornholt. It had a bone handle carved in the shape of shaggy little men casting spears at a big shaggy bear.

"I never saw a knife like that before," he said. "Where'd you get it?"

So much for royal courtesy, though not for Saxon greed.

"You want the truth, lord king, I won it off a Norsker that

didn't have better sense than to shoot dice with me. Ever played dice yourself?"

"No. Is it fun?"

"Not shot dice?" I threw up my hands in mock horror. "At your age? What kind of soldier you going to be, never rolled bones?"

"My mother says gambling's wrong 'cause it's what the Roman soldiers did with Our Lord's robe."

Now I knew for sure Ethelred would talk to me, tell me what I wanted to know. A boy whose mother forbids him to do something is a boy that can be led into temptation.

I gave him a wink. "I hear you're the king of England."

Ethelred's eyes grew wide. Then, clapping his hands together, he fairly shouted. "You bet I am! Have you got your dice with you?"

The noise brought Diggy's head up. Ordwulf's, too. In a whiny little voice, he said, "My king—"

"Leave Us, Uncle," said Ethelred. "We wish to confer with our guest."

Ordwulf made no move to go. Until Diggy stood up.

Once Ordwulf disappeared—he'd suddenly remembered important business elsewhere—I took out my dice. I kept them with my relics, where they'd be safe and get some luck rubbed off on them.

Ethelred and I knelt down on the flagged floor, Diggy watching mournfully as I let Ethelred win the first few games. Then I got serious and suggested a small wager. Right away the king cast an eager eye at my knife.

"All right," I said, putting the knife on the floor betwixt us. "If you win, you can have it. If I win, you have to answer some questions about where you found your brother."

The king took the bet—with a look that said he'd no intention of losing, never mind paying up if he did.

Next thing we knew, the boy'd beat me six rolls out of six. When I finally gave up, he hopped to his feet and went to jabbing his fists in the air. "A miracle. A real miracle."

"Damn good luck, anyhow." I reached into my boot and withdrew the other Thornholt knife. Its hilt was even more elaborately carved than the first, with long-antlered elk pursued by a brace of tall, bearded hounds. "How about double or nothing?"

When Ethelred had lost both knives, he tried to welch on his bet. "I'm not going to talk about ..."

"Your father was a gambling man. Did you know that?"

The boy nodded. "We used to play—"

"Then you must've heard him say a man always pays his gambling debts. 'Specially if that man wears a crown. It's the courtesy of kings, he used to say."

Maybe King Eadgar did say so, just never in front of me. But Ethelred must've been accustomed to being told what his father would do, or not do. He began to tell me about the fatal boar hunt. "But I wasn't there when, when, when ..."

"When what?"

The boy's face went red right up to the roots of his curly hair and he didn't answer. Maybe he'd gotten lost out there in the woods and was too proud to say so. Or maybe it was something else. I gave him a soothing smile. "Let's start earlier. How come you and your brother went off by yourselves?"

He hadn't said they did, but he looked plenty relieved when I said so. "Dward never liked Felding, but Uncle Ordwulf made him royal huntsman anyhow. Dward said

Felding couldn't find pig in a pork pie and we could do better by ourselves."

"Weren't you kind of scared in all that fog? You never know what might be lurking around."

Ethelred shrugged off the notion. "There's lupine and fennel in my charm bag and, anyhow, Dward said the elf charm."

"That do much good if you run smack into a low branch? Or maybe fall in a stream?"

"I never—" he said, bristling up. "I mean I slipped. My horse slipped. In the mud."

The boy's sudden stirring brought his dog's head up again. Ethelred looked at him. "Diggy came and got me out."

"He sure must love you."

Ethelred gave the dog's ears a good scratching. "He always loved me best. Do you think elves made Dward fall off his horse?"

Now we were getting someplace—if we could get past the elves.

Ethelred said, "I mean even if Dward said the elf prayer and everything?"

The boy didn't seem to be looking for the kind of answer it'd take Bishop Æthelwold to devise, so I said, "Elves can get up to most anything. Their spears might hit a man in the head or in the foot or in the back."

Ethelred put his arms around Diggy, peering at me with eyes as baleful as the dog's.

"An elf," I said, "is just about as evil as a being can get. When they throw spears at somebody, they never miss."

The king burst into tears.

I was saved by Ordwulf. He shoved open the door to say

that the boy's mother and Sister Hild wanted him to join them in the queen's bower. "Right now."

Ethelred hiccupped a couple times, wiped his nose on an embroidered sleeve. Then he and the dog sloped off, leaving me in the cold of Ordwulf's smirk. "Outside," he said with a jerk of his thumb. "But don't worry, you're not going to gaol again. I'm under orders to let you run loose. And, Christ help me, to tell you what happened on that goddamn boar hunt."

We now stood on the gravel walkway, out of the wind, in the lee of the lodge. Just as he had in Winchester, Ordwulf tried to use his height against me. He stepped onto a rock ledge where he could look down on me while he talked in a voice stony as the ledge.

"I found King Edward by a pond, dangling from his saddle, foot in the stirrup, leg bent all which way. Covered in blood. And grass and dirt, as if he'd been dragged Satan knows how far. Likely the damn horse only stopped when it came to the pond." He paused to tug at his beard. "Ethelred was sitting on the ground next to him, wet right through and crying his sodding eyes out."

Ordwulf said he blasted away on his horn. But no one came or even answered. "Looked like the horse had reared, then bolted for some reason, and the king's foot had gotten caught in the stirrup. Or maybe he hit a low branch—last time I saw him he was travelling pretty fast for that kind of fog."

"Could he have been in a fight?"

"Not with blades. Or at least his sword hadn't been in a fight. It was in its scabbard. And his scramseaxe was still on him."

"What did you do next?"

"By all the charcoal in hell, what do you think I did? I untangled him, stretched him out on his cloak. Then I threw my own cloak around Ethy, picked up his spear, got him mounted, and we rode back to the lodge."

Ordwulf stepped down from the ledge and tried to move past me and onto the walkway. I grabbed hold of his arms and pushed him against the rock wall. "You mean you left the king of England there? Like a deer with an arrow in its belly that you couldn't be bothered to follow. And him a king?"

Ordwulf gave a growl and pushed back, hard. He wasn't used to getting shoved around, bodily or any other way, and I could tell we'd end up in a serious battle if I didn't let go. That wouldn't sit well with his sister. She might withdraw payment when I found Edward's body. I dropped my hands and stepped away. Ordwulf let out another growl. This one sounded disappointed.

"Another time," I said.

"My pleasure, arsewipe." He started up the windy walkway toward the hall.

"Was Edward dead?" I yelled after him. I got no response.

Ordwulf sure hadn't told me much. Except that he'd abandoned his king, though I didn't think that was the way he saw it. Nor did he seem to know why or how Edward's body had gone missing. Or if he did, he wasn't about to tell me.

I wanted to kick myself. Why had I let myself get sucked into quarreling with Ordwulf? Likely that's just what he wanted—to make me angry enough not to ask him any more questions. I could've at least found out where the damn pond lay.

How could I get some clear answers here at Corfe? Not from the fine folk at the lodge. I'd have to find a churl. Somebody I could beat an answer out of.

I found Felding, the huntsman, at a table by the big wicker-sided dog pen, chopping up hare as feed for the royal hounds. He was a hulk of a man dressed in bristly wool tunic and leg-bands. His hands were covered in blood and he smelled like wet dog and dead hare. But his memory was clear and his tongue loose. He said he'd gotten the queen's order about talking to me and would obey it.

"Just lemme finish this bit first." He slit open the hare's belly and pulled out the guts, then chopped the head off and peeled away the fur.

"We was after boar," he told me as he set the fur aside to be cleaned and tanned later. "Armed to the teeth for it. Long hunting spears, sharp knives, and the king's best-trained horses. The kind that don't scare if a pig comes charging. And they had quality men riding 'em. The king and Prince Ethelred, 'course. Lord Leofric, Lord Siward, Lord Ordwulf. And Ealdorman Alvar, too."

"Anybody else? Men from the village to turn the game out?"

"King Edward didn't like using beaters to chase an animal into a net where anybody could go in and make the kill. He liked to sneak up on the brutes in their lairs, send the dogs to roust 'em out. Then he'd face 'em down and run 'em through with his spear. That's how come we decided to fan out, fog or no, and look for boar runs."

Maybe Edward wasn't the weakling I'd heard he was.

Felding pushed the hare's guts into a bucket, swiped the

blood and slime in after them. "The king and his brother took off together, riding like fury while Lord Ordwulf and me went the opposite direction. Presently, we come on a boar run. You could smell pig all over it. Lord Ordwulf said stay put and make sure the beast didn't escape whilst he went to find the king."

"Where had Lord Alvar got to in the meantime?"

Felding shrugged. "Don't know. Anyhow, after while I heard a dog baying. But not like he had something cornered. It wasn't a hunting bell, just a high howl, and I didn't like the sound of it. So I left where I was and followed it 'til I come on a couple horses by a pond. Never did find the dog, but the horses was nickering and nervous, reins tossed on the ground, and Lord Ordwulf and Prince Ethelred was a ways beyond, kneeling 'longside a man down. It was the king. I seen that right off and he was laying all still and his face was all grey, tunic all full of blood, and a bloody bone sticking out his leg."

Felding paused to cross himself, and so did I, before he went on. "Lord Ordwulf said the king was dead and he should get back up the lodge, tell 'em what happened. I said shouldn't we take the king? He just said go find the dogs."

I could hardly believe it. What was the matter with these people? "You mean to say you left that boy on the cold, wet ground and him a king?"

"I'm only the huntsman." A churl, he meant, maybe even a slave. For sure not the man in charge of a king's body. "But Lord Ordwulf covered him with a blanket."

Felding picked up a cleaver, hacked off the hare's front feet, tossed them into the bucket with the innards.

"Were you in the party that went back to bring King

Edward's body to the lodge?"

He nodded, then off came the hare's back feet.

"Know this country well, do you?"

"Hunted it since I was a lad."

"So when you went to fetch the king, you're sure you got back to the right spot."

Felding gave me an insulted look.

"Where was that exactly?"

"Big bog up Wareham way, past the old ones' barrow and the mossy cross."

"What do you think happened to the king's body?"

"It's in Wareham Church."

"You know it's not."

First, Felding looked surprised. Then his face drained and he put on that empty look churls give you when they're pretending they don't know what you're talking about. Nor was there any point threatening to beat the truth out of him. The man held a cleaver. So I simply reminded him of the queen's orders, that she had said to tell me what I wanted to know.

When he shrugged in defeat, I expected him to claim some wicked night spirit had stolen Edward's body, or elves, at least. But, as he chopped off the tail, he said, "Ask her. Ask the speaking-woman."

Queen Ælfthryth, he meant. I got out of there before his tongue turned totally treasonous.

CHAPTER NINETEEN

My own tongue had turned dry, so I decided to try out the village alehouse, think over what I'd learned from Ordwulf and Felding. Which was that they told the same tale. Edward and Ethelred had gone off together and Edward had fallen off his horse. Ordwulf found them and brought Ethelred back to Corfe Gate. He never mentioned Felding being with him. But somebody like Ordwulf wouldn't think somebody like Felding was worth mentioning. The important thing was that Felding knew King Edward's body didn't lie in Wareham Church. And if he knew, others might, too. Another good reason to visit the alehouse.

I was at the bottom of the hill before it occurred to me I'd forgotten to ask Felding if he'd seen Wynstan anyplace near the king's body. But I'd have my drink first, then I'd hike back up to the dog pen.

What they called Corfe village was a few thatched huts, some sheds, a well, an outdoor kitchen, and a hillock of garbage with dogs and chickens roaming all over it. At least the place had an alehouse, a good big one with half a dozen ale barrels lined up outside it.

As I walked into the shadow of the alehouse, that familiar stink filled the air. I still didn't know what caused it, but I knew it whirled round a brew of trouble. I grabbed my scramseaxe and slipped under the alehouse's eave, where I crouched ready to rush at whoever—or whatever—gave off that putrid reek.

From above me came the sound of something heavy scrabbling in the straw of the roof.

Then I heard the laughter of men leaving the alehouse. Around the corner came fat Siward and lean Ordwulf, friends again. Or so it would appear. You never know with Saxons.

I hadn't even known Siward was at Corfe Gate. I'd thought the *consilliarius* was still in Winchester dealing with Lord Hunwald. But I was glad to see the two of them because now I could finish questioning everybody who'd been at the hunt last year. And who might know where King Edward's body had got to.

I slid the knife under my belt and stepped out of the shadows. "Just the lads I'm looking for," I said before I realized I might sound like I was still primed for a fight. Better dampen it down for two of the most powerful men in Wessex, I thought. And for the three hard-faced fellows behind them, whose swords were already drawn.

Siward was his usual satiric self. "What a charming coincidence, since you're just the lad *we're* looking for."

Ordwulf had no time for such foolery. He just went ahead and sicked the three swords on me. My hands were above my head even before the order was on his lips

In my best whine, I said, "You know the queen has sent me on a mission."

"One you should've refused," Siward said. He sniffed the foul air. "But since you stinking Welsh do not have the word 'no' in your language, you'll need a lesson in its use."

While I wondered what that was supposed to mean, Ordwulf delivered another order. "On your knees, Welshman."

"No," I said, thinking it a fine display of courage. And well it may have been. But it was all too brief. I didn't even hear the order that landed me face down in the mud, thrown there by the three swordsmen now set to strong-arm service. I wrapped my arms around my head and said a prayer to St. Jude. Maybe I could get off with only a good hiding.

"You likely think that after your antics in Winchester we're threatening you with a slow and juicy death," Siward said. "But that would teach you nothing, in this world or the next. What I have suggested to Ealdorman Alvar might prove more persuasive."

When I didn't reply, Ordwulf said, "Get up, you filthy Welsh fart, and mind your betters for once."

He rammed a boot into me so hard I lost both my breath and my fancy for staying anywhere in range of his feet. I hauled myself up—Jesus, had the bastard broken a rib?—and slumped against the alehouse's wattle wall. I could barely breathe.

"Quit your moaning. And hand over your weapon while you're about it." Ordwulf put a fist to my chin. He was so close I could smell the ale on his breath.

I did as ordered because Siward had laid a restraining hand on Ordwulf's shoulder. And because the three swordsmen moved nearer.

"Here's a proposition for you," Ordwulf said as he stepped back and slid my knife under his belt. "And it's take it or leave it."

Why would I think otherwise?

"You have a woman back at Thornholt," he said.

The pain in my side was nothing next to my surprise. Which must've shown on my face because Siward smeared on one of his oily smiles. "There is little we don't know here in England."

"Anyway," Ordwulf said, "we know about this woman. And we know you want to take her away from Thornholt."

The next surprise came when, from his own sheath, Siward pulled out my hawk-hilted seaxe. He must've had it since I'd gotten arrested at Thornholt. Now, he yanked a hank of hair out of a swordsman's scalp and tested the knife on it.

"The woman's yours," Siward said as he ran his thumb over the blade. "I own Thornholt now. And I will trade her for this dull thing."

"And for your promise to take her and leave England immediately," Ordwulf added in a tone that told me I'd be leaving England with or without Thrima.

But that was beside the point. I turned to Siward. "You can't trade her for anything. Nor can I. She's a free woman."

"She'll be even freer when I turn her whole family out of Thornholt, right down to and including those little darlings she's so fond of."

Could he do such a thing? Surely English law protected free peasants from eviction. But who was I to challenge the king's *consilliarius*?

Instead, I tapped my sore ribs, decided nothing was broken, told Siward the knife was his. I didn't take time to figure out why they wanted me to quit searching for the king, wanted me out of England. I just asked when I could get to Thrima. "She'll need a horse, by the way. And I'll need mine."

After the two thegns shot each other a pair of smug glances, Siward said, "You'll have an escort back to Thornholt, leaving tomorrow at first light. I will send an order along allowing you to take the woman Thrima and your choice of the Hunwald stable to carry her on."

That almost took the breath out of me once again. But since they didn't need to know that, I said, "What shall I tell the queen?"

"You'll tell the queen ..." Lord Ordwulf said. "God's goat, man, tell her nothing."

He turned to the three swordsman. "Take this dog where he belongs."

They took me to the dog pen up the hill, then sent Felding away with the whole pack. The beasts barked in bitter complaint and seemed ready to bite any fool that tried to give them succor.

I growled a little myself when I went in the pen and would've gladly savaged any fool that dared come near me. Succor wasn't on offer, though, and I cursed Fortuna the rest of the day and into the night. As usual, the bitch had deserted me just when I needed her most. But I cursed myself, too. Why had I followed Wynstan right into the royal lair when we both stood accused of crimes against the crown? And where *was* the old snake, anyhow? Disappeared as completely as my mother. He could stay that way, too. I wasn't about to go looking for him.

And why did Siward and Ordwulf want to get me not only away from Corfe Gate but out of England? It was clear they didn't want me to go on searching for King Edward's body. Or asking questions. And that must be for some very important reason. Otherwise they wouldn't be defying the queen by sending me away.

What I needed to do now was find a way to turn the situation to my advantage. But I didn't think I could do that surrounded by Lord Siward's men on the road to Thornholt. I had to get out of Corfe Gate on my own—and on my own terms.

By now I had enough knowledge to look for King Edward's body on my own. I would head for that bog near Wareham where Felding said the lad's body had lain last time he'd seen it. It might take me awhile, but I'd find it sooner or later. As for Thrima, for all Siward's bluster, she'd be safe in Thornholt until I did. *She* wasn't his quarry. This in mind, I left off Fortuna and turned my trust to St. Jude, patron of the desperate.

The dog pen was round, with a sturdy, tight-woven wicker fence and a dog-proof rock base. Besides that, the soldier they set guarding me stayed so close I could all but hear his heart beat. But there was a problem in using a dog house for a gaol. The fence might be high enough to keep hounds inside, but a man the size of me? It didn't take long to prise a good-size rock out of the floor.

The guard had drawn too close for safety. His own, that is. I stripped off my tunic, found him where he leaned against the fence, half asleep. I tossed the tunic over his head. While he fumbled with it, I jumped over the fence and onto him. I pulled him into the dirt, then bashed him with my rock. He'd be asleep for a long time.

Helping myself to his soldier's kit, I got lucky again. Though his sword belt squashed my gut and I had to leave it, the hilt of the sword fit in my hand like it was made for me.

Praise St. David, so did his helmet. I even squeezed into his mail shirt somehow. All that and his red cloak would let me pass for a good Saxon loyally serving his king even in the dead of the night. Now all I had to do was fetch Tom and ride out the front gate.

I crossed the hall-yard in a slow creep, slipping from the shadow of the bower, to the kitchen, to the stable. Nobody was up and about except me. I thanked God for these hard-working, hard-sleeping royals. In the stable doorway, the stableman lay under a pile of straw, so sound asleep he never woke, even while I carried him into the tack room and left him there wrapped in a horse blanket. Then I went back to the stable for Tom.

He was gone.

Once I calmed down, I found I hadn't woken the whole of Dorset in my anger. I also knew Tom's absence was no accident. I kicked the stableman awake. "Where in hell's my horse?"

The dolt was too dumb to be scared—of me or his betters in the royal lodge. "Big chestnut? Lord Siward's man took him someplace. Over t' Kingston like as not, put him in t'royal stable over there."

I swallowed down my rage. Of course, I'd fetch Tom. Just not right now. Nor could I take one of the royal horses and get myself in even deeper trouble. It looked like I'd have to get away on foot. No easy task, that, negotiating my way down this high, steep mound on a dark, wet night—as Siward and Ordwulf well knew when they kidnapped Tom. Clever lads, these Englishmen.

But they forgot Lady Philosophy.

I'd seen her as we rode up Corfe hill. Half way up it, alone but still saddled, she'd been contentedly munching her way through the slope's thick grass. Now somebody had brought her to the stable. For what reason? I couldn't answer that. I could only look at her swayed back and skinny ribs and think about the fuss she was capable of spawning. But if I wanted to put distance between me and the folk at the lodge, I needed a mount of some kind. Besides, in unknown, dangerous hill country a sure-footed mule would be useful. I hoped.

I tossed the stableman's blanket over his head, looped some rope around him, tied him to a post. He was an old fellow and didn't fight me. I hoped Lady Philosophy would be the same.

I used some of Wynstan's soft words on her and the old girl lowered her head for me to scratch. It still took some courage to slide the bit between her teeth—they were big and yellow and mean. But maybe she knew I was Wynstan's friend, or maybe it was just a good night for ancient she-mules. She stood still while I got both the saddle and me on her back without even a mite of trouble. Even so, I should've known evil brewed 'twixt those long ears.

That would come later. Now, she trotted smartly to the gate. In my polished helmet and flowing red cloak, I looked an Englishman born. The guards, no doubt anxious to be out of the wind and back to sleep in their warm hut, waved us through. Before long, Lady Philosophy and I were making our way down the hill, she grown a little testy now that she'd been roused out of her sleep. A couple of jabs to her skinny ribs showed her the wisdom of obedience. Except now the damn mule all but minced along, one hoof more daintily planted than the last. I could have moved faster on foot.

I thought about reciting verse for her, like Wynstan did. But the only poetry I knew was in Welsh and Latin, and I was pretty sure this old mollie didn't understand either. Nor would I dare try and sing or even hum into those long ears. So once again I wooed a lady with my jaws harp. This one must've liked it, too. Lady Philosophy took to loping right along.

Then I got rid of my other problem, stripping off the tight chainmail shirt and stowing it in a saddlebag. I couldn't be squashed and lumbered by the thing any longer, but it likely cost the guard's lord a handsome sum and I knew other lords who'd pay me an even handsomer sum. I struck up a very merry tune indeed.

Once we were off Corfe hill and into the wooded valley, I pondered where to go next. From what Felding had told me and what Wynstan had said on the Frankie's boat, I should look for a boar run and then a black marsh. Trouble was, Purbeck's covered with bogs and thickets. And wolves and God only knows what else—everything from bears to elves to dragons.

It all made me pull Lady Philosophy to a halt among the protective branches of an old oak. I wanted to make sure I had enough weapons. I touched the seaxe in its sheath at my back and the sword in the scabbard laced to my saddle. Then I hauled out my neck sack. I touched St. Veronica, nestled among the healing herbs alongside St. Apollonia's tooth and the pen knife. I stuffed what was left of my silver into the pouch at my waist, along with enough gravel to make the pouch look very stuffed indeed. Satisfied I had ample security for this world and the next, I gave the neck sack a kiss and shoved it back under my tunic.

Armed body and soul as I was, I should have stormed out of those branches with blood in my eye and a Welsh battle cry on my lips. Instead, I sat tapping the jaws harp against my teeth. I had no idea where to go next nor how to find the right bog or thicket. Still, though irked with myself for not having a real plan, I told Lady Philosophy to walk on.

And I was tired, so tired that even the mule's choppy gait couldn't stop me from drifting into a doze. The breeze through the trees became a forest song, like someone making melody in the wilderness. A man's voice, deep, full of woe. He was weeping, singing into the sea-wind, lamenting lost love. Lost in the wasteland of Purbeck.

I came to with a jerk. It was Wynstan's song, the one he'd sung in the boat. His poem was his map. It told him where to travel. Why hadn't I figured that out sooner?

What was in the poem the old devil had blasted across Poole Bay? At the time I'd found it so bloated and boring that I'd nearly nodded off right there in the teeth of the sea wind. Now I summoned up what I remembered. "Ordered her within the forest grove to dwell beneath the oak ..."

What else, damn it? In my vexation, I crunched down on the jaws harp and gave it a hard twang. The thing made a noise like Wynstan bringing a drunken mead hall to heel. "*Hwaet!*" And then I had the rest, most of it anyway. "Ancient is her earth-hall ... in a valley dim, o'ergrown with briars by the lake, a black bog beyond Wareham town. Past the old ones' burying mound, past great Christ hanged. Beneath the oak, behind the briar. Joy is she who waits there."

By St. Cecilia, English poetry is awful. And a lake, a bog, a briar patch? They could be anywhere in Dorset, in England, in the whole world. But a boggy lake beyond Wareham town, a burial mound, a moss-covered crucifix—they gave me something to go on.

I searched out the moss on a big oak's trunk, then pointed Lady Philosophy in the direction it told, north toward Wareham. The opposite way, though, from Kingston and Tom Tub. I asked St. Eligius to watch over him 'til I could fetch him.

Soon we came to a wide, well kept road—the Wareham Way—and my next problem. Queen Ælfthryth took her duties as ruler of Dorset seriously and had the brush cut far back from the road, lest bandits hide there. A big Welshman aboard a skinny mule had slim hope of hiding on such a highway. I would have to go overland, over high hills, through dark woods. This for two days and two nights with Lady Philosophy's scrawny flank the only refuge for sleep.

On the morning of the third day, Fortuna returned. Wynstan had sung of the mound of the old ones. And though Dorset was full of such hillocks, not all of them had been marked with both briar and Christ's own sign.

I knew I'd found the place as soon as I saw it—a burial mound in a dark valley, a tall cross by a boggy lake, lots of oak trees and even more briars. I dismounted and, leaving Lady Philosophy by the side of the road to crop whatever greenery she wanted, pushed my way into the briar thicket I figured was all that lay 'twixt me and my reward.

The wind carried the sweet smell of death. At first I feared the return of the stinking man who'd been following me since Wilton. Then, through the thicket, I saw a glint of water and moved toward it.

I gripped my knife hard and tried not to puke. The place was shrouded in a smell far worse than the stinking man's. It could be the lair of some elf or troll or forest monster, a thing that stacked up its kill like cordwood. But I knew it was the place Wynstan had described. If I lost heart now, the whole wretched trip would've been wasted. So, shooting St. Jude a quick prayer, I pushed on through the briar.

And stepped into a clearing thick with dark figures. Huge black ones, rushing straight at me. I grabbed my cloak tails, then threw my arms up high as they'd go. Now I towered tall as any slavering beast and I told them so in a roar as loud as theirs.

They gave no answer.

Nor could they. What I'd taken for bears or elves or dragons were nothing but cowhides stretched on racks next to the reeking vats they'd tanned in. I cursed in every language I knew, so relieved and angry was I at the trick their owner'd played on me. "Come out, whoever you are, wherever you are."

Still silence. Or rather only the sound of flapping hides. A stiff wind had come up, stirring lake and sedge. It also ruffled the big heaps of brown moss scattered over the clearing. For tanning the hides, I figured. Most of the piles lay on the ground except for one in a leather coracle at the edge of the thicket. Whoever or whatever did its tanning here would use the coracle to cross the lake, so ...

Before I could finish my thought, a woman's voice came from the thicket. "You're finally here. What took you so long?"

CHAPTER TWENTY

I whirled around, knife ready to fight I knew not what. The what, though, obviously had no fear of me or my knife. She pushed aside the brambles—I now saw that they covered a hut—and stepped into the clearing.

Could this really be the fair-haired young dancing girl Wynstan had described? Or had time scraped clean his memory? Not that the woman was the wizened crone that necromancers are believed to be. But she was neither young nor fair-haired, just a dark-haired peasant woman of middling years with a thick tweed cloak draped over her stout body. She wore no headdress, but a ragged patch covered one eye.

She gripped what looked like half an oak branch. "What you want?"

"You know. Otherwise, you wouldn't tell me I'd been too long coming."

"Queen send you? No, not her. Ælfthryth strikes from behind."

It struck me that she might've been expecting someone different. Someone from Corfe Gate maybe, Ordwulf or Siward. Or Wynstan. No matter. I needed to find King Edward's body. And from what Felding said and Wynstan sang, this was the woman who knew where it lay. "I've come for King Edward. And not on orders from the queen. Her toadies neither.”

Now I tossed the dice. “Wynstan sent me.”

“Who?”

“Wynstan. Wynstan Wing-tongue.”

The woman laughed and shook her head. I asked her where the king lay once, twice, half a dozen times. She wouldn’t say.

I could’ve beaten the answer out of her. But I still had some honor in me. Anyhow, if you’ve the wit to wield it, sweet flattery will prise up even the stubbornest rock. “Wynstan said you were quite a woman.”

Her eye didn’t blink. “Wynstan? Man’s got honey on his lying tongue. If it’s him you’re here for, I’ve not seen him this year past.”

The woman’s voice didn’t have the rough burr of Wessex. Her words chimed like altar bells, like she was Welsh or Cornish.

“Your name’s Crawe.” I made it a statement she didn’t refute. “Wynstan said you were quite a healer, too.”

I began poking my nose in the crocks and vats and pails that stood outside the little house. “Mmm. Gifthrife and silverwood. Both good for wounds. And weybroed for the flying venom. And water dock for itch. Got anything for love sickness? Mine’s been kicking up bad here lately.”

Crawe put up with my poking and peeking until I came to a little wooden box with linked circles scratched on its top. “Wouldn’t open that one, I was you.”

I paid her no mind and took hold of the box.

“Make your manhood shrivel up.”

I dropped the thing back on its shelf and went on to a

little crock full of garlic. "Now here's a prize," I said as I popped a dried clove in my mouth. "Protection against lice and plague."

Truthfully, Crawe's wasn't much of a *medicamentaria*. My own mother, back in Wales, had more and better. But I could tell she took great pride in her collection. "Bet you got potions here that'll spell out past and future both."

"I'm no speaking-woman."

"Did I say you were? Hell, woman, I know you wouldn't so much as look at Satan, never mind do his bidding. I just meant you likely have the visions."

"No saint, neither."

Nor was she a fool. If she was willing to deny any ability to tell the future, getting her to tell what she knew about King Edward might take more doing than I figured.

"Well, what I am is Welsh." I pressed a hand to my chest. "And I expect you've heard us Cymry can see right into a person's soul."

Crawe laughed. "Horse apples. Ripe and juicy ones. Tell me another."

But I did see deep enough into most folks' souls to know they'll believe just about anything, so long as you dress it up in a little silver. I touched my hand to the leather pouch at my waist. "I figure you got the kind of soul that travels all over, leaps walls, glides through the hills and the forests, sees things ordinary folk couldn't ken even in their richest dreams."

Crawe eyed the bulging pouch, then gave me a shy little smile and dug her toe in the dirt. "Sometimes, at night, I do... ah... see things. And sometimes I learn from nature. It's not hard, y'know, to bring all nature right to you."

I pulled forth my last bit of silver—which Crawe plucked from my fingers so fast I wondered if it was only nature she was talking about. It didn't matter. She was finally going to tell me what she knew about King Edward's death.

She hurried into the briar-covered hut, where she stayed silent so long that my armpits went wet and cold. When she finally emerged, she juggled half a dozen bowls with one hand, while the other hooked the ear of a pitcher. Under her arm was a book so battered some of its leaves fluttered behind her.

I breathed easy. But I passed up the cup of milk she offered.

After she consulted her book, she set the bowls by the hut door, filled them with milk and a sprinkling of herbs. Animals—snakes, water rats, hedgehogs, a couple of hares, a reeking polecat—rushed from their hiding places. "You see, it's not hard to bring all nature to you."

"If that's all you mean by bringing nature to you," I said, a bit puzzled as to why she would do something that simple-minded. I'd heard of conjuring women so fen-locked they'd never even seen a book, never mind owned one, but who could prove their command of Creation by turning night to day, men to women, dogs to cats. Crawe's hares and hedgehogs just didn't measure up. But if I said as much she might never tell me about King Edward.

Crawe watched as her creatures lapped the milk, a thin smile on her lips. "Lovely, eh? I have to keep them out here, though. The queen don't care for 'em. Makes me keep 'em way away from her."

I didn't believe the queen had done any such thing. Queen Ælfthryth would be too prudent to deal with Crawe, never mind her dismal little creatures. But Crawe said it like she knew Ælfthryth well and reckoned the queen had some kink in her character that made her not want snakes and polecats and river rats squirming around in her bower house. Nor hedgehogs, neither. The little beasts were hardly rank vermin, but you still wouldn't want their spiked hides marching across your feet in the middle of the night.

"Fine beasts, these," Crawe continued as she smiled down on her collection of nasties. "But they belong not to me but to Lucifer."

She swept her arm wide, called out to the dark lord. "Hail, thou, Abdub, Siejka, Flanicutsibrab," she said in no language I'd ever heard before or ever hope to hear again.

The animals began to die, first the snakes, then the rats and the greedy little hedgehog.

In case this was one of the devil's delusions, I did as the clerics advise and crossed myself. But the creatures still lay dead before me.

I crossed myself again and started to do it yet again. But then I caught hold of myself. This was no Satan-inspired sorcery. "You poisoned 'em with those herbs or whatever you sprinkled in the milk."

Then, relieved I hadn't fallen for her trick, I began to laugh. And the more I laughed, the more I wanted to laugh—until I couldn't stop.

Crawe picked up a dead polecat by its long tail and smashed it on my head. Its stinking broth seeped into my cap, then my beard.

I've been hit a good many times, by men wielding fists and flails, spears and sticks, slingshots and shillelaghs. By women, too. A brass saucepan can put a dent in even a head hard as mine. But getting hit with a dead polecat isn't only painful. It's humiliating. No man should have to endure an insult like that, not from anybody, never mind from a woman. Whether or not she's possessed by the devil.

Crawe stood before me, triumphant, as I tossed away my reeking cap and wiped the animal's vile fluid out of my beard. I tried to decide just what do about her and her magic.

From behind came a fierce cry. I spun around, ready to pounce on Satan and all his works.

By the edge of the thicket, the three nuns—Prioress, Sister Hild, and Sister Hrothbeort—were drawn up like a shield-wall. Then they, God's spear band, marched forward shoulder to shoulder, brandishing their weapons against the devil—a linden shield, a heavy iron knife, and an open box of what smelled like dried fennel. On their lips was a psalm: "I have pursued my enemies and overtaken them. Neither will I turn until they are consumed."

I was too shocked to wonder what they were doing out in this bog or where they'd come from or how I could protect them from Crawe.

The nuns came to a halt in front of her, and Prioress stepped up like a champion ready to do single combat. The silver of her many rings flashed as she pointed at Crawe. "You, woman-fiend, show us your magic, that we can show you ours."

This was going to get unpleasant. I backed into the thicket. Thorns ripping open my flesh would be better than anything that might happen when nuns and a speaking-woman went at it.

For a moment Crawe hesitated. But her thin smile told me she was neither surprised nor scared. In her mind she was likely running through her bag of tricks. At last, she pressed her hand to her breast, then brought it to her lips. Finally, she gave a sharp nod. And let out a billow of black smoke.

I don't mind telling you, this kind of thing unmans me. I didn't like it, either, when she pulled a leather flask from under her tunic and pulled out its stopper. The wild flash that leaped forth far outdid the glint of Prioress's rings. I pushed further back into the thicket.

The nuns, though, laughed. Prioress said, "Those tricks were old when St. Hippolytus wrote about them. Crumbled stag horn moss always lights up when it hits the air, and anybody can stick an old gallnut in her mouth and blow out its soot. Show us something new."

"If you can," added Sister Hild.

Sister Hrothbeort didn't wait for anything new. She came from a line of warriors who'd held their northern lands against Picts and Scots and Vikings for half a millennium. She stepped up and punched Crawe in the nose.

Crawe's nose split open like any mortal's, blood spewing and her wailing. To add to the mayhem, Sister cursed her for Satan's whore while Crawe shouted for her creatures to come to her aid. When they didn't, she grabbed Sister Hrothbeort by the hair and for a while they reeled around like a pair of angry drunks at the fair, Crawe thrashing Sister with her oak branch, Sister punching Crawe wherever she could land a fist. Crawe cried out to the Prince of Darkness, Sister called on the Company of Heaven.

When neither appeared, Sister wrenched Crawe to the dirt, then snatched up the stick and threatened to pound her all the way to Hell's gate. Defeated, sprawled in the wet dirt,

Crawe went on calling for her friends in the netherworld.

Naturally, I couldn't hide for long. The nuns set me to guarding Crawe while they tended the animals. It did my soul good to remind her that the shadow now falling across her was Tryff Tewdwr's and not Beelzebub's.

I was about to begin a sermon on what I thought about women who serve—or pretend to serve—dark powers. But Prioress shushed me while Sister Hild touched each animal, then said in Latin, "May the beasts be healed, that are vexed in health. In the name of the Father, let this Devil be expelled through the laying on of our hands, through the invocation of all Your saints, and through Him who lives and reigns forever."

The prayer made me feel better, though I wasn't so sure about the creatures. One or two had already crawled off into the woods and the hares' eyes were struggling open. But a snake and both polecats were dead for sure. I can't say what happened to the little hedgehogs. I never saw them again.

Finished resurrecting the animals—or whatever she'd done to them—Sister Hild went to Crawe where she lay, nudged a toe into her ribs. "As you can plainly see, our magic is stronger than yours. So strong that in this very hour I could deliver you to Lucifer. And your dark lord will not be pleased by your failure here."

With a moan, Crawe burrowed her face into the dirt. Sister Hild gave a satisfied nod.

When the nuns were finally convinced that Crawe was past the reach of Satan and any weapons, animal or otherwise, they let her sit up, back against one of the tanning vats. She watched the last of her creatures hustle into the thicket.

Prioress stepped in front of her. "Now you're going to tell us what you know of King Edward's death. And when you finish that, you're going to tell us where his body lies."

Prioress then explained to the vanquished—but likely undefeated—Crawe, that you can make anybody confess to selling Jesus Christ to Pontius Pilate if you beat them hard enough or stick their head in a tanning vat often enough.

The problem is torture takes so long to get results, especially with somebody as tough as Crawe. Sidling up to Sister Hild, I whispered, "See you, Crawe knows what Pontius Pilate knew. A few pieces of silver buys an awful lot."

Sister nodded, caught Prioress's cloak and, leaving Sister Hrothbeort in charge of their prisoner, pulled her behind one of the drying racks. After considerable argument with each other, then with Crawe, they convinced Crawe she'd receive a big reward if she told them what she knew about King Edward. Prioress said the dozen silver pennies they now handed Crawe was just the down payment. She could collect the rest from Queen Ælfthryth.

Crawe counted the pennies, bit one or two, and burst into a radiant smile. "Where should I start?"

"The beginning usually makes a good spot," Prioress said. "And keep in mind that our magic can tell us if you lie."

I had to go back in the briar patch so Crawe wouldn't hear my laughter. When I came out again, she was saying, "The beginning, eh? Well, then you should know about them elves that was a-jumping—"

It's always something with Saxons. Northmen, bandits, now elves.

"Forget the bloody elves," Sister Hrothbeort said. "And get to what you seen the day King Edward died."

For a moment, Crawe's green eye went narrow as an angry cat's. Then she turned to me. "I got to tell it to these damn women?"

Why did she suddenly decide to trust me, of all people?

Sister Hrothbeort reached over and gave Crawe's arm the kind of wicked pinch she used on the oblates back at St. Finella's. It had the same effect on Crawe as it did on a ten-year-old.

Pouting and rubbing her sore arm, Crawe twisted in her bonds so that it was to me alone she spoke. "You," she said. "You I will tell because you are Wynstan's friend."

I wouldn't have gone so far as to say that, but it looked like Crawe was the kind of woman who needed to do her confessing to a man. Or maybe I just looked dumb enough to believe her.

She said, "I went out to gather some Christ lichen. It grows on stone crosses—which there's lots of hereabout 'cause this is where the priests come to say mass for the country folk when they don't have a church-house near 'em. Anyway, Christ lichen's the best thing for getting rid of elves. When you mix it with yarrow, that is, and some betony and lupine—"

"You can give us the recipe later," I said. "What happened?"

"I was at the cross by Mere pond, scraping away at its lichen, when a hare went chasing past. Running for his life, he was, 'cause right after him tore this grey dog big enough to swallow him whole. Then a pair of horsemen rode out of the woods. I figured they'd lost the dog 'cause they pulled up in the clearing and sat there yelling. I saw they was the king and his brother."

"How'd you know it was the king?"

Crawe shot me a look of disdain. "Think I could miss the royals when half a dozen times a year they come parading through on their way to Corfe hill?"

"Did they see you?"

"Don't think so. I was on my hands and knees behind the cross. Good big cross it is, too. Nor did I make so much as a peep. It's not safe for a country lass on her own with a pair of noblemen, even young ones, that near."

"Enough foolery, Crawe. Just tell me what happened."

Her story went like this:

The boys get off their horses, lean their spears up against a branch, and take a pee. Then they set to yelling at each other. King Edward says, "You stole my dog and got him killed. Thieving little bastard."

And Ethelred says, "You're the bastard. Just about, anyway. You're a thief, too. You stole my kingdom."

Edward gives out a whoop. "If that slut Ælfthryth was my mother, I wouldn't say anything about who's a bastard."

"Call my mother names, I'll kill you."

"You couldn't find a spear band big enough. You're dam's a whore. She'll lie with anybody. Lord Hunwald. Lord Siward. Even old Bishop Æthelwold. Think maybe you're a priest's whelp? 'Cause— know what?—dress you up in some fancy silk vestments and you'd look just like some prissy little priest, got his balls hid under the altar."

That sets little Ethelred blubbering. He pulls up his fur collar to hide it, but the tears come pouring out his eyes and the snot out his nose.

"Go on home, then, cry baby," Edward tells him.

"I am not a cry baby!"

"The hell you aren't," Edward says with a laugh. "And a scaredy cat. Go on home, you little shit. To your mommy."

"I don't wanna go home."

"Best place for you, mama's boy."

"No-o-o."

"Ye-e-e-s. For once, you're not going to spoil my fun. I don't give a shit what sodding Siward says, nor your slut of a dam, either." The king rams a finger toward Ethelred. "I've had bloody well enough of you."

The king mounts up, like he's going back to the hunt. But instead he pulls right next to his brother's horse and slaps his crop across its haunch. The horse takes off and Ethelred's still standing there hollering when it disappears into the trees. The king laughs and puts the spurs to his own horse. He canters away, holding high the middle finger of his right hand.

Ethelred's face goes red, then white. He snatches up a spear and flings it at the king. His aim's good. The spear hits Edward in the back. It doesn't stick, but it throws the lad out of the saddle. Spooks his horse, too. The horse gallops off with Edward's foot in the stirrup and him dragging alongside. Ethelred lets out a loud war yell or two. Then starts in cursing just as loud. And after that, he gets to bawling even louder.

About this time Lord Ordwulf rides up with Ethelred's horse in tow. When he sees how Ethelred's carrying on, he gets off his horse to try and find out what ails the lad. Ethelred keeps wailing. So Lord Ordwulf picks him up like he's a peeing puppy and tosses him in the pond. That cools the lad off quick-like.

Then that hunter man—forget his name—he rides up,

yelling so loud it's like he needs to go in the pond, too. When he calms down, he says King Edward's laying dead. Lord Siward's with him, but Lord Ordwulf, he should come and see. "Jesus, m'lord, what're we gonna do?"

At that point in her story, Crawe screwed up her brow. "He seen me, the hunter man did. He's mighty afeared of me, that one." She fell quiet.

"Then what happened?" I asked.

"They rode off into the woods. And that's the last I seen of 'em 'cause I got out of there quick as my legs'd carry me."

For once, the nuns had nothing to say. But I could tell they believed Crawe, just like I did. Crazy or no, she had no reason to make up such a story. It was worth her life not to. And worth ours not to hear it.

Now Sister Hild did what she always did as convent physician. She took charge. "We will spend Lent with the sisters at Wareham, as will Crawe. You, Tryff, need not accompany us. You have other concerns. But you will tell Queen Ælfthryth, if she asks, that this woman has an ailment I believe I can cure. Also tell her King Ethelred is a fine, healthy boy and will make a fine king."

The look on Prioress's face hovered someplace between irritation over Sister Hild seizing command and pure relief that they wouldn't have to return to Corfe Gate. Sister Hrothbeort gave a hearty nod and Crawe's rope an even heartier yank.

I didn't bother to ask Sister Hild what she planned to do once Lent was done. By then, she'd likely have not only relieved Crawe of her ailment but of considerably more information, too. As she told me, the Lord would provide.

I sure as hell hoped he'd provide for me, too.

CHAPTER TWENTY-ONE

I listened 'til the nuns' voices disappeared among the trees. Then I returned to my earlier thoughts about Crawe's stinking home. The smell of death smothered the place and by now I'd begun to wonder if the piles of moss might cover graves shallow enough to put forth the dreadful reek. If she was truly a waker-of-the-dead like Wynstan claimed, she'd surely have some corpses close to hand, King Edward's perhaps among them.

Sister Hrothbeort had flung Crawe's stick into the thicket. I fetched it because it was a stout piece of oak long enough to poke deep into the piles of moss and any grave that might be underneath. I started with the pile closest to the hut and straightaway struck something hard. Squatting down, I shoved away the cold moss fast as I could. I expected to find the late king of England.

What I found was a lyre, one marked with runes I didn't know and words I couldn't make out. But I remembered that one of the words the English have for lyre is wood-joy. On Poole Bay, Wynstan had said his Joy was blond. The instrument I held was made of some yellow wood. Dear Lord, was this the fair joy Wynstan meant when all the while I thought he was talking about a woman, about Crawe?

If that was so, then maybe Wynstan hadn't been lying

when he said he'd come on this place by accident. Maybe he'd stumbled on it while he searched for his wood-joy and wasn't the snake I'd thought he was. Maybe he really did want to find King Edward so Lady Flæda would know where her boy lay, so she could have some surcease to her sorrow. Maybe he understood, like I did, that it's a racking agony when the grave of someone you love is known only to God.

Knocking the moss off the lyre, I set it on the little table in Crawe's hut, out of the marshy dampness. I'd get it to Wynstan when I could, though I didn't think the soggy thing had much music left in it. But Wynstan had been making do without a lyre ever since I'd met up with him and claimed his voice was fine enough not to need accompaniment. Arrogant old bag of jingle-jangle. I returned to the business of shoving the stick into the piles of moss.

It sank into the soft dirt below the next pile and when I pulled it out, clinging to it was a smell so awful I puked until nothing but bile dribbled into my beard. After I wiped my mouth, I went to look for a shovel. There had to be one, otherwise how could Crawe have buried whoever was beneath that moss?

While I searched, I prayed. And not only for the souls buried here. For myself—of course—but also for King Edward and his poor mother.

I found a shovel in the little lean-to attached to Crawe's hut. It rested against a shelf lined with skulls, a dozen or so of them. Some were human, some animal, some had holes in them, and some were in pieces. Tattered flesh still clung to all of them. I said a prayer against every demon I could name.

Back digging, I turned up two or three corpses thoroughly

corrupted, another couple merely wormy, and one old and leathery. They all still had their heads, but, unlike that shelf full of skulls, none of them had yet become bone.

I'd no idea why Crawe had buried them this way. I was pretty sure, though, that they hadn't died here. They'd likely been brought across the lake in the two leather boats. Or maybe in the round little wicker one that sat on a trestle table next to the hut. The moss that filled it looked dry and brown as the stuff in the piles on the ground. But when I stuck my hand into it, I found it bog wet. It was so wet that, when I pushed it aside, some moss still clung to the young face beneath.

I recognized King Edward immediately.

How could I know a lad who'd been dead for almost a year? By now he should've been bone, or at least putrid and worm-ridden like the other corpses. But when I scraped away the rest of the moss, I saw that the king lay curled up as whole and uncorrupted as any saint in his crypt. He had on his royal ring, too, with its setting of blue-purple fluorite from Derbyshire.

I didn't know whether to take to my heels or fall to my knees.

When I came to myself, I spread the moss back over the king's body. And began to think about what had preserved him. I smelled no spices, as I often did in a saint's crypt. Nor had he been oiled, as saints sometimes were, or even wrapped in a winding sheet. He still wore the boots and leather cuirass he'd died in. His scramseaxe was on his belt. I finally decided that with his skin turned so dark and leathery, he'd most likely been smoked. Not here, though. No smokehouse stood in Crawe's camp. She had to have brought him here by boat, and probably all the rest, too. But from where?

Didn't matter, I decided. Besides, I didn't have time to wonder about Crawe's madness. I had to find Lady Philosophy, load up King Edward, collect my reward, and get the hell out of Dorset. I picked up Crawe's oak stick—I might need a heavy weapon—and walked back to where I'd left Lady Philosophy on the other side of the lake, by a wide bend in the road and a stand of yew. I'd been sure she'd stay close because all manner of greens were thrusting out of the damp dirt and though the old mule might look half starved, she'd eat just about anything that grew.

Of course, she wasn't there. I called her, traipsed up and down the track, re-traced my tracks through the thicket. No Lady Philosophy. As I stepped out of the thicket for the second time, something smacked me in the back.

Whatever it was, it dropped into the mud of the road where it stayed while I turned to look, then gawp at it. Like I said before, I've been hit by all kinds of missiles, including that dead polecat Crawe thwacked me with. But even in my trade, I never expected to be hit in the back by a human skull. 'Specially one with the hair and flesh and teeth still stuck on it.

When I got over my shock, I cast around for whoever had lobbed the rank thing at me. The thicket, the marsh, the lake were all still, and the smell from Crawe's wretched little camp was no worse.

I bent to pick up the skull. And was struck again. In the butt by another skull. Only this one was a wolf's. Or a dog's. Something, anyway, with long yellow teeth and a brown eye still clinging to its socket.

I swooped up Crawe's big stick, held it in both fists, ready to take the fight to whoever was attacking me. And just in time, too. A third skull—human—flew out of the thicket. I met this one with my stick, gave it a whack that sent teeth and bits of jaw showering over me. The rest sailed into the thicket.

"Come on out, fight like a man"—I planted myself, stick cocked at my shoulder—"or whatever you are." It had occurred to me that Crawe might've escaped the nuns and somehow gotten at the stack of skulls in her shed.

Silence. Then another skull. I swung and missed. It landed in the marsh. That's when someone started to laugh.

A man came sauntering out of the thicket, a tall, helmeted man wearing a tunic rich with gold embroidery and a stench that turned my stomach. But as the puke rose in my throat, I realized the man in the helmet must be the creature who'd pursued me all the way from Wilton. Now his reek overpowered even the stench from Crawe's graveyard.

He stopped at the thicket's edge, quit laughing, drew his sword and stepped toward me.

I called on St. Jude. Fortuna, too, if she'd have me. Then I charged him, whipping the oak stick back and forth, hoping to scythe off his head as if it were a Saxon cabbage. The stick connected. He dropped at my feet. But he wasn't dead, so I grabbed up his sword and tossed it into the marsh. Then, gulping down my gorge, I yanked off his helmet. It was a thegn's helmet, so polished I could see the reflection of my bared teeth.

Beneath it was blond hair and a face I recognized. His belt was thick with human ears. This stinking man was Lord Leofric, my friend of the meadbench—the man I'd gotten drunk with in Wilton, who'd saved me from Ealdorman Alvar's spear band, the lovesick lad who'd been so tongue-tied before Lady Edith.

Those memories made the fear drain right out of me. Now I knew why he'd laughed so hard while he'd slung skulls at me. It had all been a boyish joke. He'd found Crawe's stash and thought it would be funny to lob a few my way. Next, we'd find an alehouse and get riotously drunk. I felt bad I'd knocked him out, reached down to pull him to a drier spot. And snatched away my hand when I touched the putrid stuff round his waist. Those ears were no joke.

Which is exactly what I would've told him when he came around. Except that when he did, he wanted to talk about King Edward's body. At first I thought he'd gone foggy from our fight. Then he clearly asked, "Did you find it, Tryff? The king's corpse?"

I said I hadn't.

"Then you can help me look. It's here, you know."

That's when I began to think I should tie him up and leave him in the bog. Because when Queen Ælfthryth handed out the reward for finding Edward, she'd surely choose the handsome young thegn over the big-nosed, bushy-haired Welshman. If it even came to such a choice. More likely, once we had the body, Leofric would let his spear band deal with me while he smiled sweetly at the queen.

Leofric must've noticed that I hesitated. "Oh, I see," he said and stripped off his belt. "I suppose this thing really is rather nasty." He tossed it into the bushes.

"Why have you been following me?" I asked. "All the way from Wilton. You even jumped me once."

Leofric got to his feet, picked up his helmet and tucked it

under his arm. "I want to crown the rightful sovereign of Wessex and All England, King Alfred's heir, God's chosen," he said. "And I feared you didn't."

That was pretty high-blown, even for a royal thegn. But it sure relieved me. I said, "You didn't know Queen Ælfthryth already had me searching for King Edward's remains so Ethelred could be rightly crowned?"

Leofric gave out a sneering laugh. "Ethelred? That little worm? He's no throne-worthy successor to our great King Eadgar."

That flummoxed me. If not Ethelred, then who? King Eadgar's third son had died as a baby. So, unless one of his bastards were to be raised to royalty, there was no one left. Except— "Lady Edith? You're not talking about Lady Edith? A woman?"

"The finest lady in the land, already the greatest diplomat, the wisest counselor. Of course, Lady Edith."

A woman. A young woman. The English were even crazier than I thought. "Just how do you plan—?"

"I'm not alone in this, you know. A number of men—men of the highest rank—know her merits. They have pledged to do whatever is necessary to bring her to the throne. The Witan is already half convinced. Lord Siward will finish persuading them as soon as we've secured King Edward's remains."

Leofric's smile showed the glee of a successful conspirator. He said, "And Ealdorman Alvar will see to everyone else."

The royal *consillarius* and England's most powerful thegn? Involved in—"Treason?"

"It's hardly treason to want what is best for England. To

want a throne-worthy—"

What I wanted was to hear no more. Either Leofric had made up this wild plot or it was true. Whichever, he was dangerously mad and I had to get away from him. So I did what I always do when I'm cornered and scared. I cudgeled my way out. I rammed the big stick into Leofric's midriff, then, when he dropped gasping to his knees, I hit him again. Now I would scoop up Edward and be off to Corfe and my reward for finding him.

I got as far as the thicket's edge. Where I was met by Lord Siward and Ealdorman Alvar. They were both mounted and heavily armed, but at least they had no soldiers with them.

There wouldn't be any cudgeling now. Groveling would better suit the day. I quick-like dropped the big stick and spread wide my arms. "Greetings, great lords. May St. Christopher keep us safe here in this wilderness."

I don't know what I expected from them—an order to jail me, a spear in my gut, laughter maybe? What I got was absolutely nothing. Alvar and Siward were looking down the track at Leofric, doubled up and unconscious. "Your work, Welshman?" Siward asked.

Before I could think of an answer, Siward tossed a rope over my head and yanked it tight. Alvar dropped a second rope over me and snapped it fast. "Well, Welshman," Siward said as he and Alvar maneuvered their horses so that I had no choice but to follow or be strangled where I stood, "you seem to have saved us the trouble of killing this lunatic here."

Alvar tied my rope to his saddle, then dismounted to take a look at Leofric. He poked a toe into his side. "Lad ain't dead."

"He soon will be." Siward pulled his rope even tighter. "And this thing here will be swinging alongside him."

"Don't be a fool, man," Alvar said. "We ain't got time to hang 'em. The Welshman'd fight us like a wounded bear. A blade'll do the job easier."

Alvar pulled out his scramseaxe, knelt beside Leofric. He caught hold of Leofric's fair hair, yanked up his head, let it drop, pulled it up again. "Christ, man, you stink. Why you want to cover yourself in old ears? Like killing folk, do you? I understand that. Done some fine killing of my own. Some butchering, too. But wearing ears around when they're way past fresh is madness."

Behind me, Siward muttered a curse. "Kill him, if you're going to, Alvar. We need to find King Edward before Queen Ælfthryth does. She's likely already put Ordwulf on the hunt. And that cow-fucker knows this country like he knows his own bed."

He gave the rope a pop that cut into my throat and sent me into a fit of coughing and spluttering. "I suspect our Welshman has a good idea about King Edward's remains. Don't you, Tryff, old man?"

Meanwhile, Alvar went on yelling at the still unconscious Leofric. "Thought you'd be the king of England, you did! Once we found Edward's corpse."

Was I hearing right? Leofric king of England? I was so surprised I forgot my fear and spun around to face Siward. "What the hell?" I said.

"By St. Baglan's backside, what are you waiting for, Alvar? If we're going to get Edward's body to Lady Edith in time for the meeting of the Witan—"

Suddenly, a flaming sun must've risen in Siward's head.

He turned to me. "You've already found it, haven't you."

Straight thinking's hard when you have rope around your neck. What was all this about Lady Edith and the Witan and King Edward's body? And why did Leofric think he'd be king of England?

By then Alvar had dropped Leofric's head. But he went on yelling down at him. "You ain't gonna be no king. And you wouldn't be even if you was sane. We's had enough bad weather and worse crops. Enough Danskers raiding along the coast. We got us a throne-worthy woman now, a woman of the blood royal that'll bring England back to what it used to be when Eadgar the Peacemaker ruled."

He grabbed Leofric's hair again, yanked up his head. "And ain't no mad dog gonna marry Queen Edith. Nobody else, neither. Praise God she's a nun."

Leofric's eyelids began to flutter and he moaned a little.

Alvar cut his throat.

Next thing, it was like I was in one of those dreams where the whole world's barely moving—Alvar plodded tortoise-slow, Siward's mouth sawed up and down, the blood came out of Leofric as if it were a frozen geyser. I hovered above it all like a soul caught 'twixt heaven and hell.

The rope dragged me back to earth. "Let's go, Welshman!" Siward shouted. "Take us to Dward's body so England can be blessed with a real sovereign, one born of a king's true marriage and not of murder and incest."

That's when it finally came to me. "You two want Lady Edith to be sovereign instead of Ethelred. You're going to try and convince the Witan that she's the only one who can be consecrated because she's the one in possession of King Edward's body."

Alvar swiped his bloody scramseaxe across his thigh. "A queen full of grace, Edith'll be, a blessed woman that the Lord'll be with for ever and ever."

You ask me, no Saxon ruler, male or female, could ever be that holy. But what can you say to superstitious people? They'll believe any damn thing. And kill you if you don't, too.

Alvar pointed at me. "Some folk're too smart for their own good. They know too much."

"Our Welshman had better have been smart enough to find Edward," Siward said, just before an arrow tore into his chest.

He grunted once, then fell from the saddle, dead. Problem was, he still held the other end of the rope around my neck, so I went down, too. But Fortuna smiled and I didn't die like a throttled goose. She smiled again as I spent the next little while unloosing myself and therefore missed out on the fracas 'twixt Alvar and the attackers.

The tough old man fought hard, but even he couldn't handle half a dozen royal soldiers. By the time I righted myself, he lay with his face in the cold mud, still breathing but with Lord Ordwulf standing over him with a sword and a smirk.

For once words failed me. Just as well, too, because Ordwulf might've enjoyed killing me as much as he'd obviously enjoyed killing Siward. But instead of committing more murder, he only made sure the still dazed Alvar and I were trussed and harmless. Then he undid the hunting horn that hung from his saddle and blew a mighty blast.

An answering call came, then from around the bend in the road came soldiers, lots of them. And an ox cart big enough to haul me and Alvar, bound back to back, to Queen

Ælfthryth.

I shouted all the way that I knew where King Edward was, didn't anybody care?

CHAPTER TWENTY-TWO

We fetched up not at Corfe Gate, like I'd expected, but in the royal hall at Bere Regis. It was from there that Queen Ælfthryth ruled Dorset. And it was there, after some while jouncing our innards loose in the ox cart, that her brother Ordwulf brought me and the now fully alive ealdorman. He dumped us manacled and face down in front of Ælfthryth where she sat on a raised dais. Her son stood close by.

There, all but surrounded by a multitude of soldiers and servants, she let us sweat and fret for a while. Then she bade Ordwulf haul us to our feet so we could stand before her splendid chair like a pair of roped steers on the killing floor. But give Alvar credit, he didn't act very steer-like. He bulled his way right up to King Ethelred himself. The boy slipped behind his mother while Alvar bellowed out his fury that he, ealdorman of Wessex and Mercia, was being treated so.

Me—once I quit quivering—I just looked around to see if there wasn't a bolthole somewhere in Ælfthryth's royal butcher stall. And I needed to bolt. She'd ordered her soldiers away by now, so that only she, the king, Ordwulf, and three of the royal bodyguard remained. The guards' evil Saxon eyes never left me, even while Alvar threatened to trample their king.

I've been in Winchester's royal hall, the one King Alfred

himself raised. And I can tell you Bere Regis was much finer. Not so fine as the palaces in Cordoba and Constantinople, or some of Otto's royal halls. Nor was it as sumptuous as I'd heard tell. Still, it was damn near the size of the great cathedral at Aachen, with cedar floors that made the whole place smell like a Byzantine bazaar. It had so many lamps and candles and torches you couldn't help but notice the decorations on its limed walls—dragons slithering through intricately woven spirals, loops, whorls. Its rafters had a huge collection of animal skulls mounted on them to show off the killing prowess of the house of Alfred. Or maybe just Ælfthryth's. It was her mead hall.

While Alvar railed on, my eyes sought out the hall's few shadows for a hidden door, an unwatched store room I could somehow slip through. All I found was the queen's serving woman, Tyne, where she skulked in a corner as far away from any light as she could get.

Finally, Alvar had roared himself too hoarse to go on. Now, snorting and slobbering, he dropped to one knee and bent his neck like a good and faithful servant should. He likely thought he'd put up a pretty fine argument claiming Siward had bullied, browbeat, and badgered him into hiding King Edward's body in the marsh. "But in the end I come back for Dward. And while I was about it, I killed mad Leofric that had it in his mind he could carry Dward to Edith, marry up with her, make hisself king of England."

Ordwulf parried him. "That's as may be, my sister. But by God's grin, I wouldn't be shocked to learn Alvar and his evil confederates were responsible for Dward's death."

King Ethelred gave a little squeal, went red in the face. Ælfthryth ignored both him and Ordwulf. She cast her eel-cold eyes on the ealdorman. And smiled. "My dear Alvar, how could you have been so foolish?"

She plucked at her black dress, then at the tail of her dove-grey headdress. The woman's hands never seemed to be still. "Is being an ealdorman not enough for you? A prince of Mercia? Owning most of Gloucester? But perhaps anything can be expected from a man who has betrayed his kindred."

The king sidled up to his mother, whispered in her ear. Without turning, she waved consent. Ethelred ran the length of the hall, banged open the heavy door, streaked into the growing darkness. He never came back.

Meanwhile, the queen talked on, jeweled fingers stabbing at Alvar. "If I'm honest, I must say that what I resent most is not only that you wished to deny my son his right and his destiny, it's that you thought us, the king and me, so ill-informed as to let your wicked conspiracy come to fruition."

While Alvar took that on board, I sent up a prayer to Saint Nicholas. I'm just a thief, I reminded him, not a plotter of treason. For good measure I reminded St. Jude, too.

At least the queen hadn't thought about me yet. She was still lashing the ealdorman, whose mouth now hung slack in surprise. "Oh, yes, we knew what you planned almost from the beginning. I'm afraid Siward had to speak of it, had to strut his cunning."

Ælfthryth's pale eyes slewed toward Tyne in her dark corner. "Even if it could be to no one else but the slave in his bed."

"Don't know what you're talking about, Lady." Alvar choked, gulped, went on. "Don't know nothing about a conspiracy. I swear it. Call in my oath-helpers and I'll prove it to you."

The queen laughed. And no wonder. At a trial, the ealdorman's oath-helpers would've sworn to his innocence if he'd been caught lifting Lady Edith to the throne across Ethelred's corpse with his sword still twitching in it.

Waving Alvar into the arms of the royal guards, she then pointed a jeweled finger my way. "Let us now speak of King Edward's body with this one. Lord Ordwulf has informed me that you claim to know where it lies."

Relief spread over me like the soothing waters at Bath. "I do know. And I can tell you, when—"

Ordwulf stepped forward. His long shadow fell across his sister. "The Welshman knows no such thing. I found him wandering in a thicket not only on his own but so lost he couldn't even find his mule."

What was this now? Ordwulf found me with Alvar and Siward and Leofric's corpse beside the marsh, where Alvar's horn had brought him. Was this some scheme of Ordwulf's to keep his sister from finding out he'd conspired with them? Muddy up the water enough and you can hide a mountain of sin. But what would Ordwulf gain by making Lady Edith queen?

An even bigger question drove that out of my head and knotted up my belly—what would Ælfthryth do with me? I didn't wait for an answer. I said, "Not only, Lady, can I tell you where King Edward's body lies, I can take you right to it. And then, after I've earned your silver, you—"

The hall doors banged open again. Ethelred returning.

Or so I thought. Until behind me came an echoing, *"Hwaet!"*

I twisted around to see Wynstan with Lady Philosophy,

her reins in his hand and the two of them all but galloping around the hall's tables and benches, past the hearth, toward Queen Ælfthryth. But that was Wynstan for you. He always announced his show with every bit of tumult he could muster, even if now it was just a mule and the stringless yellow lyre he cradled in his arms. He wore a grin as big as his entrance.

Looking past him for Kyre and Beorn and little Cuthred, my glance grazed Lady Philosophy's back. And halted. Strapped on the old mule was the moss-covered little carragh that held King Edward's body.

You can guess the rest. Wynstan had King Edward, and now the others started their arse-covering lies. Ordwulf said I'd been wandering alone in the woods. Alvar swore he'd first laid eyes on me in the ox cart that had brought us to Bere Regis. "Don't know what the fellow might've got up to before that. But he sure ain't brave enough to've been looking for King Edward. Never stopped bawling all the way to here."

By now, Wynstan's grin had become a smirk so greasy I wanted to rub it off in the coals of the hearth. But I was in shackles and the lying old charlatan was beginning a long tale about the dangers he'd faced against all the wicked ones there in the woods—the female demon who'd ensnared King Edward's remains and every other evil thing that lurked behind trees, in the marsh, under the lake.

From the way Ordwulf nodded and prodded him for more, it didn't take too much wit to figure out that Wynstan had come to him at Corfe Gate ready to trade me and Crawe for ... what? During the rest of that whole long evening at Bere Regis, Wynstan never once mentioned my keg of silver pennies. On the other hand, Ælfthryth did. She said it was no longer with Wilton's bishop.

Then she went on to suggest that she and King Ethelred would be needing a skilled scop to entertain them, travel around with them, eat his fill in their royal halls. And, of course, sing their praises. And while she proclaimed it, Wynstan's grin all but cracked his chops.

So you can rest assured that King Edward's body was in the little carragh and that Wynstan got everything he wanted while I got nothing. Well, I kept my life, as Ordwulf so generously put it. And, as the queen put it, I could collect my horse from the stable at Kingston and leave unharmed. "Because you serve St. Finella's and my son is in need of the nuns' prayers." Her pale eyes flickered. "But, of course, we are all in need of their prayers."

As it turned out, Ælfthryth sure was. Nobody ever found out who—or what—killed young Edward. Nobody even asked, They certainly didn't ask Ethelred, king of England. In the end, the whole world just blamed it on wicked Queen Ælfthryth. They still do.

CHAPTER TWENTY-THREE

I'd pushed Tom Tub hard on the trip from Dorset. Now the big horse was tired. So, with only a couple of miles to go, and though I wanted to gallop all the way, I got off and led him toward Thornholt. To think over what had happened to me.

I figured Alvar, Siward, and Leofric wanted to find and destroy King Edward's body so they could claim that its absence was a sign Ethelred shouldn't be sovereign. Then they'd persuade the Witan that Lady Edith should be. Saxons will believe just about anything if it brings them more land and gold and power—and that's what the Witan would collect if they followed Alvar and Siward and Leofric. But the three couldn't manage their scheme without help. So they pulled in Wynstan and the Hunwalds. To Wynstan they promised he would be installed as the royal scop because Lady Flæda foolishly trusted him. The Hunwalds were promised vast stretches of land and, more importantly, pride of place in Edith's court.

Once the connivers learned that Ælfthryth had hired me to find the king's corpse, they decided Leofric would follow me, then grab the corpse as soon as I located it. To make absolutely sure I didn't slip out of their hands, Wynstan would keep me with him—even while, with the Thornholts' help, he tried to eliminate the queen by making her confess to Edward's murder. When that failed, Lord Hunwald had to be sacrificed and I got thrown into the crypt at Winchester for Siward to deal with.

Unfortunately, I escaped. So then Wynstan returned to the game. And, Wynstan being Wynstan, he double-crossed us all. Alvar, Siward, and Leofric had no idea that the old conniver already knew Crawe had the king's corpse.

Nor was he the only one playing by his own rules. Alvar had decided he didn't want to share the pickings with crazy Leofric and ambitious Siward. He put his own plan into motion, first arranging for Ordwulf to be hunting in the area. Then, with a few blasts of a hunting horn, he called for Ordwulf to ... um ... rescue him there in the thicket. After that, he knew he could rely on Ordwulf's murderous temper to rid him of Siward and Leofric. But Alvar, clever as he was, underestimated Wynstan.

Now my thoughts turned to what I'd tell Thrima. She expected me to return a rich man. Instead she'd have to settle for a penniless relic merchant. I might even be forced back to robbing reliquaries. I could only hope she'd take it well.

Still, it was a beautiful day. The hills were thick with sheep and cattle, the fields full of ox teams and ploughmen. The elm and beech and lime were in leaf, the scent of daffodils and dog violets tinged the air. Spring was here, and I'd be with Thrima within the hour.

Just down Thornholt's lane, I came on a churl carrying water to the plough teams. He knew me, so I asked if Thrima was in the kitchen or in the fields. He answered in a tone full of sorrow. "Gone."

"Gone? What did you mean, gone? My God, is Thrima dead?"

The churl tipped his head to one side, looked puzzled. "Not dead. 'Least, she weren't dead when she left here."

When I could speak, I said, "What do you mean, left?"

The churl stared at his shoes.

"Where'd she go?"

"Dunno."

I prayed for the strength not to rip off his head. "Does anybody know?"

He gave it some thought—if that's what goes on 'twixt English ears—'til finally, eyes still on his shit-clogged boots, he said, "Maybe. Maybe not."

I caught him round the neck and shook him like a terrier does a rat. And might surely have killed him but for an arm round my own neck. "Release the man. You can talk to me."

After I let go of the churl, and the red-haired village priest let go of me, I got some answers. The priest—his name was Father Golding—told me that a few days after Wynstan and I had left for Corfe Gate, Brother Petroc returned from Winchester. He announced that Lord Siward, as royal *consillarius*, had told him King Ethelred would pardon his father and older brother in return for Thornholt. "But he didn't. They're both dead."

Father Golding crossed himself. "Now we hear Siward's dead, too. His head's on a stake in Dorset. His body's chopped up and feeding the pigs. Didn't matter to Petroc, though. His mother neither. They left Thornholt before Easter."

Fled to Francia, I guessed. Or Brittany. Someplace safe.

But Father Golding said different. "Went to their lands up north. Took Thrima with them."

"Like a slave? Brother Petroc and Lady Bathilda took her away like a slave?"

Father Golding said he didn't think they could do that to a free Englishwoman. "She'd just be their servant, I think. Anyway, they didn't take her sons or their families. Left her acres and her oxen with them."

But I knew Saxons. They'd do most any vile thing.

My anger flared into flame then, grew so hot it all but consumed my tongue. I couldn't speak, could barely breathe. My next word seared throat, mouth, tongue, but I got it out: "Where?"

The priest shrugged. "Don't know. Only thing I heard was they took Thrima along to handle the Norskers. The ones up north, I reckon. She comes from up there, talks their language, y'know."

That gave me hope enough to say, "Maybe they'll send her home after she's dealt with the Norskers."

"I'm sure they will," the priest said, not sounding sure at all.

"What about Hunwald's hearthmen? They go, too?"

"Some. T'others still here, drinking up the lord's ale."

There was nothing left except to mount up and charge into Thornholt's mead hall. I could at least hack up a few Saxons, burn the place to the ground.

Father Golding caught me first. "Your death'll neither honor nor serve her." He pointed at a flat rock alongside the lane, handed me his water flagon.

I sat there while the fire in me lessened. But I didn't let it die. I banked it deep inside, to fan white hot when I found

Brother Petroc. Presently, I rose and thanked the priest, then knelt for his blessing, which he gave me along with the ale and cheese his wife had sent with him into the fields.

Trotting Tom away from Thornholt, I thought over what I knew. It wasn't much. A fortnight ago Brother Petroc and his mother, along with Thrima and a small host of guards, had headed north. Toward York or maybe Durham—Father Golding wasn't sure which. Hunwald had told me he owned land in both those shires, but he never said exactly where.

On the other hand, I knew the north. I'd found relics from the Cheviots to the Tyne. If Thrima was in, say, Durham, then so were St. Cuthbert's remains. And St. Aidan rested on Lindisfarne, St. Oswald in Northumbria. And in York there was the sword hand of St George. For all I knew, the Great Harp of Arthur also lay up that the way.

Perhaps my mam did, too. I hadn't forgotten about her. Of course, I hadn't.

I touched my spurs to Tom's ribs. I'd find Thrima, all right, and free her. Then I'd find my mother. I would if I had to dig up King Arthur's harp and steal every last saint in England, too.

PART II

Kingdom of All England
Anno Domini 979
Late Summer

CHAPTER ONE

The monks in Chester-le-Street were so worthless they hadn't even set up a night guard over St Oswald. All I had to do was slip inside their church-house after Compline and kick in the crypt door. The saint's coffin sat on a warped plank half sunk in the muddy floor. I cut away the coffin's hide cover, pried off the lid, and there he lay.

Or rather, there they all lay. St. Oswald's skull sits on St. Cuthbert's chest. Along with Cuthbert's gold, garnet-studded pectoral cross. My hand hovered over cross and skull a good while after I already had Oswald safely stowed in my sack. 'Twixt Oswald's holy head and that sweet little cross, I could've freed Thrima and my mam both. Throw in St. Cuthbert and I could buy half the slaves in Christendom. On the other hand, Cuthbert might've presented a problem with transport. I'd heard tell he was still whole as you and me. And maybe he was, under all the grubby linen swaddling him.

But it sure wasn't a saint that dropped a noose around my neck, threw me onto the crypt's muddy floor, then sank a heavy boot into my belly. It was a Saxon soldier's foot I puked on and another couple of Saxon soldiers that hauled me outside, where I barely got a look at them before they threw a canvas sack over my head and hoisted me onto Tom's back. The sack smelt like a sow had died in it. When I went to rip it off, one of the soldiers smacked my arm with the leaded tip of his whip. "Now, now, Welshman. You don't need to know where 'tis we're carrying you. Be more fun that way."

For them, maybe. But likely the Saxon was right about not needing to know where we were headed. Why make myself any more scared than I already was? Like the Gospel Book says, "Sufficient unto the day is the evil thereof."

Besides, I told myself, how bad could things be as long as these lads weren't horse thieves? So I settled my butt in my fine new saddle—the finest, best-cushioned one to be thieved in all England—and let Tom's smooth trot lull me to sleep.

I only woke when I heard the Saxon soldiers whispering. "Horse be worth ..." "We could say Welshman come to a bad pass at..." "You men mad? He's the queen's ... Well, you know."

By St. Valentine, had he meant what I thought he meant? I decided he had and I'd better quick-like find a reply. Queen Ælfthryth harkened to every smidgeon of scandal about herself. When she heard this—and she would—she might think I was going around saying she had a serious weakness for my charms. The queen knew her reputation and I knew what she'd do to keep it from getting worse. Being called a bishop's whore was one thing. Being a Welsh thief's was something else again.

"I ain't nothing to your queen," I said.

The three made no answer, except for what sounded like a giggle. Well, they'd think what they wanted. But if that was what they wanted to think, I'd best turn it to my advantage. I said, "If something happens to me, she'll have all your land inside a fortnight. And all your heads inside a noose."

That got me another couple thwacks with the whip-end. But I heard no more about Tom's worth, though that may only have been because we'd come to the end of our journey.

Even before they pulled the sack off my head, I knew where I was. Nowhere this side of the suburbs of Hell stinks like York. The place is nothing more than a greasy bog where two rivers meet and a lot of dirty Norskers live. It's rank even in winter and now, on this late summer day, the rivers and the bog, the streets and the roads were clogged with puke and piss and every dead thing you can imagine. It reeked. And, oh God, the flies.

We'd pulled up at the gates of York Minster—where the stink of the town was a little weaker because the monks' lair lay a bit above the rest of the cesspool. Or maybe their incense just reeked stronger.

We were met by another of those doe-eyed thegns the English army seemed full of. I hoped this one wouldn't turn homicidal like Leofric had. "Get your filthy Welsh arse inside," he said.

I said I wasn't going anywhere until I knew Tom would be properly taken care of. "And returned."

"If you're implying that Englishmen would steal your horse ..."

I wasn't implying anything, I was outright saying they

would. But before I could tell them that, another man came through the gate—a tall man with buck teeth, who I hadn't seen in more than year. Now I stood in real peril.

"See to the Welshman's horse," Lord Ordwulf said. "It was the gift of King Eadgar Peacemaker."

That bit of information made the pretty one take hold of Tom's reins, while three other soldiers—no doubt important men back home in High Mudhole or Nosepickings-upon-Avon—went through the minster gate, looking worried. How, they likely wondered, could they have murdered their chances with the royal house of Eadgar by doing something as natural as teasing a Welshman?

Ordwulf made no move to go back inside, just pulled himself to his full height and ran a dirty fingernail along his teeth. If he remembered the black eye and split lip I'd given him in Winchester, I couldn't tell. But I knew I wouldn't be throwing any head butts or fast fists here in York. My hands were still shackled, Tom was being led away. Worse, my neck sack—with my special herbs, my lucky rock, my dice, and my sliver of St. Veronica in it—had disappeared. Along with two cut pennies.

Grabbing my elbow Ordwulf marched me away from the gate and onto the lane's grassy verge, well apart from the minster's walls. "Don't be concerned about your belongings. We're not thieves," he said, stressing the word "we."

But whatever he said and however he said it, I was still his prisoner. Again. What did Ordwulf want with me this time? Wasn't it enough I'd been cheated out of King Edward's remains, not even getting a bounty for finding him in the first place?

I started to ask Ordwulf that—and add that I'd appreciate

it if he'd stop kidnapping me. But a terrible notion struck me. Had Ordwulf heard the wicked gossip about me and Queen Ælfthryth? I said, "Listen, my lord, I've never said nothing nasty about me and the queen your sister. There was nothing to say. I swear it by—"

Ordwulf waved that away. "Apparently, however, you occupy some singular spot in her heart. And by the Holy Foot Stool, I can't think why. In any case, however, she has asked me to once again offer you employment."

I wanted to let out a refusal garnished with every curse I ever knew, then repeat them all several times and in several languages. But by now I was too scared to even utter a brief, solid English "no."

"Recently," Ordwulf said, "I've been back to the crypt in Wareham church. The one where my sister ordered us to put King Edward's remains."

I always wondered why Edward hadn't been taken to Glastonbury Abbey like his father, or to Winchester Cathedral to lie in regal grandeur with King Alfred, the founder of his royal line. Instead, they'd parked him in humble little Wareham with hardly a word said or a bell rung.

Now, though, in a tone reverent as a priest's, Ordwulf said, "King Edward is gone from Wareham Church."

How many times could somebody's body go missing? Even a king's?

I was about to ask about an angel and a stone rolled away, when a terrible notion sprang up inside me. Ordwulf's hand rested on the pommel of his sword. He might be blaming me for that empty coffin.

He said, "A quaking of the earth knocked over the king's

coffin. Out fell a man's body, shroud half undone. He'd gone mostly to bone, but he still had hair. Blond hair, yes. Only it wasn't curly like King Edward's."

"Strange things can happen in coffins." As I had cause to know.

"And his royal ring was missing."

I laughed. "Well, that solves everything. His guards—"

"Shit and onions, man! Listen to me! The guards didn't steal the king's ring. Or put a straight-haired man in his coffin. His 'guards,' as you call them, were the nuns of Wareham. His body lay in their church-house. And now it's gone!"

My scalp started to crawl. Ordwulf wanted something from me. I whipped out the only shield I had. My tongue. "So what if he's not there? You don't need him any more. Ethelred's already been consecrated. He's the lawful and anointed king. No one can dispute that … Can they?"

The answer must have been "yes" because Ordwulf decided to explain the situation further. "We aren't sure just who lay in that bare-arsed box in Wareham. The problem began in Bere Regis, when my sister the queen said the body in that little carragh was Edward."

Quick-like, I said, "I'm telling you, my lord, it was King Edward I found with the necromancer. I recognized him from the time I spent in his father's court. It was him Wynstan Wing-tongue brought to the queen."

At least I thought it was. But maybe Wynstan switched corpses. There were plenty to choose from in Crawe's lair. Surely, though—

"You must've taken a look at the body yourself."

Ordwulf let out a volley of curses. Give the man his due,

he was one of the mightiest cursers I'd ever heard north of the Holy Land. "May hellfire consume me, I didn't look. I took a woman's word and may half a hundred shithouses fall on me for being that kind of fool."

What I finally picked out from betwixt the falling shithouses and the several references to Satan's cow was that only Queen Ælfthryth had looked at the body Wynstan presented her with. Later, she admitted that what she saw in the boat was the half-preserved corpse of a young man who had blond hair and wore a gold ring. When she bent to kiss the ring, she'd seen ... She couldn't remember. Was it set with a blue-purple stone? Was it the king of England's ring?

Now I joined Ordwulf in the curses until we could neither invent nor recall another. "So," he said, "you understand the problem."

The problem we both understood was Wynstan Wing-tongue. A flash of anger burned through me. But as it cooled, I began to understand the wicked riddle of Wynstan and the king's ring. The whole business was a plot to lure some unsuspecting fool into helping him earn his way back to royal favor. The fool had turned out to be me.

After the Thornholts were arrested, Wynstan had shown me a thick gold ring with a blue-purple stone. I'd often seen such a ring on the hand of Ethelred's father, so I recognized it as belonging to the king of England. Crawe must have taken the ring after she came on King Edward dead in that Dorset marsh and later given it to Wynstan. After he'd disappeared on me there in the Purbeck Hills, he'd returned it to Edward's body for me to see in Crawe's foul cemetery. All this so he could present the king's corpse to Queen Ælthryth, complete with royal ring.

Now I knew what to do about Wynstan. I thrust out my shackled hands. "Free me and I'll bring King Edward to you, my lord. And I'll only charge expenses."

I paused. "But first you'll help me find my woman. Be she at the end of the earth."

In what I hoped was a smile, Ordwulf showed teeth. He'd got what he wanted but he waited a long moment before he said, "Be careful where you search. And be careful of that damn addled scop. He has powerful friends."

It was a serious warning, of course. Ordwulf was nobody's fool. He knew I'd go after Wynstan and he knew I'd find him. I just hoped Ordwulf would take care of the old bastard's "powerful friends," Ealdorman Alvar and the other thegns who I heard still wanted to crown Lady Edith queen of England.

The deal made and royal generosity proclaimed, Ordwulf unshackled me.

"What about Thrima?" I wanted to know.

He pointed toward his pavilion set up in the shade of the minster wall. "Come. We can drink some of dirty-arsed York's fine ale and I can tell you where she is."

I dared not ask how he knew. Royals have their sources, and the less you inquire into them, the better. Besides, I didn't altogether trust the accuracy of those sources. Ordwulf might be sending me on a search as doomed to failure as a quest for the Great Harp of Arthur.

The pavilion, for all its bright flags and polished shields, was likely the one Ordwulf used every third month when he brought his tenants up from Cornwall to do their military service. I say that because when Ordwulf dropped the outside flap, we were two big men perched on three-legged leather stools and squeezed into what was barely better than an army tent. At least he served good ale.

He said Thrima was in Iceland. Said Brother Petroc had sold her like a slave to a Norsker jarl, who carried her to the top of the world so she could cook some decent food for the goat-worshipping heathen.

I jumped to my feet, shouted that I'd be off tomorrow, "To fetch her home. And with one of your ambassadors to help me sort out the Norsker, lest I serve him up for lung and lights."

Ordwulf wasn't a man for smiling, but now his lips drew across his big teeth in what looked for all the world like a grin. "That's a fine plan, Welshman. And I'll give you all the help you need. But not tomorrow."

His grin vanished. "Tomorrow—no, today—you'll be off to find King Edward."

I raved and railed. I raged and ranted. Until finally the fury drained out of me and I went calm as a mill pond. Then my mind started to grind and I soon figured out why Ordwulf had come to me. I said, "You don't want anybody else to know Edward might not be in Wareham. That's why you couldn't just unpen your hall men, never mind the Saxon army, and root up the whole of Britain looking for him. Right?"

Ordwulf shifted on the leather stool, said nothing.

It was my turn to grin. "The price, my lord, will be very high."

CHAPTER TWO

I left York the next morning, with plenty of royal gold in my saddlebags and Ordwulf's sworn oath to help me free Thrima when the time came. I was headed to St. Finella's, where the nuns ended up taking Crawe so they could cure her of her fondness for dead bodies.

By now I knew she was Wynstan's woman—or had been back when they were young. Maybe the nuns could, would, restore her to be the "Joy" he'd sung about all the way across Poole Bay. But I needed to find her, in whatever state she was in. Because if anybody'd know where Wynstan and a corpse had gone, it would be Crawe.

I don't like taking the king's highways. They're too crowded with thieves and clerics. But now I wished a highway ran southwesterly from York instead of nothing but steep paths and rutted tracks. It took Tom and me over a week to reach Manchester. Then, what with two days of hard rain, almost another to reach Cheshire.

Just after the Feast of the Nativity of the Virgin, we came to St. Finella's village—a couple of dozen farmsteads strung along a lane with a mill at one end and a green at the other. Its grain had already been harvested. Only the gleaners now filled the fields. Along the hillsides sheep and cattle grazed. In the woods on the ridge tops, herds of pigs no doubt still foraged

The convent itself sat half way up the valley's northern slope under a ridge wooded as far as the eye could see. The villagers called those woods the Dredley and said they were full of elves and night-walkers and all manner of evil spirits. Maybe so, but the Dredley had done a good job of hiding me from a killer when first I'd come to St. Finella's. The sisters had hired me to find out who was murdering nuns and even trying to steal St. Finella herself. It hadn't taken me long to ferret out the rat and the nuns were so grateful they made me their radman, their armed and mounted escort—in other words, their bodyguard and general henchman. It seemed like answered prayers at the time because a man in my business needed all the help he could get. Now, looking up at the convent with its crumbling rock wall and dreary brown buildings, I halfway wished I'd stayed that lordless man who had nothing to lose.

As I rode past, some of the folk in the village recognized me and hollered out greetings and hoots about my fancy new clothes—Norsker-made in York and very fine indeed. The churls also called invitations to join them in their alehouse come evening. I waved back, said I'd see them later. But I wanted to be away from St. Finella's quick as I could, once I found out where Wynstan had got to. A night drinking with that lot could turn into three days face down on the alehouse floor.

At the oaken convent gate, I dismounted and knocked. Its little wicket opened to show Sister Hild's glowering face. "What do you want?"

Had the poor old thing finally gone senile? I tapped a coaxing finger on the sill of the wicket. "Sister, for God's sake, I'm your radman."

"And you left us—the ones you were God-sworn to protect —in the middle of a black bog with a hell-hag poking us with Satan's own staff and howling for every demon in the Deep."

I didn't know about the demon part, but I did know Crawe's staff was barely more than a stick she'd twisted off a willow. I was about to say as much when the wicket slammed shut on my finger.

I sucked on the finger, trying not to curse the old harridan all the way to Dorset and back. I'd have to find Father Langdun, the nuns' chaplain, get him to intervene for me. But as I turned to go down to the village, the gate creaked open. Pulling its rope handle was Sister Hrothbeort, a grin of welcome on her round face. Behind her stood Prioress, beckoning me inside. Sister Hild stood there, too, clearly annoyed that she'd been outranked in the decision to receive St. Finella's servant at its door.

She was considerably more annoyed when I explained why I was there. Her response came as quick and lethal as an arrow to the eye. "You most certainly cannot speak to Crawe. She is too close to being healed. I have mixed lupine and pollegian with bramble apple and holy water for her to drink. We all have prayed. Now she is almost ready to renounce the Devil and his evil craft for the ways of God. Ready to throw down Satan's staff and don the new clothes of Christ Everlasting."

"She smells better, too," said Sister Hrothbeort.

Before Sister Hild could go up in holy smoke, Prioress began to explain what a grand healing Sister had made of it and that Crawe attended almost every church service and had even taken up spinning the miles of wool produced by

St. Finella's six herds of sheep.

I gave them the sweet, lingering smile I reserve for nuns and children. "I'll talk to her now."

"Well, no," Prioress said, "we can't allow that. Perhaps in a few weeks, a month at the outside. Meantime, Mother Eada will be so glad to see you. She's with her unicorn presently, but after Sext she'll ... "

I stopped listening and started plotting. I'd have to see the abbess and that cursed one-horned billy goat she called a unicorn. It'd always been a puzzlement to me that if Sister Hild was such a good healer, why hadn't she cured Mother Mad of her sundry delusions? Like the one about the huge flop-eared, long-nosed grey beast she thought had delivered St. Finella to the convent? Or that the little hedgehog she carried around on her shoulder was a tame imp of Satan?

But the abbess was cousin to the king of England. And since the convent's every blessing flowed from the royal coffers, Sister Hild and the rest needed Mother Eada. Besides, she pretty much left the running of St. Finella's to Prioress, and Prioress was a good steward. A tough one, too. But I knew that when on the rare occasions their abbess did issue an order, the sisters were vowed to obey.

That's why I hadn't come to St. Finella's empty-handed. Mad Mother Eada might be, but she had a collection of relics fine as any north of Winchester Cathedral. And I knew. I'd found half of them for her and sold her the rest. Today, tucked up tight in a box on Tom's chestnut rump, lay the sword hand of St George. The saint had wanted to leave York Minster for a long time and now here he was.

The nuns kept me cooling my heels in their guest lodge 'til they got good and ready to see me. Down in Winchester, the monastic guest lodges were full of ornate furniture and soft pillows. St. Finella's was just a poky little room where an oak table and two stiff wicker chairs stood on the bare rock floor and a three-legged stool sat in a corner. It had no windows, only a couple of smoky oil lamps stuck in the wall that showed the heavy door leading into the cloister yard. The room's only decoration was a gilded tapestry covering the inside wall, handsome enough, but showing a black-clad horseman entering a dark wood.

A dim, dull room. Just like the rest of the place. Once I found Thrima I'd never come back. I could earn our mead by bounty hunting, even—God help me—stealing some more saints. As I swore it for the hundredth time, a village girl brought in a brass tray that bore cups and a crock of strong cider. When the girl had set it on the table and gone, Prioress swept through the cloister door, Sister Hild limping behind.

While I explained what I wanted with Crawe, Sister Hild was in her usual pose, blackthorn stick planted in front of her, hands on its knob, chin on her hands, eyes closed. Sound asleep maybe, though you never knew—a week later she could pound you with your exact words. It was the reason I'd hesitated to tell the sisters the whole truth. Of course, I had to tell them the body that had lain in Wareham was missing. Otherwise, they'd have no part of my feud with Wynstan. But I didn't have to tell them Lord Ordwulf now feared that body might never have been Edward's.

Prioress pressed me hard about the whole business. "What kind of miracles have come to pass in Wareham?"

"Healings," I said.

"What kind?"

"The usual. Crippled folk. Lepers. A blind woman."

Prioress finished her third cup of cider, poured a fourth. "Lepers? Was King Edward's own mother taken to Wareham?"

I shook my head.

Sister Hild reared up like an angry mare. "Ælfthryth and her brother had the cure for poor Flæda and did not use it?"

I sent up praise to St. Eligius. Here was an angry mare I could ride. "And they can't 'til I find Wynstan and return King Edward to his grave. Then I'm sure the folk at Wareham church will be happy to heal Lady Flæda."

"Come, Prioress." Sister Hild struggled to her feet. "We are going to the apple orchard."

But in the end Prioress didn't go. Instead, the abbess did. The nuns had to tell Mother Eada about the situation, and when she finally understood, she ordered Prioress to stay behind. "You have other duties," Mother said, looking a bit quizzical. "Don't you?"

I was prepared for a long siege of it with Crawe. Even if she knew where Wynstan had gone and where he might've hidden King Edward, she wouldn't give up the knowledge easily. On top of that, chances were she'd lie. So I was willing to use every possible weapon short of catapult and battering ram—in other words, deception, treachery, and starvation. That's why I took along the nuns.

The apple orchard smelled like the convent cider tasted, sweet and tart and strong. At its edge Crawe sat on a little bench, wool-loaded distaff tucked under her arm, hands twisting the grey wool as she pulled it from the distaff. The attached spindle whirled at her side.

Several skeins of yarn lay in a basket at her feet, evidence of her morning's monotony. Once, when I asked my mam how she could do the same thing over and over, she told me the Gospel Book said that a virtuous wife works wool and flax with eager hands. How my father laughed when he heard that.

Sister Hild gave Crawe a sharp *"Benedicte,"* then sat beside her in the wicker chair I'd carried up the hill. Meanwhile, Mother Eada wafted among the trees, headdress catching on a branch and falling back to show copper-colored hair twisted into a thick braid. I'd never realized what a fine-looking woman she was.

I took a moment to appreciate her, then turned to Crawe. In her faraway youth she might have been called fine looking, but now she had a face coarse and creased as a peasant's sock. Her eyes, though, were an unfaded green that seemed to know me right down to my unshriven soul.

Maybe that's why I wasn't surprised when she spoke to me in Welsh. *"Ych y fi, eto!"*

So Crawe was Welsh. I'd been afraid of that.

"As you say, we meet again." I said it in English because I didn't want to give her an excuse to rake up kin like we Cymry always seem to do. "But let's not insult the nuns by speaking in a foreign tongue."

She smiled a bit as she said, "So proper now, *fy machgen.*"

Even as a little fellow I hated being called "my boy," never mind "proper." And why was she speaking in Welsh now? She hadn't when we met before.

"Where's Wynstan?" I asked.

Crawe laughed and wrapped a length of yarn onto the spindle. "How would I know that, *fy machgen?*" She slapped the spindle against her thigh, setting it a-whirl once more.

Then she turned to Sister Hild, "*Ein bachgen—*"

Now it was "our boy." But Sister didn't care to be dragged into all the sweetness. She shot a threatening forefinger at Crawe and told her to speak in English.

Crawe winked at Sister and laughed some more. "*Mi adwaen lwynog er nas goddiweddwyf.*" I know a fox though I cannot overtake one.

"What the hell do you mean by that?" I asked her.

She went on spinning. And laughing. "Wynstan has his own hiding places, a hundred in a hundred lands." At least she'd said it in English.

"Don't be silly," Sister Hild said. "A man may have hiding places, but not a hundred. Speak the truth. Where has he gone?"

What was this now? Sister Hild on my side? I thought she'd have championed her patient or at least told me to treat the poor woman with padded tongs. What I didn't expect was for Sister to up and demand answers from this unhealed waker-of-the-dead.

Crawe pulled up the spindle, took the distaff out from under her arm, put it all in the basket. In Welsh, she said, "I'd like to talk to our countryman alone."

Our countryman?

"Well, you can't," Sister said.

Crawe turned toward Hild, eyes gleaming black as a snake's. The two women stared at each other for a long time. Finally, Crawe turned back to me. In Welsh she said, "A bard must follow his lord, stand with him, praise him. A wife must do the same. And a sister—"

"Enough of that!" Hild shouted. "Just tell us where

Wynstan's got to."

We heard no more about bards or wives or sisters. On the other hand, if Crawe couldn't talk of them, she didn't want to say anything at all. She crossed her arms, pursed her skinny lips, and closed her eyes.

I began to pace in front of the two women, kicking up moss and dirt, digging at a tree root. "Don't you have some potion you can give her, Sister? Something that'll make her tell us truth."

Sister Hild pulled the blackthorn stick across her knees. "The only thing that will pry the truth out of this one is a red-hot sliver of iron under her fingernail."

That so surprised me so much I couldn't speak. 'Specially when she asked me to go down to the village and get the blacksmith. "And tell him to bring along his farrier's forge."

Just below the band of Crawe's headdress, a line of sweat broke out. But she still said nothing.

Mother Eada came out of the trees, nose wrinkled as she chewed a not-quite-ripe apple. She listened to the argument for a while, then tossed away the apple and laid her hand on Crawe's shoulder. "Warblers are on the Dorset heaths now, and stone chat and linnets. You could fly there."

Sister Hild understood Mother Mad immediately. "Eada, by all the saints, this woman is yet unhealed. And why would a Welshwoman want to go to Dorset, anyway?"

"It may be," Mother Eada said, "that Dorset is her *wyrd*, as much as it is for the birds of autumn, and we must bow—"

I hoped this wasn't going where I was afraid it might. The nuns' arguments about religion wearied me. If this one went like all the rest, Hild would talk about how not Fate but God's justice ruled the world. Then Free Will would come up and St. Augustine would be heard from, and Pelagius. Words such as "heresy" would start flying. Lord, what a bore. You ask me, it's what comes of teaching women to read.

But if an argument was afoot, Crawe cut it off. "Dorset?"

Mother Eada reached up to touch the hedgehog that usually rode on her shoulder. But today she'd left it in the little menagerie that stood by the convent's south wall. So she picked up Crawe's hand and stroked it like it was one of her creatures. Me, I wouldn't have touched Crawe if the Archangel himself bade me to.

"Tell us," the abbess said, "where Wynstan has gone and I will let you wing home like the linnet. With enough silver to build your nest and a promise from the king my cousin that you will never be hunted again."

My jaw dropped and so did Sister Hild's. But before we could get our mouths back in motion, Mother Eada said, "Once you tell us where Wynstan is, you will stay at St. Finella's until Tryff finds him and returns him here with King Edward's remains. Then—and only then—can you fly away home."

She paused to let Crawe peck at that—and me to wonder when she'd gone so lucid. "If Wynstan doesn't return with King Edward—or if he doesn't return at all—you will stay here at St. Finella's for the rest of your life."

The abbess dropped Crawe's hand and said, "Or perhaps you would rather have us send you back to Wales, to Aberffraw."

I didn't know what Crawe had done in Wales, or who she'd done it to, but now her hand went to her breast and her face turned gallows grey. Still, I figured sending her there would be a better solution than trying to keep her at St.

Finella's.

Gazing out at the valley, I said, "Crawe could escape from here easy, disappear round the ridge-end simple as the road does. And be in Chester before you know it."

Mother Eada's brow knitted up. "What would she do there, a woman alone?"

Sister Hild and I were rescued by the minster bell sounding Vespers. The abbess said she'd talk more to Crawe afterwards. But afterwards the unicorn escaped and everyone turned out to find him. Eventually he was discovered in the villagers' sheep herd trying to work his wiles on a one-eyed ewe. By then darkness had fallen and Crawe was packed off to bed in her little room in the nuns' dormitory.

The next morning she was gone.

I cursed a while, of course, but it was mostly for show because I didn't think it would take long to find her. We all agreed that she'd headed for the Dredley, though for what reason we couldn't fathom. She didn't have King Edward with her. Or, the nuns swore, anything else she could bury up there. Sister Hild suggested she might be searching for a sprig of nightshade or even henbane to use in her necromancy.

"She'll find none in this part of England," Sister added. "But that won't keep her from looking."

The nuns should send in a couple of churls, I said. "They won't have any trouble catching her."

But the churls refused. Down to a man, they said the nuns had no right to put them in the way of elves or demons or wakers-of-the-dead. And Father Langdun agreed. His own solution was to call in the Exorcist. For her part, Prioress thought someone should go to the monks at St. Finella Minor on the other side of the ridge. They'd surely help. I said not to bother. Those eunuchs would only throw up their manicured hands and lock their monastery gate.

"Well, she can't get too far," Sister Hild said.

We'd already found out Crawe had torn the gilded tapestry off the refectory wall and, in the starless night, made her way down to the village mill. There, she dumped the flour out of half a dozen sacks, then tossed her shoes and old clothes behind the alehouse. Now she'd be wearing flour sacks, the tapestry, and a pair of oxblood Spanish boots she stole from the stable. My Spanish boots.

I had no choice but to go after her.

Later that morning the churls finally did their duty and turned out to look for Crawe. They didn't find her. How could a lone woman on foot in unfamiliar territory slip past half a hundred men and dogs, every one of them born to the land they searched? I'll tell you how. Cowardice, craven cowardice. The villagers were terrified, petrified, scared shitless. And of what? A mere woman. But that's Saxons for you.

So I had to go into the Dredley on my own. Frightened? Sure. And clinging to Tom Tub, my face likely as white as the blaze down his. But though I'm not the world's best tracker, even a babe barely out of swaddling clothes could've followed Crawe—for a while, anyway. She'd left behind broken bushes and footprints sunk deep into the forest floor. Then, in one of those treeless openings that even the thickest forest holds, the prints disappeared. I circled the gap again and again. Nothing. Crawe seemed to have vanished like the will o' the wisp.

At least I could hear a faint sound—the convent bells, which were rung at intervals whenever someone wandered into the Dredley. I followed them home.

Likely, so had Crawe. And then left St. Finella's like

everyone else—by the king's highway, the moon and stars for light. I don't know how she got out of the Dredley. Maybe she doubled back over her own tracks. But I had no time to curse myself for the kind of fool who'd let such a thing slip past his notice. Not after talking to one of St. Finella Minor's monks, anyway.

He'd been up early looking for a stray cow and had seen a woman strolling along the Roman road to Chester. "Fairly a-drip in gaudy clothes, she was, and big red boots. I figured her for a nun gone over the wall. That's how come I quick-like hied myself right over here, tell you about her."

He *hadn't* hied himself any too quick-like. "Had to find the cow, didn't I?"

If Crawe was heading in the direction of Chester, then Chester was exactly where she wanted to go. She'd traveled all over with Wynstan and knew she could catch a ship there. I had no doubt, either, that she knew where Wynstan was.

By then, it was past noon. I got ready to leave for Chester straightaway, with plenty of vittles, a pile of silver—and, presently, an oxcart full of nuns. Sister Hild insisted she had to go along so she could minister to Crawe. Sister Hrothbeort volunteered to drive the oxcart. Prioress' excuse was that St Finella's needed to lay in another tun of wine.

Before Mother Eada decided to pull rank and join in, all I could do was put the spurs to Tom. Naturally, my big horse made Chester long before the nuns.

And naturally I decided I didn't want to share Crawe or her knowledge with the nuns. In Chester, I could easily use my relic thief's tricks to hide from them. And, just as easily, find Crawe. I'd soon have King Edward, no matter where Wynstan had hidden him.

Chester's a busy trading town on the River Dee, guarded by high red sandstone walls and stout Bonewaldesthorne's Tower. It has a mint and a cathedral and scores of merchants looking to sell and spend. Cloth, salt, metalwork—slaves, too—come there, then go on to Dublin and Reykjavik and wherever else Norskers have bloodied their swords.

I knew the town well, for a couple of reasons. I'd helped St. Werburg find a home in its cathedral, then come back when King Eadgar accepted submission from the Celtic kings—Iago of Gwynedd, Kenneth of Strathclyde, Malcolm of Cumbria, four or five more. He made them row him around on the River Dee, himself the steersman. That was a sight to behold, I can tell you. Still, I thanked St. David that my uncle didn't sit on one of those Saxon oar-benches.

Crowded as Chester always was, the nuns would stay at its minster, then have no trouble finding men to search for Crawe—and me. The only place I could safely hide was in Bertha the Bald's brothel. Nobody knew whether or not Bertha was truly bald because nobody'd got the headdress off her long enough to find out. Not recently, anyhow. Or so I heard when I asked which of the whorehouses strung along the river was hers.

I'd first met Bertha when we were skinny youngsters just starting out in this fallen world. She'd acquired real substance since then. I barely recognized the big, confident woman that greeted me at the whorehouse door. For her part, she said she'd know "that monster nose of yourn anyplace. Come in, you Welsh vermin. Gertrud! Get the man some mead. And don't bring that horse piss you served last night, hear?"

The mead the girl brought was a cut above horse piss, though barely. Otherwise, Bertha was a good hostess—and, I knew, a well-connected one. She'd have me on a ship bound for wherever I wanted before the nuns even passed through Chester's eastern gate.

I wanted a ship because by now I'd worked out where Crawe was headed. When she first came to St. Finella's, she'd tried to escape. But the nuns told me that instead of heading into the Dredley, she took the sheep paths along the side of the steep, rocky hill. It didn't work. She ended up bouncing down the hill on her head. After a shepherd found her and carried her back to the convent, she lay in a fitful sleep for days and talked. And talked and talked.

Sister Hild said Crawe seemed to be trying to communicate with Wynstan. She would call out, "Hear me, Wynstan!" Then she'd start a well-known Welsh story but never finish. "The fox stands above the rainbow rocks. Endless sea to the west and grey isles rising from the brine, the whole of Anglesey behind. He sees the prince seized by a fleet of Irish."

"That story's well known?"

Sister Hild ignored me. "Then Crawe would cry out, 'Hear me, Wynstan? I am there. I am there.' And she'd add, 'Tell the man the story. He will find me.'"

Sister said she had begun to think Crawe spelled out the place where she and Wynstan were headed. And maybe she was right. I'd thought the poem Wynstan sang in the hall at Bere Regis rather odd for the occasion. It was a riddle, whose answer is a sea-storm. I'd wondered just what heaving waves and shouting mere-whales had to do with King Edward. And for sure what did searching out vast caverns in the sea have to do with Queen Ælfthryth? And why had Wynstan so lavishly praised St. Patrick, not exactly your bona fide Saxon saint?

I hadn't lingered on Wynstan's peculiar poems there in the queen's hall. But now I realized, *primus*, Wynstan was most likely in Ireland, or headed there. And, *secundus*, I had only to find Crawe, then follow her to him.

I also had to get to the wretched woman before the nuns did. Fortunately, they'd be a long time getting to Chester in that pokey little ox cart, and even when they did they'd be talking to the clerics over at the cathedral. Me, I talked to Bertha.

That's how the following morning I found out Crawe had caught a ride with a churl from one of St. Finella's outlying crofts. He'd shown up in Chester with silver in his pouch. And this a man that had never had so much as a spare turnip to sell. Bertha, who always figured it paid to keep an eye on the competition, told me she knew he'd spent the night at Wily Wilma's place. I went right over there, fixing to beat Crawe's whereabouts out of him. But he was such a puny thing I settled on a bribe, a very small one.

The little scoundrel stared at the pair of cut pennies I slapped onto his palm. "They give me a lot more'n this."

I didn't bother to ask who "they" were, just added another cut penny to his collection, then another. When his fingers still didn't close around the coins, I closed mine around his skinny neck. He saw his mistake. "Come at me on the lower bridge, they did. Near run me right off it. Could be sleeping in the River Dee right now."

I pointed out that right now he was nearer death than he'd ever been on that bridge. "Who came at you?"

"Them nuns. And the old one—somebody ought tell the bishop about that'n—she laced into me with her stick while t'others grabbed the floury woman right off my cart. Then they throwed down some pennies—took off home, I reckon."

Why, dear Lord, wasn't I in Italy? A sensible land, where nuns were kept behind thick walls. Permanently.

But even English nuns have convent walls to shield them, and my nuns were likely headed toward them right now. I'd have to catch them on the road and snatch Crawe away. Only she might be reluctant to come with me. And anyhow, did I want to swoop down like some highway bandit? On the other hand, did Crawe want to go back to St. Finella's and learn how to be a proper Christian? Good thing I knew a way to solve all these problems.

The three rascals I hired to kidnap Crawe swore by St. Andrew that they'd never harm any woman, never mind a nun. They were brothers, and the eldest, a tow-headed young fellow with a thick white scar where his mustache should've been, was one of Bertha's customers. He said, "I never hurt one of your girls, did I?"

Bertha was raking smooth the straw in one of her more expensive stalls. "Nor did much else to 'em," she said. She leaned on her rake and added, "But he's good at other things, Tryff. Hire him and you'll get fine service. From his little brothers, too."

So I sent the three of them after the nuns. And got fine service. They came back long before dark, with Crawe lashed tight to a brown mule and screaming for help in both Welsh and English. No one in Chester paid her much attention. They'd seen bound women before, some wild with anger, others mad with grief.

Of course, Bertha didn't want to disturb business, but she let me stash Crawe in her stable. The brothers, all a-grin and pleased pink with themselves, said if I ever had another such chore, I should sure call on them. Said they knew Chester cathedral altar to doorstep, roof to crypt. "In case," they added with sly grins, "St. Werburg wants to move again."

After I made sure they hadn't harmed the nuns, I gave them a couple more coins and sent them on their way. At the gate to the stable yard, the oldest brother turned and called out, "Forgot to tell you. Them nuns is on the way back here. And that big 'un at the ox reins looked mad enough to eat a whole herd of oxes."

Meanwhile, Bertha—there was a good woman for you—had stripped Crawe of my Spanish boots, then pulled the ropes off her, too. Now she was trying to explain that I wasn't going to sell her for a slave. "And no," Bertha said, "you ain't for me, neither. Not that I'd have you."

When we finally took Crawe to the comfort of Bertha's bower, with its carved cedar chairs and silken wall hangings, she at last settled down. And settled even more after we got a pint or two of ale in her and I told her for the third time she was free to find Wynstan. I figured I'd wait a while before I said I'd be going along.

"You know Welsh. Let's talk in it," I said in Welsh, slewing my eyes toward Bertha as if she were just a stupid English tavern maid and not a businesswoman who did as much commerce with Cymry as Saxon. Bertha played along, slathering salve on Crawe's rope burns and trying to look like she didn't understand a thing.

By then my anger with Wynstan was burning my soul like

the ropes had burnt Crawe. But I quelled it long enough to call him "old friend" and "dear man." And, of course, to say "help you find him."

Crawe could've believed me. Maybe she did, maybe she didn't. In any case she was no fool. She recognized the easy path. I'd provide her protection on the journey, transport, too. When we got to Wynstan, she said, we'd see where the truth lay.

We'd be westward bound, she told me, so through Bertha I found a salt merchant headed to Dublin. For a price, that Saxon thief agreed to put us ashore wherever I told him. Meantime, I let Crawe think she was the one giving the orders on the merchant's solid, Norsker-made little cargo ship. Nor had it taken much to convince her. Necromancers seem to believe they can command the living as well as the dead. And the merchant was paid plenty not to tell her any different.

I reckoned my business with Wynstan wouldn't take all that long, so I left Tom in Bertha's stable. She'd treat him well and not try to sell him to some swindling Irish horse trader.

Such a good woman was Bertha. But we'd known long before that our stars would never align. Still, when I left, the taste of regret lingered on our tongues.

As the salt merchant cast off next morning in a still-starry dawn, I knew Fortuna would be at my right hand. Sure enough, we made good time up the Dee with the four sailors and me at the oars, then caught the tide to spill us into the river's estuary and, soon, into the Irish Sea itself.

The ocean's a fast road and usually much safer than the

king of England's highways. But as the morning went on, I began not to like the look of the thick grey waves and the dark, drooping clouds. The wind had picked up, too, and swung round so it came out of the north. It smelled of the ice packs of Ultima Thule.

The waves grew higher, rougher. And before long rain like mountain hail came at us. We rushed past islands grey and flat as drowned rats. Now Crawe cried out that God was punishing her for what she did with the bodies of the dead and the rest of us would be caught up in His vengeance. Not taking any chances on God's wrath, I suggested to the merchant that he bid his steersman put ashore as soon as we could. His lip curled at my cowardice. But after more silver changed hands, we headed toward the nearest cove. Through the rain, with dark cliffs looming above, it looked no bigger than Thrima's feather bed.

At the mouth of the cove, the steersman—what a mariner he was in that mean weather!—dropped sail, let the surf take us onto a sandy beach even softer and more welcome than Thrima's bed. I tumbled out of the ship, sank my knees in the sand and gave thanks for a safe landing. The salt merchant and his men did the same, but Crawe shook her fist into the storm and yelled words I won't translate from the Welsh, save to say she asked the Almighty why he'd spared the crew and me instead of providing her with a whole clutch of fresh corpses.

I wanted to throttle Crawe like I wanted to throttle Wynstan. Fortunately, the English merchant and his men laughed when they heard her cries. Misheard her, I should say. Their Welsh was so weak they thought she was one of those folk who call down the lightning on themselves to save their village from its fury. They began to treat her like the wise-women they'd known as boys, the kind that'd level a curse on your *tad* when he beat you or turn the lord's cats into savage, night-prowling dragons that'd ravage his daughters and pull down his hall.

The sailors pried the tenting off the ship to make Crawe a little hut to keep off the rain. Then they gave her their own blankets, their rations, too. Me, I went and lay down in the lee of a big rock, pulled my cloak tight around me so I wouldn't rise up in my sleep and murder the woman. In the morning I woke to find that the storm had passed. The ship, though, was gone—along with the salt merchant and his men. And, of course, Crawe.

CHAPTER FOUR

I had no idea where we'd landed. The storm could've blown us all the way to Ireland. Or, for all I knew, to the Norsker lands that lay even beyond the Faroes. Or maybe I'd come ashore on one of the eight islands of the Otherworld that the poet Taliesin sang about so long ago.

But when I crawled onto the highest rock and looked across the water at the surrounding headland, I knew exactly where I was. And, saints be praised, it was exactly where I wanted to be. Almost, anyhow. I stood on an islet off the north coast of Wales. I'd travelled along this coast many times, man and boy. So I knew I was looking out at big Ynis Môn—the island of Anglesey, as the Saxons call it. The building there on the rocky headland to the south? That would be a church-house—St Patrick's church. Below it would be St. Patrick's cave.

Part of my uncle's kingdom once lay along the north coast of Anglesey. I'd often heard the story of St. Patrick and this cave. It came from when the pope ordered Patrick to get himself over to the Irish, save their heathen souls, run the snakes off their island. On his way a storm blew him onto the rocks of one of the barren little islands off the coast of Anglesey. He was pretty battered up, but God and Fortuna were with him and he made it across the half a mile of rough water to the rocky mainland. There he crawled into a cave with a freshwater pool. When he came out, a healed man, he founded a church on the headland above.

Now it seemed obvious that Wynstan's song at Bere Regis, even Crawe's babbling about a cave to Sister Hild, didn't necessarily mean Wynstan had gone to Ireland. He would be in St. Patrick's cave, waiting for Crawe. Or she for him.

Either way, I'd find Wynstan soon. For a while I stared across the water at the headland. Once I was up there, it would be an easy trek to the church then down to the cave. But the cliffs below the cave rose steep and smooth. I could see no way to scale them.

I turned to the choppy sea. The water in that part of the world is rough even on the best of days and the tidal currents run fierce. But I was always a strong swimmer and it would be better to give the sea a go rather than stay in a place with no fresh water. I didn't want to drink herring gull blood 'til a boat happened by, who knew when. Besides, if a cleric like Patrick could brave these waters, so could I.

When the tide began to ebb, I cast away my cloak. Then I stripped off my legbands and used them to strap my knives, pouch, and boots against my body. I peered down at myself and knew how my shroud would look. That wasn't a happy thought, so I sent up a prayer to St. Christopher. "Swim with me today and I promise I'll find your grave and take you wherever you want to be." And I will yet. Sometime soon.

Even on the ebbing tide, savage waves struck me, shocked me, made me death's hostage. Worse, as I sucked down more water than air, I could hear Wynstan's laughter. Fury overcame me. Fury cold as the sea I swam in. Ahead, in St

Patrick's cave, Wynstan laughed because he had stolen not just my bounty but my honor, my *wyneb*—my face. Wynstan was the vile Dog of Darkness who stole my worth, who shamed me. And laughed.

But I would have my *wynebwerth*, my face price. Every stroke I took became a knife to his heart, every breath a shout of vengeance against him. He lurked in the rocks ahead, the cliffs alongside me. Laughing. But I would have my revenge. When I did, King Edward's would not be the only corpse in my possession.

Resolved now, I saw that on this sun-filled morning the rocks of Cemaes Bay glowed like Joseph's many-colored coat —red, black, green, yellow. But it's not exactly lamb's wool caressing your flesh when the waves slam you against those rocks. When I finally crawled out of the surf just below St. Patrick's cave, I found myself cut bloody and beaten blue. But I didn't care. I was alive. Soon I'd find Wynstan. Then there'd be blood. And plenty of it.

I knew the old man wouldn't go down easy. He'd seen battle. Lord Hunwald told me Wynstan had often dropped his lyre and fought the Norskers hand to hand. So now everything I did was preparation for war. I peeled the legbands from around my chest, laid the two knives on a rock to dry their leather hilts, pulled on my boots. Then I opened my neck pouch, touched my lucky dice, kissed the sliver of St. Veronica, gave thanks to God and St. Christopher. As I wound on my legbands and stuck my small knife down them, I sent up a prayer for Thrima. And still thought about her as I took out my whetstone and honed my scramseaxe 'til it could've cleaved an ox clean in two.

Big knife at the ready, I climbed to the cave and peered

inside. Its darkness was as total, as final as Hell. Where I would send Wynstan if he resisted me. I called his name. Once, then twice more before I got an answer—not words, just a high, thin sound. I stepped inside the cave. It stank. Crawe was in there, too.

I dropped to a crouch, then felt my way toward the sound, now a mewling little cry. I wasn't so naive as to reckon Wynstan had gotten hurt and would fall into my arms like an ailing child. I figured the squalling was just a ruse to bring me close enough so he could stick me with the scramseaxe I'd found for him at Thornholt.

As I duck-walked deeper into the cave, the sound became not louder but softer and more anguished. Finally, it stopped altogether. I kept moving 'til I stumbled against something. It threw itself on me.

Wynstan!

Only it wasn't Wynstan. A black tempest of bats surged toward the cave mouth, knocking me back onto the rocky ledge. Where they went, I don't know. But I lay on the ledge for a long time, letting the terror leak out of me and thanking God and all His saints that I hadn't bounced down the rocks and into the ocean.

There's nothing like a swarm of bats to bring you to your senses. How could I have believed Wynstan and Crawe would be in the cave? Because Wynstan talked about St. Patrick? Because Crawe described colored cliffs and told a riddle whose answer was a storm at sea? Crawe couldn't have conjured up a storm that put her ashore in exactly the right spot—and got me out of the way at the same time. A heathen waker-of-the-dead she may have been, but she was no maker of storms.

In any case my revenge would have to wait. I would have it, though, if I had to wait into the millennium.

I climbed back up to the headland, never mind how wet and slippery the rocks were. Jagged, too. Spanish cobblers claim they make soles so thick you can dance on nails. Maybe so. But they're not much good on sea-slick rock. I lost my footing often. Still, it turned out to be a successful trip, seeing as I didn't drop off the rocks, and the swarm of bats stayed away from home. I congratulated myself for a lucky lad as I crawled over the lip of the headland onto Welsh soil.

And into Welsh hands. They yanked me up by the hair.

In spite of the noise of their curses—I was obviously no prize—they weren't a sizable force, only a dozen or so, though obviously the soldiers of an important lord. A wealthy one, anyhow. Their helmets were polished, their cloaks brushed and new, their spears keen and at my throat.

One of the soldiers, likely their chief, waved a hand at the two men holding me. They let go of my arms and stepped away, though not very far away.

The chief looked me over with a lip curled in disgust. Not that I blamed him. I knew I looked like a waterlogged rat. "Who the devil are you?" he asked in Welsh. "And where'd you get them rosy-red boots?"

He was a wiry little man, with his black beard cropped short like a soldier ready for battle. Though his manner seemed that of a man who knew command, I didn't think he was lord here. His accent was mainland Wales, all right, but he'd come by it in a nobleman's village, not a nobleman's hall.

Still, no matter the man's rank, I didn't want to let on I

understood him. I gave him a look so empty and stupid that he couldn't help but mark me down as your typical Saxon. Unfortunately, the man knew English. He asked me the same two questions as his comrade—who was I and how'd I come by the boots?

"Want 'em?" I asked. "I'll trade 'em for an hour's head start." I don't know why I said something so daft.

The chief grabbed my beard, yanked me up close. He raised a fist to smack my insolent tongue down my gullet. But then he stared at me so long I began to hope my ugly face had turned him to stone. Finally, he dropped his fist, retreated a pace or two, stared some more.

Meantime, all I could think to do was hack up a gob of spit. Just as I was about to squirt it in his eye, he swept off his helmet and dropped to one knee. "My lord," he said, "we feared you was dead."

I don't know who was more surprised, me or the spear band. Anyhow, every one of our eyes near popped out. Still on his knee, the little chieftain pointed at his men. "Put away your weapons."

When they didn't, he swore at them a while, then asked, "Who you think we got here?"

If the men had an opinion, they weren't offering it. They did, though, make sure their swords still pointed my way. As a matter of fact, I had no opinion, either. But these Welshmen didn't need to know that. I glanced at the chieftain down there on one knee and made a decision.

I turned to the soldiers and, hand on hip, said in perfect Welsh and the imperious tone I'd learned in my father's mead hall, "Your commander asked you a question. Who do you think I am?"

One of the band, a man missing most of his nose, lowered his sword and stepped forward proud as a lad who'd just bagged his first hare. "I think you're Ris ap Brynmor. Look just like the king your *tad*, big snout and all. He'll be mighty glad to see you after all this time."

The man thrust his fist in the air, pumped it a few times. "And we'll be famous!"

The soldiers put away their weapons, did a little obeisance. The dolts were no doubt already counting the cattle my uncle would give them for bringing him ... well, not Tryffin ap Tewdwr, the spoiled monk that fled the monastery some twenty years past. These men believed me to be my cousin Ris, my uncle's son and throne-worthy heir.

I recalled Ris as a sturdy, courteous lad, but none too bright. So there was no telling why he'd come to be thought dead. Not that it mattered. I'd pretend to be him at least for long enough to figure out what to do next—and for sure long enough to get a good meal.

That's what I suggested we get right now. "Then I'll explain how I came to be at St Patrick's cave."

"Mount up," the chief told his men. "And keep your eyes open for King Iago's soldiers." He bade me ride his own horse, taking the extra mount for himself. "You can get a suitable horse at our camp. Rest up a while, too."

A good meal was one thing, lingering in a military camp quite another. I had no desire to get mixed up in a war, against this Iago or anyone else. But the chief—his name was Ithon—had mistaken me for somebody owed lavish and lengthy hospitality. If he found out I wasn't that somebody, or if his men did, he'd be shamed and dishonored. And I'd be dead.

I had to take action straightaway. I looked around for an escape. The headland was studded with rock and thick with ivy, rough country you couldn't exactly dash across. And I had no intention of going off a cliff into the sea. That only left talk and pretense.

I told Ithon I wanted a private confab with him. We dismounted, stood with our horses a few yards ahead of the soldiers while I explained how I could waste no time in my pursuit of a fat Saxon who'd done me a grave wrong, harmed me so that my honor could only be "cleansed by his blood."

It was the truth, after all, and if it wasn't Ris's honor ... well, as the Gospel book says, "What is truth?"

Ithon stuck a hand under his leather cuirass and scratched his chest for a long time, meanwhile glancing at his men where they stood by their mounts with the wooden faces of soldiers who've once again been told to wait. Finally, he pulled his hand free and rested it on his sword hilt. "Where's this Saxon at?"

I gave an answer right away, the one I'd fixed on while Ithon was worrying his chest hairs. "Heard he was here in Wales. Singing Welsh songs, flattering Welsh kings. I need to be off and after him."

Ithon gave out a grunt. "Old fat man? Sings good for a Saxon? Got a company with him, real pretty girl in it?"

I nodded, too astounded to speak.

"We come on him first part of summer, over Caernarvon way, him aboard a tall mule, other three on ponies. More baggage with them than a company of infantry."

Baggage King Edward's remains would be in. I hoped.

"Damned if the old man didn't up and start singing," Ithon said. "Thought he was a mad fellow, 'specially when I kenned he was singing about the bold king of the Britons, like Iago of Gwynedd calls himself nowadays." Ithon shook his head and laughed. "Got to say he didn't look worth starting no feud over. Anyhow, I says to him, 'What's the matter with you, man? Don't you know there's a war on?'"

War? What war? No one in Chester mentioned a war. It struck me, though, that I'd better not say so. Prince Ris had likely been fighting in it. And if that was so, he would hardly be looking for a battered old bard like Wynstan. `

Ithon said, "I'd have run the Saxon through for praising Iago, but his girl come up to me, give me a smile that like to broke my heart it was so beautiful." Ithon went back to scratching his chest. "Told him to quit his noise-making and get along. Don't know where that'd be, don't care."

But now I knew Wynstan would have gone to King Iago. I knew all about the "King of the Britons." Iago had been my uncle's chief enemy for eons. The enemy, in fact, of every one of north Wales's smaller kingdoms.

See you, Cymru may be just one place with one language, but it's got a bunch of parts to it—seventy odd, they say. Some of the parts are big—Gwynedd, Powys, Dyfed—but the rest are pretty much like my uncle's, just a patch of ground in the shadow of a dark mountain. I don't need to tell you that the big ones want to swallow the little ones.

My uncle's kingdom was forever under siege. No matter how often he'd fought them to a standstill, made peace, joined in defensive pacts—they came back like wolves to a fat sheep. Iago of Gwynedd was just the latest slavering king on the prowl. His main stronghold sat only a few miles away, at Aberffraw. But if Ithon's band were on patrol way out here, maybe the beast had been kenneled at last. Defeated, I hoped, and not just cornered.

But in case there'd been no such victory, I sent up a fervent prayer that Ithon and his soldiers wouldn't want their prince to lead them into battle. So I drew myself up proud as any Welsh prince and said, "I just escaped Iago's men. I don't know where they were taking me in their longship, but I jumped out, swam to shore. Hid in that cave 'til I heard you up on the headland."

Ithon had no reason not to believe me. He thought I was a prince. *His* prince, and one day his king. But now I had to find out where Iago was. Still in the field or behind his walls at Aberffraw? Because wherever he was, Wynstan would likely be with him. And maybe Edward's remains, too.

Ithon said that my uncle, King Brynmor, had sworn vengeance on Iago for what he had done to his crops, his cattle, his people. Sworn it at the altar of his own brother, the abbot. Now Brynmor was at Conwy mustering more troops, his own and those of anyone else who wanted to put an end to the havoc Iago had wrought in north Wales. On the other hand, Ithon had heard there was to be a meeting with Iago in Aberffraw, some sort of peace parley.

"Me," Ithon said, "I never put too much stock in that kind of talk, 'specially since I heard Norskers and Saxons might be in on it, too. They're not ones for too much peace."

Whatever the fact of the matter, this little unit had been sent into enemy territory to scout Iago's strength, do what ravaging they could. I didn't think they'd seen battle yet because Welsh kings are the same as English monarchs or German emperors. Most times, they like to keep their armies in the field as long as they can without ever meeting the enemy head on. Meantime, as every general knows, there's nothing like a little rape and pillage to keep the lads amused. This day, though, all the lads had found was a small herd of heifers. The creatures plodded along behind the troop, a couple of bandy-legged herding curs nipping at their hooves.

"Mount up!" Ithon yelled to his men. "And keep your eyes open."

I swung into my saddle, prepared to do just as Ithon said. I'd keep my eyes open, all right—looking for a way to escape. But Ithon wanted no harm to come to Prince Ris. He stuck so close I was tempted to offer him a generous hunk of my cousin's land as a reward for his dedication. Before I could be so foolish, though, it occurred to me that I was just lucky neither Ithon nor any of his warriors happened to notice I had a decade of years on their king's son. Some hard use, too. All they saw was a big man with a big nose. I pulled my cap down and prayed that was all they'd ever see.

From under the cap, I squinted at the green, rolling land. Though it seemed empty, I knew it teemed with creatures. Maybe I could disappear into a badger's den, a hare's hollow log, a wolf's thick tangle of brush ... Or would it be better to just take off, stay on the run until Ithon's men simply got tired of looking?

I was still trying to decide when we came to the soldiers' camp and I'd nowhere to flee. Not unless I could pass the sentries, then slog through the marsh that lay on either side of the road, and into the mountains that hovered on the eastern horizon.

The camp's smell sealed my destiny. The breeze that floated through Eden couldn't have smelled sweeter than whatever was skewered on the cooking spits. Escape could wait 'til after supper.

The camp, which lay at the edge of a stand of alder, was a good-sized one, well guarded and containing plenty of extra arms and mounts. Alongside the row of hide tents stood barrels of ale, baskets of vittles, and female camp followers, all at the ready. Today at least, the camp followers would be relieved of some duties. There'd been no battle, so they wouldn't be swooping down with the kites and ravens to pick clean the enemy dead—of swords, spears, knives, and, best of all, heads to mount on the ramparts at Caernarvon or Aberffraw or Conwy Mountain. Instead, the women already had sheep carcasses turning on the spits. The sheep had likely been stolen off a peasant yesterday or the day before. Today's pickings, the heifers, would be penned with a few skinny milk cows alongside a half dozen dressed pigs hanging from the trees.

When the women had dealt with weapons and chain mail and horses, they finally got around to serving up the vittles. I was so hungry I would've downed clumps of dirt while praising them as the pasties of Paradise. But dirt had nothing to do with this fine lamb and parsnip stew. And, oh, the mead! It was made with honey from the hills of home and I know for a fact that Paradise could have nothing to beat it.

As we sat by Ithon's tent gobbling stew and bread,

pouring down the mead, I asked a few careful questions about the war and he named the warriors King Brynmor had with him in Conwy. Some, members of his spear band, his *teulu*, I remembered from when I was a boy—Mellt Golden Hair, Owein ap Kei, Gwynn the Half-naked. I was glad to hear they still lived and would like to have asked about a few he hadn't mentioned—Ian Hog Jowl, Eri the Bald, Evan ap Mabon—men I'd loved more than I ever did my father. But Prince Ris would not have known them, so I stayed silent.

When Ithon finished his supper, he licked the last crumbs off his knife, burped in satisfaction. As he secured the knife in his belt, he said, "Last we heard, you was with Lord Tewdwr, going after Gurthrith Haraldsson."

Haraldsson, lord of the Isles? How had Norskers from Man and the Hebrides gotten into this Welsh fight? But the question answers itself. Norskers love battle and they love loot. They'll get into whatever fight comes their way and lay hold of whatever they can pull out of it.

"I'm mighty glad," Ithon said, "that you ain't come to the bad end Lord Tewdwr thought."

"What did my ... " The word 'father' was in my mouth. I spit it out and said, "What did Lord Tewdwr say?"

Ithon fished a whetstone out of his pouch and began to sharpen his scramseaxe. "Know about the blood-eagle?"

Who didn't? It's one of the Norskers' favorite games. They like to split open a captive's chest, splinter his ribs so they spread like wings. Then they yank out his lungs, lay them across his chest. And think it's even more fun if he's still alive while they do it.

"Bastards done Ian Hog Jowl that way, sure. And Evan ap Mabon and ... "—Ithon looked up—"Lord Tewdwr heard they done you, too. How'd you get away?"

It was the question I'd expected, one way or another. So I had an answer ready. "Long, long story. I'll tell you when we ride out tomorrow."

But Ithon wouldn't be put off. So I told how Wynstan had betrayed me—that is, Prince Ris—to Guthrith Haraldsson. When I finished a tale I'd made as long and complicated as I could, Ithon said, "You're telling me this Saxon that calls himself a bard, this dirty Saxon, sicked Norskers on a Welsh prince?"

I nodded dolefully. "Fought 'em, I did, though. Drew Norsker blood a-plenty."

Ithon patted my shoulder. "But there was just too many on you. Been in them situations myself."

I nodded even more dolefully, then squared my shoulders most manfully. And well I should have. Ithon had me in a corner now. Besides that, I didn't like the way he'd started to peer at me when he didn't think I saw him. Was he getting suspicious? My mind raced to work out just how I'd say I escaped being split in half, lungs flapping atop me—and, tougher yet, how I could keep Ithon believing I was indeed Ris ap Brynmor, his prince.

Fortunately, Ithon gave me some thinking room before he called his men to gather on the muster ground after supper. That was when Ithon would expect brave Lord Ris to tell how he smashed the talons of the blood eagle.

I knew how it would go on the muster ground. As a boy I'd seen it often in my father's mead hall. After we'd eaten our fill and the men had gathered by his tent, Ithon would pace up and down before them as they stood picking the lice out of their beards and wringing the cow shit out of their boots.

"Lord Ris here," Ithon would shout in his best yeoman's voice, "Lord Ris showed the Norsker assholes what a Welshman's made of!" Then he'd flick his hand my way in exactly the motion Wynstan used when calling forth the next entertainer. Hero of the day, I'd stumble forward to sing my praises.

I don't need to tell you most of my fighting's been done in the alehouse yard. Welsh poets, though, know about war and I know about Welsh poetry. More or less. When the time came, I'd plant my feet firmly as a battle bard ready to sing of Pwyll and Arawn, of Arthur and Bedwr. The bardish words would sprout from my tongue. "They first sought to enslave me, to ravage my homesteads. Then Haraldsson—he and all his host—sought to slay me, to burn my land. Haraldsson, a shrew who scratched at an oak."

Next, I'd summon up a proper figure for my sword. Say, the axe that hewed down the dark Norwegian woods. I'd even find a few other choice rhetorical flourishes, though perhaps it would be better to move straight to the peroration. "But a single tree is not a forest," I'd say and admit I'd been rescued by a troop of Welsh horsemen who rode in crying, "Woe to you, cruel Vikings who tried to gut the hawk of war, hard Brynmor's heir."

My poetry has always been dreadful, never mind how much worse my singing could make it. But by then I'd have the men's attention and it would be easy to introduce my feud with Wynstan. I'd remind them that he was the one betrayed me to the Norskers. "Find him!" I could shout. "Find him and I will reward you beyond all the dreams of all the bards!"

I'd bring it off, of course. They'd understand that my honor had to be redeemed. Besides, my tongue's dug me out of many a hard spot, some harder than this one. On the other hand, like I said, I didn't want to go galloping around Wales with a string of soldiers behind me. To hunt down Wynstan, all I needed was one horse and enough silver to pay for the kind of information any priest or peasant would have. I already had the silver—which I didn't want to spend on a horse. So the simplest course would be to wait 'til nightfall and steal one out of the pen.

But whatever else I am, I'm not a horse thief. At least not in Wales.

With the men gathered on the muster ground, I jumped up, slapped off my belt and thrust it skyward, my pouch dangling from it like a Viking's head. "This bag is full of silver I took off a Norsker jarl."

My smile was both grim and sly. "He won't be needing it anymore and I'm willing to bet Fortuna's still on my side." The soldiers gaped as silver pennies spilled from the pouch and covered the ground like mountain snow.

That's when I brought out my new dice. I hadn't been completely idle at Bertha's. I'd replaced the dice Lord Ordwulf's men had stole off me. This new pair—never mind how I came by them—seemed to have been blessed by Fortuna, if not by St. Martin of Tours himself. They'd already helped me win fine sums from Bertha's customers. And from Bertha herself, which—bless her generous soul—she offered to pay in cash or service. I'd thought about the cost of Thrima's freedom. And took the cash.

Now I didn't have to go far to again find men ready for a game. And, St. Martin be praised, Ithon decided that for his men's morale dice would beat poetry, even though it would be sung by their own prince. Of course, he and a few others just wanted to play what we Welsh call *bach gammon*—little battle—a game I don't like. There's too much maneuvering up and down the board, across those spear-shaped points painted on it. Besides, bach gammon's a game of skill and these fellows likely spent the winters of their youth honing that skill by the mead hall fire while I was honing the psalms on my knees in a monastic cell. It's straight dice for me—just roll 'em and see who Fortuna loves best.

Fortunately, I hadn't left my pouch in St Patrick's cave. Everything was there—my lucky rock, St. Veronica, a pair of new dice fresh cut from antler and raring to be tossed.

Naturally, I let the soldiers examine them. Naturally, they deemed them honest as their own—not shaved or filled with lead or drilled hollow. So I got up quite a few games, lost a suitable number, let the lads quit while they were winning. Tired, they said they were. Weary, worn out from stealing all those heifers. Maybe that's why not one of them claimed I gave Fortuna a little help by what's called setting the dice—controlling the way they fell by the way I tossed them. It's a more useful skill than knowing how to chase pips around a painted board.

The winners drifted away until the only man left was the horse pen's watchman, whose luck I'd helped run true. Like any whiney loser, I said, "Want to quit now you're ahead, I suppose."

"Now's no time to quit," he said, like the usual high-flying winner.

I suggested we'd better move our game to his post, even borrowed a horn lantern that would throw enough light to play by. "Now, then," I said as we knelt by the horse trough to cast our dice, "now I'll get back some of those silver pennies of mine."

The poor devil might have been awake there in the lamplight. But alert? Never. Nor very smart. His dice fell as dice will fall and he never noticed the shapes my fingers formed as I cast my own dice, first to his advantage, then to mine. Nor was he the sort of man who could suck down his losses and say good night. When I began to win, he just knew that on the next cast he'd be right back in the game. A foolish notion in the most righteous of games. Impossible when you play with a serpent like me. But the watchman wouldn't know that 'til tomorrow. Tomorrow, when he'd realize he'd been cheated by the man he'd believed would be his king. Tomorrow, when I'd be in Aberffraw, Iago's stronghold, with Wynstan, the most poisonous serpent ever to slither out of Eden.

I could see the sweat pour out of the watchman's hair while he lost all the silver he'd won, then his scramseaxe, his spear, his shield, his sword, his horse. But presently he began to win everything back, the pile beside him growing until it included all his things and a few of my silver pennies. Still, it wasn't enough for him. He eyed my right hefty stack of silver.

With the smug grin of a man on a winning streak, he said, "All or nothing."

I gave him back the grin. "Now what would I do with two of everything? Though your knife is mighty fine."

I reached for his scramseaxe and gave it an admiring examination, then put it back with his winnings. "How about on the next throw you just put up your seaxe and, say, one of the horses?"

The watchman gave it some thought, sorted through his scruples about gambling with his lord's property. At last, he pointed into the darkness of the horse pen. "How about that one?"

I couldn't see the horse he meant, but I took the bet. "Only if it comes with a saddle and all."

The watchman's brow wrinkled. Then greed and arrogance drove away puzzlement and he nodded agreement. After I gave him my dice to hold—"So you won't think I'm doing anything funny with them back here in the dark"—he described the horse and tack he meant.

They turned out to be a bay mare just about big enough for me and a saddle that had likely been in use since before I got sent to the monastery.

When I came back into the lamplight, I found the watchman staring at my dice where they lay in his palm. "These be funny," he said.

They weren't, of course. The man wanted to win one way or another. He threw them down and went for the knife in his legbands. I got to my scramseaxe first, slashing it across his forehead. When that straightened him up, I set its point against his belly. "Walk backward."

Blood pouring into his eyes, the watchman hesitated. I put pressure on the knife. "Move!"

He swiped at his eyes and backed up, moving right along until he pitched backward over the pile of stuff he'd just so proudly re-won.

I snatched up his scramseaxe and jumped on the little mare. I was well out of the camp before the wretched watchman managed to sound the alarm.

CHAPTER SIX

The sentries on the hills outside the camp presented a bit of a problem. The king's son would hardly be allowed to wander off into the night. Not without an escort, anyway. But again I had my answer ready. It came in the form of that dash out of the camp. As I galloped past the sentries, I yelled at them to follow me. "Saxons!"

That would likely turn the whole camp out. But the watchman would soon do that anyway. I kept pounding my heels into the little mare and praying she'd take serious heed.

She did, so much so that by the time she'd finally run out of breath and I could turn around to look, no one was behind us. Almost as good, we were still on the dirt road and not in some marsh. Just as lucky, it was still a road and not a muddy track like most of what Welshmen call roads. It had likely been built and maintained as a military way, nothing being too good for the army.

Presently, I pulled up to let the mare browse the grass by the side of the road while I considered the next part of my plan. I figured that whether or not peace had been made, Wynstan would be in Aberffraw. I'd been there once as a boy. It'd belonged to King Ieuaf then, and my uncle had taken refuge from a sea storm as we travelled to his holdings along

Anglesey's northern coast.

I recalled Aberffraw as sitting in flat land and almost on the ocean's edge. I also remembered the formidable rock walls that protected it from attack. But Wynstan wouldn't be behind them because, if Iago was like any other Welsh aristocrat, he'd make wandering entertainers camp well outside his ramparts lest his court bards be tainted by bad poetry and worse women. Wynstan and his troop would've had to raise their tents far out in the countryside. I could easily find a way to them. And just as easily take King Edward off Wynstan.

Then I'd do him serious damage because revenge is serious business.

To get to Aberffraw, I'd need to bear due south for no more than twenty English miles. In parts of Wales that could take the better part of four days. But I was on Ynis Môn, where the stars would guide me through flat country striped by only a shallow stream or two. I could be outside Aberffraw by noontide, resting up, figuring out how to deal with Wynstan, without his troupe being the wiser. Now, out here under the moon and well away from Ithon's camp, I felt so good I up and promised St. Christopher I'd build him a big shrine just as soon as I'd freed Thrima and my mother.

Putting the little mare into a trot, I mulled over a name for her. I considered Rhiannon and Branwen, fine names from fine poems, then decided that since we were on Ynis Môn I ought to call her Mona. A grand name on a grand night.

Then, life being what it is, we weren't even an hour on the road again when the stars went out. The rain started almost immediately, a thick fog falling along with it. And, of course, since wicked things come in threes, the road ran out. In a trice Mona was slogging through mud over what I now realized was definitely not flat country. But just as I started in whining to St. Christopher, I came on one of those old stone monuments, burial places, whatever they are—the things with a couple of big rock pillars holding up a capstone you could get out of the weather under. If somebody was buried there, I blessed his soul.

I'd found a full leather feed bag in the camp's horse pen and now fed Mona out of it while I listened to the rain on the rock roof and wondered how long before I'd again be in a warm bed with Thrima beside me. I must've slept some, too, because all of a sudden it was day. The rain had quit, leaving only a low rumble of thunder in the distance.

I led Mona from the rocks, was ready to mount when I realized the sound in the distance wasn't thunder. From out of the lifting fog there came men and horses, the noise of hooves, then laughter announcing them. The laughter told me they weren't an enemy host bearing down on Ithon's camp. I pulled Mona back into the rock refuge anyway.

Peeking out, I saw several dozen horsemen, too many for a simple scouting party. The richly colored banners fluttering above them told me this was a nobleman's spear band. But it didn't belong to just any nobleman. I knew those banners. This was a royal *teulu*. My father's *teulu*.

When I recognized him there at its head, my innards went loose and for a moment I thought they'd spill out my fear of the man. I pushed as far back under the rocks as I could, dropped down on my knees and prayed the place would hide me from him. I'd not known such terror since the day he sold my mother into slavery.

After a little while, I pulled myself together enough to peek out at him and his men. There was no mistaking Tewdwr ap Merfyn even though his hair, still thick as a boy's, had gone pure white, his beard grizzled as a badger. As always, he wore a red cloak so everyone would see him—"Let no enemy forget I am the son of a king. Seek me at your peril."—and rode a big black horse. How I'd looked forward to riding his horse one day. That day never came.

I hid until the sound of the hooves finally faded, then galloped Mona away from there as fast as she would go. By full daylight I felt safe enough to find a tucked away spot where we could rest a spell, eat our vittles—more oats for Mona and for me a hunk of camp bread I'd let one of the gamblers use as his stake. By mid-morning we were well on our way again.

Thank God, the sun came out and now all I had to do was ride toward the mountains in the distance, which lay many miles distant across Caernarvon Bay. They might not lead me directly to Iago's lair, but they'd bring me to the bay's coast and I could follow it to Aberffraw.

I looked over my shoulder all the way, but I'd somehow dodged whoever had come after me. If anybody had. I was beginning to doubt it. Once Ithon's band realized I wasn't Ris, they'd likely decided I was just some thieving flotsam the sea had thrown at them and gone back to the important business of making war. At least I hoped so.

Late in the afternoon, I came around a big thicket of blackthorn and elder to find myself on the bank of a river. And damn near pitched straight into it. For in the shallows below, skirt hiked betwixt her legs, stood Prioress.

I wasn't so surprised that I didn't notice those legs were just as pleasing as I always knew they would be. Still, was it Prioress, or had I fallen asleep? Or maybe last night's stew had contained bad mushrooms. I only decided I was wide awake and stone sober when I heard the peal of Sister Hrothbeort's laughter. She and Sister Hild stood on the opposite bank, their eyes on me, Hrothbeort jabbing her elbow into Hild and Hild actually grinning.

They'd seen me giving Prioress a lustful glance, though thankfully neither of them bothered to tell her how she'd come to be the morning's entertainment. For my part, I decided embarrassing her wouldn't be good for anybody. I went to the far side of the thicket and waited 'til Sister Hrothbeort stopped laughing. Then I rode up and acted every bit as surprised as Prioress.

Once her feet were dry and back in her shoes, I pressed the three nuns to tell me how they'd found me. And so quick-like. I'd only been out of Chester for three days. "You lot have some kind of magic cauldron you look into?"

"Don't be childish," snapped Sister Hild. "We are as capable of finding out Wynstan's whereabouts as you are."

More capable, looked like, since they'd got here without help from a sea storm or an army. But why were they looking for Wynstan? Did they have designs on King Edward's body? And if so, why?

Sister Hild pushed back her cloak and folded her arms across her grey bosom. "Now, then, Tryff, what have you done with Crawe?"

"More important, what you doing here?" I shot back as I joined the nuns by the stream. "And how'd you know I'd be here, too?"

By St. Anthony, if three nuns could find me, who else could? The clerics of every church I'd ever robbed might—Archbishop Dunstan, for sure. Best thing to do now would be to learn what the nuns knew about Wynstan. Or the king's corpse.

I dismounted then, and Sister Hrothbeort grabbed me in one of her big-bosomed hugs of welcome, told me the voyage from Chester had been her first. "And you should've seen all them white-maned waves trotting across the ocean."

She sounded excited as an oblate, but I cut her off to ask again, "How'd you come to find me today?" Maybe they'd answer this time.

Prioress smirked, pursed her lips, smirked some more. "We have our spies."

Sister Hrothbeort rolled her eyes and Sister Hild smothered a humph. Had some unseen scout reported me to his superiors, and they reported me to the nuns?

Sister Hild stuck her fists onto her skinny hips. "We heard you were on the way to Ireland with Crawe. Why are you here instead? And where is she?"

I could ask them the same questions. But that could wait.

I gave her my most charming look of concern. "You worry me to death, Sister, out here all by yourselves. Don't you know there's armed men on the prowl?"

Just then I heard a commotion. And saw that drawn up on the crest of the stream bank stood a whole army. Men and horses, flags and spears, sunlight flashing off the leader's iron helmet. I went for my scramseaxe.

To my surprise, the nuns waved at them. And I realized that what I'd taken for spears were only processional crosses. This was no army, and its commander wore not an iron helmet but a golden miter. I looked from the glittering crowd on the bank to the nuns and back again. Then back once more. "What the hell?"

I was close. He turned out to be a bishop. Above the crosses flew the episcopal banner of Chester. I said, "What's a Saxon bishop doing out in the middle of Anglesey? Him and his whole damn *familia*?"

The nuns told me the bishop had important business in Wales and that he and his party were encamped a mile or so outside Aberffraw. Now the whole lot had turned out to bless the countryside, rid it of war's Satanic stain.

Good thing that though country folk in Wales may be ragged and lean, they're usually not thieves. Still, that gold miter and those gold crosses could be enough to tempt the most virtuous of Welshmen.

"Prioress," I said, "it's just not safe for you here. Even with a bishop around. Especially with a bishop around. And all of you on your own, to boot."

"We're hardly alone," she said in a "how dumb do you think we are?" tone. "We came here with the bishop and his party. All of us are protected by the troops of Ealdorman Alvar of Mercia."

That's when I started thinking that not only had Fortuna deserted me, but so had the whole company of Heaven, angels and archangels included. Lord Alvar, whose tricks had almost put Lady Edith on the English throne, who'd tasted my fists in Wilton, who'd sicked Leofric onto me—Alvar was here on Anglesey. Would I ever find Wynstan now? Or the king's corpse? And, good Lord, what about Thrima?

I went onto my tiptoes to try and peer past the bishop's mob, in case the ealdorman was up there, too. When I didn't see anything that looked like a spear band, I asked where he was.

Sister stuck her cane in my chest. "What have you done with Crawe?"

Alvar I could probably take care of with brains or fists, but how would I tell Sister that Crawe had escaped from me? I glanced at the other two nuns. They'd been known to resent Hild's high and mighty ways and gallop to the rescue of whoever she had skewered speechless. Now Prioress was busy scraping a speck of mud off the hem of her cloak and Sister Hrothbeort had launched into a spirited recital of the psalm that says your mischief will fall on your head.

I couldn't tell if she was trying to warn me to be careful or just making a joyful noise unto the Lord. In any case, I could see charm wouldn't work now and no convenient lie about Crawe sprang to mind. The only thing left was bluster. And lots of it. "Those clerics up there, are you their prisoners? Have they … ? If they have, I'll …"

Prioress glanced up, a sour pout on her peach-pretty face, while Sister Hrothbeort ended her psalm with a blast of laughter. Hild's own face went blank and cold as a snow-filled pasture. "Try not to be any more foolish than you have to, Tryff," she said.

I turned to Sister Hrothbeort. She'd give me a little support. But Sister, even through her mirth, was casting a curious eye on Mona. "Y'know, Tryff," she said, "it's one thing to lose that Crawe, but what've you gone and done with Tom Tub?"

While I explained that I'd left Tom in Chester—without mentioning he was in the care of the mistress of a brothel—Sister began going over Mona with the expert hands and eye of a woman raised on some of the finest horse land in all England.

I would've joined Sister Hrothbeort next to Mona, but Sister Hild caught me by the tunic neck like my mam used to when I didn't mind her. "Crawe!"

I gave in and told the story of me and Crawe. "She sailed off with that merchant, and left me sitting all by my lonesome on some damn rock in the middle of Cemaes Bay. I don't know where they got to. Ireland, the Isles, Ultima Thule? Your guess is as good as mine."

By then Sister Hrothbeort had finished examining Mona, hide and hooves, teeth and tail. She jumped in with her report, horses being a much more important topic than whatever Sister Hild was on about. "You got a Welsh military pony there. Turned from relic robber to horse thief, have you?"

She didn't stop to hear the lie that slithered off my tongue. She rushed in with, "However you come by her, you done good. She ain't a bad bit of horseflesh. And still young enough to throw another good colt or two. If I was you, though, I'd get some good iron shoes on her soon as you can."

I thanked her, handed her Mona's reins, then swept lame Sister Hild onto the mare's back. She fussed, of course, until Prioress said, "Remember, Hild, what the Gospel book tells us. 'Charity shall cover a multitude of sins.' I'm sure you'll agree that Tryff has many multitudes he needs to cover."

Sister Hild humphed, Sister Hrothbeort laughed, and, Prioress said, "It is time we left for Aberffraw. You will join us, Tryff, to provide the protection a radman is sworn to. As you should've been doing since we left St. Finella's."

Thank the Lord she didn't sound mad enough to report my failure to the royal reeve, though I'd no doubt she'd inflict a heavy fine first chance she got.

Catching up to her as we rode along the river bank, I said, "Will somebody please explain how come you three are on Anglesey, middle of a war? The bishop, too."

To my relief, it turned out that the gossip Ithon'd heard was true—the war on the island, and in all north Wales, had ended. King Iago had been overthrown and his nephew Hywel ab Ieuaf now reigned.

The whole business had been the usual bloody Welsh mess. Seems that a few years back Iago and his brother, Hywel's father, had won a war against their cousins and for a while ruled jointly. But that hadn't been good enough for greedy Iago. He took his brother prisoner, blinded him with a red hot rod, and hanged him from the ramparts of Aberffraw.

But even when his father's body was dumped naked on the doorstep of his hall, Hywel hadn't scurried off to the safety of exile in Winchester or Rome. He'd waged a war against his uncle so serious and triumphant that Iago agreed to another period of joint rule, this time with Hywel.

I was shocked. "But no Welshman could ever forgive or forget..."—I struggled for words—"an abomination like Iago's. He'd take revenge if he had to lie in wait for a thousand years."

Prioress crossed herself, then spoke in that matter of fact way Saxons have while they recite tales of blood. "Seems Hywel didn't have to wait nearly that long. He heard Lord Alvar had turned covetous eyes on the mainland realm of Gwynedd. So Hywel covered his own eyes and let Alvar's men fall on the biggest monastery in the land, rob it bare, burn it to the ground."

Not that they'd likely found much to steal. Welsh monasteries aren't the fat prizes English ones are. Maybe Welsh clerics actually believe what Our Lord said: "Blessed be you poor, for yours is the kingdom of God." Or maybe they just don't know how to hang on to what they have. Anyway, after Alvar sacked the monastery and then the estates of some very wealthy noblemen, he repaid Hywel by joining his war against Iago.

"So did that Guthrith Haraldsson," Sister Hrothbeort put in. "He's the Norsker calls his self Lord of the Isles when he ain't nothing but the king of England's chamber pot."

That's what I liked about Sister Hrothbeort. She rode against the enemy with all the glee of a north country horse-troop.

"Silence, Hrothbeort!" said Prioress. And for a while we all were silent as we trudged along the river bank, opposite the bishop's parade but—I was glad to see—still nowhere near Ealdorman Alvar.

The sun was high by now, the morning hot. I took off my cloak, tossed it over my shoulder. "How did my uncle get involved in all this?"

"Apparently," Prioress said, "Hywel promised your uncle the return of some land he'd lost in a previous war. I don't know the particulars."

But she did know that my uncle had joined up with King Hywel, Lord Alvar, the Norsker, and my uncle to defeat Iago. He was now a prisoner in Aberffraw, where a huge peace parley was about to begin.

"Hence, the presence of the bishop of Chester, the bishop

of Bangor," Prioress said, "and, of course, Wynstan."

Why wasn't I surprised that Wynstan was in Aberffraw?

But why, I wanted to know, why would King Hywel and the others put up with a travelling entertainer like Wynstan? Hywel had his court poets and Wales was full of wandering bards, every one of them twice the poet Wynstan was.

Had Alvar arranged it? Was Wynstan here to deliver King Edward's remains to the ealdorman so he could use them to put Lady Edith on the throne after all? Maybe with some help from Hwyl and Haraldsson. I chewed that notion a bit, then pumped a fist in the air. Whatever his motive for being here, I had the old son of a bitch at bay.

I gave my fist another pump. Now I knew what I had to do. I had to find out if Wynstan was carrying around a dead man's body. Or, rather, bones—King Edward had surely gone to bone by now. Whichever, I had to get hold of whatever they were and take them to Lord Ordwulf. And it made no difference whether those bones belonged to King Edward or some thieving churl hanged at a cross-roads. What mattered was that I'd soon have silver enough to sail to Iceland and fetch Thrima home.

I was congratulating myself for having solved my problems when Sister Hild caught hold of my cloak. "Let the others go on," she said, "I have something to tell you."

Uh-oh, thought I. Sister's "something" generally turned out to be something bad. For me.

I handed Mona's reins to Sister Hrothbeort and lifted the old nun from the saddle. When the other two were out of earshot, she said, "Have you ever heard of the Great Harp of Arthur?"

I laughed at her convent-bred ignorance and said, "Every

Welshman has heard of the Great Harp. We all know"—here I turned a bit satirical—"that it'll come back to us when King Arthur does. We know that way down deep in our brave and true Cymric hearts."

The story went that after the Battle of Camlann, King Arthur, badly wounded, retired to a crystal cave. There, and to this day, he licks his wounds and plots his return, harp and hounds with him. "True or not," I said, "that's the tale told where I come from."

"You have never heard that his harp may return before Arthur does?"

It'd been a long time since I'd paid much attention to Welsh superstitions, but now I thought about it, I did recall something. "A prophecy, was it?"

Sister nodded. "It goes like this: 'When the wolf's son is laid to rest, then will Arthur's harp return, to sing in Aberffraw, for him who is supreme.'"

I threw up my hands. "That so-called prophecy's been around time out of mind. As I recall, nobody's ever figured out just who this wolf might be. His son, either. Anyhow, I hear there aren't any more wolves on Ynis Môn. King Iago killed them all."

"And sent their heads to Winchester, as tribute to King Eadgar. Three hundred wolf heads a year, they say, until all the beasts were gone. What they're saying in Aberffraw is that the wolf in the prophecy is King Eadgar, whose son has just been laid to rest."

"Slow down there, Sister. Are you telling me that everybody in Aberffraw believes it? Not just the Welsh? Norskers and Saxons, too?"

She nodded.

I fought back my laughter. "But surely you're not foolish enough to believe it yourself? That a king who's been gone for—what, 300 years?—is still alive and hiding in a cave with his dogs?"

"And his harp."

Now I bellowed laughter and Sister was forced to laugh a little herself. "Let me get this straight," I said 'twixt guffaws, "folk are saying King Arthur's harp will now return from wherever it's been these many years."

I shook my head in awe at the depths of human stupidity. "At my uncle's monastery I learned some logic along with the Psalms. So let me ask you this, Sister: How can anybody know the wolf represents King Eadgar? Lots of wolves, both four-legged and two-, have laid their sons to rest here lately."

Sister gave no answer, just let me rail on. "Far as I'm concerned, this so-called prophecy is only a story for superstitious children. Which makes me wonder why it's being told just now. You ask me, some commander's going to break this new peace and use the prophecy for his excuse. I expect he'll be holding a harp when the next war is declared."

Sister shrugged, perhaps in agreement, perhaps not. "I tell you this," she said. "Be careful. Wynstan may be involved."

That I didn't doubt. If trickery was afoot, Wynstan would definitely be involved. But I had to find him, no matter what he was up to. I'd find that cursed bag of royal bones along with him, too. Otherwise, I might never save Thrima.

Herring-bone clouds swam overhead, predicting rain. We needed to make better time. I yelled at Sister Hrothbeort to bring Mona back so we could load up Sister Hild. I'd find Wynstan quick as I could, make him hand over King Edward. Then I'd cut his throat. And be out of Wales, just like that.

For the last mile or so, I walked alongside Prioress. As usual, she had a flagon of wine tied at her waist. And, as usual, she was charitable with it. I took a couple of swigs, then a couple more, and asked if she knew where Wynstan was.

She finished off the wine before she said, "No. But he's around. I'm not sure about Crawe, though. Hild put the word out that we're looking for her—and will pay for information. The only response we've gotten was from the man in Wynstan's troupe. Said they didn't have any notion where she was. We didn't believe him, of course."

"Did you ask where Wynstan was?"

They had, several times, had even gone looking for him. So far, he'd dodged them every time. Didn't matter. I'd find him quick enough, once my silver glinted before a peasant's eyes.

Presently, Aberffraw came into view—an ordinary river

village next to what looked like any other fortified manor, Welsh or French or English, its straw-roofed mead hall and outbuildings peeking over the rock wall that surrounded them. Two things surprised me about the little place, though. *Primus*, that it was the seat of the kings of Gwynedd and, *secundus*, that I hadn't smelled it before I saw it. Nor did I smell it now. Peace truly must've been at hand, because the heads of the vanquished no longer adorned the wall.

Aberffraw sits on the deep estuary of the River Ffraw that empties into Caernarvon Bay. It's an easy distance from England and the rest of Wales, from Ireland and the Isles. That's why it's always been a great trading center. Today, though, its riverbank was full of beached warships, each surrounded by armed warriors. When the peace was made, they'd stow their spears, break out the ale barrels, and get happily drunk, thankful they'd survived yet another war.

A horn sounded. Someone important was arriving. Curious and a little excited, I told the nuns to stay put, then chased down to the stout wooden quay for a closer look, Sister Hrothbeort puffing along behind me. Welsh and Saxon troops were already there, drawn up tight and fierce as a shield wall. As well they should've been.

"The Black Gentiles have come," the Welsh said. "Spare us, oh Lord," cried the English, "from the fury of the Vikings."

Up the Aber sailed Hel Hoard, the dragon ship of Guthrith Haraldsson, lord of the Isles.

If there's one thing Norsker chiefs know how to do, it's strike awe in you, balls to brains. Today, Haraldsson had a score of his warriors lined up at the ship's gunwales banging on their shields and screaming—what? Curses? Cries of greeting? Who could tell? Whatever, Haraldsson's lads didn't need to announce themselves with such a hue and cry. The dragon ship smelled like a floating manure cart. Their Norsker stink would fell us long before their spears.

After Haraldsson and his men showed off by running down their oar shafts and onto the riverbank, the rest of his fleet sailed in from the bay. Soon, the river beach bristled with dragon ships. Reeked, too, like a barrel of dead fish, 'til a fair wind came up and saved us all.

So it was with grins and gifts that the three commanders met on the quay. For the gift-giving, hampers full of brightly embroidered tunics went to King Hywel and Lord Alvar, a pair of scrolled brooches to the Norsker. Then came the welcoming cup and an hour or so of fine speeches of praise from both sides. Finally, Haraldsson and his bodyguard were escorted to a big, striped pavilion tent well downwind.

Still waiting on the hill above Aberffraw, Prioress and Sister Hild were a bit grumpy when Sister Hrothbeort and I finally returned to them.

"What took you so long?" Prioress demanded. Then words like "duty," "vows," "obedience" got slung around. Sister Hrothbeort tried to look contrite even while she could barely tear her eyes off the Norskers. Me, I had serious matters to attend to. I'd get shot of the nuns as soon as I had them safe behind the fortress walls.

For once, that turned out to be easy. They'd insisted Lord Alvar and King Hywel lodge them in the royal bower house. Now, though, we had to wait on the hill while the troops moved away from the harbor. Excited soldiers can be dangerous. Hywel's peasants, free and bond, male and female, fled like hinds before hounds.

"They better not run too far," I said. "They might miss the joys of having Arthur's harp hereabouts. When it miraculously appears before their very eyes."

Sister Hild poked me in the arm. "Don't be sarcastic. And don't be too hard on ignorant peasants, either. They are not the only ones who believe too much, too easily."

True enough, and right now I believed the Norskers might up and take an interest in me and the nuns. I drew my scramseaxe, held it where Haraldsson's lads could clearly see it as we walked toward Aberffraw. I also said a prayer to St Andrew, who protects women and who I hoped would protect me, too. I knew my scramseaxe would. I didn't put it away until we'd passed through the oaken gate of Aberffraw's fortress.

Like I said before, Caer Aberffraw looked no different from any other fortified manor house I've ever seen—just a rock wall with a couple of wooden gates around a mead hall, bower house, and out buildings. Everything was fairly new because some ten years before Norskers had burnt the place. When Iago finally won back his stronghold, he began to rebuild. Rather, his peasants did. Iago himself was busy murdering his brother and fighting his nephew.

The mead hall, though, had escaped the fighting, so it wasn't very new at all. And wasn't Welsh, either. When the Norskers'd held the place, they'd built one of their own. Norskers always claim the bowed roofs and walls of their mead halls make them look fierce and majestic as their dragon ships. Maybe some do. But with its filthy thatch and sagging sides, this one looked more like a dead pig.

Now I knew for sure that the story about King Arthur's

harp had to be a lie. Why would a lord great and just as Arthur even consider giving his harp to Iago and his Welsh, a man and a nation shamed by—what's the Latin word?—fratricide? To a place so new the sap still leaked out of its timber buildings? One that had a mead hall built by the same Black Gentiles who'd murdered its women and children, free and bond?

I hoped this new king, Hywel, was a man of honor who, if I didn't find Wynstan right away, would heed my plea for sanctuary when Ithon and his men came looking for me. Hywel would have to. After all, I was the grandson of his greatest Welsh ally. Not the right grandson, of course. But he didn't need to know that, did he?

The royal bower house looked a little less nasty than the mead hall, even though Sister Hild—who seemed to know all about Aberffraw's history—said Iago's woman had fled long ago and Hywel had not yet installed his queen and her household. With its stout timber walls and high, wicker-roofed porch, it obviously made the safest place for the nuns. Still, I wondered if even such a solid refuge could make up for what met their eyes in the courtyard.

I closed my eyes when I saw it. A wicker cage hung from a long pole. In it crouched a naked man, bloody-mouthed and all but toothless, likely from trying to chew his way out. I'd seen such a thing often enough, but always turned away because it reminded me of what my father had done with Fynach the Funny, the man my mother had loved. Except here in Aberffraw the basket didn't hold a clown. It held a king—Iago himself.

The men surrounding the cage hurled curses and dog shit

at the naked man inside it. They laughed, too, and showed him their naked butts. These were not Saxons or Norskers but Hywel's host, because the war 'twixt Hywel and his uncle hadn't been fought over land or gold or glory or even cattle. It'd been waged out of revenge. Iago had murdered King Ieuaf, Hywel's father. Hywel had no choice but to avenge Ieuaf's honor. It was his duty.

Now, there in the courtyard, Hywel sat in an oaken chair while his men raged around the bleeding and terrified Iago. Gone was the man who called himself the prince of Wales, the king of all the Britons. Gone was the man arrogant enough to kill his own brother. What was left was not a king, barely even a man, just a quivering, shit-smeared thing.

I'd seen it all before, in Wales, in England, in many lands. Presently Hywel's soldiers would leave off heaving dung at Iago and go back to beating him with whips, sharpened sticks, the flats of their pole-axes, whatever came to hand. Soon, his screams would grow thinner, 'til he all but mewled. Soon, he would roll himself up with his head 'twixt his legs and begin to pray.

In the case of Fynach the clown, my father's men had kept at him for two days, only stopping when the cage's rope snapped and he dropped onto the hard, packed dirt of the courtyard. But Fynach had been lucky. His neck broke as easily as the rope. It was the last of Fortuna's smile, though. My father wouldn't allow him a Christian burial. He cut Fynach up and left him to the crows.

As he should have, all proper people would say. Iago and Fynach had trespassed on other men's honor, had stolen their good names, had left their reputations in tatters. And, principled people would say that for the loss of honor there can be no compensation. No amount of land or gold or cattle can restore what's been stolen. That leaves revenge—in Wales and the rest of the world, too. All right-minded people would know that the two got what they asked for, what they deserved.

As I looked at the one curled up in his cage like a smashed hedgehog, as I remembered the other in his—that's when I knew. Wynstan must be punished and suffering so all the world would know what he'd done to me—tricked me, stolen from me, stripped me of my honor.

So I watched as Iago twisted in pain, rolling and unrolling himself, screaming as a spear spiked his side. I didn't doubt he deserved his agony.

But then, thoroughly unbidden, uncertainty wormed its way into me. Did Wynstan really deserve any such punishment? After all, he'd taken neither my wife nor my kingdom.

I pushed that notion out of my mind quick as I could. Of course, I wouldn't put the old man in a cage and use a pointed stick on him. I wouldn't do such a thing to anyone. But Wynstan still needed killing.

I turned away from Iago's suffering, to find that the nuns had joined the various clerics to sing Nones in the little wooden church-house just inside the walls. As a psalm drifted over the compound—"How shall we sing the songs of the Lord in a strange land?" —I fetched Mona from the stable where Sister Hrothbeort had sent her and finally went hunting Wynstan. He couldn't be camped too far outside the walls. In the time he'd been here, he'd probably already put on several shows, trotting out the talents of Godgyth and her family for prince and peasant alike.

As I rode through the village, I asked where to find the show folk. Asked in my best Welsh, too. But the churls went dumb as donkeys. So I told them I was King Brynmor's son and if they didn't give me an answer in less than a bat of my eye they'd find his emblem tattooed on their tongues. Their eyes popped with fright but still none of them seemed to know anything about Wynstan or his troupe.

I was about to grab a tongue and start carving when a square-built man with a boil on his nose said, "You mean the stout one calls himself a poet? One with the pretty dancing girl? He's got him a camp down the other side of the river a-ways. Don't blame him going far, girl that pretty."

The camp was not only "a-ways" but hidden, too, in a thick stand of wind-warped wych elm. At its edge I stowed my pouch in Mona's saddlebag, then made my belt into a noose. I'd have the old bastard hog-tied soon as I saw him. Then I'd dangle him from one of the trees and start slicing off as many body parts as necessary 'til he gave me King Edward's corpse.

I was so absorbed in making my snare that I never noticed the small boy until he yanked on my tunic hem. "I know you," he said. "You're Wynstan's mate."

He was Cuthred, Kyre and Beorn's child. "Hush," I told him.

"And my Fa knows you, too."

"Shhh!"

"But Fa don't like you."

Cuthred had always been a quiet boy. And would be again, soon as I got his mouth stuffed full of elm leaves. Just as I went to grab him, he let go my tunic and tore through the trees, yelling for his father. "Fa! Fa! That man came back!"

From the camp I heard Beorn. "What man?"

The little boy's voice grew even more excited. "That one sent us to the jailhouse."

"Shit," Beorn said.

I followed the voices through the trees until I came to a camp so comfortable and spacious it could only have been created by people who spent their lives on the road and took their rest beside it. Around a rock-lined fire-pit they'd set up a couple of good-sized tents and a kitchen fly. The front flaps of the tents were open, showing wooden chests, three-legged stools, a goatskin rug piled with the wool blankets of their bedding. In the bigger of the tents, on one of the chests, lay a lyre. A small barrel sat on a trestle table in the empty kitchen fly next to cups and eating utensils.

Nearby, Wynstan's majestic Lady Philosophy had been joined by a couple of squat sorrel ponies, all three now tied in the trees and enjoying their feed buckets.

On a tripod over the fire, a pot of greens and porridge bubbled. Obviously, supper was on. Supper for four, I figured, since that many peeled logs sat by the fire. But only Beorn, Kyre, and Cuthred seemed to be around.

I stepped out of the trees and pointed at the bigger tent. "I see a lyre in there. Where is he?"

A smiling Kyre rushed forward to grab my hand. If Beorn hadn't sounded very glad I'd turned up, Kyre seemed to be. She served up not only her heavenly smile but a heartfelt prayer of thanksgiving for my safety. "How good it is to see you, dear Tryff. Please sit and have a cup of ale. We're delighted, aren't we, Beorn? And Wynstan will be, too. Won't he, Beorn?"

Beorn wasn't the sort to cry "Hail, fellow, well met!" under any circumstances, never mind to the man he thought got him thrown in the Winchester jail. Instead, he made a sound that fell someplace 'twixt growl and curse.

For my part, I gave Kyre's hand a gentle squeeze, then dropped it saying—yelling—"I know you're here, Wynstan! You thieving turd, show yourself!"

Now, out of Hell itself, a black tempest of rage swept through me. I began stomping through the camp like an army of Saxons. I flung stools, hurled cups, tossed blankets, all with little Cuthred's wails rising over my mayhem like a war trumpet. Beorn and Kyre reacted with the brave good sense of travelling folk who've dealt with banditry, anger, and madness all their lives. He circled me while she hustled Cuthred inside a tent. She returned with a big pot full of water. And threw it on me.

My rage died like a doused hearth fire.

When Kyre saw I was calm, she again offered the ale cup. I sank onto a log, all the vinegar gone out of me, and feeling like an ass. I apologized for trying to wreck their camp, though not for my anger at Wynstan.

To my surprise, Beorn said, "Man's a viper, alright. He'll slither past you even when you know exactly what he is and you're staring straight at him."

Well, well, a man with some sense after all. I said, "What kind of tale did he tell you, to get you to Wales? Must've surprised you when you found out there was a war going on."

They said they sure were surprised. Wynstan, too, as a matter of fact. "But the war was pretty much over by the time we got here," Kyre said.

Beorn sat down on the log across from me. "Told us his lyre was here. Song Cauldron."

"That it?" I nodded at the tent where the lyre lay. "Thought Song Cauldron was up in Orkney and likely to stay there."

Beorn shook his head. "That's not Song Cauldron, just an ordinary lyre he's had since we left Bere Regis." Beorn paused, spat in the dirt. "But it turns out he's here to find a harp alright, a magical one."

"The Great Harp of Arthur," I said. "What else would bring the conceited toad into the wilds of Wales? Likely thinks he's the one it's meant for."

Wynstan would covet the thing for the prestige of owning it. And, of course, for its magic. If it had any. "Why does he think the harp is in Aberffraw?"

"Everybody does," Beorn said. "I mean, everybody thinks it'll appear at the feast tomorrow."

"What feast?"

Beorn said that the parley was almost finished, the peace made. The bishops had blessed everybody and were now helping the commanders divide up the spoils. Tomorrow would come the celebration, a great feast in King Hywel's mead hall.

"King Arthur going to be there, too?" I said. "Oh, that's right—Arthur said the thing would come back on its own. And it would be 'For the one who is supreme.' How come folk think it's going to appear at this particular feast?"

"It's part of the prophecy."

A part I'd never heard. "Wynstan tell 'em that?"

Beorn shrugged. "I don't think so, because Wynstan says somebody stole the harp out of Arthur's crystal cave and brought it to Aberffraw a long time ago. He's going to find the harp and—"

"And get the hell out of Wales."

"He says he doesn't want it for himself." This from the man who'd just declared Wynstan a snake that would bite you before you even knew it was around. "He says once he finds it, he'll use it to make all the lords swear to keep the peace they've made. Then he'll let Arthur's harp tell who its rightful owner is. You know, 'the one who is supreme,' like in the prophecy."

Who did Wynstan think he was, to make the lords swear *anything*, never mind to keep the peace? To get that harp, every one of those men would put out his own eyes, sell his mother into slavery, cut up his firstborn and feed him to the pigs. And from the moment one of them got it, they'd all be back at war.

But Kyre and Beorn weren't completely convinced Wynstan would find the harp and make good his promise. They knew him better than that. They said they were to meet him in the morning outside the hall "ready to entertain the troops." They hadn't any notion of where he'd gone in the meantime, but they did say he'd taken his pack with him.

Of course, he had. King Edward was in there.

Maybe I could find him while it was still daylight. I got out of their camp right quick, pausing only to go through the mounts' saddlebags. Maybe Wynstan had tried to be tricky and slip the king in one of them. He hadn't.

Mona and I trudged back to Aberffraw in a cold, grey drizzle that veiled the land and foretold of winter. Huddled in my cloak, I thought about the Great Harp. Did I really believe it existed and was here on Ynis Môn? I sure believed something was going to turn up at that feast tomorrow. Because if it didn't, four disappointed armies would burn Aberffraw to the ground. Maybe it would be the Great Harp that appeared. After all, who was I to doubt the legends of King Arthur?

But I knew for sure that King Edward's bones were in Wynstan's pack and he was off searching for Arthur's Harp. The greedy old pig was canny enough to know it lay someplace close. So, to find Wynstan, I had to find the harp.

Who had stolen it from Arthur's cave and brought it here? Iago, seemed like. But on second thought, I realized that didn't matter. What mattered was where they'd hidden it. Not in a hole by some well or under a bed in the bower house, I'd bet. For one thing, it wouldn't fit. This harp would be no flat lyre, but a real Welsh harp strung with glittering wires in a fine walnut triangle. So I figured the best place for a smart fellow like Iago to have put it was where all the best Welsh harps are kept—on the mead hall wall.

If Wynstan recognized it there, he'd know he couldn't just snatch it, tuck it under his arm, and get the hell out of Wales. At night Hywel's battle companions would be in the hall, sleeping, drinking, what have you. All day women and bondmen would be in and out cooking, cleaning, stoking the fires. And even if the bondmen turned their backs on the theft, even if the warriors were blind drunk and senseless, Wynstan—all twenty stone of him—could hardly make a dash for anyplace. So he'd somehow convinced the commanders the harp would sing at the feast.

That meant the harp might still be in the mead hall. And Wynstan with it.

CHAPTER EIGHT

Back inside Hwyel's fortress, I questioned the bondman raking up filth around the mead hall's latrine about Iago's harps. He told me that when Hywel took over in Aberffraw he got rid of them. "New king hung up his own," he said. "Don't know where the others went to."

I decided to look in the hall anyway. But just then a heavy hand fell on my shoulder.

Afraid some Norsker had dared lay hold of me, I went for my scramseaxe. Next thing, I was flat on my back with somebody else's scramseaxe at my throat.

"Think you was going to get the jump on me this time, too?" said Ealdorman Alvar as he waved his man off me. "Wilton's a long way off. So's Bere Regis. Just what you doing up here?"

A dozen excuses skittered through my head. When none of them landed on my tongue, I decided to tell the truth about Lord Ordwulf hiring me to find King Edward's corpse. And part of the truth about Wynstan. When I finished I said, "So, as you can see, I'm here on crown business. And I have a travel warrant to prove it."

Alvar screwed his black eyebrows together, gave his white beard a yank or two. Then he nodded to the half dozen men in his bodyguard. "Get yourselves up on the parapets, watch them Norskers. They get too drunk, raise hell. You, Welshman. You come with me."

To my surprise, he stuck out his hand. I hesitated before I took it. You never know what a Saxon might do. But once he'd hauled me to my feet, he steered me across the compound toward a low timber building with smoke coming out its chimney. I hoped it wasn't where they kept the wicker cages.

The place turned out to be a combination of brewhouse and bakery. Beyond a stack of kegs at the door stood an oven, kneading troughs, and loaf-laden tables. At the room's other end was a big four-hearth clay brewing range surrounded by wooden tubs full of water and steeping brew. Back of the far wall was likely where the brewers kept the leavening troughs and barrels of cooling ale. The whole place smelled the way I knew Heaven would.

Alvar waved the brewers out and grabbed a couple of leather cups. He filled them from an open-ended barrel of ale, shoved one my way. "Drink up."

"*Diolch*," I muttered. Thanks.

That made him laugh. "Who you think you're fooling? You ain't been no Welshman since your father throwed you out of that shitty place. And that was twenty year and more ago."

How could I be surprised Lord Alvar knew so much about me? It's an ealdorman's business to plough up the dirt on anybody that stumbles onto his patch. More so, if that anybody's gone and beat him up in a public street.

I wanted to ask him how he'd escaped a charge of treason for his part in trying to get Lady Edith crowned queen. But I figured the answer was a brew of family, politics, and money that'd be way too strong for somebody as simple as me. I got back to business. Bolting my cup of ale, I drew another, then said, "Where's Wynstan?"

"Nuns told me you're supposed to be looking for this Crawe woman, not old Wynstan the Windy."

I decided to take a chance that Alvar might be as interested in finding Wynstan as I was. Clearly, Wynstan hadn't given him King Edward's remains or Alvar wouldn't still be in Wales, peace parley or no. He'd be in England, fighting Lady Edith's way to the throne. So I explained that Lord Ordwulf'd hired me to find King Edward's remains and Wynstan with them.

The ealdorman didn't seem surprised. He just licked a fleck of foam off his mustache, said, "That's what I like about Ordwulf. If he's got something dirty he wants took care of, he hires the dirtiest man in his nephew's kingdom."

I gave him a sarcastic bow. "That's me."

"What you going to do with Wynstan once you find him and King Edward? Turn your dirty Welsh kin on him? Let 'em cage him up, parade him in at the Christmas feast with a apple in his mouth?"

I was growing tired of the word "dirty." Maybe I'd give Alvar another good thrashing. But he had his spear band close to hand. All I had was a knife and three nuns. I loosed them on him anyhow. The nuns, I mean. "Prioress says you're protecting Wynstan."

It was a lie, of course. Prioress had said nothing of the kind.

"Ah, the prioress," Alvar said. "Still a fine looking woman. Did you know me and King Eadgar once tried to... What shall

I say? Tried to turn her loose from them silly vows they made her take when she was just a little girl."

And quite a scandal it had made. Kidnapping a nun from her convent was a serious offense, though kicking a king in the balls was also serious, even for a nun. Eventually, the archbishop of Canterbury had waved the sign of the cross over both king and nun. She got St. Finella's and the king got her cousin Flæda. I don't know what Lord Alvar got.

What he likely figured to get now was Arthur's harp. "Listen hard, Welshman," he said. "I don't know where Wynstan is. Matter of fact, I didn't even know he was in Wales 'til you said so. And I'm too busy to find him, or help you do it."

It was most peculiar that Wynstan hadn't talked to Alvar yet. Even more peculiar that Alvar didn't seem to care. "But," I said, "you want something from me, or I'd be the one with the apple in my snout."

Alvar prowled around the table that held the bread, picked up a loaf, set it down, picked up another. He gazed at it for a moment, then tore it to bits. He hurled half to the ground, crammed the rest in his mouth. When he'd swilled the bread down with another cup of ale, he said, "Just help me keep the Great Harp of Arthur away from your filthy father."

"Tewdwr ap Merfyn?" I said with a laugh. "Sure you're not talking about his brother, King Brynmor? Or maybe you've confused your Welshmen and it's King Hywel who'll get Arthur's harp."

"I been fighting you dirty Welsh most of my life. I reckon I know one cattle rustling Cymro from the next."

He went over to one of the brewhouse's steeping barrels. I

could see his rough face reflected in its surface. "There's something about that harp you maybe don't know," he said. "Its magic is going to come to pass soon, right here in Aberffraw."

Time for a bit of mock befuddlement. "Who told you that?"

"King Hywel, your own uncle, King Brynmor, and Iago, too."

"Don't tell me you believed 'em."

"It don't matter if I believe or I don't. They believe. And they all want that bloody harp. Even the Norsker does. It's damn near turned into the polestar of their peace making."

Why did so many folk believe in this harp and the silly prophecy that clung to it? The king my uncle was a hard-headed man of war. As I recalled, he barely believed in prayer. And from what I'd heard, King Iago put his faith in men, not magic. For all the good it'd done him.

"By St Cecilia, just what is Arthur's harp supposed to do?" I expected to hear that it controlled air, earth, wind, and fire.

"They say it relieves a man of his fear."

That wasn't even worth laughing at. Nor did it involve magic, just a leader that Fortuna loved. And a poet who knew how to sing the right words at the right time. I spat in the dirt of the brewery floor.

Lord Alvar's dark eyebrows twitched up, then down. He shook his head. "Like I said, it don't matter whether you or me believes it. Them kings do. They think if they owned this harp, they could send their men to storm the very gates of hell."

What do you say to a thing like that? Fortunately, I didn't have to say anything because Alvar went on. "The harp's here in Aberffraw. Or someplace close by, anyhow. Iago had it. What do you think this war was all about?"

I wanted to say, "What wars are always about—greed and blood-lust and boredom." But for once I passed up the opportunity to get my head busted open. Instead, I said, "Looks like its magic didn't do him much good."

"That's because Iago committed the sin of theft."

Iago ab Idwal, kin-killer and thief. Obviously a man no good should come to. "But what has my father got to do with it?"

"Seems he claims it's his by right. Says Arthur's men hid his harp in a cave up in your family's mountains and that's where Iago stole it from."

I laughed so hard the ale shot out of my mouth like a cataract in spring. Was there no end to my father's evil? Or his greed. Or his lies. The only question was why he hadn't mentioned Arthur and his hounds, too.

Alvar waited 'til my laughter died down before he said, "That's how come your uncle was on our side in the war. To get the harp back."

Along with the whole of north Wales, of course.

"Lord Tewdwr says his brother Brynmor and his kingdom was just taking care of it 'til Arthur comes back for it." Alvar laughed then. "If you can believe such a thing."

I wasn't sure if he meant Arthur's return or King Brynmor as selfless guardian. Whichever, I couldn't believe it either.

"So how did King Iago come by the harp? Did he just stroll up to its hiding place and stroll off with it?"

"They say one of his clerics did. And I believe it because you never know with clerics. Tricky bastards, they are, no matter how much time they spend singing to the Lord. And thieves? You wouldn't believe what all they've stole and hid in their monasteries, be they Welsh or English."

Alvar had sacked enough monasteries to know. Even ones he'd been patron of. He was a tricky bastard himself.

I said, "Iago's up in that cage now, naked and howling. Where's the harp that's supposed to protect him?"

Alvar shrugged. "Nobody knows. We've asked everybody, churl, nobleman, cleric, 'specially the clerics. Asked every which way, too. We've beat 'em blue and bloody. Dipped 'em near to drowning. Ripped out teeth and toenails. Even flayed and roasted a couple. Nobody knows."

"Looked for it yourselves, I suppose."

Alvar didn't bother to answer. Instead, he said, "Best we know is what Iago's own bard, Bran, him of the second sight, told us right before we sunk him in the tub of boiling water. Said harp'll turn up at the feast to celebrate the peace—that's tomorrow—and tell us who it belongs to."

"You mean it's supposed to just appear?"

And that is exactly what Ealdorman Alvar, the man called "West Wind, Scourge of Mercia," assured me he believed. Just as Wynstan, his troupe, and everybody else in Aberffraw did.

A noise came from behind the brewhouse's rear wall. A rat, maybe, or kittens playing. Whatever it was, Alvar grabbed my arm and pointed me toward the door. "Let's go outside. Some walls grow ears."

Neither of us wanted to see more of the bloody spectacle in the courtyard, so we went beyond the gate, onto the lane that led to the river. Everybody could see us there, but that didn't seem to be of concern to Alvar. He just didn't want anyone to hear us. He turned his sharp eyes on me. "Like I said, Lord Tewdwr and his men fought in the war. He's already here, up in the hall."

Though I'd known my father was on his way to Aberffraw, my stomach lurched anyway. *Calm down, lad*, I said to myself. *He's just a man, just flesh and blood like any other.* I touched my relic sack. And felt a little stronger.

Meantime, Alvar was still talking. "You likely know King Brynmor's heir was killed in this war."

I thought about my cousin Ris dying with the Norsker blood-eagle astride him.

"Seems Lord Tewdwr's the heir now," Alvar said. "And—"

A shout came from the parapets. "My lord! Some of them Norskers is turning berserker. And they's headed this way."

Lord Alvar pulled his sword, ready to join his men. "I want you to get ahold of Wynstan for me, the lying old bugger. You do that and I'll get ahold of Brother Petroc and his ma, take that woman of yours off 'em."

"But she's in Iceland."

"Ordwulf tell you that? Well, he's a liar, too. She's right where she's been since spring in—"

But I didn't hear where Thrima was because a shrieking Saxon battle cry rang out and Alvar took off for the Norsker pavilion.

I had no time to think about what he'd just said about the Harp, even about Thrima. Something terrible had happened and I was the nuns' radman. Whatever it was, my duty was to protect them. I raced to get through the fortress gates before they slammed shut.

By the time I made it inside, Hywel's battle companions were arrayed and ready to meet the Viking enemy. Alongside them the bishops of Chester and Bangor stood on the church-house green like true soldiers of God, their banners flying, their golden crosses unyielding as battle blades. The rest of the clerics were drawn up behind, and all of them ready to call down the wrath of heaven.

The nuns had come out to the bower house's porch, nosey as ever. I grabbed Sister Hrothbeort as she started for the parapet steps to join the church militant, then hustled all three back inside. Wishing to hell I'd stayed in Chester, I took up guard duty on the porch, scramseaxe at the ready. As it turned out, though, Haraldsson got his men under control before they'd done much more than tear apart the village alehouse and carry off a cow or two.

When it was clear the danger had passed, I let the nuns join me on the porch. Of course, it wasn't a matter of "let." They came out on their own, calm as a summer's morning, to watch the frightened and bellowing cows being led back to the village.

Just as I began to think about Wynstan again and how I'd find him, Sister Hild grabbed my arm. "Where's Crawe?"

"Damn it, Sister, how come you're so interested in that hag? Feeding her and, praise St. Peter, washing her. Now traipsing after her half way 'round Christendom."

Sister Hild was about to bat the question away like a cloud of midges. But Prioress finally came to my rescue. "Tell him, Hild."

The old nun seemed to spot something by the mead hall that warranted her close attention. She stared at it in silence.

"Aw, go on, Hild." This from Sister Hrothbeort. "He's

bound to find out anyhow."

Sister Hild closed her eyes and screwed up her mouth in exasperation. Then, she shook her head and sighed. "Crawe is King Iago's sister. Her real name, her Welsh name is Ceinwen."

"Iago's sister? But the woman's mad."

Sister Hrothbeort let out a whoop of laughter. "Everybody's got a crazy sister. Or brother. Or cousin. Even kings. 'Specially kings. Why, King Ethelred's—"

Prioress cut her off. "Never mind about Ethelred's cousins. Go on, Hild."

First casting a cold eye at Sister Hrothbeort, then turning to me, Sister Hild said, "Crawe may indeed be wit-sick. Worse, she could be fiend-sick. Whichever, I have been able to help her a little. Now God has bade me finish the job. And I would rather not have King Hywel bring harm to her beforehand."

Could this Hywel be the sort who slaughters his enemy's kin? That kind of thing made for nothing but vengeance and feud, for war and more into all Eternity. "Do not make more widows and orphans than you have to," the king my uncle used to say with a sweet smile and a lifted eyebrow. "Be generous."

What he meant was, "You can get your own back later, triple-fold." With Brynmor there was always a viper under the cloth. With Sister Hild, too. God had bade her finish the job of helping Crawe? Right. Something else was afoot here. But if I ever wanted to learn what it was, I'd have to tread lightly and take the long way around. "Why would Crawe have come here? She's been living down in Dorset a long while."

"She told me she'd like to see home again."

"Of course, she would. But tell me this, Sister. How did she get involved with Wynstan?"

Another guffaw from Sister Hrothbeort before Sister Hild gave her a look. Then Prioress started talking again. Then Hild went to talking, too, both talking at the same time and neither willing to let the pulpit go. Meantime, Sister Hrothbeort couldn't stop laughing.

When they all finally settled down, they told me a story. Some years back, they said, Wynstan had been entertaining in the mead hall at Aberffraw and he and Crawe, as Sister Hrothbeort put it, "took up with each other." More than that, they up and ran off together. And maybe they would've lived happily ever after except that in the commotion of their leaving, Wynstan forgot Song Cauldron, his lyre. Didn't miss it until they were someplace in the middle of the Irish Sea.

"So," I said, "there the bastard was without the tools of his trade and with a woman who liked to play with dead things."

Sister Hrothbeort and I busted out laughing so hard we barked and bayed and even boo-hooed. Presently, Prioress couldn't help but join in and the roars got that much worse. For her part, Sister Hild just stared at the mead hall.

After we calmed down and dried our eyes, I said, "Now Wynstan's excuse for being here is that he's come to fetch his lyre. Do you think he knew Iago was no longer king?"

Shrugs all around, until Sister Hild said, "From what I've been told, it did not matter to him who ruled in Aberffraw. He believed his lyre was still here."

"So he's just now found out that Arthur's harp is supposed to appear at the feast?"

Sister Hild nodded. "Apparently so. But we would rather not stay for that miraculous moment. Unfortunately, we won't be able to leave until we find Crawe."

She turned her hard, dark-eyed gaze on me. "However, we will soon. Because when you find Wynstan, you will send him to us. He will take us to Crawe."

Before I could object—say that Crawe was most likely in Dublin with the salt-merchant—Sister Hrothbeort and the Prioress decided it was time for their naps and took themselves off to the bower house. That left me and Sister Hild to linger on the porch—her staring at the mead hall again, me again pondering Wynstan's part in the business about of King Arthur's harp.

He'd first told it around Aberffraw that he'd come there looking for Song Cauldron. Then he heard Arthur's harp would turn up at the peace feast. Wynstan was likely in the mead hall making sure of that right now. But if I had my way, by the time the harp was supposed to oh-so-magically appear Wynstan would be leading me to King Edward's corpse.

I leaped down from the porch and headed for the mead hall to find the old reptile. To my surprise, Sister Hild called after me, "Be careful, my boy!"

When I turned to thank her, she'd disappeared.

CHAPTER NINE

I shoved past the English guards at the hall's dragon-decorated door. Except for its sleeping benches, the place was shadowy and seemed empty Then I saw a big man seated on a stool by the smoldering fire pit, alone and unarmed.

But he wasn't Wynstan. He was my father.

I halted, gulped down the fear stinging my throat, then stepped close and bared my teeth. "Who do you think I am?"

He sat down again, heavily. "Prince Ris, my lad, how'd you get away from the Norskers? I saw them ... I thought I saw the Norskers ..." Now he sprang back up, spread wide his arms. "God be praised, boy, I'm glad to see—"

But he didn't try to gather his nephew to him after all. He dropped his arms, clutched his throat while he stared at me, slack-jawed. "Who ... ?"

I said nothing, just let him look.

"Guards!"

"Too late for that, my lord father," I said, as the squad of Saxon soldiers pushed into the hall. "Ealdorman Alvar controls this place now."

The blood flooded back into Tewdwr's face, rising above his beard like a crimson tide. "I know you now. You're the thief that dares call himself Tryffin ap Tewdwr. As if you could be any son of mine. Not when that bitch-in-heat went around fucking clowns and God only knows what else."

I'd never doubted I was his son. And looking at him in the light that streamed through the open door, I didn't doubt it now. Not with my own hammer of a nose. And my own eyes that my mam used to say were blacker than an Englishman's heart.

"You dare come here," he said. "You less-than-a-fart, you lamb's prick. And not alone, like a man. With the army of a Saxon lord to stand betwixt us. Just what I'd expect from the whelp of a slut who..."

Hearing our loud voices, the English guards surged through the hall's front door. But their yeoman, seeing a fight brewing, one not his own, marched them back outside. They banged shut the door behind them. That was fine with me. I'd finish this by firelight.

I shot my fist into Tewdwr's big belly, then jumped back as he spewed soup and slime into the air betwixt us. He dropped to his knees, still spitting up his supper. I would kill him soon, but first I wanted to thrash him, whip him, leave him naked and bleeding on the mead hall floor. Make him pay for my mother. Pay and pay and pay.

I wanted him to plead for his life, too. Instead, a sneer crept out from under his grizzled mustache. "Go on. Do your worst, you ... "

What name he called me, I don't remember. But I'd heard enough. I decided to kill him on the spot. I reached beneath my legband and pulled out my small knife. I wouldn't dishonor my scramseaxe with his blood.

By now Tewdwr was trying to stand and would've succeeded had I not landed a hard kick to his chin that knocked him senseless. He crumpled at my feet. Kneeling next to him, I grabbed his white hair, yanked back his head, put the knife to his throat. I'd butcher him like the pig he was.

But the agony that came next coursed not through him but me. My head rang, my eyes watered. I was both blind and deaf. By the time I could see again, I found myself on the floor next to Tewdwr. He was moaning and bleeding and staring up at Sister Hild while she flogged him with her thorn cane.

I pulled myself to my feet. "Jesus, Sister, what—?"

"Do not take the name of the Lord in vain," she said, breathless but still pounding Tewdwr.

Who would've believed the old woman had such a strong arm? Strong enough to do him serious harm. "As long as we're talking Scripture," I said, "maybe you shouldn't be about to commit murder."

She stopped her attack then, stood—first gasping, then weeping. Finally, she threw down the cane. "I will not kill him, though God knows I want to."

Still amazed, I said, "What in hell did Lord Tewdwr do, that you'd damn near beat him to death?"

As his eyes began to flutter open, she beckoned me to her. "Look at him," she said. "Look at those eyes I always told you were blacker than an Englishman's heart."

I went as numb as if I'd been dropped into a Scottish lake in winter, then as hot as if I'd just risen from the springs at Aachen. In a trice I had her in my arms, hoisting her off her feet, dancing her across the hall, covering her in kisses. I whooped and roared and bellowed. Wept, too, while she laughed and called me "*fy machgen*," dear boy. Her dear,

dear boy.

Only once in my life had I been this happy—when I'd first lain with Thrima. Though that had been quite a different joy, the degree of my jubilation was the same. Even when my first, mad delight had run its course, I still couldn't let my mother go. Nor could I speak. She said what I could not. "I never stopped loving you and missing you and wanting you near me."

I snuffled into her ear, had all I could do not to smear it with tears and snot as I'd done as a child when she'd rescued me from the cruel man who was my father. She didn't pull away, as I might've expected the austere Sister Hild to do, until I was finally able to say, "How ... I mean, how did ... ?"

But her answer had to wait until I found some rope and tied the senseless Tewdwr to a post. When he wouldn't quit moaning, I stuck a wooly wad of sheepskin in his mouth.

Satisfied he'd disturb us no further, we sat at a trestle table and I poured us cups of strong Welsh ale. "How did you escape the slavers?" I said.

"Simple, *fy machgen*. At least it was simple once I realized that after a long march Irishmen—and not only Irishmen—will drink just about anything set before them. Especially if they think it will get them drunk."

"Oh come on, Sister ... um ... I mean ... *Mam*?" I'd stumbled over the sad fact that I'd no notion of what to call her.

She smiled thinly and said, "You may address me as Hild, as do my sisters in Christ. You are, after all, *familia*."

Even if *familia* means a monastic community and not blood kin, even if I was her community's radman, why did she have to use the Latin word and not the Welsh or English one? But what did I expect from a woman hard-boiled as a wool cape? To be covered with more tears and kisses? She'd known who I was all along. For that matter, I knew her, too. Knew she'd no more want further show of sentiment than would I. In that way, we were truly mother and son.

"All right, then. 'Hild' it is," I said with a sharp nod. "Let's get back to the Irish slavers. You can't mean all you had to do was wait 'til they got drunk, then tiptoe into the night. Nothing's that easy."

She again gave me a smile, though not so thin this time. "You might be surprised at how easy some things are. But in this case, you're right. It was not easy. Or quick. Naturally, a few days passed before I—what shall I say?—before I got my feet back under me. And I admit that took all the way to Chester. A nasty enough place, as you know, with its brothels and low taverns, never mind its slave block. But once there I was clever enough to recognize a most delightful herb—most useful, anyway—growing in the city walls. Foolishly, though, I thought all I need do was pluck a sprig or two, mash it up, toss it into the Irishmen's drink."

She crossed herself, then said, "There's no such quick bane, of course. By the time I finally found a way to poison all of them at the same time, they were negotiating my sale to an Orkney jarl. 'No public auction for a woman... ah... talented as this,' they told him."

Her mouth twisted as she spat into the rushes on the floor. But when she spoke again, she was smiling. "Fortunately, Northmen like very strong, very flavorful ale. And Irishmen like it any way it comes."

"Poison?" I clapped my hand to my head. "Poison? My God, Sister. Are you saying you killed them?"

Now she out and out laughed. "A poor choice of words, though I must admit murder crossed my mind. However, my mother had taught me well. And your father's mother, too. They were both wise-women, though each in her own way."

I was afraid to ask just what those ways might've been because I remembered Tewdwr's mother as a woman not easy to love.

"I made a lovely lot of ale that went down easy but came up hard. By the time their guts and their butts were calm again, I was under a pile of dressed leather in the back of an oxcart, bound I knew not where. Praise God, the cart stopped at St. Finella's."

I was astounded. "And the nuns took you in, just like that?"

Hild snorted, shook her head. "Oh, you of little faith."

She seemed prouder of herself than a nun perhaps ought to be, but I was proud of her, too. I was just about to tell her so when I took a whack on the head that lit up the dark mead hall in a burst of stars and pitched me to its floor, my mam stumbling down beside me.

"The bitch and her whelp," my father said as he gave my ribs a hard poke with whatever he'd used on my head. "And him still sucking her tit."

The stars in my head cleared and, as Hild rolled away, I caught hold of his legs, figuring to yank him down in the rushes with me. Then I'd rip him to pieces with my bare hands, just like I'd planned for the last score of years. But it wasn't me who brought him low. Hild once again began pounding him with her cane, hard enough to distract him while I pulled out my scramseaxe. I scrambled up, ready to rip open his belly.

"Stop!" came a shout. "Enough!"

A strong arm caught me in a choke-hold and, gagging, I dropped the knife. Then, before I could save myself, an English soldier manhandled me out the hall's back door.

I don't know what happened inside the mead hall after that. I had enough to do keeping my legs under me and my wits about me as I looked around for Hild. When I finally saw her unharmed and now making her way toward the bower house, I should have been relieved that Tewdwr had done her no harm. The problem with that was she was leaning on the arm of Wynstan Wing-tongue.

By then, the Saxon soldier had let go of me, though not before he called me some very bad names in very bad Welsh. I called him some names, too, in excellent English. And would've called him more, except Lord Alvar had come into the courtyard.

He already knew what had happened in the mead hall. "You've made a big mistake, son, taking on Lord Tewdwr. I can protect Sister Hild—God only knows why she'd do such a daft thing as help you. But she and her superior and my niece are—"

"Wait!" I said. "Your niece?" He could only mean Sister Hrothbeort. "She's your kin?"

By now my time in Aberffraw was beginning to remind me of those tedious genealogies poets so enjoy singing for their lords. I just hoped it wouldn't end like they often do— with keening women and a smoking pyre.

Alvar broke up that bad dream with, "Hrothbeort's my sister's girl. So, like I said, her and them other two nuns don't need to fear Lord Tewdwr or King Hywel, or even the Norsker. But you—you been about as stupid as a man can get, and my advice is to get the hell out of here fast as them long legs of yours can carry you. Because once they hear about what just happened in the hall, the Welsh—Tewdwr's Welsh, anyhow—will get themselves riled up. Then, vicious dogs like all Welshmen, they'll up and start a war 'twixt them and me."

"You?"

"You're under my protection here in Aberffraw, you know. My niece and Sister Hild seen to that. 'Til now, anyways." Alvar and the yeoman glanced at the hall's back door like they expected a pack of Tewdwr's men to come chasing out, swords in hand, foam at their mouths.

When no one came, the ealdorman turned back to me, a snake of a smile slithering out of his whiskers. "When you get back to England, you can tell Ordwulf I got to Wynstan first."

I had no answer for that, wasn't even sure what it meant. So I just gave him my thanks for saving me from Tewdwr, said I'd remember him in my prayers—his yeoman, too. But before I could ask about Thrima, Alvar marched off toward the parapet where his hearthmen stood watch. The yeoman lingered a moment, then with a growl, followed his lord.

Rain had threatened all day, and now came a drencher that turned the sea to greasy grey and reminded Aberffraw's churls of indoor chores.

I scurried back to the brewhouse, dipped up some ale, thought about what Alvar had said. I figured he'd have captured Wynstan by now and likely had King Edward, too. So I decided on the spot to take his advice. I'd leave Aberffraw on the morning tide and take the nuns along. It'd be for my safety, sure, but theirs, too, never mind Lord

Alvar's guarantees. Too many questions hovered over this place, questions that were likely to be answered in blood.

Would Arthur's harp appear? What would happen when only one commander gained it? What would the other three do? Turn Aberffraw into bloody ash, that's what. And then how would Lord Alvar protect the nuns?

And the most important question of all, the one I couldn't think about now—where was Thrima?

When the rain let up, I went to the bower house to tell the nuns we would leave Aberffraw in the morning. Fortunately, Wynstan had delivered Hild there. But then he'd quick-like taken off. I wasn't too pleased Hild had let him get away.

"Just what did you want me to do?" Hild said. "Toss a rope around his neck and tether him to the latrine fence?"

That's when it finally sank in that as usual she wouldn't let me—or anybody else—tell her what to do. Still, once she gave the situation some thought, she'd surely see we had to get out of Wales. Since nightfall was almost on us anyway, I'd let her sleep on it.

Me, I wanted to sleep in the warm, dry stable, but I'd sworn at St. Finella's altar that I'd take care of her nuns. And an oath was an oath, even in cold, wet, dangerous Aberffraw. I rolled up in a hairy old blanket that stank of cow shit and settled down on the cold rock of the bower porch. At least it had a roof. I dreamed of Thrima, when I dreamed at all. Then just before dawn another storm came ashore. Thunder rocked the bower house and lightning turned the darkness so white that not even love could soothe me. Now I dreamed of Thrima, chained in the snow of Iceland.

CHAPTER TEN

Next morning the rain had stopped, but the day was dark, the air thick. I hoped that yet another storm wasn't on the way, because I intended to leave Aberffraw before the peace celebration, no matter what. Standing next to the bower house with the nuns, I put my plan to them. Hild scowled while Sister Hrothbeort ate porridge and Prioress drained a cup of mead.

I tried going moral on them. "My duty is to get you out of here before all hell cuts loose. And it will, no matter what happens with Arthur's harp today."

Hild stamped her cane on the floor and rose. "It's time for Tierce." At that, Prioress finished her mead, Sister Hrothbeort slurped down the rest of the porridge, and the three marched off to the church-house. Leaving me fuming and feeble.

That's when I decided to leave on my own, to hell with oaths—and nuns, even if one was my mother. If they weren't concerned about the chaos about to suck them up ... Well, what matter duty and morality and all the rest? I'd take care of Wynstan another day. Finding Thrima was far more important. I went to saddle Mona.

Just outside the fortress walls milled a shouting,

laughing, dancing horde—the commanders' personal retinues, waiting for the peace to be proclaimed. Then they'd join their lords in the hall and make merry for a week. English hearthmen, Norse *huscarles*, Welsh *ceulu*, all of them God-sworn to stand with their lords to the death, all of them now drunk as churls on Twelfth Night.

I shoved my way through the mob as it poured through the gate, accepting drink from a Norsker here, a Saxon there. I'd pulled my cap down to my eyes, my cloak up to my nose so they'd no notion who I was, wouldn't have cared if they did. They were happy to be alive at the end of another war and happy to celebrate that fact with the whole wide world. At least they were for now. If they got much drunker, they'd be fighting each other with fists and knives and whatever timber they could rip off hall or church or bower.

Before I could reach the stable, the commanders appeared in the mead hall doorway. Their men went quiet and stood tall while King Hywel's high battle-voice rang through Caer Aberffraw. "The peace is made. Let us praise God whose mercies are without number."

After the news had been repeated in English and Norse, the hall doors opened wide and the cheering crowd pushed inside to drink some more, eat plenty, and hear their bards sing of their immense courage.

I couldn't leave the nuns to them. You never know what drunken Norskers and Saxons might get up to. While they streamed into the mead hall, I went back to the bower house.

The nuns weren't there. Or in the church-house or any of the out-buildings. Had they actually had the good sense to retreat to the village or, better yet, the bishop's pavilion? I caught hold of a bondman dragging a sled full of venison toward the hall. He turned out to be your typical Welshman, not sure just what a nun was. "You mean them funny-looking grey women, they in the hall? Seen them squatted down behind that stack of barrels—"

I didn't wait for further news before I joined the tide pouring into the mead hall.

A dozen torches showed me what I had not noticed earlier when I'd fought my father there. Now I saw that except for its bowed walls, this hall was much like the one at Thornholt, though bigger. It could easily hold half a hundred people. But it was a cruder place than Thornholt. The oak of wall and post and roof bore the marks of axes and no intricately embroidered hangings decorated the walls. It also reeked of the beds of the men who slept there. Come morning, everyone in here could count on being chewed up with their lice.

Despite its size, the hall had only the one fire pit, a large one in its middle. The four commanders sat in a half-circle around it, each with his chief poet and his battle-captain standing behind his shoulders like an eagle's wings. The rest of their retinues and the clerics sat in front of them, packed onto the crowded trestle tables jammed so close together the serving men and women barely had room to move.

As you might expect, the ale barrels took pride of place by the door. Stacked like a staircase on chocked oaken planks, the pile rose four levels high. But though I climbed all the way up it, then across the top barrels for what seemed like half a league, I didn't see the nuns any place among the hall's multitude.

That's when I should have left. But by then the doors were shut and guarded by men armed to the eyeballs. Even so, I could've found a way to melt into the crowd. Truth be told, though, I was curious about what would happen when King Arthur's harp did or didn't sing. And I was safely hidden in the smoke and darkness at the top of the hall, where I could peer down at the roiling, roistering mob below.

As I looked down at my father, backed by his bard and battle-captain and adorned with an old-fashioned gold torc, I had to laugh. One eye was swollen shut and his face looked like a burst plum, all purple and pale yellow. We'd done a good job on the murdering bastard, my *mam* and me.

I forced my gaze to King Hywel and Guthrith Haraldsson, then to Lord Alvar. In the firelight, the battle scars on their faces gleamed. Across the room Wynstan sat with the court poets, no doubt pretending to be one of them. He had his face stuck in the venison stew like a forest pig rooting the ground at the end of winter.

Presently, the Bishop of Mercia rose to give the blessing. He was a portly fellow, garbed in silk and with manicured hands raised to Heaven. "Oh loving Lord and God, ever ready to listen to the prayers of Thy servants ..."

Heads bowed in every section of the hall. Except at a table of young Norskers in the rear, where a drinking game was in noisy progress, all but drowning out the bishop as he prayed in the liquefied Latin of badly educated Saxon clerics. Of course, a little racket never stops an English bishop. "To thee do I pray, Lord, trusting in the help of the blessed and glorious Mary ... angels and archangels, the heavenly Powers, Patriarchs, Prophets, and the entire citizenry of heaven."

Since that just about covered anybody and anything short of Fortuna and his own ancestors, the bishop must've felt it was safe to get back to God. "Increase the faith," he said, flapping his soft hands heavenward. "Give peace to our rulers. Forgive our sins. Restore health to the wounded."

The ruckus at the young Vikings' table had gotten heated, with a bench tipped over and ripe Norsker oaths filling the hall. Maybe that's why the bishop began to shout out his prayer in English, which even angry Northmen can understand. "Give help to those journeying in foreign countries."

Most of the other Norskers had joined the Welsh and English in piously lifting up their hearts and hands. Only the young ones in the rear went on swilling ale, slapping their cups onto the table, clapping, yelling, laughing, too drunk to remember they were the ones in a foreign country. Haraldsson, none too sober himself, glanced their way. Then he shook his head and gave them the same soft smile you give wrestling kittens.

Meanwhile, the bishop rattled on. "Obtain freedom for those in captivity and bondage," he asked the Lord.

That made me think of Thrima, and then my *mam*. Praise God, Hild would never need such a prayer again. I wanted the same for Thrima.

At last, the bishop came to the point. He begged God to "give the blessing of mutual charity to those who are at variance." Though likely none too clear about what the bishop had just said, Alvar, Haraldsson, Hywel, and even my father nodded in righteous agreement. And all would've been well, on earth as it is in heaven, except the bishop went on to utter the words no cleric can ever resist. "And Lord, we beseech thee, bring true faith to the unbelieving."

Like any Norsker ever vigilant for insult, Haraldsson jumped to his feet. "God damn it! I'm as Christian as any man among you." His hand went to his sword. "And, by Jesus, I'll prove it with cold steel and hot blood."

Every Norsker in the hall leaped to his feet—most not sure why, but drunk enough not to care. Never mind they'd just survived a war. Any fight was red meat to their souls.

The Saxon bishop shrank back, confused and likely scared to death. But the Welsh bishop stepped forward to lay his crosier on Haraldsson's shoulder. "Of course, you're a Christian, my son," he said in Norse. "No one here doubts it. I have myself heard your confession, placed the body of Christ on your tongue, brought the chalice of His blood to your lips. And you ate and drank in remembrance that Christ died for you."

The Norsker paused, taken aback, I reckon, by this big-balled little bishop. And, to the bishop's credit, he had sense enough to press his advantage. He drew back his crosier to stand on tiptoe and with his thumb make the sign of the cross on Haraldsson's forehead. "May the peace of God that passes all understanding ..."

To the obvious surprise of everybody but the Welsh bishop and himself, Haraldsson muttered "Amen" and sat down.

"More mead!" the Welsh bishop shouted to the bondmen where they huddled by the door. "And ale, bread and pork, whatever you have. Bring it now and don't stop!"

That was enough to send the bewildered troops back to their tables. That and a volley of orders from their lords.

A few prayers later, the hall door sprang open and in hurtled Wynstan's troupe.

"It's about time," I muttered to myself as I watched Beorn and little Cuthred do a looping series of handsprings, then vault from table to table, landing lightly 'twixt the cups and horns and ewers.

Behind them came Kyre, arrayed like the Queen of the Night in a spangled white tunic, her head-dress adorned so that moonbeams seemed to leap from it. She smiled her heavenly smile, then began to sing in a voice so pure that soon even the noisiest Norsker went quiet. The song was one known the world over—at least the northern world over—and pretty soon even the Norskers had sobered up enough to hum along.

While Beorn and Cuthred cavorted through the crowd, Kyre visited the mead benches, casting the glory of her smile over each man and making every one of them believe she sang to him alone, even the clerics. Fact is, her light seemed to shine brighter on them than on anyone else. Or maybe it just seemed that way because of the dazzling crimson of their blushes.

The audience seduced, Wynstan waited until his troupe had left the hall. Then he stood and took a place in the firelight, arms outstretched as if to embrace every one there. He'd hardly begun to sing when, already all but conquered, his listeners gave themselves to the spell of his poem. I've forgotten its words, but they hardly mattered because when he came to the last of them and bowed his head in humble closing, the hall erupted in loud applause, raucous laughter and ear-splitting shouts of joy.

But maybe it wasn't Wynstan they screamed for after all. The hall door had swung open and out of the night came a bondman rolling in an ale barrel. Following it was Kyre, as solemn as if she approached an altar, hands holding not the flat, gut-strung Song Cauldron, but an upright, triangular

Welsh harp, its metal strings flashing in the firelight.

What was Wynstan playing at? And why would he have brought on this ... whatever it was? The whole business had him and his troupe at the mercy of men who were savages any time, never mind what they became when they were drunk and disappointed.

I didn't know whether to pray or curse, so I did some of both. Until finally—Oh, God, could this be the Great Harp of Arthur?

The crowd below must have thought so. Up sprang a hall full of drunken soldiers, scattering plates, spilling ale and mead, knocking over benches, colliding with each other in their haste to see the thing whose magic would allow them to storm ramparts from Ultima Thule to the far shores of Oceanus. They didn't rush the harp, though. Their chiefs straightaway ordered them to stand easy and let their betters handle whatever wonders were to come.

For the moment the only wonder was that every one of their betters—jarl and thegn, bard and bishop—simply stared at the harp where it now sat, dumb and still, on the ale barrel next to the hearth.

I stared myself, for a while, wondering how Wynstan had managed all this. How had he come by Arthur's harp? Had Crawe told him its whereabouts? And why put on this elaborate show? What did Wynstan hope to gain from its magic here? Did it truly have any magic, here or anywhere?

But I didn't have time for questions now. However the harp had landed with Wynstan, and for whatever reason, the thing was dangerous—whether it sang or not. I knew I had to find the nuns, wherever they were, and get them out of Aberffraw. I didn't know just how, but the gates of Hell were about to bust open and I didn't want the nuns to be any part of it. Nor me, either. Quickly and quietly, I crawled down the rear of the stack of barrels. Right into the iron grip of a Saxon guard. "You ain't going no place, Welshman."

He hauled me toward the back of the hall, thinking, I reckon, to shove me outside. And I surely would've found myself nose-down in the yard, sucking up mud and moss, except that soon we could go no farther. The crowd was too thick and seething and angry.

I called him a few names, tried to leave tooth marks in the arm that lay beneath his hard leather sleeve. It only got me flung against the wall, kicked by him and a couple of Vikings. To make their fun complete, they chopped off half my beard.

After I finished a right good stretch of cursing them—and their whorish mothers, too—the Saxon pointed toward the harp. "That there's going to sing for Lord Alvar presently, and when it does, I'm sworn to kill every Welshman I can lay hold of." He gave me a thin smile. "Starting with you."

He grabbed for me again but I twisted away, to take cover in the crowd as it swarmed closer to the harp.

Presently, all four of the commanders went and stood before it, first together, then one at a time. To no avail. The harp did not sing. Not for Alvar or Hywel or Haraldsson or my *tad*.

Before long, the four—too hurt and confused to be angry —fell back to become just part of the churning crowd. And were still there when I took an elbow to the ribs, followed by a Saxon curse and a clip to the ear. A hard shove sent me skidding into the barrel the harp stood on. It dropped into my arms.

The Great Harp of Arthur began to sing.

At first the harp brought forth a mere hum, followed by the thinnest of tunes. Some of the men stood stunned, some unbelieving, some just plain confused. I froze in astonishment.

When finally they all figured they understood the harp's message, the mead hall erupted in joy and rage. Joy from the Welsh—I *was*, after all, Cymru-born—rage from the Norskers and Saxons. "Fraud!" "Cheat!" "Hoax!" they roared, and again the tables went over, again the mead horns and ale cups crashed down. Norse and English, then Welsh battle cries rang out.

But before swords clashed, before blood gushed, the clerics stepped into the fray, their consecrated hands raised in peace. Very brave it was of them, too, considering those other hands, the ones that raised sword and scramseaxe. The clerics fled the field fast as they could. No faster, though, than Wynstan and his troupe, who were in such haste they tipped over the ale barrel that the harp stood upon.

Out of the barrel spilled Crawe.

In a trice she was up and laughing, then sprinting from the hall. So, as war screams filled the hall, it was me the war bands rose against. I turned to the high pile of barrels and did the only thing I could think of to save myself. I yanked out two of the chocks that kept the stack from falling. Then, harp clutched tight to me, I took off for the back door, flung it open, and fled into a hard rain.

The pile roared down like a winter avalanche—to crush three score Welsh, English, and Viking warriors beneath the heavy barrels. At least that's what I figured, and, Christ forgive me, that's what I hoped. But when I looked back inside, it turned out that I hadn't been the only one folded in the arms of Fortuna. The hall stood empty and no one lay dead. I climbed atop the barrels that blocked the front doorway and saw the four war bands out there in the hall-yard. They'd likely left the hall while I was still going up the stack, to do their fighting in the open. I'd been too busy saving my own hide to notice.

They'd marched into a fierce hailstorm, its stones big as your fist. It had sprung out of a light rain, unexpected as a dragon born of a worm, huge and fierce and deadly. Or so the poets later sang. Now, the men who'd been ready to wage mortal combat raced for shelter, shields over their heads, tails betwixt their legs, 'til finally they huddled in the safety of shed and stable, kitchen and church-house.

When the hail eased off, Alvar and Haraldsson ordered their men out of the front gate, leaving Hywel and the Welsh to clean up the mess in the mead hall. Before I could make my escape, they'd moved enough barrels to spy me out and start yelling that they'd found the *fwcar* and he had the harp and it was unharmed and he was alive and "We're fixing to haul him out damn quick."

I made for the hall's back door damn quick. I was scared

as hell and you would've been, too, if the Great Harp of King Arthur had landed in your lap and a mountain of ale barrels toppled down behind you.

Outside, hail was murdering the mud again and would soon murder me, too. Harp under my tunic, I streaked across the green and into the church sacristy.

The clerics had taken refuge in the nave after the war bands had driven them out of the mead hall and the barrels fell. Now they sang a psalm of thanksgiving. "Then the earth shook and trembled, the foundations of the hills moved ... He delivered me from my strong enemy."

I set the harp down beside me and pushed a heavy chest against the sacristy door. I didn't want them knowing I was there, but even so I finished the psalm along with them. "He delivered me because he delighted in me."

And He surely must've been delighted because not only was I safe and dry, but there on a shelf stood a big clay jar full of altar wine. Though the earth still shook and trembled, I sucked that wine down quick as I could and felt delivered for sure.

The clerics kept on singing and I kept on drinking until all of us had gone calm. The weather, too. The hail stopped, the rain softened until there was only the flat drip, drip of water draining off the eaves. As the clerics left the church-house to return to their pavilions up the river, I sank onto the sacristy floor, drank some more, and thought about Thrima.

"Your love is better than wine," I liked to tell her, quoting from the Psalter. "How fair and pleasant are you, oh love, for delights."

And she'd say, "What kind of songs, *ja*, are you learning

back in your monastery?" Then she'd laugh and we'd get to the delights.

I put that memory away quick as I could. Better to think about my predicament. I had to find out why I'd been lumbered with Arthur's harp. If I didn't, how could I know who or what would soon hunt me down? I also figured I had to hang onto the harp. It might help me free Thrima. Even folks in Ultima Thule had heard of King Arthur. Besides, if I tried to give it to anybody—King Hywel, Lord Alvar, the Norsker, even, God forbid, my father—not only would the war start up again, but I'd be its first casualty.

I ran my fingers along the harp's wires. It made that low moan the things always do when somebody besides a poet tries to strike a chord. "Not going to sing for me after all, eh? Well, what am I supposed to do with you, then?"

This time it didn't even give out a moan. And why should I expect it to? Maybe it wasn't Arthur's magical harp. Else why would it have come to me? The whole business was likely nothing but a hoax invented by Crawe—and, I had no doubt, by Wynstan. But why?

The reason would be simple. The old rogue wanted it for himself. But even though Crawe had handed it over to him, he had to show the world that the harp would sing for him alone. Only then could it bring him the power and the glory. He would've waited for the crowd in the hall to calm down, then stood in front of the harp, spoken to it. Then it—Crawe, I mean, from inside the barrel—would've sung. But I'd gone and mucked up the show. Wynstan would be as furious with me as everyone else was.

Where'd he run to? I didn't think he and the troupe would have headed back to their camp. It'd be a long walk in the rain with a small child and all their equipment. And, anyway, they'd be in danger from the angry soldiers, too. Maybe by now they were hiding in the bower house with the nuns, safe and dry. Even if Wynstan wasn't with the troupe, I could talk to Beorn and Kyre, find out where Wynstan had gone. Meantime, I'd stow the harp, whoever it belonged to, in the place I understood best—the church's reliquary.

Lucky for me the kings of Aberffraw kept their relics in a good-sized wooden box atop the altar, not under it. And, just as lucky, they had the thighbones of St. Guenissa in there. Legend had it that she died near Caer Aberffraw when her ship blew off course in the Irish Sea. An important woman was Guenissa. Not only was she St David's aunt but she was the foster sister of King Arthur, indeed grew up with him. The harp easily fit beside her.

The box, though, had no lock. Trusting folk, these Welsh. No matter, I'd be back for the harp as soon as I dealt with Wynstan. And once I found him, that wouldn't take long at all. Because by now I was convinced he'd shoved me into that ale barrel. I just didn't know why.

The storm had started up again, this time with heavy rain and hard thunder. Lightning came so close it turned the sky from black to white. But, no matter how fierce the storm—or the soldiers—I had to find Wynstan. Where to look first, stable or bower house? I chose the stable because it stood closest. On my way there, I passed the wicker cage that had held King Iago. It lay in the mud, empty. Somebody must've taken pity on Iago, pulled him out of the tempest. Or maybe he'd finally died and the cage awaited some other criminal. "Pray God, don't let it be me."

No one was in the stable except a redheaded stable boy, a scared twelve-year old left to guard the horses on his own in a thunderstorm. He took the duty seriously, though. Scared as he was, he moved among the nervous horses, calming them with a soft litany of prayer and curses. It seemed like a good idea. The storm raged fiercer than ever and Wynstan would stay wherever he was 'til it died down. So I helped the lad out with a few songs, soothing to the horses and dirty enough to delight a twelve-year old.

When the thunder slackened, we fed and watered the beasts. It took a while because the stable was crowded, and not only with Lady Philosophy, the two ponies, my Mona, and all of King Hywel's horses. My father had also stabled his men's mounts there. His own, too, fine horses likely as swift as they were sleek. Tewdwr knew horseflesh, I'll give him that.

Mona seemed glad to see me. She nickered, anyhow, and twitched her ears. The rain was still coming down too hard to ride into, so I had time to reward her with a good brushing. But when I tried to do the same for Lady Philosophy, the damn mule bit me. Only on the shoulder, but even through my cloak and heavy winter tunic it hurt like the slash of a knife. And sent me into a red fury. I grabbed the first weapon that came to hand, a braided leather rope, black and whip-like. I'd beat that sorry beast bloody, her and Wynstan both.

But every time I came close to her, rope coiled and lethal, she set to kicking. Braying, too, now. Not only couldn't I get anywhere near, her antics nearly doubled the stable boy over with laughter. I set on him, then, leather lashing. He saw the danger and hauled himself into the rafters, where he perched, laughing harder than ever. The little bastard had shape-shifted from a scared twelve-year old into a redheaded son of Satan.

I was about to pull him down and strangle him when it occurred to me that both he and the rope had a better use. My anger cooled right down, like it always does when I set to plotting. I dropped the rope, fished a cut penny out of my pouch. Stepping back, I held it up. "Want this?"

The lad dropped from the rafters and grabbed at the silver. I knocked him away, said, "Now I see why your mates left you in here on your own, middle of a storm. You're a greedy little weasel. Likely you nick their grub, eat it all yourself."

He really did look like a weasel or maybe a fox—pinch-faced, with a crafty look in his eyes. And skinny, half-starved even. Which I was glad of because a hungry boy is a willing boy. "You got a name, son?"

After he mumbled something that sounded like Sly, I told him I was going to use the leather rope in a snare. "The kind you set for hare, only this one is to catch a man."

Sly didn't take his eyes off the coin. But I could tell he was listening as I described my quarry and explained what to do after the man I called "the big fellow" had stepped in the snare and was dangling from the rafters. Then I issued a serious threat and again described the reward. "It'll be more than any cut penny," I said, flipping the coin to the boy.

I left him all a-grin and gaping at the silver in his palm. Maybe he'd do as I said, maybe not. But if he did, that would be one problem taken care of.

As I headed for the bower house, the storm came roaring back. So did Wynstan, likely looking for me and Arthur's harp. I got to the bower house porch right after him. At the top of the rain-slick steps, the arrogant bastard stopped, glanced my way, then cupped a hand to his ear. "Hear that?" he said of the rain clattering on the straw roof. "Does it not sound like the sweet applause at Bere Regis?"

I'd show him sweet. Lightning flashed as I charged up the stairs three at a time, scramseaxe drawn. Wynstan turned to make a run for the bower door. But I'd get him wherever he scurried.

Only now what appeared 'twixt him and me but the three nuns, their grey skirts flapping in the wet wind. I stopped so fast I sprawled up the staircase, skinning a knee and barking my chin so hard I damn near saw stars. What I heard was Wynstan's laughter.

I hauled myself up and mounted the slippery staircase once more. This time to stand in front of the nuns and glare over their shoulders at Wynstan where he huddled in the porch shadows. "Well, well," I said. "The ... what is it you call yourself? The great singer of valor is using women for protection."

"Women?" Wynstan's tone was both showy and astonished. "What women? These are nuns."

Prioress sighed and Sister Hrothbeort looked puzzled. Hild's head snapped around as she snarled at the old coward. "For once in your life, Wynstan, shut your mouth."

If Wynstan gave answer, it was hidden in a rumble of thunder. Hild turned on me. "Give me your knife," she said, thrusting out her hand.

"My God, Hild, do you think I want to kill Wynstan?" I put on my most distressed and innocent face. "Of course, I don't. I ..."

What did I reckon I could tell her as I stood there with a foot-long scramseaxe in my fist and blood in my eye? Before I could decide, Prioress entered the fray. "You know, Tryff, the trouble with revenge is that you become no better than the demon you pursue. That's why Christ said those who take the sword will perish by the sword."

Sister Hrothbeort grinned and added, "In the Proverbs it says him that digs a shit hole will fall in it."

Just what I needed—a few passages from the Gospel-book while Wynstan inched toward the porch railing.

"Give me the knife," Hild said again. And this time, I did. Because if I didn't, Wynstan would be in Ireland before these women quieted down.

"The one in your sock, too."

Along with that they took the pouch from my belt and even my relic bag. Lest I sic St. Veronica on the old viper, I suppose. By the time they had me plucked clean, Wynstan was on the far side of the hall-yard. Didn't matter. I could throttle him as easily as dismember him. I'd trap him against the wall like a terrier does a rat.

I took off after him and was on his heels when the gate went and swung open, to let in a goose-girl and her gaggle. Wynstan leaped over, through, on top of the squawking birds and into the wide meadow beyond. I kicked through right behind him, the wretched geese striking back as hard as snakes in a pit.

The sky had grown darker, the wind stronger. Closer and closer came the crackle of thunder and the streak of lightning. At least the rain had let up a bit. Nor had it yet turned the little meadow to mush or blurred the straggle of trees on the other side. I closed the distance betwixt us.

I'd have him right quick now. First, I'd wring the truth about King Edward out of him. That would be for gold. Then I'd wring his neck. That would be for honor. Soon Wynstan would lie dead at my feet, his soul headed to hell.

I was so excited the hair on my arms stood on end. When I leaped onto his back, the whole world lit up.

Next thing I knew I was on the wet ground, my ears ringing. Wynstan sprawled beside me. Three grey geese hovered over us. "Raise a joyful shout," one squawked.

"A miracle ..." It was Sister Hrothbeort. "He's been spared from the lightning by the Lord."

CHAPTER TWELVE

They say lightning shoots down from the sky and burns you up. If that's right, the Good Lord—never mind Fortuna and all the saints—must've put out those flames. I saw the flash, I remember. And that's all. I didn't know anything else 'til I came around, lying on my back and feeling like you do when you hit your funny bone. Except I felt that way all over and my ears were full of twittering baby birds. I got over the numbness quick enough, but the damn birds nested in there for years.

I don't know who watched over Wynstan, but he didn't die, either. He sat in that muddy meadow squalling like he was a baby himself. He was still at it when Sister Hrothbeort and Prioress hauled the both of us to our feet and hustled us back to the bower house. They pulled off our wet clothes, threw a grey horse blanket over me and a bearskin over Wynstan, then stepped back to watch us shiver ourselves to sleep.

That's not all they were doing. From under my blanket, I could hear the hissing whispers of conspiracy. Their plot hatched next morning when I woke, still sore and sick, on a pallet in a room bare except for the iron brazier that warmed it. The three nuns sat on stools beside me, but both Wynstan and his bearskin were gone.

"The old bastard dead?" I asked, hoping so.

"He left a while ago, but you're to stay here. Under the blanket."

I was sore tempted to do just that, I don't mind telling you. I'd barely slept, and when I had my dreams'd been full of flashes and screams and birds, birds, birds. A bad night, and a bad day would follow, if the nuns had anything to say about it. And they did.

From behind her Sister Hrothbeort produced a clay pot. "Better get up and use this now, Tryff. You won't be able to later because you're going to be playing dead."

What the hell?

"Need we tell you," Hild said, "the lords are not happy about what happened in the mead hall yesterday? You are in serious danger. They've already set up the gibbet."

I tossed off the blanket. I had to get up, get my knives, get out of there. But I was bare naked. And tempted to give Prioress a good long peek before grinning Sister Hrothbeort swept up the blanket and threw it back over me.

"Fortunately," Hild said, "the lords and their war bands think you're dead. So a bit of pretense may save you from their wrath."

I yanked the blanket up to my nose and peered at her. "Just how d'you plan to make me look dead? I've got to breathe, you know."

"I have herbs."

Some physician was my *mam*.

"And," she added, "we will trust in the Lord."

Me, I trust in the Lord better with my clothes on. I jumped up, twisted the blanket into a skirt, demanded to know where they'd put my pants and tunic.

Hild slapped a hand to her forehead. "What are we thinking? We wouldn't have undressed a dead man. Give the man his things, Hrothbeort, so we can get on with it."

She held a little cloth bag. "You may need this," she said and stuck it in my neck pouch.

Prioress's peach-pink face went purple as a plum while I pulled on my clothes—and thought over the nuns' mad plan. Mad it was, too. *Primus*, the commanders would never believe I was dead, especially after they stuck a thumb in my eye or a knife betwixt my ribs. *Secundus*, even if the nuns somehow kept them at bay, what would happen to my so-called corpse? Would they let the commanders shroud me up and pay some Welsh churl to drop me in a distant ditch like an unwanted infant?

Anyway, I didn't have time to pretend to be a dead body. I had to find Wynstan and King Edward. To be on the safe side, though, I asked the nuns about the situation in Caer Aberffraw. It was as bad as I expected and they said they had already hired a ship to take us home. It would board at the tide. I didn't wait to hear the rest of their plan. I grabbed Sister Hrothbeort's cloak off the peg by the door and barreled bare-footed down the high porch steps, into the dark gold of dawn.

Before the guards on the parapets could see me, I ran behind the bower house where I dropped the blanket and threw Sister's cloak around me. Praying I looked like a peasant so poor he had to go barefoot in mud cold as the grave, I pulled down my cap and slouched toward the stable.

There, the red-haired boy sat on a three-legged stool

twanging a jaws harp. Its noise couldn't cover the angry howls of the prey caught in the leather snare. My father. But no matter how loud his cries and curses, he wouldn't be getting free of that tangle for a very long time. He went quiet, though, when he saw me, a man back from the dead.

"Help me," I said to the boy. Tewdwr ap Merfyn was a big man and it wouldn't be easy to haul him through the mud to the courtyard. I'd also need help stuffing him into the wicker punishment basket and hoisting it up the pole, where he'd dangle while men struck at him with stick and spear.

The boy and I had the cage about half way up the pole when Tewdwr came to, blinking in blue-eyed bewilderment. Seeing me, he pulled himself to his knees and said, "What the fuck are you up to, slave's whelp?"

For that heartfelt welcome to his son, I gave him a smack on the head with a farrier's hammer. For fun, the boy threw a fist to his nose. Tewdwr collapsed onto the basket floor, moaning and clutching his battered head.

When we'd raised the basket and secured the pole, I pointed out of the courtyard. "Here," I said, giving the boy a handful of silver. "Go someplace far away and thrive. Never look back and, for God's sake, never come back."

His brow wrinkled like he was a bit puzzled, but then he strode off without so much as a "*diolch*."

"And take the little bay mare," I called after him. "Her name is Mona."

Once the boy had ridden out of sight, I called up to my father. "Oi, there! Your brother is going to be plenty interested when he finds out just what his new heir—you, in other words—got up to in this war. What you did to his only son."

Tewdwr cursed me pretty good, but I kept on talking. "The Norskers bragged about it at the meadbench, you know. Bragged how King Brynmor's son and heir screamed when they ripped open his chest and yanked out his lungs. They claimed Prince Ris was nothing but a coward because he went and died on 'em. They think a real man would be proud and grinning while they made him into a blood-eagle."

"That's got nothing to do with me!" Tewdwr yelled down.

"The Norsker king said you sold Ris to him."

More curses from the basket.

"Haraldsson said he was surprised how cheap the prince came. Just one silver penny. But you didn't need the money, did you? Not when the transaction would buy your brother's kingdom."

Tewdwr began yelling for his *teulu* to come and rescue him. But I knew they wouldn't, not after what they'd heard from the seven Welsh war prisoners Haraldsson released at the peace parley. "I saw him, my lord," each had said to King Hwyel, one after another. "I saw him sell his prince."

Now those men and the rest of King Brynmor's Welsh had already sailed for home. So I would leave my father to King Hywel's Welsh. They, too, knew what he'd done and were already fixing to put Iago's rotting corpse in the wicker basket with him. "Then we gonna have us a time!"

I smiled as I yanked his boots off him and put them on.

And I was still smiling in the church-house as I shoved the top off St Guenessa's reliquary. Before long I'd be safely hidden in the belly of the ship the nuns had hired to carry us back to Chester, all snuggled up to the Great Harp of Arthur.

The stone top slid away far more easily than when I'd

dealt with it the day before. For a moment I thought it would go crashing to the flagstones and summon half the monks in Wales to aid the saint. But I caught it, eased it to the floor, reached for the Harp.

And came away with St. Guenessa's thighbone. In the darkness I scrabbled through the other bones, hauling them out one, two, three at a time—all but heaving them over my shoulder, I was in such a fright. As well I should've been. The Great Harp of Arthur was gone. Only Guenessa's bones and a woolen sack remained.

I didn't need to ask who could've known where I put the Harp. Who could've gotten there before me. Not kings or lords or warriors—they'd had their troops to worry about— nor churls nor slaves nor clerics. Only Wynstan would've known. Crawe—or Kyre or Beorn—would've followed me through the tempest of hailstones. Or perhaps the old fox'd simply bought the eyes of churls or slaves or clerics.

I pressed back my rage. I was in God's house, after all. Besides, anger would be neither balm nor cure for what had befallen me. I should've dealt with Wynstan long since. Now only blood would do. I leaped up, scramseaxe pulled, ready to find him and cut him into tiny scraps.

Nor did I care if Lord Alvar or King Hwyel or the Norsker found me as I tore along the road to the quay. Wynstan had to come there eventually. Crouched behind a fishing shed, I waited for him—and tried not to think of Thrima.

Presently, Welsh and English troops came to gape at the Norskers boarding their dragon ships, bound for their stronghold on the Isle of Man. They swooped down the estuary like evil seabirds. In Hel Hoard's prow, King Haraldsson stood with his fist raised in triumph. On the deck behind him was Beorn, Cuthred on his shoulders, Kyre beside him. Next to them came Crawe, then Wynstan. Even Lady Philosophy had gone aboard.

Suddenly, the gulls' raucous chatter stopped. The dragon ship seemed frozen, the world motionless—except, for all to see, the sun-struck and glittering strings of the Great Harp of Arthur clenched in Wynstan's hands.

The nuns went home to England by sea, with Lord Alvar and the Bishop of Chester in Alvar's longship. I was supposed to trudge back with Lord Alvar's army. But I had business elsewhere. A fisherman took me down the coast to Ynys Enlli, the island Saxons call Bardsey.

They say 20,000 saints lie in Bardsey's rocky ground. If that's so, the monks weren't going to miss one or two—four, as it turned out—who wanted to be elsewhere. Indeed, the four were delighted with their new resting places in Clnno Fawr, Bangor, Abergele. One even found a new home with a bald old hermit near Flint. So all parties—the saints, the monks of north Wales, and, most of all, me—were pleased with this holy enterprise.

After the fuss over the Harp, Ealdorman Alvar hadn't found time to tell me where Thrima was. He'd left Aberffraw on the next tide, so anxious was he to be back in England, plotting to make Lady Edith queen. He'd left no message for me, either. Nor did the nuns leave orders that I was supposed to come to St Finella's and fix a bridge or chase down some pig rustler. So I had the freedom to find Thrima. But first I had to fetch Tom Tub.

Bertha welcomed me with a kiss and sly grin, then had Tom brought from the stable to her sprawling courtyard. He came right to me, nickered as I handed him a dried apple I'd brought from Bardsey. They say the island is King Arthur's Avalon and its apples full of sweet juice and powerful magic. Tom wrapped his big soft lips around this one, gave it a chomp, and promptly spat it out.

Bertha laughed. "So much for Cymric fancy. Tom's got good English horse sense. By the way, some nuns came to see me. Said you know them."

I sent Tom off with the stableman, then hustled Bertha inside before she blurted out God knows what. Business, of course, was conducted elsewhere. Bertha lived alone in a little timbered house, her quarters much finer than Lady Flæda's. The walls were hung with the kind of elaborately woven red rugs I'd only seen in Constantinople. On her cloth-covered table polished silver cups sat alongside a tall filigreed drinking horn. Her storage chests were made of iron. And lest a visitor not notice this grand show of prosperity, the room had a glass window.

I had no time for the wine Bertha now poured into her silver cups and I didn't need to ask where the nuns had come from. "What did they want?"

"To give you something," she said, and opened one of the iron chests. "Come look."

Inside, nestled in lambs wool, sat my barrel of silver coins.

"They said some bishop had it sent to our cathedral but that it was definitely yours and I should—"

I scooped up the barrel and made for the door.

"Wait!" Bertha called after me. "Don't you want to know the rest?"

She said Lord Alvar had also stopped by, on his way to his manor in Gloucestershire. "And Alvie said tell you— "

Alvie? No wonder Bertha had glass in her window.

The ealdorman had explained that after Lady Bathilda had been arrested, she ordered Thrima to bring some kind of potions to her in the Winchester convent where Queen Ælfthryth had her held.

"Your woman didn't have no choice but to go with the soldiers that come for her. But she give them potions to the queen instead."

Potions? *Eitr* for Ælthryth? But—"I don't care about the blasted potions! Where is Thrima?"

"Alvie said she's been back home all summer long."

Late October found me astride Tom Tub, galloping up Thornholt's lane. It had taken me another month to get there, what with stops at Chester and St. Finella's, then at Winchester. But here I was at last, galloping to Thrima, fearing she wouldn't want me back after all this time. But my fears turned out to be foolish. I'd barely pulled Tom to a halt before we'd fallen into her feather bed.

We got married right after St. Elizabeth's Day. Well, not married exactly. Not by a mass-priest anyhow, though we could have if we'd wanted to. Father Golding certainly wanted us to. But priests will marry anybody as long as they promise to stay together till they die.

"Like anybody should promise such foolish thing!" Thrima said when she told me how her sons had all but insisted we let Father Golding say his words over us. "Like anybody should *do* such foolish thing! *Could* do it."

I gave a brief thought to her late husband, smashed and dead at the foot of the bell tower. Then I put my arms around her, said that daft nonsense about promising to stay together forever was something we agreed about. And so we had a handfasting ceremony, which only bound us to each other for a year and a day like any other contract. That's the way a lot of folk feel about marriage in Wales. England, too. And, I reckon, in Ireland and even those mountains on the back side of the Euxine Sea.

It was a simple enough ceremony so I didn't fuss, even if I wanted to jump over the broomstick like we did in my part of Wales. We'd worked everything out one morning while we were slaughtering chickens. "I am not wanting birch twigs tearing my good dress," Thrima said as she selected a rooster from the cage, grabbed it by the legs. "I am wanting red ribbons like folk get tied around their hands when they say contract words."

I beheaded the rooster, then watched it go flopping and bleeding around the yard. "I've seen those ceremonies. The ribbon's always just out of the dye pot and still wet. You don't want that nasty thing slopping up your pretty dress, staining your pretty hands."

Thrima had seen those messy weddings, too. So I gave up my broomstick and she left off hankering after red ribbon. As for the ceremony itself, I did like some parts of the church service—for better for worse, for richer, for poorer, in sickness and in health. And 'specially the part where the bride promises to be "bonny and buxom in bed and at board." But even without the church words, handfasting was as legal as any other form of marriage. King Eadgar's first, the one that produced Lady Edith, was a handfasting.

Nor is a handfast ceremony held in some dank hidey hole with nobody to see it but the mice and the spiders, though I think Thrima might've preferred that. Me, I wanted the whole of Thornholt gathered, the whole of Wessex. I threw the gates wide open. And except for Father Golding and his family, all of Thornholt turned out, from the oldest widow woman to the tiniest breast baby. Lady Wilma even came from her estate down the road, the whole village in tow. And from the other side of the Narrow Valley came Lord and Lady Augustine. To my surprise, Lord Carlyle of Monteagle also appeared. Not only was he the richest man in the neighborhood, but his brother was abbot of the richest minster in London.

So many folk came I decided we'd been right not to hold the wedding feast in the mead hall. All our guests would never have fit in there. But that was the only reason we didn't. After all, who would've stopped us? The heads of both Lord Hunwald and his heir still decorated a bridge in Winchester. By royal decree Lady Bathilda was now exiled someplace in the dark of Frankie-land. And Brother Petroc? I'm glad to say his skinny knees were permanently planted on the hard rock of the abbot my uncle's monastery, condemned to spend the rest of his miserable life in that bleak place.

Queen Ælfthryth had put a wool merchant named Ine in charge of Thornholt until she could bestow it on some worthy arse-licker like me. But Ine preferred to tend to royalty in Winchester, not a passel of peasants someplace in the back of beyond. The villagers hadn't seen him since June. We didn't see him that day, either.

And the feast? Ah, the feast.

Fortunately, the farm year had been good, late October warm and dry, the cider and ale full and delicious. Our feast could go on for days if anybody had head and stomach enough to handle it. But I had something I wanted to do on the first day, right after the ceremony. And I wanted everybody to be sure and see me do it, both Thornholt's churls and the neighboring gentry. 'Specially the gentry.

I had what the English call a morning gift for Thrima that I wanted the whole world to know about. Morning gifts of land or stock or jewelry are what even the stingy Saxons give their wives to keep forever. Depending, 'course, on how they spend their first wedded night. Since that wouldn't be a problem for me and Thrima, I wanted to give it to her as soon as possible.

The villagers had strung trestle tables all over the meadow that lay 'twixt hall and village, conveniently close to both kitchen and brewery. They'd risen before dawn to decorate the tables with evergreen and mistletoe, cover them with roast pork and stewed eel and roasted chicken. They rolled out the ale and cider barrels, tapped them, drew off a few cups for themselves. "Just to sample, mind you. See it's fit for our Thrima's wedding day." And they kept on sampling until the neighbors arrived and it was time for the ceremony.

Thrima had been as busy as any other villager all morning and only now stopped to straighten her head-dress and scrape the chicken shit off her shoes. That was when her sons' wives pleased her by giving her a blue woolen shawl they'd woven. It was also when I went out to see if Wynstan was lurking in the lane.

The King's Corpse

I was sure that even up in the Isles he'd found out about this day and would come slithering into Thornholt like the snake he was. But the armed men I'd left to guard the gates, prowl the woods, and patrol the village assured me they hadn't seen the old bastard anywhere. And if he did come around, they said, he wouldn't get past a force tough as the village hundredmen. I thanked them by having ale and eel carried to the woods and into the lane. For which they toasted me and my bride with loud shouts and louder laughter.

Presently, the pipes began their merry hoot and it was time to get married. On the way back to the meadow, I dunked my hands in a rain barrel and ran them through my beard. I wanted to be at least as presentable as Thrima. And I wanted her approval, too. So I moved my weapons to my back. Maybe she wouldn't notice I was armed with not one but two very big, very sharp scramseaxes. If Wynstan showed up, I'd slaughter him on the spot, wedding day or no.

That done, I took a deep breath and joined my bride. No priest, no official, nobody at all would say words at our handfasting. Only us. We had witnesses, of course. This was a contract, after all. We stood in front of the crowd, and Thrima's witnesses—her two daughters-in-law and Old Horsa—stood beside her. Next to me were my own witnesses—the farrier, the miller, the stable master. I found myself grinning like any Saxon yokel as Thrima and I joined hands and said the traditional words. First, I promised her my keys, half my bed, and a third of my goods "acquired or to be acquired."

The ceremony stopped while everybody laughed. I had no keys, my bed was her bed, and Thrima said goods "stolen or to be stolen" would be a better description of what I had on offer. But like I had a hundred times since I'd gotten back to Thornholt, I promised her I'd quit my thieving ways. "Honest to God."

"I know," she said. And promptly promised to be bonny and buxom in bed, though I noticed she said nothing about in board.

Finally, we both said the words that sealed our contract. "I take you Tryffin ap Tewdwr for my husband." "I take you Thrima of Thornholt for my wife."

And that was that. We ignored the shoes tossed our way and I told the crowd that if any young idiots tried to throw dirty water on Thrima, like the savages I knew Saxons to be ... well, they should notice I was the kind of man who got married carrying a pair of scramseaxes.

Just then a ripple of excitement ran through the crowd. Wynstan! I reached for my knives.

But it was only Father Golding and his family joining us after all. He was smiling and not only blessed everybody in his thin Latin but, to my surprise, settled himself and his sons on one of the men's benches. His wife joined Thrima and the women in heaping mountains of fried greens on the tables. There followed rivers of smoked eels, herds of hot pork, flock on flock of roast chicken.

But after Father had given the food a quick blessing and ploughed into it, his presence made everybody go quiet. For a while, anyhow. Till a young girl spilled a kettle of marrow soup in the brewer's lap. The man jumped up yowling that he'd been gelded. A whoop of laughter shook us back to life. Pretty soon, everybody was chewing and chattering away, me leading the pack.

Even when the after-meal sweets came on—wine-soaked curd, apple custard, rock cake with calves-foot jelly—Father and his family did us the honor of staying. He wasn't one of those self-righteous clerics that think sweets lead not only to gluttony but to lust besides. He was working on a third rock cake when the entertainment started.

Thrima joined me at the wedding table while Straethford played his whistle and Osmond blasted on his bagpipe. Then everyone sang a while, and presently Thrima's elder son and the priest's wife told jokes. I won't bother to repeat them. If you've heard one wedding joke, you've heard them all.

When the food was mostly gone—but not the drink, thank God—Thrima's sons and I hoisted a barrel of our special Frankish wine onto a wheelbarrow. With the boys pushing the barrow and Thrima by my side, I began a slow amble around the green, stopping at every table to pour wine and thank the householder for his kind hospitality in allowing me, a stranger in their land, to celebrate my wedding with such a fine, rich supper, may the good Lord bless and keep them every one.

Then I stood on a trestle table and hollered out a few Welsh riddles that set them slapping their knees and holding their bellies. In other words, I laid it on like a Christmas pudding, thick and sweet and rich. When I started on the women, it got even deeper. I raved about their clothes and their cooking and their hair and their homes. I patted their children's heads and praised their husband's potency.

"Now," I said when I had ever so reluctantly finished, "Now, I want to show you Thrima's morning gift."

Naturally, the guests were shocked I'd do such a thing before our wedding night. Thrima seemed surprised, too.

And a little disappointed when all that came out of the leather bag at my waist was a piece of parchment covered in writing and hung all over with ribbons and sealing wax. The writing wasn't Latin but plain English, though no one but me and the gentry could know that, and the wedding guests were clearly bored when I read out its words.

First came a flowery invocation followed by lawyer words stiff as a frozen pond. When I came to the next part, though, a few folk came around enough to recognize "First to the ring pit through the narrow valley, then along the lynchet and past the heathen graves to the greenway..."

The stable master jumped up. "That's Thornholt you got on that there scrap of paper."

Thrima must've agreed, because while the crowd began to buzz like disturbed bees, she threw me one of her looks. It didn't grind me down and when I could get everyone quiet enough, I read on. "Thornholt is granted to Thrima of Thornholt by my seal—Ethelred, king of Wessex and all England."

Into the stunned silence that followed, I read out the names of the witnesses—Queen Ælfthryth, Lord Ordwulf, Lord and Lady Tuck, and half a dozen more names of the highest rank.

When I was finished, I handed the deed to Thrima. She stared at it for a long time, hands stuffed in her apron pockets. My stomach lurched. Was she going to refuse my reward for finding Edward's body?

King Ethelred had been surprised when I'd turn down the reward of a mint full of silver and three fine, fat estates that lay next to Wales. "You want what instead? Thornholt? That weeny place?"

Weeny? With a church, a kitchen, a bell tower, and enough land to support ten families? Hunwald had been a thegn, after all. And so would I.

The king's mother was against it, of course. She likely figured I'd be too close to Winchester. But young Ethelred had not yet found an occasion to defy his mother, to demonstrate just who was sovereign of all England. Lucky for me, he chose just then to do it.

And what could Ælfthryth say, after I dropped the bag of bones at her feet? After I reached in my relic sack and brought forth a gold ring set with a blue-purple stone? After Ordwulf and two archbishops accepted that ring as the one King Edward had worn when he was buried?

Was it that same ring? Had Hild somehow gotten it away from Wynstan as he lay lightning-struck in the bower house at Aberffraw, then given it to me? Or had she only handed me a bag of herbs and this was a stone I'd bought in the back streets of Chester and had set by a Norsker goldsmith? Were those King Edward's bones in the sack at Ælfthryth's feet? Or were they those of the good Welshwoman Guenessa, St David's own sister?

Come to all that, had that ring ever been the king of England's? Or was it just a trinket Wynstan traded for a song and story in some tavern deep in Derbyshire?

Whatever the truth of the matter, in Winchester King Ethelred had listened carefully while I told him about Thornholt and that I'd be giving the place to Thrima. Smothering a grin, he ordered the deed drawn up, then gathered together witnesses, and that very day signed and sealed it.

Here at my wedding feast, the guests were likely as

confused as King Ethelred had been. But, like him, they seized the occasion to their own purposes and got good and drunk. I helped them. Nor did Thrima turn away the ale horn. She was sharing a cup and chattering away with her daughters-in-law when Lord Carlyle squatted down behind me. He whispered into my ear. "St. Mary Magdalene that's in Frankie-land has sent word she wants to be in London at my brother's minster."

The Magdalene? She'd always been trouble. I ignored him.

"It'd be a hard quest, I'll admit. Though not as hard as searching out the king's corpse. But there's gold in it." His whisper grew even softer. "Enough to pay the taxes on this place."

He nodded toward the laughing crowd of churls. "Enough to pay their tithes and their Peter's Pence for years to come."

That made me think hard about the villagers. They were happy now, but how about when they woke tomorrow? Sore-headed, still poor, and jealous of Thrima's good fortune. What if all of a sudden the mead hall burnt up, the horses kicked down their stalls, the drovers didn't return from market? Envious people can be mighty vengeful.

I gave Thrima a quick kiss, then escorted Lord Carlyle to the mead hall where a man could discuss business in private.

And woo Fortuna.

The End

M J Jones

MJ Jones grew up in an old town in an old house with a father who read history and a mother who told stories. That may explain why she took a BA in English and history, then a PhD in English literature. She has taught college English in the South and Midwest. She has also been a technical writer, an antiques dealer, and a visiting professor at Pyatigorsk [Russia] State Linguistic University. She travels often in the UK and Ireland.

Although she has published fantasy as well as contemporary and historical crime fiction, she now concentrates on crime fiction set in Anglo-Saxon England. Her story "The Witch and the Relic Thief," published in *Alfred Hitchcock's Mystery Magazine*," received the Mystery Writers of America's Robert L Fish Award for Best First Short Story. It is included in *Crime In Its Time*, a collection of her crime fiction. MJ Jones lives and writes in Wisconsin.

An ARGUMENT OF BLOOD

BY

MATTHEW WILLIS AND J. A. IRONSIDE

William, the nineteen-year-old duke of Normandy, is enjoying the full fruits of his station. Life is a succession of hunts, feasts, and revels, with little attention paid to the welfare of his vassals. Tired of the young duke's dissolute behavior and ashamed of his illegitimate birth, a group of traitorous barons force their way into his castle. While William survives their assassination attempt, his days of leisure are over. He'll need help from the king of France to secure his dukedom from the rebels.

On the other side of the English Channel lives ten-year-old Ælfgifa, the malformed and unwanted youngest sister to the Anglo-Saxon king Harold Godwinson. Ælfgifa discovers powerful rivalries in the heart of the state when her sister Ealdgyth is given in a political marriage to King Edward, and she finds herself caught up in intrigues and political maneuvering as powerful men vie for influence. Her path will collide with William's, and both must fight to shape the future.

An Argument of Blood is the first of two sweeping historical novels on the life and battles of William the Conqueror.

PENMORE PRESS
www.penmorepress.com

A Congress of Kings

BY
James Boschert

The Year 1191

Under the vigilant protection of Lord Talon and his companions, the land of Kantara enjoys peace even as the tyrant Isaac Komnenos continues to plunder the rest of Cyprus. However, dark clouds are gathering and great storms bring with them unwelcome Norman visitors. Soon Talon is embroiled in the invasion of Cyprus, assisting King Richard of England who, en route to Acre for the Third Crusade, must save his royal sister, Queen Joanna, from Isaac's clutches.

Talon is forced to accompany Richard I to the besieged city of Acre—a city which holds painful memories for Talon. There, quarreling kings, men who once were kings, and men who want to be kings form the leadership of the Crusading armies. Their lust for power blinds them to the threat posed by Salah ad Din, the skilled general who fights on the Arab side, continuing the tragedy that started with the terrible defeat at Hattin.

And lurking out of sight is yet another implacable foe who prepares his own assassins for a mission of revenge. Talon has eluded the *Fidai* of The Master Rashid ad Din for nearly twenty years, but his luck may be running out.

PENMORE PRESS
www.penmorepress.com

ÆGIR'S CURSE

BY
LEAH DEVLIN

A thousand years ago, the Viking colony of Vinland was ravaged by a swift-moving plague ... a curse inflicted by the sea god Ægir. The last surviving Norseman set the encampment and his longboat ablaze to ensure that the disease would die with him and his brethren.

In present-day Norway, a distinguished professor is found murdered, his priceless map of Vinland missing. The ensuing investigation leads to the reclusive world of Lindsey Nolan, a scientist and recovering alcoholic who has been sober for five years. Lindsey reluctantly agrees to help the detective who's hunting the murderer, but she has a bigger problem on her hands: a mysterious disease that's spreading like wildfire through the population of Woods Hole. As she races against a rising body count to discover the source of the plague, disturbing events threaten her hard-won sobriety—and her life. Will Lindsey be the next victim of Ægir's curse?

Leah Devlin is rapidly establishing herself as a writer of modern day mystery-thrillers. This story is as tight as a piano wire. Life at a seaside town in New England is full of treacherous undercurrents and peril, as residents are threatened by a menace from a thousand years ago. Murder, romance and deceit are a potent mix in this gripping novel, which I didn't want to put down.—James Boschert, author of the Talon Series and *Force 12 in German Bight*

PENMORE PRESS
www.penmorepress.com

ASSASSINS OF ALAMUT
BY
JAMES BOSCHERT

An Epic Novel of Persia and Palestine in the Time of the Crusades

The *Assassins of Alamut* is a riveting tale, painted on the vast canvas of life in Palestine and Persia during the 12th century.

On one hand, it's a tale of the crusades—as told from the Islamic side—where Shi'a and Sunni are as intent on killing Ismaili Muslims as crusaders. In self-defense, the Ismailis develop an elite band of highly trained killers called Hashshashin...whose missions are launched from their mountain fortress of Alamut.

But it's also the story of a French boy, Talon, captured and forced into the alien world of the assassins. Forbidden love for a princess is intertwined with sinister plots and self-sacrifice, as the hero and his two companions discover treachery and then attempt to evade the ruthless assassins of Alamut who are sent to hunt them down.

It's a sweeping saga that takes you over vast snow-covered mountains, through the frozen wastes of the winter plateau, and into the fabulous cites of Hamadan, Isfahan, and the Kingdom of Jerusalem.

"A brilliant first novel, worthy of Bernard Cornwell at his best."—Tom Grundner

PENMORE PRESS
www.penmorepress.com